GNOSIS

ALSO BY

Tom Wallace

What Matters Blood

The Devil's Racket

Heirs of Cain

GNOSIS

TOM WALLACE

Hydra
Publications

Printed in the United States of America

ISBN 978-0615563459
Hydra Publications
337 Clifty Dr
Madison, IN 47250

www.hydrapublications.com

DEDICATION

For Amy Reynolds,
whose voice and spirit will never be silenced;
and
Marilyn Underwood,
always and always

PROLOGUE

April 5, 1982

The only thing Bruce Fowler loved more than having sex with Darleen was smoking weed. Most of his friends would say his priorities were all screwed up, but, of course, none of them were getting laid on a regular basis. Being perpetually horny, it was only natural for those guys to prefer sex over . . . well, just about everything. Not so with Bruce. True, Darleen was a tiger in the sack—by far the best sex he ever had—but as terrific as she was, she simply couldn't compare to smoking pot. It wasn't even a close call.

Bruce took his first toke seven years ago, when he was twelve. His older brother, Daryl, was smoking a joint in his room when Bruce barged in unannounced. Daryl asked his kid brother if he wanted to take a hit. Bruce refused. That changed when Daryl called Bruce a chicken. No one called Bruce Fowler a chicken, because Bruce wasn't afraid of anyone or anything, not even his older brother, who had a reputation for being a tough guy. He grabbed the joint from Daryl's hand, and before Daryl had time to show him the proper way to smoke marijuana, Bruce took a long, deep hit. The impact was immediate. His throat and lungs burned, he felt slightly dizzy, and his eyes watered, but . . . there was something else happening as well. Something positive, nice, and calming. He had the strangest sensation that he was floating like an angel high above the scene below, looking down at Daryl, who was sitting on the bed laughing at the boldness of his younger brother.

It was a memorable moment in Bruce's life; a pivotal moment, a life-altering moment. From that initial taken-on-a-dare toke, he swore to make it his life's goal to find and smoke the best pot he could lay his hands on. It was a goal he achieved with admirable success.

Tonight, with the first drops of rain beginning to fall, Bruce and his best buddy, Carl Osteen, were standing in front of the Kentucky Theatre when Bruce noticed the big car pull up to the curb. The window on the driver's side went down, and the man behind the wheel asked where he might score some good weed. Naturally wary, Bruce looked at Carl, shrugged, and told the man he had no clue where to buy weed, either good or bad. Of course, this was a lie—Bruce knew a dozen pot dealers in the city. He simply wasn't about to take a chance that the guy was an undercover narc looking to make a bust.

However, despite his instinct for caution, Bruce couldn't help but be intrigued. The guy was driving a Lincoln Continental, a pricey car for a narc. And he was dressed in an expensive suit and tie, like a business man or a lawyer. Certainly nothing like the clothes worn by any cop he knew. Most narcs dressed like street bums, hoping to make you think they were ordinary Joes out looking for a score. More often than not, it was the dumb-ass outfit that gave them away. But this guy was different. He didn't give off a narc vibe, didn't look like a cop. Maybe he was legit, someone who could be trusted. Bruce was torn, unsure what to do. His gut feeling that the guy was okay waged an interior battle against his fear that he might be wrong. And with so much at stake, this was not the time for an error in judgment. You never roll the dice when dealing with law enforcement.

But when the man reached into his pants pocket and pulled out a wad of bills the size of a softball, well . . . Bruce never saw a narc with that much cash. Hell, he'd never seen *anybody* with that much cash. Bruce was still unsure what to do until the man peeled off two one-hundred dollar bills and said he would give them to Bruce and Carl if they would direct him to the best pot dealer they knew. Seeing all that cash made Bruce's decision an easy one to make.

Bruce and Carl climbed into the big Lincoln and informed the man that Eddie Martin sold the best pot in the city. Rarely did Bruce recommend strangers to Eddie. On a couple of occasions he had done so, but only after the stranger was vouched for by someone Bruce knew and trusted. Eddie seldom sold to anyone outside his known clientele.

To Bruce's way of thinking, pot was harmless. Unfortunately, the idiots who make laws saw things from a different perspective. They didn't distinguish pot from deadly heroin. Both sins were equal in their stupid eyes. Getting busted for selling pot meant jail time, and Bruce didn't want to think about that. He wouldn't last two hours in prison. Therefore, he had to be safe. Taking unnecessary risks was not an option.

To protect Eddie's address, Bruce told the man to park two blocks from Eddie's house. The man gave Bruce five hundred dollars for the purchase. Bruce was only gone fifteen minutes before returning with the pot. The man took the bag, thanked Bruce, and then asked if they would like to smoke some with him. Bruce and Carl both nodded in the affirmative.

With rain coming down harder now, the man drove out of the city and into the county. Neither Bruce nor Carl knew where the man was heading, nor did they care. They were going to smoke some seriously great shit, and it was not only free, they had each been given a hundred bucks. Pot and cash for doing nothing—sometimes dreams do come true. This weird dude in the big car could be taking them to Siberia, for all they cared.

The Lincoln stopped next to a barn seconds before the rain went from steady to serious. The man cut the engine, reached into the glove compartment and extracted a bag filled with pills. He asked the two boys if they wanted to try one of the blue ones before smoking the pot. He promised them it would intensify the experience. They declined. He then told them to go into the barn, and that he would join them in a few minutes.

Bruce and Carl were standing with their backs to the barn door when the man came inside. When they turned around, they were confused by what they saw. The man had a pistol in one hand and several pieces of rope in the other hand. Bruce felt a shudder run through his body, but he felt no real fear. This had to be some kind of a joke, right? They didn't know this man, and they had done everything he asked them to do, so why would he have any reason to harm them? He didn't have a reason, which is what made this so confusing. It had to be a joke, Bruce thought. Some kind of weird game. Nothing else made sense. As the man moved closer to the two boys, Carl muttered something like "what the fuck is this all about?" but his question was met by silence.

The man ordered the two boys to turn around and lie face down on the barn floor. He knelt behind Carl and tied his ankles together. Then he moved behind Bruce and performed the same procedure on him. After binding Bruce's ankles, he told Bruce to get onto his knees and put his hands behind his back. He bound Bruce's hands, and then did the same to Carl. When the man completed his tasks, the two boys were on their knees, hands and feet bound, facing away from the man.

Bruce was staring straight ahead when he heard the pop and saw Carl's body tumble forward. Turning his head slightly to the right, he saw blood spurting from the back of Carl's head. He also noticed that Carl's eyes were open.

Only now did fear engulf Bruce. Fear and panic combined with bewilderment. He knew he was about to die, but he didn't know why. He wanted to ask the man why this was happening. What could possibly be his reason for murdering two innocent young kids? What had they done to deserve this? Instead, Bruce chose to remain silent. He knew it was too late to ask the man anything. Anyway, what would be the point? Some questions are beyond answers.

I'll never smoke pot again was Bruce Fowler's last thought before the bullet entered his brain

CHAPTER ONE

Present Day

Warden Thad Curtis entered his office like an angry water buffalo, moving with great haste and determination from door to desk. Once he'd reached his destination, he removed his coat, loosened his tie, and dropped like a fallen boulder into the soft leather chair. From door to chair took less than five seconds. Not bad for a man whose weight hugged three hundred pounds.

Curtis coughed, shuffled mindlessly through a handful of papers and looked up, a no-nonsense expression on his freckled, moon-like face.

"Thank you for being so prompt, Detective Dantzler," Curtis said, taking off his glasses. "I appreciate those who are on time. I have little or no patience for the tardy."

"No problem."

Curtis leaned back in his chair. "You don't remember me, do you, Detective?"

Dantzler shook his head. "No. I'm afraid you have me at a disadvantage."

"We squared off against each other in the second round of the state tennis tournament," Curtis continued. "I was seventeen or eighteen, and you were maybe thirteen or fourteen. I took one look at you and figured if I couldn't whip a scrawny kid like that, I had no business on a tennis court. You beat me six-love, six-love. Guess you could say I overestimated my ability somewhat."

"I got lucky."

"You won the damn tournament, Detective. You weren't lucky, you were good. Plenty good. Way out of my league."

Dantzler nodded but didn't respond to the compliment. He was in no mood to ransack his mental archives for the purpose of discussing a thirty-five-year-old tennis match, especially one against a player he crushed. Anyway, what could he say? The double-bagel said it all.

"Any idea why Eli Whitehouse wants to see me?" Dantzler asked, shifting the subject to why he was at the prison in the first place.

"I was about to ask you that very same question, Detective."

"I'm as baffled as you are."

Curtis opened a brown file folder that looked to be five inches thick. "What do you know about John Elijah Whitehouse? Or, as he's more commonly referred to around here—the Reverend?"

"Probably a lot less than what everybody else knows. I did some research last night, went through his file, the murder book and the trial documents, so I'm familiar with the basics. Beyond that, I don't really know much."

"Were you on the force when it all went down?"

"No. I was still in college."

"Strange, him asking specifically for you," Curtis said. "I mean nothing personal by saying that. But it is intriguing, wouldn't you agree? You're a homicide detective, yet you had nothing to do with his case. I would have expected him to ask for a detective familiar with his situation, if any are still around."

"Does he have many visitors?"

Curtis shook his head. "Not so many, anymore. Early on he did. You know, church members would visit on a regular basis. But . . . over the years, the number has dwindled. I suppose members of his flock either died off or found a different shepherd. Either way they stopped showing up. These days you can count his visitors on one hand. Close family members, mostly."

"According to the file, he has two sons and a daughter."

"That's correct. The boys never visit, but the daughter sees him regularly. She seems to be closest to him."

"That's not surprising."

"A couple of others come by fairly often. His attorney and a former business associate." Curtis put his glasses on and searched the folder. "Yeah, here they are. Colt Rogers and Johnny Richards. Rogers is the lawyer."

"I'm familiar with him."

"Don't know Johnny Richards?" Curtis said, taking off the glasses.

"The name doesn't ring a bell."

"Probably shouldn't. He's not from around these parts. Judging by his accent, I'd venture a guess that he's the New York or New Jersey type."

"Whitehouse isn't from Jersey or New York, is he?"

"Nope. The Reverend is an Eastern Kentucky boy all the way. Harlan County, which is deep in Appalachia. He told me once his roots go back seven generations in those mountains. That translates to a multitude of snake-handling relatives." Curtis closed the folder and leaned forward, both elbows on the desk. "He's dying, the Reverend. Has the Big C, both lungs, inoperable. Three to six months is what they're giving him, but I say that's highly optimistic. I'll be surprised if he lasts to the end of this month."

"What kind of prisoner has he been?"

"Model. Of course, he had some age on him when he got here, and older guys tend to cause less trouble. It's the young ones that give us problems. Punks, assholes, scumbags. Half of 'em pumped on steroids, half just plain mean and crazy. Still . . . I've known some old-timers who delighted in causing us grief. The Reverend wasn't one of them, though. He's been easy to handle."

Dantzler closed his eyes and let his mind sift through last night's research, hoping to find some bit of logic, some reason why Eli Whitehouse would request a meeting. From his brief study, Dantzler learned that Whitehouse was accused of murdering two young men in what, the detectives concluded, was a drug deal gone sour. Cocaine, heroin, and an assortment of pills were found at the crime scene, an old barn located on property owned by Eli. He also knew Charlie Bolton was the lead detective on the case, and that it was one of Dan Matthews's first Homicide assignments.

Whitehouse was brought in for questioning the day after the bodies were discovered. Less than twenty-four hours later he was arrested and officially charged with the crime. The trial only lasted two days. A guilty verdict was handed down after the jury deliberated for less than an hour. John Elijah Whitehouse, the Reverend, was sentenced to life in prison with no possibility of parole.

Dantzler remembered one more tidbit of information gleaned during his research: the Reverend said very little in his own defense.

"If you're ready, Detective Dantzler, then we should go," Curtis said, rising from his chair. "I scheduled the meeting for three and I don't want to be late. I have no patience for those who cannot be on time."

"Yeah, I think you said that, already." Dantzler stood. "Where are we meeting?"

"The gym."

"Will Colt Rogers be there?"

"No. The Reverend insisted that no one other than the two of you should be present. He also insisted on no recording devices, either ours or yours. If you have one, you'd better hand it over."

"I don't."

"He also insisted that I allow as much time as necessary."

"He does a lot of insisting for a convict. I'm surprised you cave to his demands."

"Hell, he's a dying man," Curtis said, gruffly. "Might as well let him have a few small victories before his time is up. Contrary to popular opinion, even a prison warden can show compassion."

CHAPTER TWO

Dantzler was escorted out of the Administration Building by Warden Curtis and a beefed-up guard who looked like he could handle the toughest NFL linebacker on any given Sunday. Handle with ease. The man was a mountain, easily six-seven, his muscled upper torso and arms pushing against a brown shirt that looked like it had been painted on. Dantzler doubted many inmates would want any part of this behemoth. He certainly wouldn't.

They walked down three flights of stairs, across an open courtyard, toward a large Quonset hut Dantzler guessed to be the gym. No one spoke during the trip. The warden, despite his weight, moved with an ease and grace that belied his size. He hardly broke a sweat, and his breathing was steady and even. Clearly, Dantzler decided, the man was in good shape for someone carrying so much weight.

The guard, Leroy Henderson, began searching his key ring while the men were still several yards from the gym. After shuffling through what had to be fifty keys of various shapes and sizes, he found the one he was looking for. When the trio reached the back door, Henderson inserted the key, turned the lock, and pushed the door open.

"Like I said, Detective, you have as much time as you need," Curtis reminded. "Or, as much time as the Reverend wants. When you've finished your meeting come back here. Leroy will be inside, in the open area to your left as you enter. If you need to speak with me again, he will bring you to my office. If there's no need to meet, he will take you to your vehicle. Any questions?"

"Just . . . why am I here?"

"I suspect you're about to find out."

*****

Dantzler entered the gym, which was dark except for a single row of lights that arced across center court like a 50,000-watt rainbow. Every window was shut and covered by metal shades, all other exit doors closed. An eerie silence dominated the building, that strange quiet unique to large, empty spaces. In this silence, this dark, the place felt more like a mausoleum than gym.

Dantzler waited until his eyes adjusted to the darkness before moving slowly and silently toward the man who had summoned him. For some unknown reason he felt a strange mixture of intrigue and dread. Something was about to happen, something big, and he wasn't sure he wanted it to. Rarely did he question his own judgment; second guessing wasn't in his nature. That wasn't so on this occasion. This time he had doubts, questions. Buried somewhere deep inside was a nagging feeling that this was one invitation he should have declined.

John Elijah Whitehouse, the Reverend, sat in a wheelchair at mid-court, the light above him glowing like a halo. He was flanked on both sides by IV towers, each one with a bag dangling from the top. A tube trailed down from each bag, into a needle, through which the medicine was dispensed into his hands and arms. Behind the wheelchair a green oxygen tank stood like a lone guardian angel. A clear tube snaked its way around the left side of the chair, leading to the Reverend's face, where two vents supplying oxygen had been inserted into his nostrils.

As Dantzler drew closer, he was struck by two aspects of the old man's appearance: the Reverend's hair and beard were long and white as cotton, and he couldn't have weighed more than ninety pounds. His thin, bony body seemed almost lost inside his ill-fitting striped pajamas and blue housecoat.

"They tell you I'm dying?" the Reverend barked in a voice stronger than Dantzler would have expected from someone so frail. "If they didn't, you ought to be able to tell just by looking at me."

He laughed but it lacked mirth. "You don't even have to be a particularly good detective to see what pathetic shape I'm in."

Dantzler sat in the chair, leaned back, and nodded at the old man. "Sorry to hear about your situation. Cancer's a tough break."

"Cancer's not tough! *I'm* tough. One of the toughest old birds you'll ever run across. I've survived twenty-nine years in this hell hole, so I know I'm tough. Now, cancer . . . well, that's something entirely different. Cancer is from the dark regions, an evil Satan loosed upon the world to make us question God's love for his children." He shifted in the wheelchair, careful not to dislodge the IV needles. "You believe that, Detective?"

"I don't know why I'm here," Dantzler answered, "but I doubt if it's to discuss theology or the nature of good and evil."

"We'll get to why you're here in the good old by and by," the Reverend said. "Do you believe in God, Detective Dantzler?"

"Come on, Reverend. I didn't come here—"

"Answer the question, Detective. It's simple enough. God—yes or no?"

"I believe in a Creator, yes."

"But not the God of the Bible? Yahweh?"

"No."

"Why not?"

"The biblical Yahweh is a fictional character created by the J writer."

"Fictional? Like Superman?"

"Yes."

"That would make Yahweh a very special fictional character, wouldn't it? Last I heard, no one prays to Superman."

"Look, Reverend—"

"Let's see . . . you believe in a Creator but not Yahweh. Unravel that for me, will you?"

"I believe there is a God beyond the God of the Bible."

"And how would you characterize your relationship with this God beyond the God of the Bible?"

"Strained."

"Any chance it will improve?"

"That's up to him."

"You've got it all wrong, Detective. It's your task to find him, not his task to find you."

"That's letting him off too easy. He needs to do some work."

"Do you believe God loves us, Detective?"

Dantzler shook his head. "In the entire Bible, do you know how many people God actually says he loves?"

"Enlighten me, Detective."

"One. Jacob."

Eli smiled and nodded approvingly. "Malachi, first chapter, second verse. God said, 'I loved Jacob.' What do you make of that?"

Dantzler shrugged. "He also said, 'and I hated Esau.'"

"God loves you, Detective Dantzler, regardless of your inclination to disbelieve it." Eli paused for several seconds, then said, "Since you are a fan of the J writer, I take it you don't subscribe to the belief that Moses authored the first five books of the Bible. The Torah."

"That's a marvelous myth, but I doubt any real biblical scholar believes it."

"Scholars have no claim on the truth."

"Nor do religious leaders."

Eli nodded in agreement. "You're not a Christian, are you, Detective?"

"More of a Gnostic, I'd say."

"Do you know where the term Gnostic comes from?"

"Gnosis. Greek for knowledge."

"Do you possess gnosis, Detective?"

"I chase it, but I don't always catch up to it."

"I like you, Detective Dantzler. We don't have much in common, and I think you're dead wrong, but at least you're a thinker. That's more than I can say for most folks. They tend to be non-thinking sheep."

"Isn't that what religious leaders want? Sheep, blind followers?"

"Religious leaders, politicians, merchants, generals—blind followers are precisely what they want. Not me. I always appreciated those few who challenged my beliefs. Kept me on my toes."

"Look, Reverend—"

"Charlie Bolton still kicking around these days?"

"Yeah. Charlie is very much alive. Retired about ten years ago. Spends most of his time fishing."

"I always respected Charlie. Thought he was fair with me when all that nonsense was happening. He was fair because he wasn't sold on my guilt. His partner, what was that rascal's name?"

"Dan Matthews."

"Yeah, that's him. Tough hombre, he was. Certainly not the warm, friendly type. How is he doing these days?"

"He's dead."

"Murdered, correct?"

"If you knew, why did you ask?"

"For the sheer fun of it, Detective."

Dantzler stood. "Have fun at someone else's expense, Reverend. I'm leaving."

"No, you're not. There's no way you leave now."

"Awfully sure of yourself, aren't you?"

"You couldn't handle it if I called your bluff and let you walk out of here without knowing why I asked to meet with you. I doubt you would make it ten paces before your curiosity got the better of you. You would spin around like Fred Astaire, dance back in here like you had been summoned to God's throne, and fall into that chair. Sit down, Detective. We both know you're not going anywhere."

"Enough chit-chat, Reverend. Why am I here?"

"To prove my innocence."

That wasn't an answer Dantzler expected. "You're putting me on, right?"

"I'm as serious as this cancer inside me."

"Why should I believe you're innocent?"

"Because I'm telling you I am. I may have many negative qualities, Detective, but being a liar isn't one of them."

Dantzler sat, stared at the floor for several seconds, and then looked at the Reverend. "You've been here since, what . . . 'eighty-two, and you're just now declaring your innocence? In all those years, not one squawk, not one appeal. You never once cried foul. Something about that doesn't ring true."

"I didn't kill those two people, Detective Dantzler. That's the truth."

"Why now? Why me?"

"Why now? Let's just say circumstances have changed within the past two weeks. Changed in a positive way from my standpoint. As for why I chose you, simple. I checked up on you, and from everything I could learn, you're a first-rate detective."

Dantzler reached into his coat pocket and took out his notepad.

"What are you doing?" Eli asked.

"I'm gonna take some notes."

"No, you're not. You don't need notes. You're young . . . your memory is fine. Put that away."

"Notes ensure accuracy."

"You're not preparing for an exam, Detective. Lose the cheat sheet."

"You don't like it, tell me to leave," Dantzler waited for the Reverend's response. When the old man remained silent, Dantzler flipped the notepad open, and said, "Tell me about the circumstances. What changed?"

"Can't do it, Detective. Sorry."

"Why not?"

"Silence is golden."

"Clever answer, but not very helpful," Dantzler said, shaking his head.

"It's all you get."

"I don't work closed cases."

"Then open it," the Reverend said. "Give it a fresh look through a new pair of eyes. Who knows? Maybe you'll get it right this time."

"They got it right."

"No, they didn't."

"The evidence—*all* the evidence—says you were guilty."

"That evidence is much like some of your religious beliefs, Detective. It's dead wrong."

"What's wrong about it?"

"That's for you to find out."

"You're not doing much to convince me to take this case."

"You're already convinced, Detective. You just haven't admitted it to yourself yet."

"Let's say I believed you, Reverend, which I don't. But for the sake of argument, I'll pretend I do. You would have to give me a lot more than your assurance that you are innocent before I would agree to pursue this. A whole lot more."

"I'll give you two reasons, Detective. First, the drugs. They found heroin, cocaine, and pills at the crime scene. I had nothing whatsoever to do with drugs. In any way, shape, or form. Ever. Wouldn't even know what they look like or how they smell. They were planted at the scene."

"Not good enough. Anyone in your situation is going to say exactly that. Your second reason needs to be much better or we have nothing else to discuss."

"The gun. Do you really think I would leave the murder weapon at the scene? Do you think I'm that stupid?"

Dantzler shook his head, said, "That's still not enough."

"Check the *Herald-Leader* for the past two weeks. The obits. You'll find your answer there."

"The obits?"

"Dead people do tell tales, Detective."

"That's it? Check the obituary page? That's all you've got?"

"It's all you need. Trust me."

Dantzler stood. "Whose obit am I looking for? And why?"

The Reverend shook his head and closed his eyes.

"Why not give me the name?" Dantzler asked. "If it's that important?"

"Those circumstances I mentioned earlier? The change was positive, not perfect."

"So, you won't give me the name? Or you can't?"

The Reverend shrugged.

"Are you afraid of someone?"

Silence.

"What you are giving me is awfully thin, Reverend."

"No more talk, Detective. I've given you enough. You either do it or you don't. Won't make much difference to me, because I'll likely be dead by the time you figure it out. It would be nice to see my name cleared before I'm gone, but if it doesn't happen, so be it. When I face my Maker—your Creator—I'll have to answer for my share of sins. But murder will not be in the book."

"You're smooth, Reverend. I'll give you that. I almost believe you."

"Look into it, Detective. If you don't, you're letting a murderer run free."

"I'll think about it."

"You do that."

Dantzler turned and walked out of the light and into the darkness.

"Oh, Detective," the Reverend said. "You *do* believe me."

CHAPTER THREE

Dantzler made it back to Lexington just after nightfall. As always, the Saturday night in-town traffic was a nightmare, a whirling mass of far too many people in far too much of a hurry to get to far too many places. Everyone, it seemed, was always in a rush. Always on the go. Dantzler often wondered if Americans were somehow wired for constant movement. Maybe it was part of our DNA, like the color of our eyes. Whatever the reason, the evidence was clear that taking life easy, stopping to smell the roses, or appreciating Nature's beauty were quaint concepts that had long ago vanished in this mad-dash country.

He gave brief consideration to making an appearance at the police station, but decided not to. It was out of the way, and he didn't want to fight the traffic any longer than necessary. Also, he knew there was no need to check in, not in today's cell phone, text message, Twitter world. Had anything happened demanding his attention, he would have heard about it ten seconds after it occurred.

After making a quick stop at the Liquor Barn on Richmond Road to buy a bottle of Pernod and some orange juice, he headed home, the small ranch-style house on Lakeshore Drive he bought in the mid-1990s. Home sounded good, especially after the craziness of the past few months, in which there had been four homicides and three suicides. God knows, he could use the down time, the quiet, being alone. There were books to be read, music to be listened to, tennis to be played, personal issues to be dealt with. In the blur of work, too many important items had been neglected or pushed aside. Like most Americans, he seemed to be trapped on a speedway going nowhere fast. It was a feeling he didn't like.

With each passing year, he became more aware of the reality that time charges relentlessly forward, never yielding, grabbing your life by the throat and carrying it toward its inevitable end. We are all weary and reluctant travelers hanging on as best we can, engaged in a futile attempt to outrun the clock, to win the mad dash to the finish line. But no matter how hard we fight it, how strong our resistance, or how swiftly we run, time always wins the race. Time is undefeated and always will be. That will never change.

An hour later, sitting at home alone, he recalled a line written by the great T.S. Eliot: *all time is unredeemable*. The old poet got that one right, Dantzler had long ago concluded. True, work was important, and what he did mattered, but . . . he had to pay more attention to life outside the job. Time lost is time gone forever.

He wanted off the speedway.

Maybe that was why he felt such ambivalence toward his meeting with the Reverend. Did he really want to open that can of worms? Dig into a crime now almost thirty years old? Help a man who would surely be dead within a matter of weeks, possibly even days?

Did he really want to invest his time and energy in a closed case?

Dantzler's silent answer to every question was no. And yet . . . he couldn't simply dismiss it outright, no matter how much he might want to. The old man was right—Dantzler tended to believe him. Dantzler had interviewed his share of liars in the past, but the Reverend, though smooth-tongued enough to be a superb liar, was hitting at some truths.

The detective instincts in Dantzler were screaming that this was a case with legs. It was, Dantzler conceded, and he admitted this with some reluctance, one he would probably look into. Like it or not, his interest had been piqued. His detective juices were flowing.

There was yet another, ever greater reason for his interest—the possibility that an innocent man was in prison. That was unacceptable.

*****

Dantzler spent Saturday night drinking Pernod and orange juice and listening to Leonard Cohen CDs. On Sunday, he rose early, put himself through an hour of torture on the treadmill and Stairmaster, showered, and read the newspaper. After paying a couple of bills, he gave thought to playing a few sets of tennis with Randall Dennis, but quickly brushed them aside. He also toyed with the idea of phoning Laurie, but cast that notion out just as quickly. Their relationship had cooled during the past few months, which, both of them agreed, was for the best. Richard Bird, their captain, was in equal agreement. He was dead set against co-workers being involved romantically, and he had not been afraid to make his feelings known.

Instead, Dantzler opted to dig into the stack of unread books, beginning with Harold Bloom's *Jesus and Yahweh: The Names Divine*. He had read several of Bloom's books and had always found the celebrated Yale professor and literary critic to be interesting, provocative, and enlightening. An hour into this one and Dantzler wasn't disappointed. It was, he felt, Bloom's best book to date.

By three-thirty, however, Jesus and Yahweh had been usurped by Eli Whitehouse. Dantzler couldn't get the Reverend's words out of his head: *I didn't kill those two people, Detective*. He set the book aside, looked up Charlie Bolton's number, grabbed his cell phone, and punched in the numbers. Charlie answered after the first ring.

"Jack," he yelled, "if this isn't life-or-death important, I'm gonna shoot you dead."

"You'd do better to shoot those fish you're trying to catch. From what I hear, you can't land one with a rod and reel."

Charlie laughed. "Much as I hate to admit it, there's a good deal of truth in that statement. I'm an old man who can't see."

"Clever, Charlie. Didn't know you were up on your Hemingway."

"Hell, Jack, I met him once. Down in Key West a couple of years before he ate the shotgun. Shook his hand."

"You and Papa. Hard to envision."

"I only shook the man's hand, Jack. We didn't share a beer."

"I assume you're at the lake. Correct?"

"Yes."

"When will you be back?"

"Tonight, around midnight. Why? What's up?"

"Meet me at Coyle's tomorrow. Say around one-thirty. Lunch is on me."

"What's this about, Jack? Something important I need to know about?"

"Relax, it's nothing big. I simply want to talk to you about a few things."

"That has an ominous sound to it."

"You worry too much, Charlie. There's nothing ominous about it at all."

"Worrying is what made me a good cop."

"See you tomorrow, Charlie. And don't smell like fish when you show up."

*****

After hanging up, Dantzler returned to the Bloom book, spending the next hour reading and contemplating the author's suggestion that Yeshua of Nazareth and Jesus Christ were not only different personages, but were, indeed, totally incompatible with one another. According to Bloom, one was a rather dark and mysterious human, the other a theological God. One longed for his father, the other was his father's anointed son. The great irony, Bloom was quick to point out, was the transformation of Yeshua, the Jew of Jews, into the centerpiece of a new religion—Christianity. Bloom took that paradox even further, saying that had Yeshua of Nazareth somehow survived the Crucifixion and lived on into old age, he would have regarded Christianity with amazement. Dantzler found himself in complete agreement with Bloom's assessment.

At six, with more than half the book finished, Dantzler's growling stomach reminded him he hadn't eaten all day. Yahweh would have to wait, Dantzler decided. Food, not esoteric literature, was now the top priority.

He quickly threw together one of his instant "left-over specials," this one consisting of spaghetti and meatballs, and what remained of a Caesar salad. Not an award-winning meal by any standards, but at least it was filling.

There was nothing in the house that would even remotely pass for dessert, so he mixed another Pernod and orange juice and was about to head for the deck when his phone rang. He put his glass on the counter and picked up the phone.

"Jack Dantzler."

"Forget everything the Reverend told you," a man's voice ordered. "That's for your own good, and I will not repeat myself."

"Who is this?" Dantzler asked, but the man ended the call without answering.

Dantzler punched in the caller ID, only to be informed by a mechanical voice that the number was not accessible.

He hung up the phone, stood there for several seconds, then grabbed his Pernod and orange juice and went out onto the deck. The night was warm and breezy, the sky filled with countless stars. A gold moon reflected off the lake that bumped up against his back yard. Damn near a perfect night, he thought to himself.

Dantzler sat in a lounge chair and pondered the phone call. Specifically, the questions it triggered. How did the caller know about the meeting with the Reverend, which took place less than thirty-six hours ago? What was the caller's relationship to the Reverend? To the crime itself? Was he a family member? Could it have been Colt Rogers, the attorney? And how did he get Dantzler's unlisted home number?

One other question had to be considered: could the call have been instigated by the Reverend as a way of increasing the odds Dantzler would get involved?

Dantzler had no answers to any of his questions except the last one.

He discounted the possibility that the call was made at the Reverend's behest. The Reverend had made it absolutely clear during the meeting that he didn't need outside assistance. He was certain Dantzler would re-open the case.

With that one out of the way, Dantzler was left with one final thought, one that had nagged at him since leaving the prison: an ever-growing belief that the Reverend may well be an innocent man.

CHAPTER FOUR

Dantzler was in his office by six-thirty Monday morning. He had no particular reason for the early arrival, other than the need to feel like he was doing something constructive. Idleness wasn't his cup of tea. He was like the shark that must keep swimming or die. It wasn't lost on him that his much-longed-for leisure time had once again become a victim to his work, his need for action. So much for getting off the speedway.

Dantzler was surprised to find Eric Gamble standing by the coffee pot, holding an empty Styrofoam cup in his hand. The bags under his eyes were testament to his lack of sleep.

"I hope you don't feel as bad as you look, Eric," Dantzler said, plucking a cup from the stack on the table. "Because if you do, you might as well be pushing up daisies."

"Do I really look that bad?"

"Dead man walking."

"Man, I'm this close to finishing my novel," Eric said, pinching his thumb and forefinger almost together. "I just can't get the ending the way I want it."

"Maybe you need to step away from it for a while, put some distance between you and the story. Then, at some point, attack it again. Maybe you'll come back to it with a new and fresh perspective."

"I tried that, already," Eric said, shaking his head. "Didn't work. I put it away for two days, tried to forget about it, but then I felt compelled to get back at it. It's like a fire in my brain and it's consuming me. I have to finish the damn thing."

Eric poured coffee into his cup before filling Dantzler's. "Did I tell you I finally landed an agent?"

"No, you didn't. That's huge, right?"

"Oh, definitely. She's with a big-time New York agency. Loves what she's read so far. Thinks it has definite potential." Eric sipped at the steaming coffee. "She's the one who recommended a different ending. Initially, I was resistant, didn't think the ending had problems. But she convinced me. She gave me two or three possible endings. So . . . now here I am, struggling to come up with a different finish."

"You'll do it."

"Would you read it, Jack? Take a look, see what you think? Let me know your verdict on the ending I'm going with? I mean, only if you have the time."

"Not unless you make the lead character white, base him on me, and let Daniel Day-Lewis play him in the movie."

"Well, you ain't reading it, then," Eric said, laughing. "Because the guy is as black as my ass, and no one but Denzel plays him in the movie."

"Bumped by Denzel Washington. I can live with that. Sure, Eric, I'll be happy to take a look at it."

"Thanks." Eric looked at his watch. "We have a meeting this morning?"

"Not unless Rich has one planned."

"I haven't seen Captain Bird in a week or so," Eric said. "I think maybe he's been out of town."

"He's been in D.C. attending a big-time conference on homeland security. But he should be back today."

"Well, a Monday morning without a meeting is fine with me," Eric said, dumping his cup into the wastebasket.

*****

A few minutes after eight o'clock, Laurie Dunn and Milt Brewer walked in. Laurie, stunning as always, wore a blue pants suit, white turtleneck top, and black flats. Her long brown hair was pulled back in a ponytail, and if she had on any makeup, it wasn't noticeable. Not that she needed any help. Nature had treated her extremely well. By any standard, she was a natural beauty.

She moved past Milt, went to the table, pulled back a chair, and took a seat. "Morning, guys," she said. When no one responded, she said, "Well, aren't we a grumpy bunch today?"

As always, Milt, a ten-cup-a-day guy, headed straight for the coffee pot. After filling his cup, he claimed his usual seat at the table, first one on the right. He spied Eric yawning.

"You know, Eric, for such a good looking dude, you look like crap. Another late night with the ladies?"

"I was writing."

"When are you gonna finish that damn book, anyway? You've been working on it for, what, five years now?"

"Three."

"You know, God created the Earth in six days. Surely . . ."

"Yeah, yeah, you've told me this before, Milt. I'll finish it when I finish it."

"Yogi Berra couldn't have said it better."

Dantzler moved to the table and sat down next to Milt. "How did trial go Friday?" Milt had been the lead detective on a murder case that finally found its way into the courtroom after two years in legal limbo. "Any glitches?"

"Piece of cake," Milt answered. "Puckett's attorney only asked me three questions on cross. Ask, then sat. He knows this isn't a battle he can win."

Milt finished off the coffee and tossed his cup into the wastebasket. "Funny thing is, everyone, including the defense attorney, has been begging Puckett to take a plea. He won't do it. Keeps saying, 'we're gonna win this thing at trial, just like O.J. did.' Who's he kidding? Lonnie Puckett has about as much chance of winning as I have of getting a date with Ashley Judd, which, we all know, ain't gonna happen. He may be the most stupid moron I've ever encountered. It's just a damn shame all criminals aren't that dumb."

"That would certainly make life easier for all of us," Dantzler said. "You put in your papers, Milt?"

"Not yet. They're filled out, lying on the kitchen table, just waiting for me to hand in. But . . . I haven't been able to bring myself to do it. A coward, I guess."

"Thirty-five years chasing bad guys. You've earned the right to kick back and relax."

"Yeah, I have. And with Dan gone, it's not the same for me. I love you guys, and you know it, but me and Dan, we just had so much history together. Vietnam, here, the cases we worked—it's just not the same."

Dan Matthews, Milt's long-time partner, was murdered while working the Victor Sammael case, strangled and mutilated at the Marriott Inn. He and Milt had been more than mere partners. They were drinking buddies and close friends for almost forty years. They were like brothers, a perfect pairing of brains, tenacity, and toughness. For Milt, losing Dan was akin to losing a family member.

Milt looked away, said, "I always assumed Dan and me would call it quits together. Start together, finish together. Then we would spend our remaining time drinking and playing cards. Never thought I'd finish solo."

"What do you remember about the John Elijah Whitehouse case?" Dantzler asked.

Milt seemed puzzled by the question. "Eli Whitehouse?"

"Yeah."

"Man, you're taking me back a few years with that name."

"What can you tell me about the case?"

"Mainly, it was Dan's first homicide case. He worked it with Charlie Bolton. Why do you ask?"

"Did Dan ever talk about it?"

Milt shook his head. "Only that Eli was guilty, and the case went down easy and quick. Not much else, best I recall. If you want details, check with Charlie. He has a memory like a computer."

Milt filled another cup with coffee. "Why are you asking about Eli's case? That's ancient history."

"You know me, Milt. I'm a real history buff." Dantzler stood. "Come on, Laurie. Take a ride with me."

"Where are we going?"

"To kneel at the shoes of the fisherman."

CHAPTER FIVE

Charlie Bolton lived in a cozy brick house in the Palomar Estates subdivision, a standard three-bedroom, two-bath, two-car garage model he purchased a few years before retiring. Charlie, a cop for thirty-five years, was the grand old man in Lexington law enforcement circles, and the detective who served as mentor and rabbi for virtually every detective working there today, including Dantzler and Laurie.

No one was held in greater esteem than Charlie Bolton.

Charlie was in the front yard watering plants when Dantzler and Laurie pulled into the driveway. He cut the water, let the hose fall to the ground like a dead snake, and walked slowly toward the car. A huge smile creased his tanned and craggy face.

"Dunn, how many times did I warn you to stay away from stray dogs?" he said. "Especially a big mutt like this fellow?"

"You know me. I'm not keen on following orders." Laurie pinched her nose. "I would hug you, Charlie, but you smell like rotten fish."

"Indeed I do," he answered. "It's the smell of victory."

"I'd hug you, Charlie, but you're just too damn ugly," Dantzler said, grinning.

"You've been with uglier, Jack," Charlie said. "And don't tell me otherwise."

"Can I take the Fifth on that one?"

"The prudent thing to do, I'd say." Charlie frowned. "Thought we were meeting at Coyle's."

Dantzler shook his head. "Nah. This way, I don't have to buy you lunch."

"You always did have alligator arms when it came time to pick up a check." Charlie looked at the thick folder in Dantzler's hand. "A murder book? You did get the memo saying I had retired, didn't you?"

"A detective turns in his shield and his weapon. He never retires."

Charlie laughed. "Where did you get that slice of wisdom? A fortune cookie?"

"Where can we talk, Charlie?"

"Sun's gonna get hot shortly, so I vote for the kitchen."

"Then let us tarry no longer."

Charlie draped an arm around Laurie. "Tell me again how you put up with this mutt."

"It ain't easy."

*****

Charlie handed a can of Diet Pepsi to Dantzler and a glass of water to Laurie. "I know it's not cool these days to drink water straight from the tap, but I don't have any of the bottled stuff. Simply won't buy it. No need to pay for water because someone slaps a fancy name on the bottle. H_2O is H_2O."

"You're a true Spartan, Charlie," Laurie said. "If you were just a few years younger, I would—"

"Yeah, yeah, that's what all the young and beautiful ones say." Charlie held out his left hand, fingers spread. "See this ring finger? Ain't never been one on it. Know why? Cause I never fell into the female trap."

"Ah, Charlie," Laurie said, clasping both hands over her heart. "A Spartan *and* a heartbreaker."

"Nope. Just a sensible man, that's all." He looked at the folder resting on the middle of the table. "What did you bring me, Jack?"

"John Elijah Whitehouse. What do you remember about his case?"

"Eli Whitehouse? You're here about him?"

"I am."

"Hell, Jack, that was twenty, twenty-five years ago. I—"

"Twenty-nine, to be exact."

"Okay, twenty-nine. That's a long time ago."

"Tell me about it."

"You're joking, right?"

"You don't see me laughing, do you?"

"What do you want to know?" Charlie asked, his fingers drumming the murder book.

"Anything. The basics."

"It's all in the murder book. I kept detailed notes."

"And I'll study them in great detail. But . . . for now, off the top of your head, what do you remember about the case?"

"He killed two people. Shot them both in the back of the head, execution style. The murder took place in an old barn on a piece of property owned by Eli."

"Go on," Dantzler prodded.

"The two vics were a couple of local street kids. Drugs were found at the crime scene, so we figured it for a drug deal that turned ugly." Charlie sipped some coffee. "Why are you inquiring about Eli Whitehouse?"

"I met with him."

"When? Where? Why, for God's sake?"

"Saturday, at the prison. At his request."

Charlie set the coffee cup on the table and shook his head. "Why did he request a meeting with you? You didn't work the case. Hell, you weren't even on the force back then."

"He heard I was a first-rate cop."

"No argument there. But, why did he want to meet with any cop?"

"Says he's innocent. Wants me to re-open the case."

"After all these years? Why now?"

"He's dying. Inoperable cancer."

"Huh."

"He said something else, as well, Charlie. Said you thought he was innocent."

Charlie shook his head. "That's not exactly accurate. I never said he was innocent; I was just never convinced of his guilt. Dan, on the other hand, had no doubt about it. He was certain Eli was the killer."

"Why did you have doubts, Charlie?"

"Damn, Jack, I need time to think about this."

"No, you don't. You remember every detail of every case you ever worked. Why the doubts?"

"Well, the method the killer used always troubled me. Back of the head, single shot. Like I said—execution style. That seemed awfully professional to me. Something you might see from the Mob or the KGB. But not how a civilian—a preacher—would do it."

"Go on."

"The drug aspect. We never uncovered any evidence connecting Eli to drug trafficking, production, sales, or distribution. None whatsoever. And the two victims were another stumbling block for me. A couple of local street-wise punks who had each been arrested a number of times for possession of marijuana. Typical weedsters, you know? Neither was a big-time druggie, and neither had a prior connection to Eli. At least, none that we found. There just didn't seem to be a legitimate motive for Eli to kill those two guys."

Dantzler leaned forward. "Let me ask you a couple of questions. If it was a drug deal gone bad, then why were any drugs left there in the first place? Second, why leave the bodies in such an open place, where they were sure to be found?"

"Your drug question is one that bothered me as well, and it's one I have no answer for. Either they were left there inadvertently, or they were planted. Take your pick. As for your second question, the killer did make an attempt to get rid of the bodies. He torched the barn, but it rained like hell that night, effectively putting out the fire. A young couple was out parking, saw the smoke, and went to check it out. They found the bodies."

"You had doubts; Dan didn't. Why was he so convinced?"

"Fingerprints. Eli's prints were all over the murder weapon."

"A twenty-two, correct?"

"Yep. And it belonged to old Eli, too." Charlie sipped more coffee. "Those fingerprints—that's what did him in. When the D.A. stood in front of the jury, held up the murder weapon, and stated the prints on the gun belonged to Eli, well, that closed the lid on the coffin. All reasonable doubt got washed away."

"According to your notes, you found the gun at the crime scene."

"Yes. Right next to the bodies."

"That didn't bother you?"

"Of course, it did. I mean, why would Eli leave the murder weapon at the crime scene, where it was certain to be found? Why not toss it into an incinerator? Or into one of the ponds on his farm? Hell, there must've been five or six of them. And if he was stupid enough to leave it there, why not at least wipe it clean of prints? Finding it where we did, with those perfect prints on it, just didn't make sense to me."

"Sounds like he was framed."

"My instincts always said so." Charlie looked at Laurie, then back at Dantzler. "You gonna look into it?"

"I'm considering it."

"Those damn prints, Jack. That's nearly impossible evidence to overcome." Charlie rose, refilled his coffee cup, and stood next to the counter. "Something else also troubled me. During the lead-up to the trial, Eli said very little in his own defense. Was almost silent, in fact. Even Dan was troubled by Eli's silence. Dan kept saying, 'if I was innocent, been framed, I would be screaming so loud they would hear me in heaven and hell.' But not Eli. He remained stoic through it all."

Charlie sat back down. "What did he say to you during the meeting?"

"Not a lot. Only that he didn't do it, and that I should check the obits page in the *Herald* for the past two weeks. He said the answer is there."

"Did he give you a name?"

"No. Said he couldn't."

"You think he couldn't, or he wouldn't?"

"Both. I think the man is afraid of something. Or someone."

"You said he's terminal. What's a dying man got to be afraid of?"

"He has three kids. Six or seven grandkids. Could be he's worried about their safety."

"And it could be he's just yanking your chain. Running one final con before he ventures off to the Great Beyond. He wouldn't be the first murderer to pull that stunt."

"This is no stunt. He's afraid, and I think he has reason to be. Last night, not long after we spoke, I got an interesting call. The caller, a man, said I should forget everything the Reverend told me. He said it in a very threatening tone. It was definitely a warning, not a request."

"You trace it?"

"Couldn't be accessed."

"That is interesting."

"What can you tell me about Colt Rogers?" Dantzler said.

"He's a lawyer—what else needs to be said?"

"You had any dealings with him?"

"Couple of times he's questioned me in court or for a deposition. Nothing serious. Why are you asking about him? He wasn't Eli's attorney. Abe Basham was. Abe's been dead for years."

"Rogers and a guy named Johnny Richards visit with Eli on a fairly regular basis. I'm curious about their connection."

"Well, Rogers operates out of the same building Abe was in. Maybe even the same office, for all I know. Could be he took over Abe's practice and sort of inherited Eli."

"And Johnny Richards?"

"Not familiar with him."

"Is there anything else you can tell me?" Dantzler said, closing the folder.

Charlie shook his head. "You're gonna pursue this, aren't you?"

Dantzler shrugged.

"You've got no choice." Charlie started to say something, hesitated for several seconds, then said, "There is only one thing worse that letting a guilty guy go free and that's sending an innocent man to prison. God, I hate to think I let that happen. But—"

He looked up at Dantzler.

"Those damn fingerprints. That was the clincher."

CHAPTER SIX

At five-thirty, Dantzler left the police station, walked several blocks down Vine Street, turned onto South Upper, crossed the street, and went into McCarthy's Irish Bar. The place, crowded as usual, was crawling with attorneys, most of whom were standing together, chatting and drinking. Several nodded at him as he walked past.

Near the back, sitting alone, was Sean Montgomery. When he saw Dantzler, Montgomery picked up his empty pint glass and called out to the woman tending bar.

"Make it two of these," he said, putting the glass back on the table.

Montgomery was an ex-Homicide detective who quit the force, went back to school, and earned his law degree. He was now a partner in one of the city's biggest, most-prestigious firms, having moved up fast due to his great skills as a trial lawyer. He and Dantzler had worked several cases together in the early '90s, and had remained close over the years. Even though Sean had gone over to the "evil empire" and become a defense attorney, he was one of the few people Dantzler trusted completely.

Dantzler sat just as the bartender placed a pint of Guinness in front of each man. Montgomery lifted his glass and downed half the contents in one long guzzle.

"Best darn Guinness outside of New York, Boston, or Chicago," he said, putting down his glass. "Some days it's even better. Of course, if you want the *really* good stuff, you have to go to Ireland. I've been there twice, and I can promise you the Guinness there is to die for."

"This is good," Dantzler said, after taking a drink. "I need to come here more often."

"That you do, laddie. That you do."

"Aren't you Scottish, Sean, rather than Irish?"

"Which I suppose makes me first cousins to the Irish. Can't say for sure. What I do know, though, is we both have a strong dislike for the Brits. The colonial bastards." Montgomery took another long pull, almost emptying the glass. "Have you noticed how everybody in this country claims to be either part Irish or part Native American? Those seem to be the two 'in' ethnic groups to have in your background. I once dated a beautiful, blonde, blue-eyed, fair-skin lady—pure Scandinavian from head to toe. Could've easily been Miss Sweden or Miss Denmark. Anyway, we started discussing ethnicity and she claimed to be one-eighth Cherokee. I'm thinking, well, of course you are, my dear. How could you not be? Isn't everyone?"

He laughed and said, "If that woman has a drop of Cherokee blood in her, I'll give you a kiss on the lips out on Main Street."

"I'll take a pass on that," Dantzler said, grinning, "regardless of her bloodlines."

"Ready for another one?" Montgomery asked, holding up his glass.

"Not just yet. I'm savoring this one."

"One more for me," Montgomery said to the bartender. "And keep an eye on this guy. Get him another one when he runs dry."

"Listen, Sean. What can you tell me about Colt Rogers?"

"He's an asshole, not to be trusted. Why? Is he representing you on some matter?"

"No."

"Good. I'd make you buy the next five rounds if that were the case."

"You don't like him?"

"Don't like him or respect him."

"What's his reputation within the lawyer community?"

"Mediocre attorney, world-class bullshitter, master manipulator, courtroom coward."

"Why do you refer to him as a courtroom coward?"

"Because he never goes to trial," Montgomery said. "He always has his clients plead out. Convinces them they don't have a chance to win, then has them cop a plea. He scares them into accepting the sentence recommendation rather than fight it out at trial. Then he takes credit for winning while his clients head off to jail without having been given a chance to beat the rap. They get four years instead of six, when, in many instances, with a little luck and a good attorney, they might have been acquitted. And most of them are dumb enough to believe he's done them a big favor. Poor schmucks."

"What types of cases does he normally handle?"

"He'll take on pretty much anything, so long as the money is right."

"You ever cross swords with him?"

Montgomery shook his head. "We're both defense attorneys, so the chances of us crossing swords are nil. I have dealt with him a few times, but nothing serious. Like I said, he tends to dodge real challenges. If I did face off against him at trial, I would eat his lunch. Now, that I would savor."

"Did he take over Abe Basham's practice?"

"Oh, hell, no. 'Honest Abe' would have had nothing to do with a guy like Rogers. Trust me, Abe and Rogers were at opposite ends of the morals spectrum. Abe was revered, Rogers is reviled. They operated in different galaxies."

"Doesn't Rogers have an office in the same building where Abe's practice was located? On West Short Street?"

"Yeah, but Rogers moved in after Abe died. Prior to that, Rogers had an office in Chevy Chase."

"Has Rogers ever been in trouble?"

"You mean, with the Bar?"

"Any kind of trouble?"

"If he has, I've never heard about it. I figure him for one of those slick types who knows just how far to go without going over the line. Caught or not, I'm sure he's done his share of shady dealings."

"You know Johnny Richards?"

"Nope. What's going on here, Jack? Why are you inquiring about a slimeball like Colt Rogers?"

"You remember the Eli Whitehouse case?" Dantzler asked.

"Vaguely. I was a kid when it happened. He was a preacher or evangelist—something along those lines, wasn't he? Killed a couple of guys."

"Yeah, well, I'm thinking about re-opening the case. Give it another look."

"I know you pretty well, Jack. You wouldn't do that unless you were convinced something was off. Are you?"

"No, I'm not convinced, and won't be until or unless I find evidence that will convince me. But I do think there is reason for doubt."

"Who was the lead detective on the case?"

"Charlie Bolton."

"You're pissing in the wind, my friend. Charlie *never* screwed up."

"No. But I talked to him about it, and he admits he was never one-hundred percent certain Eli was guilty." Dantzler got the bartender's attention and ordered two more pints of Guinness. "Dan Matthews worked the case with Charlie. It was his first homicide investigation. Dan had no doubt about Eli's guilt."

"After you, Dan's the best homicide detective I've ever run across. If he was convinced, and if Charlie didn't prove the man's innocence, I'd say you really are pissing in the wind."

"I don't know. My gut says otherwise."

"A cop's instincts can sometimes be more persuasive than the evidence. We've both known that to be the case. And no one has better instincts than you. If you feel it, give it a whirl."

Dantzler finished off his Guinness, stood, and put two twenty dollar bills on the table. "By the way, Sean. I've never asked you what it's like making your living defending assholes you used to put away."

Montgomery chuckled. "It's easy, Jack. I just hold my nose when they hand me the money."

"Just make sure the stink doesn't rub off on you."

*****

Dantzler left McCarthy's and walked back to the station. He stopped briefly at the front desk, engaged in a few minutes of small talk with Bruce Rawlinson, and then headed for the stairs. When he reached the second floor, he saw Eric standing outside of Captain Bird's office.

"Hey, Eric," Dantzler said. "You serious about wanting me to take a look at your novel?"

"Sure. If you have the time."

"For you, Eric, I'll make time."

"Okay, what's the catch?"

"No catch."

"Oh, yeah, there's a catch," Eric insisted.

"I'd prefer to call it a Hannibal Lecter-type exchange."

"What?"

"I give you advice, you give me information. You know, *quid pro quo*. Like with Hannibal and Clarice."

"What information? Specifically?"

"I want you to check the *Herald's* obit page for a specific two-week period. Make it the two weeks prior to last Saturday. Really dig into the background of those who died. I want to know everything you can come up with."

"What's this about?"

Dantzler spent the next fifteen minutes bringing Eric up to speed on the Eli Whitehouse case. Eric listened intently as Dantzler gave a quick overview of the murders, his being summoned to meet the Reverend, discussing the matter with Charlie, the threatening phone call, and his intention to re-open the investigation.

Eric shook his head, a look of deep skepticism on his face. "I don't know, Jack. Sounds to me like you're fishing for minnows in the ocean."

"No. The phone call changed everything. It convinced me the Reverend is telling the truth. When a stranger orders me to shut down an investigation I haven't even begun, it can only mean one thing—something is going on."

"Any parameters on the obits thing?" Eric said.

Dantzler thought for a second, then said, "Start with males, Lexington or Fayette County residents. If we need to branch out, we'll do that later on."

"What do you want me to look for? Besides a criminal background, of course?"

"Anything you find that might smell. Check finances, family members, business dealings. Pallbearers, if you have the time. Did the family request donations rather than flowers? If so, where did they want the money to go? It's gonna require you to dig through a huge pile of manure in order to find the diamond."

"If there even is a diamond."

"It's in there somewhere. We've just got to uncover it."

"Okay. I'll get on it first thing in the morning." Eric laughed. "*Quid pro quo*, huh? It's more like *quid pro I got suckered*."

"Could be I made a fool's deal, Eric. Depends on how good your book is."

"It's a helluva lot better than the obits page. I can promise you that."

CHAPTER SEVEN

Eli lay in his bed in the prison infirmary, eyes closed tight, as though by so doing he could miraculously shut out the pain along with the light. Lying there, with a half-dozen needles jabbed into veins in his arms and the back of both hands, extremities now black and blue from the relentless torture, he felt like a pin cushion. No human should experience such indignity.

He wanted to curse God, to rail against a Maker who would allow such misery, such affliction, but he couldn't. He wouldn't dare, never, regardless of the circumstances, however grim and horrible they might be. Eli knew better, knew that despite the intense and bitter feelings he now felt, nothing could erase his awe for the Almighty. Awe . . . and fear. To love God is required; to fear him is the true beginning of wisdom.

The pages of history are replete with cautionary tales about men and women who voiced angry displeasure at God and the consequences they suffered. Eli often told his parishioners—and his own children—the story of Kierkegaard's father, Michael, who, while still a young boy, cursed God. That single moment of anger, only a split-second in the space of a full lifetime, placed such a heavy burden on young Michael that he never cast it away. He remained throughout his life a sad, broken, and remorseful man.

Never, Eli warned, admonish the Almighty, no matter how bad or tragic or dire the circumstances that fire your anger. His ways are not our ways, and no matter how hard we try, we can never comprehend them. His plan for each of us is his alone. We are merely his instruments, his humble servants.

And yet . . . at this moment, it took all of Eli's will and strength to contain the angry feelings that roiled inside him. The pain he felt now was unbearable. His lungs burned like they were in flames. It felt like a mad wolverine was in his chest, chewing relentlessly at his insides, consuming his very being inch by inch. The cancer was, Eli knew, eating him alive.

The morphine available to him could ease the pain, but Eli wasn't ready to go that route. Yes, the pain was unbearable, yet at this point he preferred suffering to being doped up and out of it. Once you choose to bury the pain behind a cloud of drugs, you also choose to abandon life as you know it. That option wasn't acceptable . . . yet. Eli did not want to be dead while still alive.

Still, he couldn't help but wonder why God had placed such a heavy burden on him. He had always been God's faithful servant, a true believer. Yes, he had sinned, fallen victim to temptation, to lust, but he was cleansed through God's love and mercy. He had tried to obey the Commandments, to live a pious life, to be a loving husband and devoted father. A protective father. He had taken the blame for sins he didn't commit. Spent three decades in prison for a sentence that wasn't rightfully his to serve.

Eli wondered if perhaps this was the sin that caused God's wrath. Maybe he shouldn't have taken the blame. Maybe he should have pointed fingers at the real perpetrator. Maybe, by allowing a murderer to go free, he was, in God's eyes, as guilty as the killer.

Maybe—

But he had taken the only path available to him at the time. He had but a single option then and he had taken it. Any loving father would have made the same decision. Eli simply did not believe God would elect to punish him for following his conscience in a matter involving the safety of his wife and children. God could not be that cruel and uncaring.

God had to understand.

God *must* understand.

Tears rolled down Eli's cheeks as he drifted off to sleep.

CHAPTER EIGHT

Dantzler spent the next day studying the murder book for the Eli Whitehouse case. The report was detailed, thorough, clean, and as easy to read as a Michael Connelly novel. Exactly what you would expect from Charlie Bolton.

The specifics of the case were simple: On the night of April 5, 1982, Greg Spurlock and Angie Iler saw smoke and flames rising toward the sky. Curious, they drove in the direction of the fire, eventually arriving at the site, an old barn located next to a small pond. By this time, around midnight, a hard rain had begun to fall, effectively putting out the fire. The couple went into the barn, where they discovered the bodies of Carl Osteen and Bruce Fowler. The couple then drove to a small gas station several miles away and phoned the fire department and police.

Charlie Bolton had Dan Matthews contact Eli and ask him to come to the site. Eli arrived at two forty-five a.m. Eli was told the names of the deceased, and asked if he knew them. He stated that he did not. He was asked if he was aware of any reason why drugs would be on the property. He did not. He was also asked if he owned any weapons. He said he owned a Winchester rifle and a .22 caliber pistol. At approximately four-fifteen, Eli was allowed to leave the scene.

At five p.m. that same day, Charlie and Dan met with Eli at his house. During their talk, Dan showed a .22 pistol to Eli and asked if the weapon belonged to him. Eli said no, his was locked inside the safe. Dan asked Eli to open the safe, which he did without hesitation. Eli expressed disbelief when he saw the .22 was missing. Charlie informed Eli that the weapon now in police possession would be turned over to the ballistics experts for testing.

At approximately ten on the morning of April 6, Eli was brought to the station and officially interrogated by Charlie and Dan. The interrogation lasted more than three hours and covered a surprisingly wide range of topics.

Dantzler read the typed transcript of Eli's initial conversation with Charlie and Dan several times, eventually returning to the section in which they discussed the .22.

Charlie: Tell us again. When was the last time you used

the weapon.

Eli: Two weeks ago.

Charlie: What were the circumstances?

Eli: Circumstances? There were no circumstances. I simply took the pistol to the lake by the barn and fired several rounds. I do that periodically to ensure that it is in working order.

Charlie: Was it in working order?

Eli: It worked perfectly, as it always did.

Dan: Here's where we run into problems, Mr. Whitehouse. Your fingerprints are on the weapon and . . .

Eli: Of course, my fingerprints are on the gun. I told you. I used it two weeks ago.

Dan: But the gun had been fired more recently than two weeks ago. And I'm betting ballistics will confirm that it was the weapon used to kill those two boys in your barn.

Eli: That can't be. It just can't be. The gun was locked in the safe. I would swear to it. I had not removed it since I last used it. If I had used it to commit murder, do you think I would be stupid enough to leave it at the crime scene? Or to let you look into the safe without a search warrant?

Charlie: Who besides you knows the combination to the safe?

Eli: My wife, of course. My two sons. And Abe Basham, my attorney.

Charlie: That's it? You've positive of that?

Eli: Yes.

Dan: I have to tell you, Mr. Whitehouse. This does not look good for you. And if ballistics does bear out my suspicions, things are going to look a lot worse. What it's going to mean is, you committed these murders.

Eli: I did not. As God is my witness, I did no such thing.

Dan: Well, let's wait and see if the evidence has the same eyes God has.

Several pages later Dantzler read the transcript of Eli's second interrogation. This one took place the next day, after he had officially been charged with the crime. For this meeting, Abe Basham, Eli's attorney, was present.

Charlie: Do I need to read you your rights again, Reverend?

Eli: It's not necessary.

Abe: Why don't you do it anyway, Detective? For the sake of protocol.

Charlie: John Elijah Whitehouse, you have . . .

Eli: This is not necessary, Abe.

Abe: Have it your way, Eli. Proceed, Detective.

Dan: Mr. Whitehouse, it appears as though God and the physical evidence are not on the same page. We have your prints on the murder weapon discovered at the crime scene. That pretty much makes it a done deal. Why not confess? Tell us how it went down?

Eli: I can't confess to a crime I did not commit.

Charlie: Then give us a scenario that backs your story.

Eli: I can't.

Dan: You claim you were at the church when the murders occurred? Right?

Eli: Yes. I was working on Sunday's sermon.

Dan: What time did you return home?

Eli: I'm not positive. Around midnight, I would say.

Dan: Can anyone verify that you were at the church?

Eli: No.

Dan: You made no calls to your wife or kids? No one called you?

Eli: No.

Dan: The evidence points directly at you and you have no alibi. You did it, Mr. Whitehouse. There can be no other explanation.

Eli: I did not do it.

Charlie: Convince me.

Eli: I have nothing else to say.

Dan: Why not confess, Reverend Whitehouse? I've always heard confession is good for the soul. You, being a man of God, should know that better than anyone.

Abe: Don't say another word, Eli. That's it, fellows. We're done here.

Dantzler briefly scanned interviews with Eli's wife, children, Abe

Basham, and several members of the congregation. The verdict was unanimous—Eli could not have committed these murders. Unfortunately for Eli, not one of them could provide an alibi proving his innocence. At the time of the murders—estimated by the medical examiner to have occurred between nine-thirty and eleven that night—no one could remember seeing Eli Whitehouse.

Charlie and Dan had every right to arrest Eli for the crime. The full weight of evidence pointed directly at him. The murder happened on his property, the murder weapon was his, it had his prints on it, and it was at the scene. That alone was damning enough. Throw in lack of an alibi and the case became, as Dan said, "a done deal."

Dantzler had seen plenty of suspects convicted on much less evidence.

Still—

Three areas troubled Dantzler. The first was motive. Or, more specifically, lack of a motive. Why would Eli kill two young men he did not know? During the entire investigation, Charlie and Dan never established a connection between Eli and the victims. What could possibly have been his motive for ending the lives of two complete strangers?

The second troubling factor was the one that also bothered Charlie—why would Eli leave the murder weapon at the crime scene? Why not toss it somewhere? Or at the very least, wipe it clean of fingerprints? Only an idiot would leave it next to the bodies, in plain sight, and Eli was no idiot.

Dantzler, like Charlie, had a problem with how the murders were carried out. Single shot, back of the head, small caliber weapon—that had professional hit written all over it. Was it reasonable to believe Eli Whitehouse, a man who had not committed a violent crime in his life, had suddenly morphed into a cold-blooded Mafia-style hit man? That a man of God had suddenly become Bugsy Siegel? Dantzler wasn't buying it.

Eli Whitehouse, the Reverend, did not commit these murders. Dantzler was now all but certain the man was innocent.

And that conclusion brought Dantzler face to face with the biggest puzzle of all—why would Eli take the blame, then silently spend the next three decades behind prison bars? Why didn't he fight it with greater vigor? What was the reason for his silence? What was he afraid of? Who was he protecting?

Who was the real murderer?

CHAPTER NINE

Dantzler's background check on victims Osteen and Fowler yielded nothing new or enlightening. Both were 1980 graduates of Lafayette High School, both came from broken homes, both had spent one semester at a technical college before dropping out, and both were unemployed at the time of death. Both had twice been arrested for smoking pot, each arrest stemming from police raids at the home of schoolmates after neighbors complained of outdoor partying, loud music, and unruly behavior. Those two incidents were their only run-ins with the law.

In short, there was nothing serious or legally noteworthy in either man's background. These were not hardened criminals or serious drug offenders. They were lost, misguided youth, nothing more.

This was attested to in Charlie's report by Malcolm Sherwood, a teacher at Lafayette. Sherwood knew the boys well, and had them in class when they were juniors. He didn't hesitate to give them a mostly thumbs-up review.

"Neither had it easy, and neither was a saint by any means," Sherwood had said at the time. "But given their difficult home situations, I would say they turned out fairly well. Neither one ever caused me a whit of discipline problems. And to the best of my recollection, neither was ever in serious trouble during their high school years.

"Bruce was an extremely bright young man; he was especially strong in math, which I taught. Carl was an above-average student, but not quite as strong as Bruce. Like many young people from lower middle class backgrounds, they were not predisposed toward learning. As a result, given their mental capabilities, I would classify Carl and Bruce as classic underachievers. Both could have been so much more, given proper guidance. Not unlike many, many students I have encountered during my years as a teacher."

Sherwood went on to say he had no idea who would have wanted to kill his two former students, or why. He couldn't fathom them being involved with the criminal element, although he did acknowledge the two boys were "probably not unfamiliar with certain aspects of the drug culture." However, Sherwood expressed surprise when told drugs other than marijuana were found at the crime scene.

Next, Dantzler went over the testimony of Greg Spurlock and Angie Iler, the young couple who discovered the bodies. Neither had anything relevant to offer, although Dantzler was struck by one statement made by Greg.

I don't think they were killed in the barn.

That was a peculiar observation, especially from someone who spent perhaps a minute at the crime scene. What did he see that caused him to say that? Why would he pick up on that detail? And why hadn't Charlie or Dan followed up on it?

Dantzler grabbed his phone book and began searching for a Greg Spurlock listing. He found four, including one with home and office listings for Gregory Spurlock, M.D. For no particular reason he chose that one first. He dialed the home number and got the answering machine. Choosing not to leave a message, he then tried the office number. After patiently listening to a long list of numbers for connections to various departments, he was instructed to dial zero for the front desk.

A harried-sounding receptionist answered, quickly informing Dantzler that this was the office of Doctors Eades and Spurlock, specialists in internal medicine, and would he please hold. Two minutes later she came back on the line.

"Sorry for making you wait," she said. "It's been a real zoo around here today. What can I do for you?"

Dantzler identified himself and asked if Dr. Spurlock was available. He was told that the doctor was currently with a patient, his last of the day, but he should be free within the next half-hour. Dantzler left his name and number and asked the receptionist to have the doctor give him a call at his earliest convenience.

Milt Brewer was standing in the doorway when Dantzler hung up. He closed the door and stepped inside the office.

"A doctor, huh?" he said, taking off his coat. "Personal or job related?"

"Greg Spurlock was the young man who found the bodies in the Eli Whitehouse case," Dantzler answered. "I'm trying to track him down."

"Man, you've sure got a hard-on for this case. You really think it's worth your time and effort?"

"I'm convinced Eli Whitehouse is innocent."

"Let me tell you, Ace. If you're right, it means Charlie and Dan, two of the finest homicide investigators this department has ever had, were both wrong. It also means they sent an innocent man to prison. Any way you slice it, I don't like the sound of that particular tune."

"Neither do I. But . . ." Dantzler opened the murder book, found the section where Greg Spurlock was interviewed, turned the book around, and pointed to an underlined sentence. "Take a look at this."

"*I don't think they were killed in the barn.*" Milt looked up and shrugged. "Okay, so what's got you so buzzed? It's just an observation made by a kid. What the hell could he possibly know?"

"Yeah, but why did he make that observation?" Dantzler asked, pulling the murder book toward him. "What did he see? And why didn't Charlie or Dan follow up on it?"

"Maybe they did and it led nowhere. Maybe Dan looked into it and decided it wasn't worth noting. Not every single detail makes it into the murder book."

"Dan wasn't the lead detective—Charlie was. And Charlie was notorious for writing down everything. If it's not in there that can only mean they didn't notice it, or if they did, they didn't check it out. Either way, I don't like the sound of *that* tune."

"All I can say is ask Charlie about it," Milt said. "With the memory that old coot has, he'll have an answer for you."

*****

Twenty minutes after Milt left for home, Dantzler's phone rang. The caller was Dr. Spurlock.

"Yes, Doctor," Dantzler said. "I'm trying to locate a Greg Spurlock who discovered two bodies in a barn back in nineteen eighty-two. Would you by any chance be the person I'm looking for?"

"One and the same," Spurlock said, chuckling. "That was certainly the most memorable date I ever had."

"No doubt," Dantzler said, adding, "if you can spare me a few minutes, I would like to ask you about that night."

"What . . . you writing a book about the case?"

"No. I'm just looking into it, and I have a handful of questions I'd like to ask. Get certain loose ends cleared up."

"Loose ends? After almost thirty years? What loose ends could there be?"

"Can you spare me the time, Doctor?"

"Sure. Let's see, it's a little past four-thirty. I have rounds at Central Baptist Hospital, beginning at seven. What I need now is nourishment. If you don't mind talking while I feed my face, I'll be more than happy to meet with you now. Say, thirty minutes."

"Sounds good. Where?"
"What about Paisano's, on Nicholasville Road?"
"See you in thirty minutes."

CHAPTER TEN

Paisano's, a quaint, quiet, dark Italian Ristorante, was virtually empty when Dantzler walked in. Two women sat at the elevated bar to the left, and an elderly couple was seated at a table to his right. Straight ahead he spied a lone male sitting in a booth against the back wall. The man waved as though Dantzler was a long-lost friend he was seeing for the first time in years.

"Greg Spurlock," he said, motioning for Dantzler to join him. "You're Detective Dantzler. I've seen your picture in the paper numerous times. You're something of a tennis legend around here, aren't you?"

"Legend may be taking it a bit too far."

Dantzler sat across from Spurlock, who was tall, thin, and completely bald. He wore gray slacks, blue shirt, and a light yellow sweater tied around his neck. A pair of white Nike running shoes completed the aging Yuppie ensemble.

"Have you dined here before, Detective?" Spurlock asked.

"It's been a while."

"Terrific food at a reasonable price. If you're hungry, dinner's on me."

"Thanks, but I'll pass."

"Glass of wine, maybe?"

"No, thanks."

"So, what do you want to know about my memorable date from hell?" Spurlock said, smiling. "I remember every detail . . . like it happened an hour ago."

"I can imagine. It must have been a traumatic experience for you."

"Scary more than traumatic. And exciting in an odd way. After all, it's not every day you see two murder victims." Spurlock leaned back. "Fire away with your questions, Detective Dantzler."

Taking out his notepad, Dantzler said, "Approximately how far do you estimate you were parked from the barn when you saw the smoke?"

"Hmm. I've never really thought about that."

"How long did it take you to get to the barn from where you were parked?"

"Oh, less than ten minutes, I'd say. No, maybe closer to fifteen. It had been raining hard most of the night, so visibility wasn't all that great."

"At any time did you hear gunshots?"

Spurlock shook his head. "I was pretty much into the making out scene at the time. Between that and the rain, I probably wouldn't have heard shots if they'd been fired next to the car." Spurlock waited until the waitress placed a half-carafe of red wine on the table before continuing. "I'm no hero, Detective. If I had heard gunfire, I would have gone away from the barn, not toward it."

"Describe the condition of the barn when you arrived," Dantzler said.

"There had been extensive damage near the section closest to the pond, but by the time we arrived, the fire was all but out."

"What did you do when you got there?"

"I told Angie—Angie Iler—to wait in the car while I went inside. I wanted to make sure no one was in there, needing help. But Angie said there was no way she was staying in the car alone, so she followed me in. Big mistake on her part."

"How far into the barn were you before you discovered the bodies?"

"I saw them the second I went in. They weren't more than ten feet away from me. They were laying side by side, face down, hands tied behind their back. Not as much blood as I thought there might be, but still a gruesome sight.""Did you consider the possibility that the killer—or killers—still might be in the barn? That you could have been putting you and Angie in danger?"

"No, I don't think it ever crossed my mind. I just went in without thinking, really. Stupid thing to do, huh?"

"Anything about the way they were tied up that caught your attention? The knots, maybe? Or the rope?"

"Nope. Their hands were tied behind them, and they were bound around the ankles."

"In reading through your statement to the investigators, you stated that you didn't think the victims were killed there. I'm curious. Why did you say that?"

"Because I thought it was damn obvious."

"Why?"

"There were drag marks behind each body. You know, like they had been killed somewhere else, then dragged to the spot where I saw them."

"You're positive?"

"You bet. And I told that to the detectives when I spoke with them. Why? They didn't believe me?"

Dantzler shrugged.

"Damn," Spurlock said, setting down his glass of wine. "I thought they would be all over that. I mean, those two guys were not killed where they fell. I'm no homicide investigator, but even I could see the two victims had been relocated."

"They probably did look into it and decided you were mistaken."

Spurlock shook his head. "No way was I mistaken about that. Those bodies had been moved."

"You see, the problem is, there was no mention of a blood trail in the report, which indicates the bodies had not been moved," Dantzler said. "According to the detectives, all blood was pooled around each victim's head. A head wound tends to bleed quite profusely, so there should have been a blood trail had the victims been moved from some other location."

"I'm a physician, Detective. Before going into private practice, I spent many years working in the emergency room. I know a thing or two about gunshot wounds. Sometimes you get a lot of bleeding, sometimes you don't. That's true of head wounds as well."

Spurlock sipped wine, and then put down the glass. "Tell me, Detective. Was there an exit wound?"

"No."

"On either victim?"

"No."

"Well, that could explain why there might not have been heavy bleeding. Oftentimes, a gunshot victim loses more blood from the exit wound than the point of entry. And the bullet was small caliber, which could also be a contributing factor concerning lack of blood."

"The girl you were with—Angie Iler—you still keep in touch with her?"

"Haven't seen Angie since high school. Couldn't tell you where she lives now. Back then, she lived on Longview Drive." Spurlock leaned back as the waitress placed a plate of chicken parmesan in front of him. "I seriously doubt if Angie could tell you very much. She got out of there in a hurry when she saw those two dead guys. Went straight to the car. She was still shaking when I got there."

"You didn't touch either body, did you?" Dantzler asked.

"There was no need to touch them. I could see they were goners. I stayed in the barn maybe forty-five seconds to a minute after Angie left. Then I got in the car and went in search of the first phone I could find."

Dantzler thought for a second, said, "What about the gun? Did you see it?"

"No."

The timber of Spurlock's voice changed slightly, and he glanced down and to his right. Dantzler could tell he had just caught Spurlock in a lie.

"You are positive about not seeing a gun?"

"Yes."

"You mentioned earlier that the bullet was small caliber," Dantzler said. "In fact, the bullet came from a twenty-two. If you didn't see the gun, how did you know that?"

Spurlock put down his fork, picked up his wine glass, and emptied its contents. "Simply a surmise on my part. You know, from the obvious absence of an exit wound."

A second lie.

"A moment ago you asked me if there was an exit wound. Now you're telling me there wasn't one. What am I supposed to believe?"

Spurlock poured wine into the empty glass. "Or it could be I'm remembering it wrong. Maybe I heard it from one of the detectives."

Now the lies were starting to pile up. And, Dantzler could tell, the doctor was not a polished or comfortable liar.

Dantzler nodded, said, "I sense you're leaving something out, Doctor. Something you saw or something you did. Either way, I need the truth."

"I'm telling you the truth," Spurlock said, a little too quickly. "The gospel truth. I saw the bodies, hung around for a minute, then booked. I didn't touch or disturb anything. I swear."

Dantzler was always suspicious when an individual being interviewed ended a statement with "I swear." There was an unmistakable whiff of desperation about it, like the person was begging you to believe him. And when a person begs to be believed, it usually means he is dodging the truth.

"You're sure about that?" Dantzler asked.

"Yes, I'm positive. I swear."

Spurlock used his napkin to wipe the perspiration beads from his forehead. When he finished, he picked up the glass and took a long drink.

"Think about what you've told me tonight, Doctor," Dantzler said, getting out of his chair. "If you remember events differently, regardless of the circumstances, give me a call. I'm investigating this case and I'm going to uncover the truth. The last thing you want is for me to find out you have been less than forthcoming. And I have to tell you, I don't think you're being totally honest with me."

"Yes, yes, I have been truthful," Spurlock insisted. He took another drink. "One-hundred percent truthful."

Dantzler pointed to the now-empty carafe. “You might want to slow down with the drinking. Remember, you have rounds to make. I doubt your patients want an inebriated doctor checking them out.”

CHAPTER ELEVEN

Dantzler made a quick stop at a grocery store, purchased some bread and sandwich meat, then headed home. He thought about putting in a Leonard Cohen CD, but didn't. Instead, he used the short drive across town to mentally replay his chat with Greg Spurlock.

It was obvious the good doctor had been hedging on various aspects of his story. To state for certain the bullets were small caliber could only mean one thing—Spurlock had seen the gun. How else could he have known? The bullets were still in the victims and there were no shell casings found at the scene. He didn't hear it from the detectives, nor did he make a lucky guess. Those explanations defied credibility. Yet he stated it as fact and with absolute conviction.

No. Dr. Spurlock knew more than he was telling.

So . . . why was he lying? What was he covering up? Or leaving out? Was he protecting someone? If so, who? And what about those drag marks? Was that an honest assessment by Spurlock, or was it part of the lie?

Dantzler let his thoughts go deeper, which only led to more questions. Did Spurlock play some role in the killings? Was he the shooter? This seemed farfetched, Dantzler concluded, since Spurlock was with Angie Iler when the murders went down. But could she have been an accomplice and the whole story about "discovering" the bodies was bogus? Was she somehow in on it? She wouldn't be the first female to partner with a cold-blooded killer. Clyde had Bonnie, Charles Starkweather had Caril Ann Fugate. It was unlikely, but not beyond the realm of possibility.

But going in that direction only triggered a broader question: If Spurlock and Iler were the killers, what was their connection to Eli? What reason could they have for setting him up as the fall guy? And if they committed the crime, and if Eli knew they were the shooters, why would he cover for them? Why would he spend his adult life behind bars for that pair? What could have persuaded him to do that? Or who could have?

The more Dantzler thought about it, the more outlandish the notion became that a pair of teenagers possessed the moxie—the cunning—to murder two people, pin that murder on an innocent man, then for whatever reason present enough of a threat that the innocent man would remain silent while meekly accepting a life-without-parole jail sentence. It simply didn't make sense.

There were two mysteries at play here, Dantzler realized. Who and why? Who committed the murders, and why did the Reverend take the blame for a crime he didn't commit?

Dantzler made a mental note to have Laurie track down and interview Angie Iler. He was still far from convinced that Angie was involved, but he now deemed her a person of interest. To move the investigation forward required more information from her. He would also need to meet again with Charlie Bolton, to query him about those alleged drag marks seen by Spurlock. That part of the story was particularly troublesome to Dantzler. If those bodies had been moved one inch, Charlie and Dan would have mentioned it. A fact that important would not be omitted from the murder book, especially by a detail-obsessed cop like Charlie.

But . . . what if it was an oversight? Even great detectives are capable of screwing up. Or what if that detail was, for whatever reason, intentionally omitted by Charlie and Dan?

What if . . .

Turning onto Lakeshore Drive Dantzler was surprised to see Laurie's car parked in his driveway. This was most unexpected. She hadn't been to the house for almost four months, not since they had officially called it quits. Why now? he wondered.

But at this moment, as he pulled his Forester up behind her car, the why didn't really matter. The reality was he had missed her more than he might care to admit. There were some nights when he ached to be with her, to make love to her, to hear her voice, to feel her in the bed with him at night, to just know she was there. Now, for whatever reason, she was here. That she had decided to break the ice was a gutsy move on her part, and one he wasn't going to argue with.

He cut the engine, grabbed the bag of groceries, and went inside. Laurie was sitting on the sofa, a bottle of Smithwick's in one hand, the TV remote in the other hand, and a Cheshire-cat grin on her face.

"Keeping some late hours, aren't you, Detective Dantzler?" she said, the smile widening. "Are you becoming a fortyish-something Tom Cat?"

"I'd say the better question is, when did you become Willie Sutton?" Dantzler set the bag on the kitchen table. "How did you get in here?"

Laurie tossed the remote onto the sofa, set the Smithwick's on an end table, and began searching through her purse. After several seconds of digging, she found what she was looking for.

"You never asked me to give it back," she said, holding up a single key. "Was that intentional, or did it just slip your mind?"

"Nothing slips my mind," he said, picking up the Smithwick's. "And nobody drinks my beer without asking."

Laurie stood. "Ooh, is the famous detective really pissed? Or is he acting?"

"It's better to keep you guessing."

She moved closer and kissed him on the lips. Stepping back, she said, "Tell you what, Jack Nicholson, I think you're acting. I think you love it that I'm here. I think you've missed me like crazy."

"And I think you're a little too full of yourself tonight. Too much self-assurance in a lady can be a dangerous thing."

"Does that mean you want me to leave?"

"You can't," Dantzler said, pulling her close to him. "I parked behind you."

"Good boy."

*****

At a little past midnight, Dantzler eased out of bed, careful not to wake Laurie. He slipped on a robe and went downstairs to the kitchen. After filling a glass with orange juice, he sat at the table, grabbed the phone book, and began looking for a listing for Angie Iler.

This was, he knew, a quest virtually guaranteed to fail. After almost three decades, what were the chances Angie still resided at 590 Longview Drive, or even in Lexington, for that matter? If she did still live in the city, the odds were great that her last name was different now. She could have been through any number of marriages or divorces during the intervening years. And if she did have Iler for a last name, she would probably have an initial rather than her first name in the phone directory. Many single women preferred that listing as a safety measure against unwanted male callers. Or she might not have a landline, only a cell phone, which meant her number wouldn't be listed.

Dantzler's search didn't come up completely empty. There was a listing for L. Iler on 590 Longview Drive. Not Angie, but maybe her mother or a sister. At least it was a starting point.

He ripped a piece of paper from a legal pad and wrote down the name, address, and phone number. First thing in the morning he would dispatch Laurie to make contact with L. Iler. Then he would get with Eric and find out what pertinent information, if any, had been gleaned from the obits page. Hopefully, Eric would uncover the clue Eli only hinted at.

Later in the day, Dantzler was scheduled to meet with Brother Isaac Whitehouse at the Church of the Holy Father on Southland Drive. Isaac was Eli's oldest child. Thinking about that meeting, Dantzler couldn't help but wonder how close—or how far—the apple had fallen from the tree. How alike or different were father and son. Judging by Isaac's chosen profession it appeared they were more alike than different. Both were men of God. That a son followed his father into the ministry wasn't all that unusual. It was rare but it happened. The Reverend Billy Graham had a son *and* daughter follow in his giant footsteps. But Dr. Graham had never been found guilty of a double murder, either. Eli Whitehouse had been. And yet his son, Isaac, followed his father's path.

The path Isaac Whitehouse chose was not much different from the one taken by the biblical Isaac, who continued to love and honor his father, Abraham, even though the old man had been willing to offer his beloved son as a sacrifice to Yahweh. Despite their fathers' questionable and unholy actions, the two Isaacs did not turn their backs and walk away. Their love and devotion remained steadfast. On the surface, at least.

But, Dantzler wondered, what feelings and emotions did the two Isaacs keep buried deep in their heart of hearts? Was love for their father enough to drive away other more natural, more human feelings? Feelings that had to accompany them throughout the remainder of their tormented lives? The terror, confusion, and memories that surely lingered from those horrible moments the biblical Isaac spent bound on that altar of death, waiting to be executed, mystified by his father's actions? The pain and embarrassment young Isaac Whitehouse carried like a yoke on his shoulders for having a father sent to prison for murdering two innocent men?

How does anyone cope with such dreadful, life-altering experiences? It couldn't be easy, not even for the best of children. Yet, both Isaacs somehow managed to do so.

The biblical Isaac went on to become a dutiful son, but one much closer to his mother than to the father who was ready to kill him. So, apparently, had young Isaac Whitehouse. But at what cost? What price had he paid for his father's sins? How scarred was he by his father's actions?

Having lost both parents at a young age—his father killed in Vietnam, his mother murdered—Dantzler knew plenty about pain, suffering, and the scars left by certain events, especially those beyond your control or understanding. Tomorrow, hopefully, he would find out how well the son of Eli Whitehouse disguised his own scars.

*****

Dantzler grabbed a pen and legal pad and began jotting down random thoughts concerning the case:

- two vics murdered execution style
- Eli's .22 the murder weapon; his prints on the gun; gun found at scene
- Eli had no alibi for time of murders
- vics had no apparent connection to Eli
- drugs found at scene; a decoy? Yes. Why?
- Eli put up little in way of defense; accepted his sentence quietly
- Charlie/Dan—did they look at all possibilities? Did they miss something? Were bodies moved?
- Greg Spurlock—hiding something?
- phone call warning me off case; how did the caller know about meeting with Eli?
- obits, obits, obits—that's where the answer is

Dantzler put the pen down and closed his eyes for more than a minute. This was standard procedure when he worked a difficult, complex case like this one. First, he would rapidly make a list of known facts or lingering questions, let his mind digest what he'd written, and then circle the one fact he deemed the most crucial at this stage of the investigation. He opened his eyes and smiled. The choice this time was easy.

Greg Spurlock—hiding something.

He drew a circle around the entry and underlined it three times.

CHAPTER TWELVE

While on his way to work the next morning, Dantzler reflected on the previous night with Laurie. What did it mean, her showing up unexpectedly? Did it mean anything or nothing? Was she looking to kick-start the relationship, or was what transpired last night nothing more than an isolated evening of passion? A one-night stand for old time's sake? Dantzler could only ponder his many questions. Answers eluded him. Laurie had never been particularly hard to read, but this time she had him wondering.

There was no denying they each had strong feelings for the other. And he certainly enjoyed her company. She was smart, sexy, and talented, and she gave as good as she got. Independent-minded and strong-willed, she could hold her own with the toughest of men. And, damn, she was beautiful. There were plenty of upsides to having a relationship with Laurie Dunn.

Still . . . despite those feelings, Dantzler always had serious reservations regarding their relationship. For one thing, there was the twelve-year age difference. Not a major issue for her, but one that nagged at him. More troublesome, though, was the fact that he was her superior at work. In-house love affairs were always dicey at best, disastrous at worst. Richard Bird, head of Lexington Homicide, made no bones about how he felt, advising them both in no uncertain terms that it was a no-win proposition, and one he strongly suggested should be stopped before things got out of hand.

Dantzler's instinct was to agree wholeheartedly with Bird. His heart, however, tugged in the opposite direction. He wanted a relationship, unwise as it might be. Maybe the best approach to take was to let matters unfold as they will. Don't force the issue either way. That seemed to be the smart thing to do. Give it time and space, see what happens. He resolved to do exactly that.

*****

Bruce Rawlinson, the desk sergeant, looked up when Dantzler walked into the building. Rawlinson, a world-class needler, never missed an opportunity to crack wise with Dantzler.

"Hey, Ace," Rawlinson yelled. "How come I haven't seen you

hanging around with the lovely Miss Dunn lately? She wise up and put your ancient ass on the pavement?"

Dantzler was in no mood for inane early morning banter. "Is Eric here yet?"

"Just left," Rawlinson said, shaking his head. "Told me to let you know the information you need is on the table in the War Room. Said he would call you later, in case you have any questions."

"Thanks."

"Hey, Ace," Rawlinson said. "If the lovely Miss Dunn ever decides to look my way, she won't be disappointed."

"Bruce, if the 'lovely Miss Dunn' ever looks your way, it could only mean the End Times have finally arrived. God would not tolerate such a mismatch."

"Yeah, yeah, whatever."

CHAPTER THIRTEEN

Judging by the number of Inter-Department envelopes and manilla folders lined up on the table, it was obvious to Dantzler that Eric had not been wasting his time. The man had put in many hours on this project. This came as no surprise to Dantzler, who had been the first to recognize Eric's gift for police work. From the first day he joined the Homicide crew, Eric's work had been consistently thorough, professional, and superb. With this effort, he had once again justified Dantzler's faith in him.

There were nine very thick Inter-Department envelopes bound together in stacks of three, each with an identifying note attached to the top envelope.

- Obits for week of 4/5/11—4/11/11 (22 total)
- Obits for week of 4/12/11—4/18/11 (18 total)
- Pallbearers (196 total)

Lined up directly beneath the larger envelopes were three manilla folders. On top of the middle folder was a typed note from Eric:

> Jack:
>
> Ran all names through every possible data base as per your orders. Male relatives, preachers, ministers, and funeral home personnel can be done later, if necessary. As expected, most were solid citizens who stayed out of trouble. However, I did find three nuggets that got my interest. You'll see why when you dig into it. Will contact you later.
>
> E

Dantzler was impressed. By looking into the backgrounds of pallbearers, which Dantzler hadn't specifically requested, Eric had clearly done far more than expected. An additional two hundred background checks was nothing to take for granted. Dantzler made a mental note to mention Eric's extra effort to Captain Bird.

Next, Dantzler turned his attention to the three manilla folders lying in a straight row. The first thing he noticed was that Eric lined them up alphabetically by last name. He also noticed the folders were not particularly thick, which meant Eric had printed only the information he deemed important or noteworthy. Dantzler trusted Eric's judgment, so he had no problem with not getting everything in the various local, state, and federal data bases relating to each man. If he needed more he could always get it later.

Dantzler pulled back a chair, sat, and picked up the first folder. On the outside, Eric had typed:

Lawrence Edward (Larry) Gadd
2/10/56 -- 4/9/11
Lexington, Ky.

Leaning forward, Dantzler opened the folder and began reading. The information consisted primarily of the individual's obituary notice, arrest records, prison records, bank statements, and employment records. There were mug shots from the time of arrest, as well as driver's license photos.

According to the *Herald's* obit, Larry Gadd had peacefully been "taken up to his Lord" after a lengthy illness. He was survived by his wife, Karla, two brothers, and a sister. Cause of death was not specified. It needn't be. The answer could be found near the end of the obituary notice, where those wishing to make a financial contribution were asked to send money to The Markey Cancer Center.

Dantzler continued reading, jotting down notes as he did. Before reaching the halfway point in the file, he had become convinced Gadd was not the killer. Gadd was no saint by any stretch of the imagination, but he wasn't a cold-blooded murderer.

The records indicated Gadd served a stint in Eddyville State Prison from 1977 to 1979 for armed robbery. Prior to committing that crime, he had been arrested twice, once in 1975 for selling drugs, and again in 1976 for breaking and entering. Both charges were pleaded out by his attorney, Colt Rogers. Gadd served no time for either offense.

There were no recorded arrests or run-ins with the law subsequent to his release from prison. For the past twenty-five years, Gadd worked as a mechanic at a local automobile dealership. Straight-arrow, solid Joe-Citizen stuff. Apparently, hard time in prison made an impact.

Dantzler thought about this for a while. Gadd probably was a long-shot candidate at best, but Eric was right to include him. And he knew why

Eric did so. He also knew why Eric included the other two as well.

He put down Gadd's file and picked up the one in the middle.

Bobby Lee Maxwell
11/15/61 -- 4/14/11
Lexington, Ky.

Maxwell's obituary notice was brief, consisting of a single paragraph. He died of natural causes, although the exact cause of death was not given. No surviving family members were listed, nor were pallbearers named. There was also no mention of his being "taken up to his Lord." Had he been, Dantzler concluded, it would not have been peacefully.

Bobby Lee Maxwell was anything but peaceful. He was a bad dude with a strong propensity toward violence. And the records attested to that fact.

On nine separate occasions, from 1978 through 2002, Maxwell had been arrested for assault and battery. The victims ranged in age from eighteen to forty-seven. Their injuries ran the gamut from a simple black eye to serious head wounds. In one instance, the victim was beaten so severely he was in a coma for three days.

Despite the damage he inflicted, Maxwell never did serious jail time and no prison time whatsoever. In each instance, he pleaded to the lesser charge of simple assault. Served a few days in jail, paid a small fine, and then was sent on his way, no doubt on the prowl for the next person to smack around.

Maxwell's lawyer? Mr. Cop-a-Plea himself. Colt Rogers.

Sean Montgomery had been right on the money about Rogers. He was a plea-bargaining machine.

Dantzler picked up the third file and began reading, only half expecting to find information that would trigger his interest. He couldn't have been more wrong. Before he finished reading the first page, he had concluded that this man was a definite possibility. Eric might have struck gold with this guy.

Douglas Keith Reynolds
7/6/51 -- 4/16/11
Lexington, Ky.

Unlike Gadd and Maxwell, Reynolds did not die of natural causes. He died in an automobile accident while returning from a trip to Florida, leaving behind a wife, three children, and five grandchildren. There were other differences as well. For one, Reynolds was not originally from Kentucky. He had been born and raised in Chicago. Also, Reynolds's obituary notice was lengthier than either Gadd's or Maxwell's, due mainly to a long paragraph detailing his military accomplishments.

Reynolds served two tours in Vietnam, distinguishing himself in such a manner that he earned a bountiful harvest of combat commendations, including the Purple Heart (twice), Bronze Star, and Silver Star. The article also said he single-handedly took out two enemy machine gun nests, and though severely wounded, he managed to carry a badly injured fellow GI to safety. The paragraph ended with a quote from an ex-soldier, Chris Daniels, stating that he was one of many who felt that "Doug deserved the Medal of Honor for his heroic efforts in Nam. It is criminal he didn't receive it."

"Criminal" was definitely an appropriate term for Doug Reynolds. His rap sheet, dating back to his teenage years, chronicled a life filled with violence, death, drugs, and other assorted anti-social acts. Here was a man whose behavior was that of a jungle predator, a man lacking judgment, restraint, kindness, or respect for his fellow citizens. There was no line he wouldn't cross to get what he wanted.

Reynolds had been arrested and tried for murder in 1983, then re-tried in 1985. In both cases, he was acquitted when the jury failed to reach a verdict.

He was also arrested in 1981 for assault and battery; 1987 for burglary; 1988 for rape; 1991 for possession of a controlled substance; and 1998 for spousal abuse. In each case, he pleaded to a lesser charge. Reynolds's punishment for committing these acts? A grand total of thirty-nine hundred dollars in fines and a three-month stay in county lockup.

Talk about punishment not fitting the crime.

And the magic man who engineered Reynolds's escape from serious punishment? None other than Colt Rogers.

Reading this information, seeing hardened, violent offenders get off with little more than a slap on the wrist, caused Dantzler's stomach to churn and his anger to rise like bile in his throat. How many victims could have been spared injury and harm had thugs like Reynolds and Maxwell been taken off the streets and placed behind bars like they deserved. Why were men who thrived on violence continually allowed to walk away untouched by the hands of justice? How can a system even call itself just when the innocent suffer and the criminals go unpunished?

In moments like this, Dantzler wondered who committed the more egregious sin—the criminal or the attorneys who defended them. Right now, he rated it a toss-up.

Going through each file, he extracted a picture of the three men and carefully studied their faces. Maxwell was the smallest of the trio, standing five-six and weighing one-fifty. He had blond hair, blue eyes, and a scarred face that bore testament to a lifelong battle against acne.

Dantzler had seen plenty of guys like Maxwell, hot-headed runts who were quick with their fists, and who were always ready to inflict hurt on another person, usually someone physically bigger and stronger. They tended to throw the first punch, and they weren't above grabbing the nearest available weapon, a bat, club, or tire iron, if they felt the need to stack the odds in their favor.

Size, or more specifically lack of size, played a key role in a mutt like Maxwell's psychological make-up. From childhood on, he had been driven by a need to prove his toughness, his manhood. He would never, under any circumstances, back down from a physical challenge. That would be seen as cowardly. Being small helped in yet another way—opponents tended to underestimate him. They saw his small stature, not the giant chip on his shoulder or the fierce anger in his heart.

But was he a killer? Someone who could tie up two men, put a gun to their head, and squeeze the trigger? Dantzler didn't think so. Bobby Lee Maxwell was a violent punk, but not a murderer.

Neither was Larry Gadd, a man who made mistakes early but somehow managed to turn his life around in his later years. He was that rare bird, a man who came out of prison a better person than when he was locked up. That didn't happen often. Most criminals only harden their anti-social attitudes while behind bars. Prison is like a college for bad guys, the institution where even the most stupid inmates can earn a PhD in criminal behavior.

Somehow, Gadd had defied the odds and gone straight. *Good for him.*

Dantzler looked at Gadd's photo, taken for his driver's license when he was thirty-four. By this time, Gadd was almost completely bald, and what little hair he did have had gone gray. His bearded face was beefy, indicating he was probably a heavyset man. His DL weight was listed at one-ninety but, Dantzler knew, that wasn't accurate. He estimated it to be closer to two-twenty.

Gadd's eyes caught and held Dantzler's attention. Unlike Maxwell's, Gadd's eyes contained a twinkle, a spark of kindness or gentleness. There was no hate or hardness in them. No look of rage or an impending explosion so often seen in the eyes of most criminals. Perhaps by this stage of his life,

Gadd had found the inner peace that eluded him when he was a troubled young man.

Larry Gadd was no executioner.

The irony did not escape Dantzler: Gadd, the only one to serve hard prison time, was the only one of the trio who lived a productive life.

Doug Reynolds was another matter altogether. Looking into his eyes was like peering into two empty holes, two cold pieces of black ice. They were chilling, yet somehow strangely hypnotic. You were drawn to them even though you wanted to look away. Even though you knew you should look away. They were evil eyes that advertised danger and violence.

Based on the record, Reynolds was a definite possibility. He resided in Lexington at the time of the murders. He had a long history of violent behavior, including rape and assault. He had twice been tried for the murder of a gas station attendant who, it was alleged, was killed for failing to pay Reynolds a large sum of money lost in a poker game. Since both trials ended in a hung jury, there was no way to know for certain whether Reynolds committed the murder or not. A hung jury did not equate to innocence.

From Dantzler's perspective, the outcome of those trials was irrelevant. What was relevant was the fact that Reynolds had taken human life in the past. He had blood on his hands. He had killed, with the medals to prove it. If nothing else, his combat experience provided uncluttered evidence that he would not hesitate to pull the trigger.

You don't get the Bronze Star for kindness.

The next step, Dantzler knew, was linking Reynolds to the two murder victims. Or to Eli Whitehouse. If no connection was found, it likely ruled out Reynolds as a suspect. Finding that link, if one even existed, wasn't going to be easy. Too much time had elapsed, potential witnesses were either dead or had relocated to God knows where. And tracking down the live ones would be virtually impossible. They could be all over the map.

Regardless of the long odds against success, Dantzler knew a detailed study of Reynolds was the only logical approach. Conversely, he saw no value in digging into the background of Gadd, Maxwell or the two young victims. To do so would be a colossal waste of time and resources. No, if a connection to the murders or to Eli did exist, it would have to come through Reynolds.

Dantzler looked at his watch. It was closing in on noon, giving him just enough time to grab some lunch before his one-thirty meeting with Isaac Whitehouse. He was eager to meet Eli's oldest child, the son who had followed his father into the ministry. He wanted to learn more about their relationship. About those scars Isaac surely carried with him. Dantzler also hoped Isaac could shed some light on why his father would silently suffer in prison for a crime he didn't commit.

If, indeed, he didn't commit it.

CHAPTER FOURTEEN

The Church of the Holy Father was housed in an old building that had once been a hardware store. The one-story structure, which was at least seventy years old, was made of concrete and had recently been given a fresh coat of white paint. The roof was black, and three large silver crosses rose from the front facade. The parking area was small, requiring most parishioners to park in an adjacent restaurant lot.

When Dantzler arrived there were only two cars in the church parking lot. He pulled up next to a blue Honda, cut the engine, and got out. Walking toward the front entrance, he recalled that as a young boy he had come here with his father to purchase a ladder and some paint. Less than three months later his father was killed in Southeast Asia.

Dantzler entered the building, looked around, saw no one. As he was about to head toward the pulpit, he heard sounds coming from his left. Turning, he saw a plump middle-age woman standing on tip-toes dusting a large picture of Jesus. Upon seeing Dantzler, she took one last swipe at the picture frame, and then came toward Dantzler, right hand extended.

"Name's Clara," she said, shaking his hand. She looked back at the picture. "You wouldn't think the Son of God could collect so much dust, but he does. I spend half my time keeping this picture and frame dust free. Well, I suppose it's the least I can do for our Savior."

"I remember when this was a hardware store," Dantzler said, looking around. "A guy named Walters owned it."

"You have an A-one memory. Buddy Walters. He was my first cousin."

"How long has the church been here?"

"Let me think. Since about nineteen ninety-two. Maybe 'ninety-one. You'd have to ask Brother Isaac to be sure." She put down her dust rag. "I'm assuming you are Detective Dantzler."

"I am."

"Brother Isaac is in his office in the back. Follow me and I'll show you the way."

*****

Isaac Whitehouse stood when Dantzler entered the office. He was of medium height, somewhat on the stocky side, with dark eyes, jet black hair, and a full beard. He wore a blue suit and white shirt, with the collar open, and a pair of loafers. Except for the area around the eyes, he bore little resemblance to his father.

"Clara tells me you're a Homicide detective," he said, motioning to a chair across from his small desk. "I don't see many of those around here. Am I safe in assuming you are not here on a spiritual quest?"

"That would be correct."

"Why are you here?"

"I'm here to talk about your father," Dantzler said, sitting.

"Ah, an Eli quest. Been years since I trod that path."

"I'll make it as painless as possible," Dantzler said.

Isaac nodded. "I must confess up front that I am more up to date on Holy Scripture than I am on my unholy father."

"You aren't close?"

"How can you be close to a man who has been absent for much of your life?"

"I'm sure it's been a difficult situation."

"Every family, every individual, will at various times come face to face with trials and tribulations. It is God's way of testing us. His way of challenging the strength of our faith. Haven't you been tested, Detective?"

"On occasion."

"And how do you handle your trials and tribulations?"

"One at a time."

"A wise approach." Isaac brushed a piece of lint from his coat sleeve. "What do you want to know about Eli, Detective? And why?"

"I'm looking into your father's case."

"Really?"

"Really."

"There isn't much I can tell you. It was a long time ago."

"I understand. But you may know more than you realize."

"I doubt it, but . . . okay, fire away."

"Where were you when the murders occurred?" Dantzler said, taking out his notepad and pen.

"Asleep in my dorm room."

"At the University of Kentucky?"

Isaac nodded. "I was awakened in the middle of the night when my aunt phoned to tell me two men had been shot to death in the old barn. That was really all she knew. I immediately phoned the house, but got no answer.

A few minutes later, my aunt phoned again and told me Eli had gone to the crime scene. I dropped by the house later in the day, after classes, but no one was there. By the time I did see Eli, he had been arrested for the murders."

"How long before you were able to speak with him?"

"I think it was the next day."

"What did he say?"

"He told me not to believe the things I was about to hear."

"Did he tell you he was innocent?"

"Sure. He swore to me there was no way he would ever commit a double murder."

"Did you believe him?"

"I did, initially," Isaac said. "But when I was told they found his pistol at the murder scene, with his fingerprints on it, I went in the other direction."

"Do you still think he's guilty?"

"I've seen no evidence to convince me otherwise."

"Your father swore the gun was in the safe."

"But it wasn't, was it?"

"You don't seem too torn up about any of this."

"The incident happened twenty-nine years ago, Detective. I was seventeen at the time, a freshman in college. Whatever I felt, and my feelings have varied over the years, I've had plenty of time to come to grips with what happened that night. I've had to live with the knowledge that my father, a man of God, is in prison for committing a double murder. It hasn't always been easy, but I've dealt with it."

"Did you know the two victims?"

"No."

"The original detectives thought the killings resulted from a drug deal gone bad. Do you think your father was involved in drugs?"

"No. He wouldn't know the difference between a joint and a Camel."

"Can you think of any members of his congregation who might have wanted him out of the way?"

"Get real, Detective. I was a teenager, I hated being a preacher's son, and I paid absolutely no attention to Eli or his congregation. Back then I worshipped Bob Dylan and James Dean, not Our Lord Jesus Christ."

"And yet you followed in your father's footsteps."

"Hardly. I answered God's call, not Eli's."

"Even a preacher can have enemies. Can you recall your father ever having trouble with any church members?"

Isaac shook his head. "Those people loved my father. They hung on his every word like it had been faxed down straight from heaven. To them, he was like the thirteenth Apostle. And Eli loved them as much as he loved his own children. Maybe he loved them more than he loved us. He always said, 'I am the one who shines God's light into their dark hearts.' Saving souls was his mission, and he took it seriously. No, Detective, he had no enemies within the congregation."

"Had to be tough sharing your father with so many strangers."

"You learn to deal with it," Isaac said, looking away. "Why are you asking these questions?"

"Because I think your father might be innocent."

"Well, you have now become the second person to hold that belief, the first being my sister."

"Rachel?"

"That would be correct. She has never wavered in her belief that Eli is an innocent man. But I would say to you the same thing I have always said to her—show me the evidence that proves his innocence."

"How old was she when it happened?"

"Eight or nine. And the apple of Eli's eye. They have always been extremely close."

"What about your brother?"

"You would have to ask him. I learned long ago not to speak for Tommy."

Dantzler stood and looked at a large gold plaque on the wall. Inscribed on the plaque were the names of deceased church members. "How many members do you have in your congregation?"

"Almost two hundred."

"I was told that in his hey-day, Eli's congregation numbered around six hundred."

"That's a fairly accurate estimate, I would say. He was a very powerful, very charismatic evangelist. To this day, he remains one of the finest I've ever encountered."

"That's a rather generous assessment of a man you seem to have so little regard for."

"As Eli often said, the truth is the truth, even when it might be distasteful." Isaac smiled. "If you are asking whether or not Eli was a better preacher than me, the answer is, yes, he was. By many miles. However, my preaching skills are not inconsiderable. I'm no slouch when it comes to spreading the Word, Detective. If you're wondering why my congregation numbers are small, it's because of changing times, not because I lack talent. We are old school here. The men and boys wear a coat and tie, the woman wear dresses. Here, we still sing Rock of Ages, not rock 'n roll. I have little or no use for these so-called mega-churches. They are like Wal-Mart—big and loud and offer everything. But at their core they lack soul."

"Who owns the property where Eli's church was located?"

"Eli."

"And what about the property where the murders occurred?"

"It's all Eli's."

"He's the sole owner?"

"Yep."

"And when he dies?"

"I assume it will be jointly owned by his three children."

"Does Eli have a will?" Dantzler said.

"I suppose he does, but I've never seen it."

"That property has to be worth some serious money? Ever had any offers for it?"

"We are besieged with offers on an almost-weekly basis, some of which are rather hefty. One developer wants to put in a shopping center, condos, and a water theme park. There's certainly more than enough land to do it. But Eli won't sell, and no amount of money is going to make him budge."

"Why?"

Isaac shrugged. "No one but Eli can answer that. What I can tell you is that once he passes on, the three of us will sell it in a New York minute."

"You've discussed the matter, then?"

"No. But we're not fools, Detective. We can use the money. We'll listen to all offers, choose the best one, and sell."

"Who pays the property taxes now?"

"You would have to ask Eli's attorney. I don't actually know."

"Colt Rogers?"

"Yes."

"Have you ever had dealings with him?"

"Never. I've only met him once or twice."

"What about Abe Basham?"

"I met with him several times during the lead-up to the trial. After the verdict, I maybe spoke to him a half-dozen times. Tell me, Detective. What makes you think Eli might be innocent?"

"Instinct, mainly."

"That's a rather tenuous thread to hang a belief on, isn't it?"

"No more tenuous a thread than faith in a God who lives in the heavens, or belief in life after death."

"I like my thread better than yours, Detective."
"Well said, Brother Isaac."

CHAPTER FIFTEEN

The L. Iler at 590 Longview Drive turned out to be Louise, Angie's talkative, emotional mother. Louise informed Laurie that Angie's last name was Claybrooke, she was divorced, and she now lived with her daughter, Nicole, on Cooper Drive. Her voice cracking with emotion, Louise went on to say Angie had never really gotten over the "horror of discovering those two slain boys."

"An image like that can stay with a person forever," Laurie agreed.

"Oh, my dear, you have no idea," Louise said, crying into the phone. "She had horrible nightmares for years. We took her to a psychologist, paid a lot of money, but that quack didn't help her at all. That was money wasted. I think Angie's life was altered that night. She was never the same person."

"I'm sorry to hear that," Laurie said.

"Is it your intention to ask Angie about that terrible night?"

"Yes."

"Oh, my, my, my. Is it absolutely necessary? Can't you get your information from some other source?"

"I'm afraid it is necessary," Laurie said. "But I promise to make it as easy for her as possible. You know, I won't ask her about certain specific details. Just general information."

"I would be most grateful if you would do that. Angie needs to forget, not remember."

"What can you tell me about the young man she was with? Greg Spurlock?"

Louise snorted. "Huh, I thought he was a bum. A jerk. I had no use for him at all."

"Why did you have such negative feelings toward him?"

"Because he treated Angie like crap, that's why. He would take her to a movie and make her pay for her ticket. Sit out in the car and honk rather than come to the door and pick her up like a real gentleman would. Things like that. Angie never would say it, but I suspected he did some heavy drinking. Probably did drugs, too."

"Did you have evidence he used drugs?"

"No. Just a feeling, that's all."

"How long were they together?" Laurie said.

"They were never together. They only had four or five dates. I don't think they went out again after that night."

"The night when they found the bodies?"

"Yes, that horrible night," Louise said, more angry now than upset. "He never called again, which was fine by me. And I think by then Angie had come to see what a loser he was. She was happy to be rid of him."

"He's a doctor now, you know?"

"So I heard. Well, all I can say is, I hope he treats his patients better than he treated my daughter."

Laurie had to endure another ten minutes listening to Louise berate Greg Spurlock before she was finally able to get Angie's home address and phone number. Laurie thanked Louise for her help, promised once again to be gentle with Angie, and closed her cell phone. She was exhausted by the conversation, which felt like it had lasted a week.

Laurie wondered if perhaps the shrink had seen the wrong Iler woman.

*****

Nicole Claybrooke was as concise and together as her grandmother was scattered and talkative. In a matter of seconds, she let Laurie know that her mother was a real estate agent with Rector-Hayden, she was showing a house in McMeekin Place, she should be finished at any moment, and, by the way, here's her cell phone number.

Laurie thanked her and hung up. She thought about grabbing a bite of lunch, but decided to go ahead and call Angie. With any luck she might catch her between showings. Angie answered on the second ring.

"This is Angie Claybrooke."

"Miss Claybrooke, this is Detective Laurie Dunn, with Lexington Homicide. I—"

"Homicide? I give my word that I haven't murdered anyone lately. Not that the thought hasn't occasionally crossed my mind."

"That's good to know. The reason I'm calling is to see if you have some free time this afternoon. If you do, I would like to get with you. Ask you a few questions about that night in nineteen eighty-two."

Laurie immediately regretted the way she had broached the subject with Angie. It was clumsy and insensitive. She cringed, unsure how Angie was going to respond.

"No prob," Angie said, cheerfully. "I've just finished showing a house, and my next showing isn't for another two hours. If you like, we can meet here. It's a terrific house. Who knows, maybe you'll like it enough to buy it."

"In McMeekin Place? On my salary? I wouldn't hold my breath if I were you."

"As Don Corleone so famously said, 'I'll make you an offer you can't refuse.'"

"Yes, and as Sam Spade so famously said, 'it's the stuff that dreams are made of.'"

Both women laughed.

"When you turn into McMeekin Place, it will be the third house on the right," Angie said. "You'll see the 'For Sale' sign out front. You can park behind my black Volvo."

"I'll see you in about fifteen minutes."

CHAPTER SIXTEEN

Angie Claybrooke was standing next to her Volvo, a hammer in one hand and a thick folder tucked under her arm. She wore a blue pants suit, white turtleneck, and black Michael Kors loafers. The ensemble was tailored to accentuate a still-impressive figure. Her auburn hair was long and pulled back into a ponytail, which gave her a youthful look. She wore no noticeable make-up, and the only visible jewelry was a gold chain necklace. Chic and professional without being pretentious was Laurie's assessment.

Upon seeing Laurie drive up, Angie tossed the hammer and folder into the front seat, moved away from the car, and waved.

"Sam Spade—it's nice to meet you," she said, once Laurie got out of her car.

"Same here, Don Corleone." Laurie motioned toward the house Angie was showing. "Nice spread. And you really thought I could buy it?"

"I had to give it a shot," Angie said. "It's how I make a buck."

"I couldn't afford this crib if I earned twice what I'm making now. This place is a palace."

"And for a million-two this palace can be yours."

Laurie whistled. "Knock off the million and we'll talk."

"I'm afraid that in my line of work, another movie line always comes into play—'show me the money.'" Angie pointed at the house. "Let's talk inside. There's a marvelous antique table in the kitchen. We'll sit there and pretend we're wealthy."

"I feel like a criminal just entering this mansion," Laurie said.

She followed Angie up the walkway and around to the side of the house. Angie walked quickly, almost aggressively, as if she was striding toward a neighborhood donnybrook and wanted to be among the first to arrive. There was real purpose in every step she took. She moved with great intent, and with the grace of a superb athlete.

Laurie was struck by the fact that in no way did this Angie resemble the Angie portrayed by her mother. This Angie was a strikingly beautiful woman, tall, with a trim figure and a confident demeanor. There was nothing about her that said victim. No outward signs of a shattered or tormented psyche. Of course, Laurie knew, the exterior oftentimes lies in order to protect an individual by hiding the pain and hurt within. She wouldn't know that until she spoke with Angie. But simply based on a first impression, Angie was a far cry from the pathetic woman described by her mother.

The sliding glass door opened to the kitchen, which was bare except for the antique oak table and six chairs. A stack of papers and several of Angie's business cards lay scattered on the table. Angie gathered them up, paper-clipped them together, and put them on the counter.

"Have a seat," Angie said, pulling a chair away from the table. "Make yourself at home. At the very least, pretend this is your kitchen."

"This kitchen is half as big as my entire apartment. I'm not sure I would want a kitchen this big. Too much cleaning involved."

"I can assure you the people who purchase this house will never pick up a dust rag. They'll pay someone to do the cleaning."

Laurie laughed. "Well, there's one thing I have in common with the rich. I would hire someone to do my cleaning if I could afford it. But I can't, so—"

"The cleaning doesn't get done, right?"

"Right." Laurie looked out at the swimming pool, then back at Angie. "You're not at all like how I had you pictured."

"How *did* you have me pictured?"

"I don't know. More fragile, maybe. Less confident."

Angie seemed puzzled for a few seconds, then her eyes widened. "Ah, now I get it," she said, shaking her head. "You met my mother. That's how you got my home number."

"We didn't meet, but I did speak with her on the phone."

"And she told you I was a wreck of a human being because of what I saw that night. That I had to see a shrink and had nightmares and cost the family a small fortune and blah, blah, blah. She's been telling that story for so long I'm sure she actually believes it."

"It isn't true?"

"Please! Do I look like someone who is a wreck of a human being? I'm very successful at my job, I've raised a wonderful daughter, and I live a happy, contented life. Do I wish I made more money and was in involved in a steady relationship with Mr. Right? Sure, I do. But all in all, my life is pretty darn good. Don't get me wrong. I love my mother dearly, and I have tremendous respect for her, but the truth is, she's a first-class drama queen."

"No shrink, no nightmares?"

"I had a couple of bad dreams after the incident. So what? I'd had bad dreams before, so to me it was no big deal. Besides, I didn't necessarily connect those dreams with what I saw that night. As for seeing a shrink, it's simply not true. My father, God rest his soul, had a close friend who was a counselor at the VA hospital. I'm not sure what credentials he had, if he had any at all, but that's who I spoke with. He was one of those guys who worked with veterans, especially the ones who had been in combat and had trouble adjusting when they returned home. Anyway, I met with him maybe two times. We talked about that night, what I saw, and how I felt about it. He could tell I wasn't all that shook up or in need of serious counseling. And that's what he told my father. The matter was dropped by everyone except my mother, who continues to tell anyone who will listen that I'm damaged goods."

"She was also pretty tough on Greg Spurlock."

"I know. He's a bum, a loser, a druggie, treated me like crap. Again with the drama."

"You got along with him okay?"

"Sure. He was a guy I went out with a few times in high school. Nothing serious, by any stretch."

"What was he like?"

"Very cocky, very sure of himself, a daredevil kind of personality. Not all that unusual, I suppose, for someone who came from money."

"His family was rich?"

"Not rich, rich. But very well off. I think his mother's family had money."

"Your mother mentioned drinking and drugs. Any truth to that?"

Angie rolled her eyes upward. "Beer and pot, maybe. But I couldn't swear to it, because he never did any of that stuff around me. He was not a serious substance abuser, regardless of what my mother says."

"Tell me about that night," Laurie said. "From the beginning."

"Greg and I went to a movie. We saw *On Golden Pond*, with Katharine Hepburn and Henry Fonda, which I thought was terrific. Jane Fonda was also in it. After the movie, we went to Pizza Hut to get something to eat. Then we drove around for a while, eventually ending up somewhere in the boondocks. We had been parked maybe twenty minutes when we saw the smoke. I remember telling Greg that it looked pretty serious, that maybe we should check it out."

"What time of night was it?"

"I'd say close to eleven. Maybe a little after."

"What happened next?"

"We drove to the barn."

"How long did it take you to get there?"

"Ten or fifteen minutes."

"Was it raining when you arrived at the barn?" Laurie asked, scribbling in her notepad.

"No. But it had been raining cats and dogs an hour earlier. I remember being worried that Greg's car might get stuck in the mud and we'd have to call someone to come pull us out. That would have been beyond embarrassing."

"Describe the barn when you guys got there."

"One end was badly damaged, but the other end, the one closest to where Greg parked the car, wasn't damaged at all. I guess the rain put out the fire before it spread to that part of the barn. It was in the undamaged section that we saw the bodies."

"Tell me about that."

"Greg told me to stay in the car, but I said no way I'm staying in the car, not in this darkness. It was really creepy. The dampness, the flickering flames, the smoke. Oh, the smoke was so thick you could slice it with a knife. Just a real boogie-man, Stephen King kind of night."

"So you and Greg went into the barn?"

"Yeah, unfortunately we did. That's when . . . I took one look, turned around, and got the hell out of there."

"Back to the car?"

"You bet. And locked all the doors."

"How long were you in the barn?"

"Ten seconds."

"What do you remember about the victims?"

"Not much, really. Only that their hands and feet were tied, and their eyes were open."

"Was there much blood?"

"If there was I didn't notice it," Angie answered.

"Did you see a gun?"

"No."

"Anything else about the victims—or the scene—that caught your attention?"

"No. But like I said, Detective, I didn't stick around long enough to take notes."

"Greg said he remained in the barn for maybe a minute before he returned to the car."

"That's not accurate. Greg was in that barn for a good ten minutes before he came out."

"You're sure?"

"Absolutely. I was petrified sitting in the car alone. In the darkness, with two dead guys thirty feet away? Are you kidding me? Those ten minutes felt like three hours. I let him have it good when he did get in the car. For making me sit out there alone for so long."

"Did he say anything?" Laurie asked. "Give a reason why he stayed in the barn that long?"

"Not that I recall. He was just hell-bent on getting to a phone and calling the police."

"Did you see any blood on him?"

"On Greg? No. Why do you ask?"

"I'm wondering if he touched or moved the bodies."

Angie shook her head. "I doubt if he did that. That would be stupid on his part, and Greg wasn't stupid."

Maybe not but he is a liar. Laurie thought for a while, and then said, "Did you mention to the detectives who interviewed you that Greg spent that much time in the barn?"

"I never spoke to a detective."

"You never spoke with a Detective Bolton or Detective Matthews?"

"The only person I spoke to had on a uniform. The detectives talked with Greg."

Laurie started to ask Angie if she remembered the officer's name, but didn't. That information would be in the file. She tapped her pen on the tabletop, thinking about what she had just learned from Angie. She didn't like what she was hearing, that was for sure. Angie should have been interviewed by one of the detectives, and it was almost impossible for Laurie to believe that neither Charlie nor Dan had seen fit to do so. Those guys didn't screw up like that.

Maybe Angie was remembering it incorrectly, Laurie reasoned. Maybe Charlie or Dan did interview Angie and she had forgotten it. That was a definite possibility. After all, twenty-nine years is a long time. Memories fade, details can get shuffled around, lost, or re-imagined entirely. This was especially true during stressful, emotional, and chaotic moments in a person's life. To be sure, finding two dead bodies and being interrogated by the police was more than enough to cause stress and emotional chaos. Angie could be forgiven for not remembering events in perfect order.

Despite her concerns, Laurie decided to reserve judgment until she spoke with Charlie. At the very least, Charlie and Dan deserved to be accorded the benefit of the doubt. Both were decorated, celebrated cops. They had earned that much.

"Sam Spade—you have the look of a very troubled woman," Angie said, softly, breaking nearly a minute of silence.

Laurie nodded. "As the prison warden said to Cool Hand Luke, 'what we've got here is failure to communicate.'"

*****

Sitting alone in O'Charley's, her thoughts racing a hundred miles an hour and in fifty different directions at the same time, Laurie felt like she was being beaten up by some invisible force inside her. An inner tornado had been unleashed, resulting in a war among competing options, possibilities, and scenarios, none of which were positive or pleasant to contemplate. 'What should be her next move?' she silently asked herself. Her instincts said she should call Charlie and have him verify Angie's recollection of what happened that night. She should also ask him to explain why neither he nor Dan had spoken to Angie at the crime scene. Her curiosity screamed the same thing. That those two excellent detectives had not done so was more than puzzling; it went against everything she knew about both men. Until that puzzle was pieced together to her satisfaction, she could not—would not—allow herself to believe that Charlie Bolton and Dan Matthews committed such a bonehead rookie mistake.

She speared a piece of lettuce from her Caesar salad, held the fork suspended above the plate for several seconds, and put it down. Her appetite had vanished, a victim of the swirling mass of thoughts and emotions ripping through her. She drank some water, took out her cell phone, and began to punch in Charlie's number. Halfway through, she closed the phone and dropped it back into her purse. The voice in her head told her that calling him now would be making that rush to judgment she wanted to avoid.

There was an alternative option, one that made far more sense. She would phone Dantzler, fill him in on what she had learned, and find out how he wanted to proceed. That would relieve her of having to make the decision concerning Charlie. Let it be Dantzler's call. Besides, there was always the possibility he had uncovered some information in the murder book that would contradict Angie's memory of not being interviewed by one of the detectives. Laurie hoped that was the case. If it wasn't, then Dantzler had no choice but to ask Charlie about it.

For now, though, she wanted to go home, put on a sweat suit and running shoes, and go jogging. Running was her way to escape the shackles of her job while also serving as the mechanism by which she calmed the storm raging inside her. Ultimately, she ran in order to remain sane.

Charlie Bolton, Eli Whitehouse, and Angie Iler would have to wait. Top priority now was Laurie Dunn's mental well being.

She grabbed her purse and the check, paid the bill, and headed home.

CHAPTER SEVENTEEN

Dantzler was surprised to learn that he knew Rachel Whitehouse, Eli's daughter. She was now Rachel Foster, wife of Kirk Foster, a former circuit judge who currently held the position of chief of staff to the governor. The Fosters also owned and operated RKF Farm, one of the most successful thoroughbred farms in the nation. They were politically powerful, very wealthy, and highly placed among the social elite. The Fosters were, in every respect, an A-list couple.

Dantzler only knew Rachel in passing; he couldn't recall ever having had a conversation with her. He was more familiar with Kirk, although he wouldn't include the man among his coterie of friends,. A nodding acquaintance at best. Primarily, he knew the Fosters from the Lexington Tennis Club, where they were members, and where Dantzler was part owner.

As a young man, Kirk experienced some success as a junior tennis player, having once been ranked in the top ten in several age divisions. His love for the sport carried over into adulthood. So did the confidence he gained as a youngster. Three years ago, Kirk, yielding to a burst of self-assurance, challenged Dantzler to a set of tennis. Dantzler, arguably the best tennis player in Lexington, won six-love. Like many powerful, successful men, Kirk did not graciously accept defeat. He quickly challenged Dantzler to a second set. The result was the same. It took two subsequent sets, both ending at six-love, before Kirk finally raised the flag of surrender.

"Come on, fellow," Kirk said when the two men met at the net. "Couldn't you at least have given me a sympathy game?"

"I would have," Dantzler replied, "if you hadn't been so damn sure you could beat me."

Dantzler enjoyed few things more than humbling a cocky opponent.

*****

After learning that Rachel Foster was Eli Whitehouse's daughter, Dantzler went to the Tennis Club in search of Kirk. Arriving at seven-fifteen p.m., Dantzler went downstairs to the courts, where Kirk was involved in a doubles match. Dantzler waited until the changeover before approaching Kirk.

When Kirk noticed Dantzler heading in his direction, he stood, and said, "Have you finally seen fit to apologize for the beating you gave me?"

Dantzler shook his head. "I never apologize for winning." He waited until Kirk's partner walked past before continuing. "Listen, Kirk, I need to speak with your wife. Would she happen to be here tonight?"

"No. She's out of town," Kirk answered, wiping his face with a white towel. "If you don't mind my asking, why do you need to speak with her?"

"Some questions regarding Eli."

"You know her father?"

"I don't know him. I met him once, at the prison."

"That's where she's been today, visiting him. She should be home around nine, maybe a little later. When would you like to meet?"

"Tomorrow, if possible."

"Is something going on that I should know about?"

"I need to get some information from her, that's all. Clear up a few things."

"Come to the farm in the morning. Ten, if that's okay. I'll leave your name with the guard and he'll let you through. Go to the first barn on your left. That's where she will be."

"Thanks, I really appreciate it."

"Still no apology, though, right?"

"Never."

*****

Dantzler identified himself to the guard and was immediately waved through the gate. Following Kirk's directions, he drove slowly toward the main house, his eyes on the lookout for the barn. It wasn't until he crossed over a wooden bridge that the barn came into view. Turning left, he traveled another hundred yards, eventually stopping and parking behind a white Cadillac Esplanade.

Rachel Whitehouse Foster was standing just outside of the barn, cup of coffee in one hand and a clipboard in the other hand. She was dressed in Levis, a sweatshirt, leather boots, and a white baseball cap with RKF Farm on the front. A stopwatch dangled from her neck.

"My husband tells me you show no mercy on the tennis court," she said, tucking the clipboard under her arm. "What was it, six-love times four?"

"I like bagels."

"Probably did him some good, being cut down to size like that." She extended her free hand. "Hello, I'm Rachel Foster. I've seen you around for years. It's nice to finally meet you."

"Thanks for taking the time," Dantzler said, shaking her hand. "And for meeting me on such short notice."

"Let's go inside," Rachel said, gesturing toward the barn. "To my grand air-conditioned office. You may not care much for the smell of horse manure, but at least you'll be cool."

"Fair enough," Dantzler said, following her into the barn. Once he was seated in a leather chair across the desk from her, he said, "How long have you and Kirk owned the farm?"

"We bought it in 'eighty-nine," Rachel said. "Back then it was known as Limestone Stables. We got it for virtually nothing, which is exactly what it was worth at the time. Took a lot of hard work and tons of money to get it back into working shape. We killed ourselves, sometimes working twenty hours a day for weeks on end. Finally, we managed to turn it around. And we were also very lucky. Not long after we got into the business, the price for thoroughbreds went through the roof. The big American owners and trainers began bidding wars against each other. Then the Europeans came, especially the guys from Ireland. That pushed up prices even more. And to top that off, the Saudi sheiks suddenly decided to use all that oil money they make off us to get into the horse business. Sales prices skyrocketed. It was insane. Still is, if you want my honest opinion. Our first group of foals, this was in 'ninety-six, turned out to be very successful, put us on solid footing within the industry."

"Hard work, good luck, and timing—that tends to translate into success in any endeavor. I know it's certainly true in my profession."

Rachel got out of the chair, opened a small refrigerator, and took out two bottles of water. She handed one to Dantzler, then sat back down. After opening the bottle and taking a drink, she said, "So, Detective, what can I do for you?"

"I'd like to talk to you about your father."

"Kirk mentioned you wanted to talk about Eli. Well, about the only thing I can tell you is he's terminally ill. Cancer in both lungs."

"Yes, I know. Sorry."

"You know my father?"

"I met him last week at the prison."

"Did he send you to see me?"

"No. Until two days ago, I had no idea Eli Whitehouse was your father."

"You would have had no reason to."

"I understand you visited him yesterday. How is he holding up?"

"Better than expected," Rachel replied. "But . . . it's obvious he's beginning to go downhill."

"Any idea how long he has?"

"His oncologist said three weeks at best. I'm hoping he is wrong."

"What was your relationship with Eli?"

"*Was*? He's not dead yet, Detective."

"Sorry, I misspoke. What is your relationship with Eli?"

"I love my father very much," Rachel said. "We've always maintained a close relationship, even after his incarceration. Rarely do I go a week without visiting him."

"I understand you are his favorite."

"Not even close, Detective. I was the baby, the only girl, so I was his little darling. His pet." She smiled. "You know, I was what you might call a redemption baby."

"What does that mean?" Dantzler asked.

"Eli was a man of God, but he was also a man. A flawed man in many respects. About three years prior to my arrival, he had an affair. As you can imagine, when my mother found out about his indiscretions, she was angry, hurt, and embarrassed. She threatened to leave and take the boys with her. Given Eli's reputation and the reverence his congregation had for him, a divorce would have been devastating. He would have been ruined. So he pleaded with my mother to forgive him and take him back. She loved the man, so that's what she did."

Rachel laughed, as though she had just recalled some private and humorous moment.

"Some babies are accidents, some born out of wedlock. Me, I was born because a sinful man was trying to redeem himself." She shook her head. "Eli loves me very much, but I am nowhere close to being his favorite."

"Isaac?"

"He wishes. No, Detective, Tommy is Eli's favorite. Always has been, always will be. It's not even a close contest."

"When I spoke with Isaac, I asked about Tommy. Isaac didn't have much to say."

"They aren't close. Not since . . . Looking back, I don't think they ever were close. Are you familiar with the Bible, Detective?"

"I know my way around it."

"Do you know the story of how Jacob, with his mother's help, manipulated his blind father, Isaac, into granting him the Blessing that rightfully should have been bestowed upon Esau, Jacob's twin?"

"Yes, I know that story."

"Then I'm sure you can appreciate the irony that in real life, in our house, Isaac was Esau and Tommy was Jacob. Isaac desperately wanted my father's blessing and never received it. Tommy couldn't have cared less yet it was bestowed upon him every day. The irony becomes even greater when you factor in how their lives turned out. The rejected son follows in his father's footsteps, while the chosen son becomes a lost soul."

Rachel turned away and blinked back tears. She withdrew a tissue from her purse and wiped her nose.

"Tommy truly was a golden boy, Detective," she continued. "That's not exaggeration, or baby sister idolizing big brother. Ask anyone who knew Tommy back then. They'll agree. He was handsome, smart, personable, kind, the best athlete in school—there was simply nothing he didn't excel at. And it all came so natural to him, so easy. Isaac studied diligently and made B's; Tommy phoned it in and made all A's. Isaac worked harder at sports; Tommy was the superstar. If Isaac wanted to date a beautiful girl, he had to keep his fingers crossed that Tommy didn't ask her out first. You get the picture, Detective. Tommy was special."

"Did Eli encourage the rivalry?"

"You aren't listening, Detective. There was no rivalry. Didymus Thomas Whitehouse had no competitors."

"Interesting name," Dantzler said. "Both mean twin. Didymus is Greek, Thomas is Aramaic."

Rachel applauded. "I am impressed, Detective. You've obviously studied subjects other than criminal investigation, police procedure, and tennis strategy. Am I correct?"

"Philosophy."

"Wonderful field. Which brings me to the obvious question—how did a budding Jean Paul Sartre become Sherlock Holmes?"

"My mother was murdered when I was fourteen. Her killer was never caught. I knew the day after she was killed that being a detective was what I wanted to be."

"Doesn't take Dr. Freud to untangle that plot."

Dantzler said, "Back to Tommy. You speak of him in the past tense. Is he dead?"

"The golden boy certainly is."

"What happened to him?"

"You turned your family tragedy into something positive, Detective.

That's admirable. Unfortunately, Tommy wasn't able to overcome our family tragedy. It devoured him, changed him completely, turned him into another person, one none of us knew or could every really get close to again. He became this dark, quiet, melancholy loner. His grades went from all A's to far below average. Sports no longer meant anything to him; before the incident they were his passion. After high school, Tommy joined the Marines. Did eight years before the alcoholism got so out of control they had no choice but to discharge him. I can't begin to explain the change, Detective. I don't have the vocabulary for it. It was just . . . a one-hundred and eighty degree turn."

"You've made it clear that Eli worshipped Tommy. Did Tommy feel the same about Eli?"

"Tommy was fifteen when it all went down. Sure, he loved Eli, but Tommy was like some solitary planet circling in his own galaxy. People gravitated to Tommy, not the other way around."

"Does he still live around here? I will need to get in touch with him."

"We own quite a bit of rental property, and one of the places is a duplex off Redding Road. We let him live there. I'll get you the address and phone number before you leave."

"Thanks. What does your brother do to earn a living?"

"Nothing of real consequence. Along with letting him live rent free, we let him manage some of our properties, pay him a small salary. He's been clean and sober for six months now, and that's a long stretch for him. I do think he's trying, making some progress. But we've been down this road before and . . . he always lets us down. Always lets himself down."

"What's your husband's relationship with Tommy?"

"Kirk has been more than patient with my brother, cut him miles and miles of slack. He really likes Tommy, and would love to see him get straightened out. He really would. But—"

"Does Isaac help out?"

"Prays for him, maybe, but not much else."

"In all this time, you haven't asked why I wanted to talk about your father," Dantzler said. "Aren't you curious?"

"I deal with horses and politicians, Detective. I've developed two things over the years—thick skin and patience. You'll tell me when you feel like it. But, yes, I am slightly curious."

"I think there's a chance your father may be innocent."

"I have maintained from the beginning that he did not kill those two young boys," Rachel said, fighting back tears. "I have been the lone voice crying in the wilderness. There is no way my father is a cold-blooded killer.

Can you prove his innocence?"

Dantzler shrugged. "Not unless I can dig up something new concerning the case. The evidence against him is fairly overwhelming. I've seen plenty of people convicted on a lot less."

"Why do you think he is innocent?"

"I didn't say he *is* innocent. I said he might be."

"But there has to be some reason why you feel this way."

"I do, but I don't have time to get into specifics right now. What I need is to ask you a few questions."

"Yes, yes, go ahead. Ask me anything."

"If your father is innocent, he has spent twenty-nine years behind bars. And he's done so without complaining, without appealing the decision, without trying to find the real killer. Why would he do that? Throw away his life like that? He should have been the loudest voice crying in the wilderness."

"How many times do you think I've asked myself those very questions, Detective Dantzler? Fifty times a day, every day of my life. And I have no answer."

"Did you ever ask Eli?"

"A million times. He never answers, just looks away."

"This woman he had an affair with. Was she married?"

"Divorced."

"Were there other women?"

"My mother said no, but maybe that was just wishful thinking on her part. There very well could have been other women she didn't know about. All I can tell you is that I'm not aware of others."

"Is your mother still alive? If she is, I'd like to speak with her."

Rachel shook her head. "No. She died in nineteen ninety-three. Why? Do you think my father might have been set up by an angry husband or boyfriend?"

"Not unless the husband or boyfriend was a professional hit man."

"Are you saying this was a professional job?"

"Has all the earmarks, yes. That's one of the reasons why I have doubts that Eli committed the murders."

"Then my father's silence makes sense. He kept quiet to protect his family."

"Okay, let's assume that's true. My next question is, how was Eli Whitehouse mixed up with a professional killer?"

Rachel closed her eyes and shook her head. "I can't imagine how he could have been. That would make no sense."

"Can you recall any members of his congregation who were suspicious? Maybe someone who joined the church a short time prior to the murders?"

"God, I was only nine at the time, Detective. That was such a long time ago. I knew most of the members, but there were new ones showing up all the time. Some stayed, some didn't. But if you're asking me if I remember anyone who could have been a professional killer, the answer is no."

"How well do you know Colt Rogers?"

"The attorney?"

Dantzler nodded.

"Not at all, really," Rachel said. "I've dealt with him on a few occasions over the years, mainly to sign some documents. Why are you asking about him?"

"Just gathering information, Rachel. What about Abe Basham?"

"Nice man, superb attorney. He really tried to help my father. But his hands were tied by my father's silence."

"There's something we're missing here, something critical," Dantzler said. "And unless I can uncover it, I can't prove Eli's innocence."

"Can't you take another, closer look at the evidence?" Rachel asked.

"That's not where the answer is."

"Where is the answer, then?"

"Not where. Who." Dantzler thought for a few seconds, and then said, "Eli told me to check the *Herald's* obit page for the two-week period of April fifth to April eighteenth. He said I would find the answer there. Do you have any idea who he might have been referring to?"

"I have absolutely no clue," Rachel said. "Why wouldn't he give you the name? If he wants you to prove his innocence, it's the least he could do."

"I suspect he's afraid to."

"What did my father get himself into all those years ago? How could this have happened?"

Dantzler had no answers.

CHAPTER EIGHTEEN

"We struck out with Doug Reynolds," Eric said, as Dantzler came into the War Room. "He has an alibi and it's solid."

"Out of town?"

"Hospital. He went in for an emergency appendectomy on the day before the murders. Wasn't released until three days later."

"He was a long shot at best," Dantzler said, sitting. "But it's good to eliminate him as a suspect. Knowing for sure allows us to move forward."

"Jack, are you still sold on all of this?" Eric asked. "I went back and checked the murder book and the trial transcript again last night. Went over it hard. And I have to tell you, I can't find anything to contradict the verdict. The evidence says guilty."

"You may be right, Eric. But . . ."

"You're challenging work done by Charlie and Dan. Think about it. Those guys were good detectives. They didn't botch things."

"I can't disagree with anything you're saying," Dantzler said. "But something isn't right about this case. It smells. And I can't walk away from a case that has a sour odor to it."

Dantzler took the Doug Reynolds folder from Eric.

"Ask yourself this, Eric. Why would a guy warn me to keep away from a case that I hadn't even begun looking into? He wouldn't, unless there was a reason for him to be worried. And why would he worry if Eli is guilty? That's one area that troubles me. Another is the fact that I caught Greg Spurlock in a series of lies. Why would he lie? What is he covering up? I need answers to those questions. The evidence, yeah, it points to Eli. But the circumstances of the crime do not. This was a professional hit, and I just cannot bring myself to believe Eli Whitehouse is a professional hit man."

"Maybe not. But I can't see a seventeen-year-old kid like Greg Spurlock as a professional hit man, either," Eric said.

"Greg Spurlock didn't kill anybody. But he knows more than he's telling. That much I'm sure of."

"Want me to check him out?"

Dantzler shook his head. "Milt is. Once he's put everything together, I plan on having another chat with the good doctor. Only this time it won't be at Paisano's, he won't be drinking wine, and I won't be so nice."

"What do you want me to do?"

"Go back to the obits and check the females. You don't have to be so detailed this time around, though. Mainly, I want to know if any of them had criminal activity in their past."

"You think the shooter could've been a woman?"

"Anything's possible."

"Those two guys were tied up, Jack. If the shooter was a woman, she had to have an accomplice. No way she could have done it all by herself."

"Well, just look into the female obits, see if anything hinky pops up. If nothing does, then I'll probably need to throw in the towel and walk away from the case, sour odor or not."

"I'll get on it first thing tomorrow."

"Did I tell you what a terrific job you did gathering information on those obits?" Dantzler said, standing.

"If you did, I didn't hear it."

"It was excellent work, Eric. You went above and beyond on this job. I want you to know I really appreciate it."

"And I'm sure you've read every word of my manuscript."

"Gonna start on it tonight."

"Yeah, right."

CHAPTER NINETEEN

Devon Fraley answered the phone at the same time the gentleman walked into Colt Rogers's office. Devon, desperate to make a good impression, had been sent over by a temp agency yesterday to fill in for Barbara Tanner. Barbara, Colt's longtime receptionist, was out with the flu. If Devon could perform well on this job, earn Colt's respect—and a possible recommendation—she had a chance to find the full-time employment with benefits she needed. To move up the ladder and provide a better life for her and her young son was her goal. Working here could be the ticket.

She held up her hand to let the visitor know she would be with him as soon as she finished with the call.

"Colt Roger's office, Devon speaking. How may I help you?" She listened for several seconds. "No, Detective Dantzler, Mr. Rogers is not in. He is meeting with a client. I expect him back around four-thirty or five."

The man standing by the desk turned and walked away. He went to a table, picked up a copy of Time magazine, and began leafing through it.

"Well, Detective, I know Mr. Rogers has a meeting here tonight at seven," Devon said. "Yes, I will put you down for six. And, yes, if there is a conflict, or if Mr. Rogers can't make it, I will have him give you a call. Is there anything else? No? Then I will make sure Mr. Rogers gets your message. Thank you."

When Devon finished writing on her message pad, she looked up. The man who had been standing there was gone.

*****

Colt Rogers plopped down in the leather chair, opened the brown paper bag, and took out his supper. Egg salad sandwich on marble rye, chips, a generous slice of cheesecake, and a can of Dr. Pepper. Not a meal to rate very high on the nutrition scale, but one he was anxious to dig into. It had been a long, eventful day, and he was famished. At this point, bologna and crackers would have been acceptable supper fare.

Rogers was alone in his office, having let Devon leave thirty minutes before her five p.m. quitting time as a reward for her excellent work. Devon was, he judged, an energetic and enthusiastic worker, far superior to the standard replacements usually sent by the temp agency. He would definitely keep an eye on her. She was someone he would consider as a permanent replacement if Barbara followed through on her promise to retire within the next couple of years.

Rogers had a much more muted opinion of Cheryl Likens, his firm's paralegal. Cheryl, twenty-six, was lazy and condescending toward virtually everyone she came in contact with. A mediocre paralegal at best, she was an uninspired writer, totally lacking imagination, cleverness, or insight. Her research skills, such as they were, also left much to be desired. Were she not so hot in the sack, Rogers would have fired her months ago. Like it or not, he knew it was only a matter of time until he would have to let her go. Despite her prowess in all matters sexual, she was too much of a liability to the firm to keep on board much longer. He could not allow his carnal desires to cost him money or clients.

He took a swig of Dr. Pepper and sighed out loud. The prospect of severing ties with Cheryl was more than a little disheartening. It was downright depressing. After all, how often does a fifty-nine-year old man have a sexual relationship with a twenty-six-year-old woman, especially one with the looks and body of a Playboy playmate? Once in a lifetime, if the man gets lucky. And if he were being completely honest with himself, he would admit that he hired Cheryl for her body, not for her brains. It had been a regrettable mistake, one that had to be rectified. Saying goodbye to Cheryl was going to be more painful than paying alimony. But he had no choice. It had to be done.

Sandwich and chips devoured, Rogers dug into the cheesecake. It was smooth and creamy, exactly the way he liked it. Plain, too, without some nonsensical chocolate syrup or strawberries lathered on top like an unwanted oil spill. That would only ruin it. No whipped cream, either. Cheesecake was meant to be eaten plain, sans any and all adornments. He had always preferred it that way.

When he finished the cheesecake and Dr. Pepper, he dumped everything back into the brown sack and dropped it into the wastebasket. Leaning forward, he shuffled through the notes Devon had given him before leaving for the day. Three related to phone calls he needed to return; those he would put off until Monday morning. There was a message reminding him of his seven o'clock meeting with Lance Ford, a stockbroker who was embroiled in a war of wills with the Internal Revenue Service. Lance, it seems, had conveniently neglected to list all of his income for the past three years, an oversight the IRS frowned upon. Lance was, Rogers knew, fighting a losing battle with those vultures. His best bet—confess his sins and beg for mercy, not that he should expect any. Those IRS folks are notoriously short on forgiveness.

The last note informed him that Detective Dantzler would be here at six. Rogers looked at his Rolex—it was now five twenty-five. He stood, went to the window, and looked outside. Night was rapidly closing in, those dark clouds off to the east bringing with them the threat of rain. West Short Street was deserted, not a soul in sight. Unusual, especially for a Friday.

Rogers felt like the only person left on the planet.

Standing there, deep in thought, he began to feel a strange heat rushing through his body, scorching his insides. He had the peculiar feeling that his blood was on fire. Butterflies suddenly fluttered in his stomach, a battalion of imaginary winged creatures gone berserk. His legs grew weak, and his breathing became quick and shallow. For a split second, he was certain he was going to pass out.

And he knew why his nerves were so unsteady.

Dantzler.

No secret why he's coming—to talk about the Reverend. To stick his detective's nose where it doesn't belong. To dig up skeletons from the past. To uncover secrets buried by the passage of time.

To shine a light into dark places best left alone.

Rogers struggled to calm his shaky nerves, to get control of his emotions and thoughts. This was no time for weakness, not when facing a guy like Dantzler. He's a cop, and like everyone else in law enforcement, he sees weakness as one of the absolute signs of untruthfulness. And he has a reputation for sniffing out weakness the way a shark sniffs out a drop of blood miles away in the ocean. Dantzler was known as a furious, hard-edged investigator.

Falter ever so slightly and Dantzler will know. Then he'll pounce, relentlessly, until you cave in.

Rogers felt as if he were about to lose his supper. He swallowed hard, took several deep breaths, and sat back down. Perspiration dripped from his chin to the desk. The butterflies continued to swarm inside him.

Stop this, Rogers silently admonished. *Okay, so Dantzler wants to talk. Big deal. What questions could he possibly ask that I can't answer honestly? None. I know the Reverend's story, know it by heart, which means I am fully aware of what I can reveal and what I must keep secret. Dantzler has only speculation to go up against my knowledge and that gives me the clear advantage. He cannot win against me. I can handle anything he throws my way. I am superior.*

Rogers felt his nerves begin to settle and the butterflies disperse. He had won the internal debate against the coward that lay deep inside him, that quiet but often persuasive voice he continually had to battle, to silence, to drive away from the dark places in his soul.

He was ready for Dantzler. *Let the great detective bring on the questions. Let him probe and dig for my weaknesses. He won't find any.*

I am superior.

At that moment, Rogers heard a knock at his door. He glanced at his Rolex. Five-forty. Dantzler, true to his reputation, was eager for confrontation. So be it, Rogers murmured to himself. I am also ready for confrontation.

Striding confidently forward, Rogers moved through the outer office and opened the door. Surprise and confusion registered in equal amounts when he saw the man standing in front of him. It was not Jack Dantzler.

It was—

"What are you doing here?" Rogers asked.

The man said nothing as he slowly raised his right arm. In his hand was the most beautiful pistol Colt Rogers had ever seen.

"What the hell?" Rogers said, backing away.

Those were his last words before his face exploded.

CHAPTER TWENTY

What had once been Colt Rogers's face was now a grotesque mixture of blood, flesh, bone, and brain tissue. One eye, blown out of its socket, dangled down his cheek like a ball on a string. The other eye had been obliterated upon impact. His nose was gone, along with virtually all of his lower jaw. The back of his head had fared no better, having been utterly destroyed by the blast, which blew open a gaping fist-size hole that exposed a small segment of brain that miraculously had survived intact. Brain matter, blood, and tissue had sprayed across the office to the back wall, where, Dantzler knew, they would likely find the bullet that had inflicted such damage.

Mac Tinsley knelt next to the body, his gloved hands bloody from inspecting the massive wounds. A diminutive man famed for his black horn-rimmed glasses and his meticulous work ethic, Mac had been the coroner for almost four decades. The joke was that Mac had been around so long he performed the autopsy on poor, murdered Abel. But Mac's days on the job were numbered. With his sixty-fifth birthday less than a month away, he had recently made the decision to call it quits at the end of the year. He had concluded that enough was enough.

"Tell you one thing for certain, Jackie-boy," Mac said, removing the bloody Latex gloves. "There will be no open casket at Colt's funeral service. In all my years doing this nasty work, I can only recall two occasions when I've seen such extensive damage to a man's face. Both were suicides, and both victims used a shotgun."

Dantzler helped Mac to his feet. "Any guess as to how long he's been dead?"

"The man's still warm. This happened within the past ninety minutes."

"The shooter cut it close," Dantzler said. "I couldn't have missed him by more than a few minutes."

Richard Bird entered the office, glanced down at the body, and quickly looked away. Bird, head of the Homicide division, had no stomach for the ugliness of the job. His talent was administrative, not investigative detective legwork. Politics rather than police procedure was his strength. He much preferred his cool office to a vulgar crime scene.

"Damn, I could have gone a lifetime without seeing that," Bird said, shaking his head. "What a mess."

"Am I clear to take the body, Jackie-boy?" Mac said. "Did you get everything you need?"

Dantzler looked toward the back of the office, where Milt was overseeing one of the crime scene tech's efforts to retrieve the bullet. "Milt, any reason to keep the body here?"

"Nope. Feel free to take Mr. Rogers out of his neighborhood." Milt held up his right hand. "Got the bullet, Jack. Big sucker, too, just like we suspected. In fairly good condition considering the road it traveled. I'm guessing this came from a forty-four or a three-fifty-eight."

"That makes Clint Eastwood our prime suspect," Bird said.

"For taking out a lawyer, I vote to give Clint an award." Milt laughed. "I always felt one of Clint's old flicks perfectly summed up my feelings toward our barristers—*Hang 'Em High*."

"That's not funny, Milt," Bird said. He looked at Dantzler. "But Rogers was a lawyer. I'm sure he had plenty of enemies."

"I'm sure he did. But this wasn't done by an angry client. This is connected to the Eli Whitehouse case."

"You don't know that for sure, Jack."

"Come on, Rich. Think about it. I'm supposed to meet Rogers at six, to talk about Eli's case, and when I get here, he's dead. That's more of a coincidence than I care to accept."

"What time *did* you get here?"

"Six, straight up. Mac says Rogers couldn't have been killed more than fifteen minutes before I got here. That—"

"How did the killer know you were going to be here?" Bird asked, shaking his head. "And how could he possibly know what you were planning to discuss with Rogers?"

"Don't know. What I can tell you is this has to do with my re-opening the Eli Whitehouse case."

"But there are differences. You've said from the beginning a professional hit man took out those two boys in 'eighty-two. This doesn't look professional to me."

"Well, you're wrong, Rich. We've been all over this place and we can't find a shell casing. That tells me the shooter, despite being in a time pinch, acted in a cool and collective manner. Like a pro. He didn't panic."

"You could be right, Jack. But you could also be dead wrong. I don't want us heading down one path at the exclusion of all others. You want to continue with the Eli Whitehouse case, that's okay with me. But I'm assigning Milt and Eric to look into Colt Rogers's murder as a separate case. We clear on that?"

"Perfectly. That's the way we should approach it."

Dantzler and Bird watched as the covered body of Colt Rogers was loaded onto a gurney and taken out of the office. Mac Tinsley closed his medical bag, picked it up, and followed the body outside into the darkness.

"Damn, a bullet in the face," Bird said. "That'd be a hard way to go."

"Is there ever an easy way?" Dantzler asked.

*****

West Short Street, deserted two hours ago, was now a buzz of activity and energy. Curious onlookers, having learned via the gossip grapevine that a murder had occurred, poured out of the nearby bars and restaurants eager to see what happened. Within a matter of minutes, they were three deep behind the blocked off section and multiplying fast. Nothing draws a big crowd quicker than yellow crime scene tape and rumors of a grisly murder.

Microphone-toting reporters from two local TV stations were on the prowl for interviews, moving rapidly toward anyone who looked even remotely official. A female scribe from the newspaper had Richard Bird cornered against an adjacent building. Bird, at six-six, towered above his inquisitor, who was scribbling at a furious pace, certain she was being given inside information about the murder, when, in fact, she wasn't. No reporter ever got a scoop from Richard Bird. He possessed a great talent for saying nothing relevant or important while giving the impression he had recently descended Mount Sinai with the Ten Commandments. Bamboozled reporters, eager to uncover the big scoop, confused gibberish for gospel.

Outside, in front of Colt Rogers's office, Dantzler huddled with Milt and Eric. A strategy needed to be put in place, he knew, and now rather than later. While Dantzler didn't necessarily buy into the long-held consensus that if a murder isn't solved in the first forty-eight hours, it likely never will be, he did agree that time is of the essence. The killer already had a head start. The trick is to not let him get so far ahead he can't be caught.

"Ah, shit, man, here come the jackals," Eric said. "Bad idea coming outside to talk."

Eric was referring to the two TV reporters running in their direction, one male, one female, both being trailed by hefty cameramen struggling to keep pace. The female, a reed-thin blonde with a mouthful of perfect pearly whites, won the race, easily beating her opposition by five full seconds.

"Detective Dantzler," she said, three seconds before the cameraman caught up, turned on his light, and focused. "What can you tell us about the murder of Colt Rogers?"

"No comment."

"Is it true that he was shot to death?"

"No comment."

By this time the male reporter had joined the group. Breathing hard, he rammed his microphone within inches of Dantzler's face, causing Dantzler to push it away.

"Look, guys," Dantzler said, clearly peeved. "You're not going to get anything from me worth reporting, because at this stage I don't know much more than you know. We've just begun the investigation. We're not even twenty minutes into it, yet. When we have anything worthwhile to report, you'll hear about it. Until then, back off and give us room to breathe. And one more thing. In the future, if you have questions, ask the tall guy over there."

Dantzler pointed toward Richard Bird.

"One more question," the persistent female reporter said. "Is—"

Dantzler glared hard at her. "Are you hearing impaired? I said no fucking comment. Now get away from me and let me do my job."

Milt and Eric were both laughing when Dantzler walked away from the reporters.

"Ah, Ace, such atrocious language to use in front of one so young and innocent," Milt said. "You probably scarred her for life."

"Somehow, I doubt that, Milt." Dantzler turned serious. "Rich wants us to keep the investigations separate, which we'll do. We need to keep the boss happy, because when he's happy, he's not climbing up our rectums. But we all know this killing is linked to the Eli Whitehouse case."

"I'm not as sure about that as you seem to be," Milt said, shaking his head. "Truth is, I have serious reservations about it. I don't think they are linked at all."

"They have to be, given the circumstances."

"Jack, you're asking us to believe the shooter of those two kids in 'eighty-two is the same shooter who took out Colt Rogers. A twenty-nine-year gap between killings. That's stretching credibility and reason beyond the breaking point, don't you think?"

"I'm scheduled to meet Rogers and talk about Eli's case. Rogers is gunned down fifteen minutes before I show up. And you don't see a connection?"

"Let's say it is the same shooter," Milt said. "Why kill Rogers? Why now?"

"Because Rogers had information or knowledge about the case and the shooter was afraid I might squeeze it out into the open. He couldn't take that chance. Dead men don't give away secrets. So, Rogers had to be done away with."

"Still a stretch, Jack." Milt grinned. "But, hey, you're the Ace, right? And who can argue with the Ace? You tell me what you need and I'll do it."

Before Dantzler could lay out his plan, his cell phone rang. He looked at the caller ID. Sean Montgomery.

"Hey, Sean, thanks for getting back to me in such prompt fashion," Dantzler said. He listened for a few moments, then said, "Yep, right in the face, too. Pretty damn messy. Listen, Sean, do you know Rogers's receptionist? I think her name is Devon. Barbara Tanner? You positive? The lady I spoke to was named Devon. Yeah, I'll check it out. And thanks."

Dantzler closed the phone and put it in his coat pocket. Looking up, he saw that Milt and Eric had moved several feet away and were standing next to Scott Crofton. Scott, recently promoted from patrolman to the Homicide crew, was engaged in a conversation with a man Dantzler didn't recognize. The man was fidgety and nervous and talking a mile a minute. Scott was scribbling furiously in his notepad. When the man finished speaking, Scott gave him a pat on the shoulder and the three detectives watched him walk away.

"Who was that?" Dantzler asked.

The question had been directed at Scott, but the rookie detective remained silent, certain Dantzler was addressing one of the veterans. After several more seconds of silence, Milt elbowed Scott in the ribs.

"Are you a mute, Scott?" Milt said, chuckling. "Answer the man's question before we all die of old age. And keep in mind that it's Detective Dantzler doing the asking, not God."

"Right, sure," Scott said, looking down at his notes. "Lance Ford. He's a stockbroker, and he had a seven o'clock meeting with the deceased. But—"

"Deceased?" Milt interrupted. "You're one of us now, Scott, so you don't have to be so damn proper. Call it like it is. Say, the guy had a meeting with the poor schmuck who had his face turned into cherry pudding. Make it sound a little more colorful."

Scott looked up, unsure how to respond.

Dantzler came to his rescue. "He's busting your chops, Scott. It's Milt's way of welcoming you aboard. Now, proceed."

"Well, Mr. Ford said he had car trouble," Scott continued, "which is why he was almost an hour late for the meeting. When he heard what had happened, he spoke with one of the patrolmen. Then he was sent to me."

"What was the purpose of the meeting?" Dantzler said.

"Mr. Ford is apparently in hot water with the IRS, and he was meeting with the deceased . . . with the late Mr. Cherry Pudding Face to see what, if any, options he might have." He looked at Milt. "Is that better?"

Milt nodded. "That's why we brought you up to the A team, Scott."

"Any reason to suspect him as the shooter?" Dantzler asked.

Eric laughed out loud. "Lance Ford? No way. I went to school with him, and I can promise you he ain't no killer. He was the all-time king of nerds. A certified meek geek."

"Not everyone is a basketball or tennis great," Scott said, his eyes going from Eric to Dantzler.

"Oh, a double zinger," Milt said. "Way to go, Scott."

Dantzler, a serious look on his face, put a hand on Scott's shoulder. "You know, Scott, you looked awfully spiffy in that patrolman's uniform. Would you like to walk a beat again?"

"No, sir, I—"

"Cut him a break, Jack," Eric said. "After all, he did call us great."

"I don't know. A double zinger from a rookie. That's fairly serious."

"But I was just—"

The three veteran detectives burst out laughing.

"Relax, Scott," Dantzler said. "We're just having some fun with you. There's always a lot of ribbing going on, and you being the new kid on the block can expect a disproportionate amount hurled your way. Stand your ground and send out as much as you receive."

Scott let out a sigh of relief. "I thought I'd pissed you guys off. Thought maybe I was in big trouble."

"When you really piss me off, you'll know it," Dantzler said. "Milt, you and Scott dig into Rogers's files, past and present. He's an attorney, so there are bound to be dozens of clients he's angered over the years. Concentrate on his clients who went to jail. Sean Montgomery says Rogers was a master at plea bargaining and his clients usually got the short end of the stick, even though they probably didn't realize it at the time. Could be one of those clients figured out Rogers didn't have his best interest at heart and came back to square the account. Sean also told me Barbara Tanner has been Rogers's receptionist since forever. Have Laurie speak with her. When I phoned Rogers's office, I spoke with someone named Devon. She was probably filling in, sent over by some temp agency. Have Laurie make contact with her as well."

"What are you gonna do?" Milt asked.

"Meet with Eli Whitehouse again. Convince him that if he wants this thing solved, he needs to give me more than he already has."

Eric shrugged his shoulders. "What am I supposed to do, Jack? Work on my jump shot?"

"What you were doing before Colt Rogers bought it—keep looking through the obituaries. If Eli refuses to give me more information, then it's up to you to find the answer."

"If Eli refuses to help," Milt said, "you need to say to hell with you, Reverend, have a nice eternity."

Dantzler nodded and slowly walked away.

CHAPTER TWENTY-ONE

It was almost eleven and Dantzler was concerned. He had spent much of Saturday afternoon and evening trying to get in touch with Charlie Bolton, without any luck. Repeated phone calls had gone unanswered, both on the cell phone and the landline. It was not like the old detective to be incommunicado for such a lengthy period of time. Charlie, a life-long bachelor, always let someone know when he left town.

Dantzler reasoned that Charlie must have taken off for the lake and had either left his cell phone behind or had it turned off. If Charlie was at the lake, that was the most likely scenario. Then he remembered that Charlie had told him he wouldn't be going to the lake until Tuesday or Wednesday. This left yet another possibility, one he tried hard to dismiss. Charlie, nearing eighty, could be lying stone cold dead in his house.

Thoughts of Charlie dead shot Dantzler's concern up to the worried level. After one more unsuccessful attempt to reach Charlie by phone, he decided to hop in the car and drive over to Palomar Estates.

Worry became panic when he saw Charlie's red pickup truck parked next to his Ford Explorer. Both vehicles in the garage meant Charlie was in the house. Charlie at home, not answering the phone—that had to translate into something bad. Dantzler's panic now registered as fear.

Dantzler jogged toward the house, and was almost on the porch when the light went on and the front door opened. Charlie met Dantzler, looked at his watch, and shook his head.

"Kinda late for a social call, isn't it?" Charlie said, opening the door wide enough to allow entrance. "Must be something mighty important for you to come here at this time of night."

"I was worried," Dantzler said. "Been calling you all day. How come you didn't answer the phone?"

"Didn't have it with me. And I just got home a few minutes ago."

"Where have you been?" Dantzler asked, flopping down on the sofa. "Or would I be better advised to not ask?"

"I've been consoling a certain Miss Danforth."

"Emily Danforth? Pete's wife?"

"Pete's widow."

"What does she need consoling for? Pete's been dead for ten years."

“What can I say, Jack? She loved the man.” Charlie grinned. “We all know grieving can be a long and painful process. People handle it in different ways. Some seek solitude, while others, like Emily, seek companionship. Therefore, I feel compelled to do all I can—as often as I can—to help her get through the pain and suffering that accompanies the death of a loved one.”

“And just how long have you been performing this Christian deed?”

“For many years now.”

“Does it include years prior to Pete’s death?”

“I think it prudent on my part to plead the Fifth on that one.”

Dantzler shook his head. “You old dog. How come I never knew about this?”

“Because not everything belongs in the public domain.”

“Forget about something coming out of left field; this is coming from another continent.” He laughed. “You know, Laurie will be blown away if she ever gets wind of this. She sees you as a celibate saint.”

“She’s been aware of it for nine or ten years. She found out back in the days when I was training her. I swore her to secrecy then, and Dunn, being an honorable lady, has faithfully fulfilled the vow she made to me. Although I’m aware that you are less honorable, I fully expect you to keep this tidbit of salacious information quiet. I ask not so much for the sake of my reputation, but rather for Miss Danforth’s. Can I count on your silence concerning this matter?”

“Would I be so heartless as to darken Emily Danforth’s name? Rest easy, Charlie, your secret is safe with me.” Dantzler pointed at the TV. “You hear about Colt Rogers?”

“Yeah. Heard he took one right in the face. That had to hurt.”

“What do think?”

“One less lawyer in the world. I’d say things are looking up.”

“No, Charlie. What do *think*?”

“I try not to think about matters that don’t concern me.”

“Answer me, Charlie.”

“What do you want me to say, Jack? That his murder is somehow connected to the Eli Whitehouse case? Okay, if that’s what you want me say, I’ll say it. There is a connection. Now, are you happy?”

“But do you believe it?”

“What is this, voodoo detective work? Come on, Jack. I’m old school. And I taught you better than to assume without first having all the facts in hand. You want me to believe there’s a connection? Then show me the evidence that *makes* me believe it. Otherwise, I’m an agnostic.”

Dantzler laughed. “You’re a tough old coot, that’s what you are.”

"And don't you ever forget it." Charlie sat in the recliner across from Dantzler. "If you've been calling all day, it can only mean you have certain issues you want to discuss. What is so important that it couldn't wait until tomorrow?"

"There are a couple of things about Eli's investigation that trouble me. Discrepancies I need straightened out."

"My investigations didn't have *discrepancies*."

"Good. Then let's clear up the two areas that bother me, starting with Greg Spurlock's assertion that the two victims had been moved, that they were not killed where they were found. That was not mentioned in the murder book. Why wasn't it?"

"Spurlock said the bodies had been moved?"

"Relocated was how he phrased it."

"Jack, in all the years we've known each other, I have never once been pissed off at you. But I have to be perfectly frank. Right now, I'm pretty damn close. You're challenging my professionalism, my experience—and Dan's—based on the word of a kid who stumbled upon a crime scene. That not only pisses me off, it hurts."

"I'm not looking to piss you off or hurt you. You know that. But I have questions, and you are the guy who can give me answers."

"Well, here's my answer. Those two bodies were not moved an inch, I don't care if God himself tells you they were. If they had been moved, I would have noted it in the murder book. What that kid saw, or thought he saw, or imagined, or dreamed up, I can't say. It was a barn, after all. Barn floors get swept, raked, have all sorts of people, animals, and vehicles constantly moving across them. He very well could have seen dust, dirt, hay, or horse manure that gave the impression the bodies had been moved. But they were not. Those two boys were bound at the wrists and ankles, they were made to kneel, and they were shot in the back of the head. They died where they fell. End of story."

"Okay, Charlie, that's good enough for me. I just needed to hear you say it."

"What's your second 'discrepancy'?"

"Angie Iler, Greg Spurlock's date that night, said she never spoke to a detective, only to a uniformed officer. Don't you think either you or Dan should have questioned her?"

"Not necessarily. When we questioned the Spurlock kid, he told us Angie wasn't in the barn more than two or three seconds. Dan and I felt she wouldn't be able to provide us with anything more pertinent or relevant than he could, so we concentrated on getting his account of what happened. But

I'm positive the Iler girl was questioned."

"Yeah, she was. According to the murder book, she was questioned by Dale Larraby. And we all know what kind of cop he was."

Larraby, recently retired, had a reputation for being lazy, boorish, and inefficient. Someone once said Larraby couldn't find a Jew in Tel Aviv, much less a murderer. He and Dantzler despised each other, and had clashed on numerous occasions after Larraby had been assigned to the Homicide squad. No one in Homicide wept when Larraby turned in his gold shield.

"Tell me, Jack. Have you spoken to Angie Iler?"

"I have."

"And did her account of what she remembered about that night differ greatly from what Larraby wrote in his report?"

"That's not the issue. What troubles me most is what Larraby didn't put in the report."

"What did he omit that you feel was important?"

"If you'll recall, Greg said he was in the barn for maybe a minute or two before he returned to the car. Now, that differs from what Angie told me. According to her, she was in the car alone for at least ten minutes before Greg came back. If Angie's account is accurate, what was Greg doing in that barn those extra eight or nine minutes? And if she told this to Larraby, why didn't he put it in his report? Why didn't he tell you and Dan about it?"

Charlie frowned and leaned forward. "Because Dale Larraby was a lousy cop from day one, that's why. He should've told us, and, yes, maybe Dan and I made a misstep by not questioning Angie. I suppose we trusted Larraby's judgment more than we should have. But, hell, you just take it for granted a professional law enforcement officer has enough common sense to get important information to the lead detectives working a homicide case."

"Larraby was an idiot, Charlie. He shouldn't have been trusted to write a parking ticket."

Charlie stood. "Want a beer? I have Bud Light and Anchor Steam. Take your pick."

"No, thanks. I'll pass."

"Suit yourself." Charlie left the room for no more than a minute before returning with a bottle of Anchor Steam. "Tell me, Jack, do you believe the Iler girl's account of that night?"

"I don't know. Sitting in the car alone, after having just seen two dead bodies, I can see how it might affect your perception of time. Two minutes could easily seem like ten. So I think it's possible she's wrong. But one thing I can tell you—she's not lying. And that's more than I can say for Greg Spurlock."

"Yeah, Milt told me you found some 'discrepancies' in Spurlock's story." Charlie took a long pull from the bottle and set it on a coaster. "Okay, he's a liar. But is he a killer?"

"No. The person who killed those two boys also killed Colt Rogers. Spurlock couldn't have done it. I had Eric check Spurlock's whereabouts at the time Rogers was murdered. He was performing surgery at Central Baptist Hospital."

"Which puts your ass firmly planted back on square one." Charlie finished off the beer. "Where do you go from here?"

"Talk to Greg Spurlock again. Try to find out why he's lying."

"That's a start. Anything else?"

"Go back to the prison and talk with Eli. If he really wants to prove his innocence—if he is innocent—he has to give me more than what he's given me so far."

"When are you going to see him?"

"I'm leaving at nine this morning."

"Want some company?"

"I don't know if that's a good idea, Charlie. He might not be too thrilled to see one of the detectives who put him away for life."

"Well, I'm going, so thrilled or not, Eli will just have to deal with it."

CHAPTER TWENTY-TWO

Today had been a good one for Eli Whitehouse. Better than good, really, considering the violence taking place inside his body. What had once been a healthy temple was now a battleground for those traitorous cancer cells gnawing at him like starving rodents, devouring the remaining healthy tissue inch by inch. But that wasn't the case on this particular day. Today, the holy Sabbath, the two hostile factions rested, just as God had done after creating the world and all that was in it. As a result of this temporary truce, the excruciating pain that kept him on the edge of madness had blessedly taken a few hours off, allowing him to enjoy the best day he'd had in weeks. This was a rare moment, and he was thankful for it.

Eli felt strong enough to get out of bed without assistance and sit in a chair next to the window. This was the first time in weeks he had been able to perform such a simple task, and he was delighted that he could pull it off. No buzzing a nurse for help, thank goodness. No need to seek assistance from an orderly. Today, he was his own man. Pain and the certainty of death were terrible burdens to shoulder, but what he detested in equal measure was the loss of independence that went hand in hand with a terminal and debilitating illness like cancer. He had always been strong and independent; now someone had to clean him after he used the toilet. On certain days, he had to be fed like a baby. He no longer controlled the simplest of functions.

He was a prisoner behind bars and a prisoner to his illness.

Sitting in the chair, gazing out the window into the bright sunlight, he thought about his children. How much he loved them and missed them. How different they are, especially the two boys, neither of whom he had seen in years. Isaac had stopped visiting more than fifteen years ago; Thomas had never set foot inside the prison. He had often marveled at those differences, Isaac with his desperate need for approval, Thomas with his casual lack of concern toward virtually everything and everyone. How could two children born of the same parents be so dissimilar? Esau and Jacob had nothing on his two boys.

And there was Rachel, his lovely flower, the loyal one. His heart burst with joy every time he thought of his precious daughter. She had been steadfast in her belief that he was innocent, never wavering, never questioning or condemning. Her regular visits to the prison kept him going, providing him with the strength to survive today and the courage to face tomorrow. Were it not for Rachel, he would have withered and died long ago.

She had been like Saint Peter, the rock, the one who held the family together and kept him sane.

Rachel was also his primary lifeline to the outside world, particularly in regards to family affairs. Through her he kept up with his two absent sons, and although he was fully aware that her reports were far from truthful, he drank in her words like expensive wine. Not once did he challenge anything she said to him about the boys, even though he knew much of her account was pure fiction.

Isaac is an evangelist like you, Father, she told him. He has his own church, a nice one on Southland Drive. He has many members in his congregation—more than two hundred—and they love and respect him. He is happily married to a lovely woman named Rebecca—yes, just like Isaac in the Bible, what a coincidence!—and they have two sons, David and Matthew, and a daughter, Mary. You should be proud of him, Father.

Eli was proud of Isaac, but more than anything he was surprised by him, by the path he chose to take in life. Never in a million years would he have guessed that his eldest son would become a preacher. Not Isaac, who, as a young man, would go to any lengths to put distance between him and the church. He wanted to get as far away as fast as possible. Isaac had no time for sermons, or the Word of God, or Holy Scripture handed down like thunder by his old man. He got more than enough of that nonsense at home.

However, as Eli reflected upon it now, he wondered if he should have been surprised by Isaac's decision to follow him into the ministry. Perhaps it wasn't such an outlandish or extreme decision. After all, preachers are nothing more than performers, actors upon a stage, playing to an audience. And what are all performers desperately seeking? Love. They all want to be loved.

No one sought love more than Isaac Whitehouse. Where better to get it than the pulpit?

Through Rachel, Eli kept up with Tommy's career in the Marines. Rachel told him Tommy had been awarded many commendations, having served with distinction in the First Gulf War and in Afghanistan. He had been wounded once, but it wasn't serious. Now a colonel, Tommy worked at the Pentagon, but would soon be shipping off again for another tour in Afghanistan. He was single, never having found a woman willing to accept his nomadic existence.

When Eli asked why Tommy had never once visited him, Rachel

said it was because "it would break his heart to see you behind bars."

Of course, Eli knew she wasn't telling the truth. He knew it from the sorrow in her voice and the sadness in her eyes. He also knew why she was lying, and he loved her all the more for it. She was protecting both father and son.

No brother could ask for a better sister. No father could expect a better daughter.

Eli played along with Rachel even though he had long been aware of the real truth about Tommy, the sad, heart-breaking truth about his beloved son. Early on, various members of the congregation, while visiting Eli, would relay news of Tommy's downward spiral. Later, it was Colt Rogers who delivered the ever-depressing stories of Tommy's decline.

Tommy had been booted out of the Marines long ago and was now a full-fledged alcoholic. He was unable to hold a steady job for any substantial length of time, had never been married, and would likely be homeless were it not for the kindness of Rachel and Kirk Foster. He was a sad, lonely, broken soul.

Eli's heart ached at the realization that Tommy, his special child, his golden boy, had fallen so deep into the depths of despair. Why it happened was no mystery. The murders, seeing his father sent to prison for life; therein lay the root cause for Tommy's decline. But Tommy's downfall wasn't simply a matter of the son not being able to deal with the sins of his father. Or that his father was exiled to a prison cell for life. That was only part of the story, not all of it. The truth, Eli knew, was yet to be uncovered. And only when the truth is finally revealed will the world know why Tommy Whitehouse descended into his own private hell, taking with him all but a precious few fading memories of the beautiful child he had once been.

From the time he was very young, Tommy had been strangely aloof, indifferent to the judgment and opinions of others, emotionally shut off (by his own choice) from any part of the outside world that failed to interest or intrigue him. He did not suffer fools or boredom lightly. Those with special gifts rarely do. And yet, at any given moment, with the quicksilver flash of a smile and the twinkle in his eyes, he could draw you to him with the suddenness of a lightning strike. His was a magnetic personality.

"You are like the serpent in the Garden," Eli once told him. "Wily, cunning, charismatic, and . . . maybe a little dangerous."

Thoughts of Tommy only added more crushing weight to the guilt Eli felt for what had transpired. To see his talented, gifted son fall like beautiful Lucifer from God's heaven inflicted upon Eli far more pain and hurt than the cancer inside him. It ripped at the very core of his soul.

He closed his eyes and prayed.

CHAPTER TWENTY-THREE

By two in the afternoon, Eli could feel his strength and energy levels begin to ebb. He still felt better than usual—just being out of the damn bed was enough to lift his spirits—but he could feel the fatigue begin to set in. In a couple more hours he would once again be a prisoner in his bed, too tired and too weak to move, a pitiful shell of the once-formidable man he had been.

Earlier in the day he had received a call from Rachel informing him that Colt Rogers had been murdered. He had acted surprised when Rachel broke the news, but in truth he wasn't. There was no reason to be surprised. Colt Rogers operated in that shadowy world between right and wrong, living a dangerous existence while also consorting with men of questionable character. Eli had never harbored any illusions about Colt Rogers. Colt was a man constantly in search of trouble, and in Eli's experience, men who seek trouble usually find it. That Colt met a violent death came as no shock to Eli.

Being a man of God, Eli felt duty bound to say a prayer for Colt. After all, even the worst sinners are deserving of a few kind words directed at the Almighty. If Jesus was magnanimous enough to grant the thief on the cross entrance into Paradise, then the least Eli could do was pray for Colt Rogers. But this particular prayer would not be a lengthy one. Only a few words followed by a quick Amen. He would not take up much of the Almighty's time advocating for Colt Rogers, a man he had little use for.

Eli now understood that Colt's death was the reason why Jack Dantzler requested a second meeting. When Dantzler phoned Warden Curtis late yesterday afternoon, he had offered no particular reason for the meeting, other than the usual "to tie up a few loose ends." He didn't mention Colt's murder, or if he did, Warden Curtis kept the news to himself. Either way, it didn't matter. Eli had granted Dantzler's request. Truth be told, he liked Dantzler, and would enjoy visiting with him again.

Sitting in his chair, the warm sun shining through the window, Eli felt his eyelids begin to grow heavy. He fought sleep as long as he could, wanting to be awake and alert for his chat with Dantzler, but by two-thirty, with fatigue closing in faster than he expected, Eli nodded off.

He wasn't sure how much time had passed before he was startled awake by the door opening and the shuffling of footsteps in his room.

Looking up, clearing the sleep from his eyes, he saw two men standing in front of him. A smile crossed his lips.

"Well, well, Charlie Bolton," Eli said. "A ghost from my long-ago past. This is quite the surprise."

"Eli."

"It's been a long time, old friend."

"That it has."

"Lie to me, Charlie. Tell me I'm looking good for a man my age."

"You look better than I expected."

"For someone with a terminal illness, right?"

"Right."

"Are you enjoying your retirement? Your 'golden years', as they say?"

"My knees ache constantly, and I would like to catch more fish. But all things considered, I have no complaints."

"Lucky you." Eli nodded at Dantzler. "Detective Bolton, are you aware that your young partner is a Gnostic?"

"No kidding. What's a Gnostic?"

"Someone with heretical beliefs."

"Huh. And all this time I had him pegged as a Democrat."

Dantzler stepped in front of Charlie, cutting short their private chit-chat. This was not the time for small talk. He wanted to ask his questions, get his answers, and leave as quickly as possible. The prison infirmary, like all hospitals, smelled of sickness and death. It was a smell—and an environment—that made him uneasy. The sooner he could get out, the better. He certainly didn't want to stick around listening to these two gabbing about the past.

"You get the news concerning Colt Rogers?" he said.

"Rachel called this morning to inform me of what had transpired. A harsh way to meet your Maker." Eli grinned. "Excuse me, Detective Dantzler. Your 'Creator'."

"Any thoughts on who might have pulled the trigger?"

"Well, I didn't do it, that much we all know."

Dantzler reached in his coat pocket, took out a small tape recorder, and held it in front of Eli. "I'm taping this conversation, Eli, whether you like it or not. I want accuracy."

"So be it, Detective. I am too weary to argue with you. Turn it on and let's get started."

"What was your relationship with Colt Rogers?" Dantzler asked.

"Relationship? I had no relationship with the man. None."

"He was your attorney, wasn't he?"

"Are you insane, Detective Dantzler? I would never have a man like Colt Rogers as my attorney."

"That may come as a shock to Isaac and Rachel. They are both under the impression that he's your attorney. According to them, Rogers has handled your affairs since Abe Basham died. Are they wrong?"

"Not wrong, just not aware of facts as they are. Let me assure you of one thing, Detective. Colt Rogers was a two-bit hustler, a con man, and in all probability an outright thief. Why would I dare have someone like that as my attorney?"

"You're telling me he didn't represent you after Abe died?"

"That's precisely what I'm telling you." Eli stroked his white beard while taking several deep breaths. "Colt knew from having talked with Abe that I have property and holdings worth a lot of money, somewhere in the neighborhood of seven million dollars, in fact. A neighborhood like that tends to attract a lot of flies. Well, when Abe died, Colt was on me quicker than a vulture swooping down to a rotting carcass. Came to me with all these grand ideas, elaborate plans to parlay the money—*my money*—into an even greater fortune. And, of course, he volunteered to be my partner, the guy on the outside making all the deals. He always brought a stack of papers for me to sign, including one granting him power of attorney, thus making him executor of my estate. 'Please sign here, Eli,' he said. 'This deal will be worth millions.' Now I have never claimed to be the brightest bulb on the Christmas tree, but I'm not dumb enough to ever sign anything that man stuck in front of me."

"Okay, so who does handle your financial affairs?" Dantzler asked.

"My son-in-law."

"Kirk Foster?"

"Your mouth to God's ears, Detective. That is not public knowledge."

"Given the fact that neither Rachel nor Isaac know, it's not even private knowledge. Why the secrecy?"

"They will find out in due time."

"Why Kirk?"

"Because I trust him. And because I know he will do the right thing when I'm gone. He loves Rachel very much, he's friendly with Isaac, and he has been exceptionally kind to Thomas. He was the perfect choice and the logical choice."

"Was Colt aware of this?"

"Don't be absurd. If my own children don't know, do you really think I would tell him?"

"Warden Curtis said Rogers visited on a regular basis. How often did he see you?"

"Oh, maybe once a month back in the early days. But as my health began to deteriorate, he came more frequently. He became more desperate for me to sign those papers he brought with him. He was very persistent. Criminals usually are."

"Warden Curtis said Johnny Richards often accompanied Rogers when he came to see you. What's his deal?"

"He's an associate of Colt's. I really don't know him at all."

"Define associate."

"That would be a question for him. I can't answer it for you." Eli turned his attention to Charlie. "Ask your question, Detective Bolton. The one that has been gnawing at you for twenty-nine years."

"Why did you lie about the gun being in your safe?" Charlie said without hesitation.

"I didn't."

"Yes, you did. You knew whoever took the gun killed those two kids. You knew the identity of that person, and you lied to protect him."

"Detective Bolton, you couldn't be more wrong."

"I don't think so."

"Cling to your belief, then, if you must. Just know that your belief, like that of the apostate, is far from God's truth."

Dantzler moved closer to the chair and looked down at the withered, dying old man. "Who murdered those two boys, Reverend? If you do know, tell me."

Eli shrugged.

Dantzler knelt in front of Eli until they were at eye level. "Whose obituary am I looking for? Give me that name, at least."

"We've danced this dance before, Detective. Nothing has changed. You'll have to find it without my help."

Dantzler stood. "If you are serious about having your name cleared, you might want to re-think your stance on this matter."

"You have all you need. It's right in front of you."

"What I need is something concrete, not hints."

"The light of truth always prevails, Detective Dantzler. You'll uncover it. Maybe not while I'm still around, but you'll eventually find the answers." Eli closed his eyes and sighed heavily. "Gentlemen, I think it best we end this conversation. I've suddenly grown very tired and feel the need to get some rest. I apologize, and I ask that you not judge me to be discourteous."

Dantzler turned off the tape recorder, went to the door, and opened it. After waiting until Charlie was out of the room, Dantzler turned back toward Eli, who now appeared to be smaller and older than he did only moments earlier. He started to tell the old man goodbye, but didn't. Instead, he just looked at Eli for several silent seconds.

Dantzler turned to leave, and was almost out the door when he heard Eli's frail voice.

"Think of Jesus's empty tomb."

Dantzler wasn't sure who Eli was speaking to.

*****

For the first hour on the ride back to Lexington, neither Dantzler nor Charlie spoke. Both men stared straight forward, lost in thought, reflecting on what the Reverend had told them and what he hadn't told them. Each man also wondered what the other was thinking.

After a while Charlie closed his eyes and pretended to be sleeping. Dantzler wasn't fooled; he was familiar with this ruse. Charlie was using sleep as a pretense, a reason for not engaging in conversation. He simply did not want to talk.

But it was Charlie who, a few minutes later, opened his eyes and broke the silence.

"I'm telling you, Jack, the man is a seer," Charlie said. "He has special powers, exactly like those ancient prophets. Isaiah, Daniel, Ezekiel—he sees just like they did. How did he know the gun and safe question was the one that has been troubling me all these years? How could he have possibly known that?"

"It's what he knows that he's not telling that troubles me."

"I knew back in 'eighty-two that he wasn't being truthful about the gun being in the safe," Charlie continued, now awake and fully alert. "But I never once challenged him on it, never brought it up. He knew before he opened the safe that the gun wasn't in there. I should have pressed him harder, but I didn't. That will always haunt me. It was not good detective work."

"Don't beat yourself up on that issue, Charlie. Questioning him about the gun wouldn't have changed the outcome. Like you said, his fingerprints on the gun were powerfully persuasive evidence. Given those circumstances, I might not have asked the question, either."

"Then *you* wouldn't have been doing good detective work. I was suspicious, I should have asked. Simple as that."

"You have to drop it, Charlie. What's done is done. You can't change the past."

"Oh, really? Seems to me that's precisely what you're trying to do."

Dantzler was happy to see the lights of Lexington on the horizon. Although he loved Charlie like a father, he was growing weary of hearing him whine about what he should or should not have done. It wasn't constructive or enlightening. Whining didn't help move an investigation forward.

It would be much different if Dan Matthews was in the car. Dantzler smiled at the thought. If Dan was sitting beside him, they wouldn't dwell on past mistakes. There would certainly be no whining; Dan would slap a whiner. Instead, they would be tossing ideas and scenarios and possibilities back and forth like a tennis ball. They would challenge each other to come up with better ideas. They would be digging and digging until they reached the bottom of the case, where the answers are found.

"Are you doing any consoling tonight?" Dantzler asked, changing the subject.

"It's too late for that. Besides, I'm in no mood to console anyone. I'm gonna have a couple of drinks, then I'm hitting the sack."

"Sounds like a plan," Dantzler said, adding, "although I'm sure Emily Danforth will be disappointed."

"Yeah, well, she'll get over it," Charlie grumbled.

CHAPTER TWENTY-FOUR

Devon Fraley didn't find out about Colt Rogers's murder until early Sunday afternoon, the only day in the week she bought a newspaper. She made the purchase not for the news or entertainment, but to check the Lotto numbers. She spent five dollars every Saturday, always on Powerball, "the big one" as she liked to call it, hoping like millions of other dreamers to hit the once-in-a-lifetime jackpot. If she could only match those six numbers she wouldn't have to scrounge around looking for full-time employment. She and her son, Mark, would be set for life.

She spent all day Saturday accompanying Mark's fourth-grade class to Kings Island, an amusement park north of Cincinnati. It was the end-of-the-year school trip for all three fourth-grade classes, and it had been predictably chaotic. Keeping nearly one hundred wild and energetic kids in check at that place was no easy task. It took a battalion of eagle-eyed adults to manage it. No Child Left Behind took on real meaning in a situation like that. Blessedly, no child was left behind, lost, or injured. It had been a terrific day for everyone. She and Mark didn't get back to Lexington until almost nine p.m. Both were so tired they immediately went to bed.

On Sunday morning, she asked Mark what he wanted for breakfast even though she knew what his answer would be—McDonald's, of course. She would have a coronary if he chose some place other than Mickey D's. She didn't understand the fascination with the place—she rated the food only so-so—but try telling that to kids. To them it was a five-star restaurant.

After they finished eating, Mark asked if he could spend the afternoon with his cousin, Jordan, whose mother, Terri, was Devon's older sister. Although Mark was almost two years younger than Jordan, the two boys had always been close. Mark was also extremely fond of Terri and her husband, Kevin, so much so in fact that Devon couldn't help but wonder if perhaps her son saw in Terri's stable family environment the very thing he sorely missed in his own home.

Mark had never known his father. Devon had only dated the man four or five times when she found out she was pregnant. It was on the night she broke the news to him that he informed her he was married, that he and his wife were separated but had now "worked things out" and were getting back together. Devon was devastated, but she held herself together, swore she wouldn't ask the bastard for one red cent, and promised to raise her child by herself, regardless of how difficult the circumstances might be. And she had done exactly that, providing a loving home and a safe environment for Mark. It hadn't been easy. There were many days when she wondered how she would make it financially, and an equal number of nights when she cried herself to sleep. Once or twice she had to borrow a few dollars from Terri, but for the most part she got by.

After dropping Mark off at Jordan's, Devon drove to a convenient store and bought a paper. When she got back in the car, she immediately went to the page listing the Lotto results for Saturday's drawing. Taking out her ticket, she began comparing numbers, her forefinger moving slowly across all five lines. One number in two different rows and that was it. Damn, she mumbled under her breath, what a bummer. Wadding the losing ticket up and tossing it into the empty seat next to her, she resigned herself to yet another week of accepting whatever crummy jobs the Pro-Temp Agency sent her way. It was better than nothing, she had to admit, but she simply had to find permanent employment.

Almost two hours later, while scanning the paper, she saw the article about Colt Rogers. She was stunned, couldn't believe what she was seeing. Colt Rogers, dead? How could it be? What could possibly have happened?

The article was brief, six paragraphs wrapped around a mug shot of Rogers, and it didn't offer much in the way of details. Devon read it three times, finally zeroing in on a quote from Captain Richard Bird.

We estimate that Mr. Rogers was killed sometime between 4:45 p.m. and 5:45 p.m.

Devon put together a timeline for Friday afternoon. Mr. Rogers gave her permission to leave at four-thirty, saying he was letting her go a half-hour early because she had done outstanding work. He did ask if she could swing by the Post Office and drop off the day's mail. She had gathered up the stack of mail from the outgoing tray, thanked Mr. Rogers for the opportunity, adding that she would love to work for him in the future if at all possible, and walked out of the office at precisely four-thirty.

Between 4:45 p.m. and . . .

A wave of fear swept through Devon when she realized she had possibly missed the killer by a mere fifteen minutes. Had she stayed on the job until her actual quitting time—five p.m.—her name might have ended up in the newspaper article. There would have been two murder victims and she would have been one of them. The thought terrified her.

She phoned Terri and told her about Rogers's death. She asked Terri if she should call the police and talk to them about it. Terri recommended holding off on that, arguing it wasn't a good idea for Devon to get involved, especially since she really didn't have any important information to offer. Besides, Terri said, if the police feel the need to speak with you, they'll be in touch.

Devon really didn't know anything worth telling. That had been her one and only time working for Mr. Rogers, and he had been out of the office for much of the day. The paralegal, a woman named Cheryl Likens, had been off all day as well. Devon spent most of the day alone in the office. She recalled that three of Mr. Rogers's clients came by to pick up documents he had filled out. Two others came in asking to set up appointments with him, which Devon did. And there had been maybe a dozen phone calls, some from clients, still others wishing to speak with Mr. Rogers about him possibly representing them on certain legal matters. She had logged every caller's name and message, and promised to give them to Mr. Rogers when he returned.

One of the last calls she took on Friday afternoon was from a Detective Dantzler, who asked if he could meet Mr. Rogers later in the evening. She remembered telling the detective she would schedule him for six p.m., give the message to Mr. Rogers, then have him get back in touch if there was a conflict and the meeting couldn't take place. When she relayed Detective Dantzler's request to Mr. Rogers, he said it wouldn't be a problem, he would arrange his schedule so the meeting could take place.

Between 4:45 p.m. and 5:45 p.m.

Detective Dantzler was to meet with Mr. Rogers at six. Could he be the killer? Devon wondered. No, no, no, that's a preposterous notion, she said to herself. A police detective wouldn't kill Mr. Rogers. Clear that thought out of your head, girl, this instant.

Then Devon remembered something else—the man who came into the office while she was speaking with Detective Dantzler, the one who stayed a few minutes and then mysteriously disappeared. Could he have been the killer? Or was he one of Mr. Rogers's clients, perhaps one who was in such a hurry he didn't have time to stick around until she got off the phone? The man didn't give his name, and she had not mentioned him to Mr. Rogers when he returned later in the afternoon. Thinking about it now, she wondered if she should have.

Devon spent the rest of the day trying her best to block out thoughts of what happened to Mr. Rogers, or how close she may have come to being murdered. It was frightening and unsettling to realize the difference between life and death for her boiled down to a mere fifteen minutes. If she hadn't been given permission to leave early, she would be dead.

The realization brought tears to her eyes.

It was almost dark when Terri brought Mark home. Seeing Terri's car pull into the driveway, Devon went outside and spent fifteen minutes talking with her sister about the Rogers murder. She told her about the phone call from Detective Dantzler, and about the man who mysteriously vanished. Then she asked Terri again whether or not she should contact the police. Terri suggested that if the police had not contacted Devon by noon tomorrow, she should call Detective Dantzler and speak with him about it. Devon agreed to do that.

By eight-thirty, Mark was sound asleep, a rare occurrence for him. Under normal conditions, Devon had to fight to get him in bed by nine or nine-thirty. It was a nightly battle getting the child to give it up. But not tonight. The all-day Kings Island excursion on Saturday, and a Sunday afternoon spent romping around with Jordan were more than enough to wear him down. He was yawning at seven, droopy-eyed at eight and completely out of it thirty minutes later.

Devon undressed, put on her pajamas, poured a glass of ginger ale, and stretched out on the sofa, eagerly awaiting the start of her favorite Sunday night TV show, *CSI:Miami*. When it went off at eleven, she would have to hit the sack. She was scheduled to be at work tomorrow morning at eight. A local dentist's office needed a receptionist, and Susan Lloyd, owner of the Pro-Temp Agency, had called to see if Devon was interested. Initially, Devon was reluctant to accept the offer, but when Susan told her the job was guaranteed for a week, Devon couldn't say no. A week-long gig—that was like permanent employment. It also meant a decent paycheck.

At ten, Devon cleared her mind of all thoughts, choosing instead to focus only on *CSI:Miami*. No more thinking about what happened Friday, or how close she may have come to losing her life, or the mysterious stranger, or Detective Dantzler. Nothing to keep her from enjoying the show to the fullest.

She settled back, upped the volume one notch, and began watching.

Devon was so focused on her favorite TV show she failed to hear the noise coming from the kitchen. It was barely detectable, first a quiet pop followed by a soft shuffle of feet. Had she heard it, she would have suspected that Mark had gotten out of bed and was getting a drink of water. Or maybe he had gotten out of bed to pee. But she didn't hear it, didn't lose focus on the TV, on *CSI:Miami*, where detective Horatio Caine was questioning a suspect about a murder that occurred during a South Beach party.

Devon smiled when Horatio shrewdly trapped the suspect into telling a lie. But, Devon knew, this suspect wasn't the murderer. She guessed

Horatio knew it, too. But the suspect was somehow involved, and Horatio would eventually sort things out. He always did. Horatio Caine was the best.

Devon reached for the ginger ale, never taking her eyes off the television, not missing a word Horatio spoke. She didn't want to miss anything. After taking a sip, she placed the glass back on the end table.

Suddenly, from behind, a gloved hand covered her mouth and violently yanked her head backward. She tried to turn her head, to see the person behind her, but she couldn't. The person's grip was too powerful.

What's this? What's happening here? What's going on?

As she tried to struggle against her captor, to free herself from his grasp, she felt a sharp prick at the base of her skull.

Then Horatio Caine went black.

CHAPTER TWENTY-FIVE

Laurie Dunn was sitting in Barbara Tanner's kitchen when Eric phoned to tell her Devon Fraley had been found murdered in her home. Laurie listened intently, scribbling notes as Eric explained that Devon was the temp worker who filled in for Barbara at Colt Rogers's office on Friday. Laurie didn't interrupt while Eric was speaking, and she asked no questions when he finished. Her only comment before closing her cell phone was to tell Eric she would try to find out if Barbara could shed any light on the matter.

Barbara Tanner was forty-eight going on seventy. At least, that's the way she looked on this Monday morning, and she was the first to admit it. When Laurie arrived at a little past nine, a very tired-looking Barbara, dressed in a blue robe and white pajamas, her hair uncombed, apologized for her shabby appearance, adding that she simply didn't have the energy or the will to get dressed and face the world like a normal person should.

Barbara laid the blame for her malaise on flu-like symptoms that had stayed with her for almost a week. Laurie wasn't so sure about Barbara's self diagnosis. She couldn't help but wonder if Barbara's red and swollen eyes were the result of illness or from crying. Laurie leaned toward crying, because from the start of their conversation, Barbara made it clear that she cared deeply for Colt Rogers, and that she was devastated by his death. Laurie had no reason to doubt her.

Laurie decided to wait until later in the interview to tell Barbara about Devon Fraley. She knew it would be yet another shock to Barbara, who was already showing signs of sinking into depression. If Laurie could somehow spare her the bad news concerning Devon, she would. But she couldn't. She had no choice but to ask, and Barbara would have to answer. Sometimes being a detective really sucked.

"How long have you worked for Colt Rogers?" Laurie said.

"Since nineteen eighty-five," Barbara whispered. "I went to work for him right out of college. He's the only real boss I've ever had."

"Was he a good boss?"

"The best. He was never anything but fair and kind and generous to me. If I needed time off, either for illness or personal situations, he let me have it, no questions asked. Once, when I was being hounded by a collection agency, he loaned me the money to pay off the bill. Told me to take all the time I needed to pay it back. Took me three years, but I paid him every penny. To me, he was a wonderful person and a terrific boss."

"Was your relationship ever more than employer-employee?"

"You mean, did I sleep with him?" Barbara almost managed a chuckle. "Good heavens, no. And even if I had wanted to, it never would have happened."

"Why not? You're a very attractive woman."

"Let's just say I'm not exactly Mr. Rogers's type, if you know what I mean. He prefers his women to be a lot wilder and more flamboyant than I could ever hope to be. I'm a little too plain, too drab, and too conservative for his taste. Also, I'm now too old. He likes them young."

"Did he have a lot of women?"

"I would say he did." Barbara blew her nose into a tissue, wadded it, and dropped it into a wastebasket. "His current paramour is Cheryl Likens, our paralegal. They've been cozy with each other for the past year or so. I certainly hope she's better in bed than she is on the job, because that's the only way Mr. Rogers is getting his money's worth. The woman is dumber than a bag of nails."

"Is it possible they had a falling out and she killed him?"

"I seriously doubt it. To be perfectly honest, I'm not sure Cheryl has enough intelligence to load and fire a gun."

"What about past employees? Did Mr. Rogers have trouble or conflicts with any of them?"

"There haven't been all that many. Since I've been with the firm, there have been six paralegals prior to Cheryl. Three of them went on to law school and are now practicing attorneys. One left to get married, the other two left to take jobs elsewhere. They all left on good terms with Mr. Rogers."

Laurie thought for a moment, then said, "Any clients, past or present, you can think of who might have enough anger toward Mr. Rogers to want him dead?"

"None that I can think of. I have to say, most of his clients seemed happy with his services. We received very few complaints."

"Did you know Abe Basham?"

"Sure. He was one of the most-respected attorneys in town. After he passed away, we moved into his office on West Short Street. Prior to that, we were located in Chevy Chase."

"Were Abe and Mr. Rogers close?"

"No. I wouldn't say so. They certainly weren't enemies, but they didn't run in the same circles, either. Remember, Abe was quite a few years older than Mr. Rogers. Aside from the law, they didn't have much in common."

"Do you know Eli Whitehouse?"

"Well, I know of him, but I don't know him personally. Mr. Rogers did some work for him over the years, so I've handled paperwork involving Mr. Whitehouse. But I've never met him in person, not that I ever could, since he's in prison. When I was in high school, I did have a couple of classes with Isaac Whitehouse, Eli's oldest son. He was known as Ike in those days."

"What was he like?"

"Basically a good guy, smart, nice. He'd do anything for you." Barbara grinned. "Now, that younger brother of his. Tommy. He was one seriously handsome and sexy young man. With his looks he could put movie stars to shame. Every girl in school wanted to jump his bones, and that included me."

"I've known a few guys like that," Laurie said. She tapped her pen against the table top. "Can you think of anyone—*anyone*—who would want Colt Rogers dead?"

Barbara shook her head, tears beginning to roll down her cheeks. "No. I've racked my brain and I can't think of anyone who would do such a thing."

"He had no partner, so what will happen to the firm now that he's gone?"

Barbara burst into tears. "I don't know. I suppose we'll have to close it down."

Laurie waited until Barbara composed herself before asking the next question. "Did the Rogers firm use the Pro-Temp Agency very often?"

"We had no need to use any temp agency very often," Barbara said, "because I very seldom miss any work days. Friday was my first day off in years. I can't remember the last time I missed because of illness."

"What about when you go on vacation?"

"On those occasions, a woman named Maggie Richards usually filled in for me. She was a friend of Mr. Rogers."

"Was?"

"Yes. She passed away not long ago. Breast cancer."

Laurie hesitated, not wanting to drop another bomb on Barbara. But she had no choice.

"Barbara, do you know Devon Fraley?" she finally said.

"No. Who's she?"

"Devon Fraley is the lady sent by the Pro-Temp Agency to fill in for you on Friday. This morning, she was found murdered in her duplex. We have every reason to suspect that whoever killed her also killed Colt Rogers."

"Oh, my God, the poor girl, the poor thing." Barbara began to cry harder. "This is a nightmare, just a horrible nightmare. Tell me I'm going to wake up and none of this will be true. Please, tell me this is all just a bad dream."

Laurie closed her notepad and gently touched Barbara on the arm. She left without saying another word.

CHAPTER TWENTY-SIX

Dantzler opened the door to the interview room, moved briskly to the table, and sat down across from Greg Spurlock. Milt Brewer followed Dantzler into the room, eased to his right until he was directly behind Spurlock, and leaned against the wall. This positioning was standard procedure when interviewing a suspect. All cops know most humans are not comfortable when someone stands directly behind them, and contrary to what the movies and TV shows portray, detectives doing the interviewing want their subjects to be nervous and on edge, not comfortable.

Greg Spurlock was nervous and on edge long before Dantzler and Milt came into the room. He'd been in there alone for almost thirty minutes, sometimes sitting in the chair fidgeting with his tie, other times pacing the room like a scared puppy. At all times, he appeared to be on the verge of bursting into tears.

Dantzler slapped his notepad on the table, flipped it open, and glared across the table. Spurlock seemed to flinch when his eyes met Dantzler's. He looked away and shifted in his chair in an attempt to see where Milt was standing. Milt reached down, took Spurlock by the shoulders, and turned him back toward Dantzler.

"Eyes front," Milt said, harshly. "Don't look at me unless I ask you a question. Got it?"

Spurlock nodded.

"Okay, Greg," Dantzler said, "the last time we . . ."

"Do I need a lawyer?" Spurlock interrupted.

"That's up to you," Dantzler answered. "If it takes a lawyer sitting next to you in order for you to be honest with me, then by all means call one. You can use my cell phone."

"I just don't want you guys to trick me. You know, get me to fall into a trap."

"The best way to avoid a trap is by telling the truth. Lying to me, like you did the first time we spoke, will not serve you well. I can promise you that much."

Milt put his hands on Spurlock's shoulders, bent down, and whispered in his ear. "Didn't your parents ever tell you honesty is the best policy? That the truth shall set you free?"

"Yes," Spurlock mumbled.

"Well, then, this is the perfect time to heed their advice," Milt said, letting go of Spurlock's shoulders and leaning back against the wall.

"So, Greg. Do you want to call an attorney?" Dantzler said.

"No, I guess not."

"You're sure? I don't mind waiting if you do."

"No. It's okay. Let's just get this over with."

Dantzler said, "Greg, the three of us are not leaving this room until we clear up a few things about your actions on that night in nineteen eighty-two. If you're truthful with us, we can get this over and done with in a relatively short period of time. However, if you persist in being dishonest, we'll be here until the Messiah shows up. Do you understand?"

"Yes."

"Okay, let's begin with the gun that was at the scene. You told me you didn't see it, correct?"

"Yes."

"Was that a lie?"

"Yes."

"You're telling me now you *did* see the gun?"

"Yes."

"Why did you lie about that?"

"I don't know. I just . . . did."

"Where was the gun when you saw it?"

"Between the two victims, but closer to the victim on the right."

"Did you touch the gun?"

"No, absolutely not."

"You're sure about that?"

"Yes, yes, I am."

"How did you know it was small caliber?"

"My grandfather was a big gun collector. He had dozens of guns—rifles, shotguns, pistols—every kind you can think of. He taught me all about the different types of guns. I could tell from looking at the gun in the barn that it was probably a twenty-two."

Dantzler nodded. "This is good, Greg. See how much smoother things go when you tell the truth?"

"You'll want to stay on this path," Milt said from behind. "Don't stray from it one inch and we'll all get along fine."

"When we first spoke," Dantzler continued, "you told me you were only in the barn for a minute after Angie went back to the car. That doesn't square with how Angie remembers it. She claims you were in the barn for ten minutes. Which is it?"

"Well, uh . . ."

"Come on, Greg," Milt said. "This is no time to get squirmy on us. Focus on that path I talked about."

"I would say Angie is closer to being accurate," Spurlock admitted. "I don't agree that it was ten minutes, but it was longer than a minute."

"How long?" Dantzler asked.

"Between five and ten minutes, I would say."

"All right, Greg, we're now getting to the heart of the matter. *Why* did you lie about that?"

Spurlock's face and neck turned beet red, and his entire body began to tremble. He looked like a man having a seizure or a stroke. His eyes clouded with tears.

"Because I, well, I, uh, sort of touched the bodies," he finally managed to say. "I know it was stupid, but I did."

"Why did you touch them?" Milt asked.

"When I bent down next to the bodies, I noticed some money in one of the victim's jacket. I took it."

"Jesus Christ," Milt barked. "How did a numbskull like you ever become a doctor?"

"How much money?" Dantzler said.

"Seven hundred and fifty dollars. It was in a big wad, you know, all rolled up with a rubber band around it. I just . . . took it."

"Which victim had the money?"

"They both did. The other victim, the one on the left, had more than six hundred dollars on him. It was in his pants pocket."

"So, let's do some accounting here," Milt said. "You pilfered more than thirteen hundred bucks off two corpses? That's despicable."

"I'm sorry, really sorry."

"You say you 'noticed' the money," Dantzler said. "Is that true, or did you go digging through their pockets and find it?"

"It was in plain view," Spurlock said. "Like, half in the pocket, half hanging out."

"Did you also take drugs from the scene?" Milt said.

"No."

"Plant any?"

"No. The pills were in a small plastic bag in one of the victim's pocket. It fell out when I took the money. I never touched those pills, much less steal any of them."

"Why did you tell the investigators the bodies had been moved?"

Dantzler said.

"So no one might think I'd been around the bodies." Spurlock lowered his head. "Am I in trouble?"

"Well, let's see, Greg," Milt said. "You tampered with a crime scene, you stole evidence, and you lied to the police. By taking the cash, you prevented us from possibly getting fingerprints off the money, which might have helped us catch the killer. So, yeah, I'd say you could be in some trouble."

Spurlock slumped in his chair, as though he was being crushed by a heavy weight. Tears began to stream down his cheeks.

"Will I be prosecuted?" he said. "Am I going to jail?"

"I can't say right now," Dantzler said, closing his notepad. "It depends on what kind of mood I'm in when this is all said and done."

"Good thing you didn't ask me," Milt said, sitting next to Spurlock. "If it were left up to me, you'd spend the next few years getting butt injections rather than giving them."

"Please don't send me to jail," Spurlock whined. "I couldn't survive in there."

"You can go, Greg," Dantzler said, standing. "Just don't go too far. And be available if I need to speak with you again. Is that clear?"

"Yes, sir."

The minute Spurlock was out of the room, Milt burst into laughter. "I'd say we scared that poor putz into going straight. From this day forward, he'll be the most honest person in this town. We'll never have to worry about him again."

"I only wish he'd been truthful back then. Had he been, Eli Whitehouse would never have spent a day in prison."

"Maybe, maybe not," Milt said. "Those fingerprints on the murder weapon—that was powerful evidence against Eli. Nothing Spurlock did in the barn would have changed the outcome."

"I hope you're right." Dantzler opened the door. "The cash and pills—obviously the killer planted the stuff."

"Thirteen hundred bucks," Milt said, draping an arm around Dantzler. "Pretty good haul for a kid. Sure hope he spent it wisely."

CHAPTER TWENTY-SEVEN

After concluding his interview with Greg Spurlock, Dantzler jumped in his car and drove to Devon Fraley's duplex on Crosby Drive. He made the short trip from downtown in less than fifteen minutes, arriving just as Devon's body was being loaded into the ambulance. Mac Tinsley, the coroner, was standing in the yard conversing with the driver. Dantzler nodded at the two men as he walked onto the small porch and entered the duplex.

Rarely did he arrive at a crime scene after the body had been removed. Given his choice, it would never happen. Like all good homicide detectives, Dantzler felt there was much to be discerned from seeing the murder victim in his or her original death position. Photographs were fine, video even better, but neither was a match for seeing the scene prior to the body being taken away. The human eye almost always trumped technology.

But on this occasion, Dantzler's late arrival couldn't be prevented. His interview with Greg Spurlock had been scheduled for nine a.m., and he didn't hear about Devon until five minutes before entering the interview room. Knowing he would likely get to the scene after the body had been removed, he dispatched Sammy Turley, a videographer, to work with Eric and Scott.

Dantzler needed no visual aids to tell him where Devon Fraley had been murdered. One look at the beige sofa told him this was where she had taken her last living breath in this world. Devon had been sitting directly in the center of the sofa, obviously watching television, when her attacker struck from behind. There was dried blood on the top pillow, and a dark stain trailed down the back of the sofa, eventually forming a small puddle of blood on the wooden floor.

"Man, the hits just keep on coming," Eric said, moving alongside Dantzler. "And this poor lady never knew what hit her."

"What did hit her?"

"Mac says either an ice pick or possibly a screwdriver. Base of the skull, into the brain. She died instantly."

"Did Mac venture a guess as to time of death?"

"Between nine and midnight."

"Who found the body?"

"Her nine-year-old son. Mark."

"Ah, don't tell me that."

"He woke up, checked the alarm clock in his room, knew he was gonna be late for school, so he started running around looking for his mother, wondering why she had failed to get him up on time. Found her down here. He ran next door and told the neighbor. She called nine-one-one."

"Where's Mark now?" Dantzler said.

"With Devon's sister, Terri, and her husband."

"What about the Mark's father? Anyone spoken to him yet?"

"According to Terri, Mark's father has never been in the picture. She says Mark doesn't even know who his father is. Apparently, the father split when Devon told him she was pregnant, went back to his wife, and has had no contact with Devon or Mark. Terri says the guy was a sperm donor and nothing more."

"Okay," Dantzler said, moving closer to the sofa but careful not to step in the blood, "let's figure out how this went down. Devon is sitting here, eyes on the tube, and her attacker comes from . . . where?"

"The kitchen," Scott said, entering the den. "Through the back door."

"It wasn't locked?" Eric said. "I can't imagine a single mom not keeping her doors locked at night."

Scott shook his head. "Nope. But Devon probably thought it was. The killer used tape on the dead bolt, which kept it from locking. Devon didn't check it last night—she probably assumed it was locked like always—so the killer just waited until the right time, then came in and did his business."

"Which means he staked out the place," Eric said. "Are the techies looking for shoe or fingerprints?"

"They're on it now," Scott answered.

"Scott and I will start a canvass of the neighborhood," Eric said. "If we're lucky, one of the neighbors saw someone suspicious back there."

"Folks, we're dealing with a real pro here," Dantzler said. "This guy is good, damn good. And smart. He killed those two kids with a twenty-two, Colt Rogers with a bazooka, and Devon Fraley with an ice pick. Different murder weapon each time, not a single hair or fiber or fingerprint left at the scene, no witnesses, nada. Does anyone still doubt that we're dealing with a professional hit man?"

No one answered.

*****

Later, as they were finishing up, Dantzler pulled Eric aside. "Are you making any progress on the female obits?"

"Wrapped it up late last night. My plan was to give everything to you this morning after you finished with Spurlock. Then this came up. It's all in a big envelope on your desk."

"Find anything worth mentioning?"

"Are you kidding? I found nothing of interest. Not even one jaywalker in the bunch."

"Saints and vestal virgins, huh?"

"I don't know how many virgins there were, but I can tell you there's not a criminal in the group."

"I'll give it a glance when I get some free time. And listen, Eric, I really do appreciate it. I'll make sure certain people up the food chain are aware of the time and effort you put in on this. It won't go unnoticed."

"Don't worry about it. I only regret that nothing positive came of it."

"We gave it a shot and it didn't work out. It happens. I don't like coming up empty any more than you do, and I especially don't like it when the man who sent us on our quest knows the answer and won't reveal it. That pisses me off."

"You think Eli knows who the killer is?" Eric said.

"Oh, yeah."

"And do you believe the same person killed those two boys, Colt Rogers, and Devon Fraley?"

"I'm positive they were all killed by the same person."

"Then it doesn't take much to understand why Eli is keeping secrets. He's protecting himself."

"Or others."

CHAPTER TWENTY-EIGHT

The man sitting in the chair next to Eli's bed was late middle-age, thin, with dark hair and piercing blue eyes. Handsome by any standard, with chiseled features and an unusually clear complexion, he looked much younger than his actual age, thanks to the extensive facial surgery he underwent more than three decades ago.

Surgery deemed necessary in order to remain alive.

He was a killer, a stone-cold assassin with more than thirty major hits to his credit. Before his twenty-first birthday, he was already considered the ace of aces among hit men. If a target had to be eliminated, or an old score needed to be settled, he was the preferred choice to handle the task. Operating as an independent, owing loyalty only to the person paying the bill, he was among the most respected men in the Organization. And the most feared. Legend holds that Jimmy Hoffa once wet himself when elevator doors opened and he found himself standing face to face with the Mob's top mechanic.

He had the reputation and the credentials to back it up.

Then, almost overnight, following the death of his benefactor and mentor, things changed and his world went topsy-turvy. Allegiances were shattered, contracts broken. Old friends became enemies. Enemies sought revenge. Suddenly, almost without warning, the most feared hunter of them all became the hunted.

His choice was simple: change or die.

Now, all these years later, sitting in this room on a late afternoon, watching the dying Eli Whitehouse sleep, the man could only reflect on the circumstances that brought them together. The cruel winds of fate were responsible, a moment, a split-second in which the innocent became a prisoner to evil, and silence became the difference between living and dying.

Chance, providence, bad luck, shitty karma—call it what you will. It didn't matter. In his world, words meant nothing, actions everything. He had been forced to act and he did, in the only way he knew. He killed.

When danger threatened, old habits kicked in. Survival trumped everything. People had to be eliminated.

He thought the killing had ended thirty-one years ago when he laid down his gun and walked away from the business. At the time, even though his life was in danger, a voice in his head said no more, this is enough. It wasn't his conscience whispering to him; in truth, he had no conscience. Nor was it fear or burnout. He couldn't explain what it was, other than a desire deep inside him to stop taking money for killing. He wanted no more blood on his hands.

So, he left it all behind. He relocated, changed his appearance, made arrangements for his wife to join him, and became what he had previously despised—a civilian.

Despite the changes, he understood that men like him are never truly free from the past. Those who operate in shadows forever remain in shadows. Then or now, theirs is a world of dark places where the light, if it is allowed to penetrate, means death, either for them or for those unlucky enough to get trapped in its glare.

Like those two nameless victims in the old barn twenty-nine years ago. He did not want to kill them, but he had no choice. A light threatened his shadow, an invasion that was not acceptable. Light equaled death for him. Killing those two innocent, luckless kids made a point to certain people—silence equals life.

Now the silence had been broken. He had been betrayed, and this betrayal had set in motion a series of events resulting in the death of two more innocent, luckless victims. And now, in this prison infirmary, as the evening shadows crept across the room, he looked at the innocent, luckless man sleeping peacefully in his bed.

Eli Whitehouse.

The man did not claim to really know Eli. They had no real relationship, then or now. Not friends, not enemies. Only two men from different parts of the world thrown together forever by the oldest of reasons: a whisper overheard, a secret revealed. Knowledge, as it often does, became the X factor, the invisible chain that bound them to one another.

Knowledge was the light that could penetrate shadows.

His instinct was to kill Eli, to make him pay for his betrayal. In the past, he would have done so without hesitation. But killing Eli now was not only dangerous, it made no sense. Eli was already dying, slowly being assassinated by those cancerous cells inside his body. In this instance, nature was doing the dirty work. Eli's silence was guaranteed; what the man had to do now was find out if there were others who needed silencing.

He rose from his chair, went to the bed, and gently touched Eli's shoulder. Several seconds passed before Eli awoke. Even then, it took more time before he recognized the man standing above him.

"Have you come to kill me?" Eli said, his voice barely audible.

"That's up for grabs," the man responded. "Depends on the answers I get."

"Why did you kill Colt Rogers?"

"I don't learn anything by answering your questions, Eli. So I'll do the asking, you do the answering?"

"As you wish."

The man pulled his chair closer to the bed and sat down. Leaning forward, he quietly said, "Why did you bring the detective into this, Eli? And what have you told him?"

"Charlie Bolton mentioned some things to . . ."

"I don't know Charlie Bolton," the man interrupted. "I'm talking about Detective Dantzler. Why did you bring him into this?"

"I didn't," Eli lied.

"You requested a meeting with him. Why? I thought we had an understanding, Eli. Everybody stays quiet, everybody stays alive. Seems to me you've broken your promise. Now everybody and everything is in play."

"No, you have it all wrong," Eli protested. "I didn't request a meeting with Dantzler. He asked to see me. That's the truth. If you've heard otherwise, you've been given bad information."

"Why would he want to meet with you?"

"Like I was saying, Charlie Bolton, the lead detective on my case, mentioned a few things that really got Dantzler interested. Dantzler is writing an article on homicide investigative procedure and he thought my case would be worth mentioning. As a study tool, you know? He only asked me procedural questions. How Charlie and his partner, Dan Matthews, went about investigating the case, that sort of thing. I told him nothing about you. I swear to you. I would never make that mistake."

"It was a mistake talking to him at all, Eli. And I'm not sure I believe what you're telling me. Dantzler is doing more than writing an article."

"You shouldn't have killed Colt Rogers. That was a mistake."

"I had no choice, now, did I? Rogers was weak. I couldn't take a chance and let him talk to Dantzler."

"But Dantzler knows nothing."

"You don't want this to go any farther, Eli. It's in everyone's best interest for you to make sure it doesn't. Should Detective Dantzler continue pursuing this, certain people are going to die. And first on the list is your lovely, precious daughter. Make no mistake, Eli, her death will not be quick and painless. She will suffer."

"Please, you can't do that."

"I can and I will."

"Not Rachel. She's innocent."

"Do you really think that matters to me?"

"You gave your word. You promised."

"Make it all go away, Eli. Or else."

Eli turned away, tears in his eyes, his thoughts on Rachel. He realized now that he had unleashed a storm by bringing Dantzler into this. It might have been a mistake, a grave error in judgment that could easily lead to disaster. But it was the right decision to make. He believed it then, and despite the potential for a tragic outcome, he believed it now. If Dantzler was as smart as Eli believed him to be, it would all turn out for the best.

If . . .

Dantzler held the fate of Eli's family in his hands. And he didn't even know it.

CHAPTER TWENTY-NINE

Think of Jesus's empty tomb.

What had Eli meant when he uttered that statement? Was it a cryptic message, his way of directing Dantzler to the mysterious name in the obits? Was it even a message at all? Could it be Eli, overwhelmed by fatigue and fear, had confused Jesus's empty tomb with his own, which, in a matter of weeks, would no longer be empty? Had the words been directed at Dantzler, or was Eli, a man of God, conversing with a higher authority?

He wanted to dismiss Eli's statement as little more than the incoherent ramblings of a dying man. But he couldn't persuade himself that the words were meaningless. It was the timing that wouldn't allow him to simply write off the five words spoken by Eli. The timing, he felt, was crucial. He had been pleading with Eli to give him the name in the obits, yet Eli steadfastly refused. Then, at the last minute, Eli spoke:

Think of Jesus's empty tomb.

Dantzler was convinced of two things: Eli had directed his statement at Dantzler, and the answer to the puzzle could be found in those five words. But how to go about unraveling the mystery, that was the question. Eli had given him very little to work with, not a Proverb or a Psalm or one of the thousands of familiar biblical quotations. No particular book, chapter, or verse. Only five simple words:

Think of Jesus's empty tomb.

What are you trying to tell me, Eli? Dantzler said to himself. And why do you persist in making this so difficult?

It was well past midnight, and Dantzler sat on his back deck, watching the moon slowly make its way across the lake that backed up against his yard. The CD player was on, the volume down. Leonard Cohen, his favorite singer-songwriter, was singing a song titled "The Law" that had a lyric Dantzler now associated with Eli Whitehouse.

"*You just don't ask for mercy while you're still on the stand.*"

This was surely true in Eli's case. In twenty-nine years behind steel prison bars, the old man had never once asked for mercy, never once pleaded his case. Even now, with death banging on his door, he refused to provide information that in all likelihood would set him free. The name that held the answer to this mystery, along with the reason why Eli took the fall, would soon be locked away forever. Eli was taking it all to the grave with him.

You're a damn fool, Eli, Dantzler whispered out loud. One stubborn, insane Reverend.

*****

After nearly two hours of solid drinking, Dantzler was more than halfway through a bottle of Pernod. He had long ago zoomed beyond buzzed and was now well on his way to completely drunk. The night air was warm, almost muggy. In the darkness, around the lake, a chorus of crickets and loons sang, competing with Leonard Cohen for his musical attention.

The alcohol, the night, Eli's cryptic words, Cohen's music . . . they had conspired to send him into a dark, funky mood. It was territory he knew well, a place he visited often, and had since he was a small boy.

Next to him, on a small wooden table, was an 8x10 photograph in a gold frame. Picking it up, he brushed off some dust and held it under a lamp. It was his favorite photo, taken in Florida when he was six years old. In the photo, he was standing between his parents, Sarah and Johnny Dantzler.

Johnny Dantzler was only twenty-eight when the picture was taken. Tall, muscular, proud, more handsome than a movie star, he was a man who seemingly had everything within reach.

Everything, that is, except time.

Less than four months after the picture was taken, Johnny Dantzler was dead, killed in Vietnam.

Dantzler was barely six then, yet he'd felt a depth of sadness and hurt he doubted could ever be rivaled. But he had been wrong. He would feel it again. Eight years later when his beloved mother was murdered.

After staring at the photo for several more minutes, he gently put it back on the table. He took another drink and stared out at the shimmering water. Leonard Cohen sang "If It Be Your Will."

"Let your mercy spill on all these burning hearts in hell."

Those were the last words he heard before passing out.

CHAPTER THIRTY

Dantzler was flagging pages in the Bible when Milt and Scott came into the War Room. Several seconds later, Eric strolled in, carrying a bag overflowing with bagels. He tossed the bag onto the table, went to the coffee pot, filled a cup, and sat across from Dantzler.

Milt eyed the Bible in front of Dantzler, turned to Scott, and said, "Know what this reminds me of, Scott?"

Scott shook his head.

"A story I once heard."

"Oh, yeah? What story?"

"The great W.C. Fields was an alcoholic and quite the reprobate his entire life," Milt said, dragging a chair away from the table and sitting. "He was anything but a man of God, that's for sure. Well, one day, late in Fields's life, when he was old and near death, a friend of his walked into the room and was stunned to find Fields reading the Bible. 'Why are you studying the Bible?' the guy asked. 'You're not a religious man.' Know what Fields's reply was?"

"Don't have a clue."

"Old W.C. said, 'I'm looking for loopholes.' " Milt laughed. "Now, that's one terrific line, don't you agree?"

Scott shrugged. "Yeah, I guess so. One question, though. Who's W.C. Fields?"

"You gotta be kidding me," Milt said. "You don't know who W.C. Fields is? That's criminal. You ought to be busted back to traffic cop for an answer like that. Don't you young kids know anything at all?"

"Hey, Milt," Scott said. "Who's Lady Gaga?"

"Hell, how should I know?"

"You gotta be kidding me. Don't you old farts know anything at all?"

"*Zing*," Eric said, taking a bagel from the bag. "You've been severely neutered, Milt. And by a rookie, at that."

"He'll never last as a Homicide dick." Milt gently cuffed Scott on the side of his head. "He's too ugly, he's a wise ass, and he's a dummy when it comes to cinema history. I give him two more months and he's back walking a beat."

"Nah, Milt, I think the kid's got a future with us," Eric said, turning toward Dantzler. "Why are you studying the Good Book, Jack? Are you looking for loopholes?"

Dantzler shook his head. "When Charlie and I went to see Eli, just before we left, the old guy said something interesting. He said, 'think of Jesus's empty tomb.' At first, I wasn't sure if he was speaking to me or mumbling to himself or maybe hallucinating. But after thinking about it, I've concluded he was trying to tell me something. Those five words hold the answer to this mystery. I'm convinced of it."

"Jack, are you sure this guy isn't playing mind games with you?" Milt asked. "Hell, if he really wants this thing solved, all he has to do is give you a name. How difficult can that be?"

"Dammit, Milt, he can't. He's protecting his family."

"You like that cantankerous old bird, don't you?"

"Like, dislike—they don't factor into this. I simply can't stand seeing an innocent man locked up behind bars."

"None of us can," Milt said. "But he had the option to do something about it long before now. He didn't have to wait until the Grim Reaper was on his doorstep before seeking help. Spending unnecessary years behind bars—that's on him."

Eric picked up the Bible and leafed through the four pages Dantzler had flagged. "Find anything worthwhile? Any idea what Eli was trying to tell you?"

"Not really," Dantzler answered. "The four gospels are all fairly consistent in their narratives concerning the women finding Jesus's empty tomb. But they do differ on who those women were. Mary Magdalene is the one consistent; her name appears in all four accounts. Mary, the mother of James, is in Matthew, Mark, and Luke. Salome is in Mark's gospel, and Joanna is in Luke's. Luke also says there were other women with them, but gives no names. John mentions only Mary Magdalene. Like I said, there's not much to go on."

"A female shooter?" Milt said. "Are we wrong to discount that possibility?"

"I never discount anything, Milt. But the likelihood . . . I just can't see it."

"Okay, so where do we go from here?" Eric said.

"Back to the obits," Dantzler said. "Men only, forget the women. Scott, you help on this. This is gonna sound nutty, but here's what I want you to look for. Matthew, Mark, Luke, and John are obvious names to check for. Peter is mentioned in Mark's and John's versions, so look for anyone with that name. The stone was rolled away from the tomb—that was a big deal—so look for someone named Stone. Anyone named Lord or James. I know this is asking a lot, but right now it's all we have to go on. The answer is in those five words. I'm positive of it. The name is buried somewhere in the obits."

"What's your next move, Jack?" Milt said.

"I need to speak with Tommy Whitehouse, but he's a hard dude to pin down. I have his sister, Rachel, trying set up a meeting. That's my first priority. Then at some point, I want the two of us to talk with Johnny Richards. See if he can shed some light on all this."

"Did you ask Eli about him?" Eric said.

"Yeah, but he doesn't know the guy all that well. Richards was Colt Rogers's friend, not Eli's. Still, I don't think it would hurt to meet with him."

"Colt's funeral is tomorrow at ten," Milt said. "You want us there?"

"You bet. Sean Montgomery and I are going to the visitation tonight to see if anyone interesting or suspicious shows up. Laurie, Eric, and I will attend the service tomorrow afternoon. Milt, you and Scott find strategic and discreet locations near the gravesite. Photograph everyone who attends. Sammy Turley will be there to get it all on video."

"Can you handle a camera, Scott?" Milt asked, smiling.

"Better than Annie Leibovitz."

"Who?"

"It's true. You old farts really don't know anything."

CHAPTER THIRTY-ONE

Sean Montgomery was right—Colt Rogers was not highly regarded by his peers. During the two hours Dantzler and Sean spent at the funeral home, not more than a dozen people showed up for the visitation. If Rogers did have friends and professional colleagues who respected him, they were no-shows on this particular night. Judging from this turnout, the man known for his plea-bargaining tactics was a pariah within the legal community.

Dantzler and Sean stopped by McCarthy's for a few pints of Guinness before driving out Harrodsburg Road to Kerr Brothers Funeral Home. The before-visit drinks were at Sean's insistence.

"I want alcohol before the visit and a good long shower after I get back home tonight," Sean said. "Maybe if I'm a little drunk, I can tolerate the slime until I'm able to wash it off."

"Such a horrible thing to say about the deceased," Dantzler joked. "You're supposed to show respect for the dead."

"Colt Rogers was a horrible person when he was alive," Sean countered. "As for respecting the dead, I say a person gets in death what he or she earned in life."

"You're a hardcore philosophical bloke, Sean. No wonder you made a great defense attorney."

"Come on, Jack," Sean said after finishing off his third pint. "Let's do this before I change my mind and order another round."

*****

The handful of visitors who did show up at the funeral home included three or four of Rogers's fellow attorneys, all of whom looked to be in the senior citizen age group, and none of whom gave the slightest hint they wanted to be there. Each one signed the register, spent a few brief moments by the casket, then quickly departed, head down as though they were afraid they might be recognized. Their haste to leave seemed to be propelled by extreme embarrassment for having known Colt Rogers.

Several others trickled in during the two hours Dantzler and Sean were there. Most were middle-age women who came not so much to pay tribute to the dead man, but rather to console the one person in the room who was a genuine mourner—Barbara Tanner.

Barbara sat alone, dressed in black, obviously distraught by the death of her long-time boss. Her makeup had long since been washed away by her tears, and her eyes were red and puffy. She paid several visits to the beautiful oak casket, which was closed and covered by a blanket of red roses. A folded American flag and a single 8x10 photograph of a smiling Colt Rogers rested on top. After looking at the photo of Rogers for several seconds, she would wipe the tears from her eyes and return to her chair.

"That's Barbara Tanner," Sean said to Dantzler. "How she survived all those years working for such a sleazeball is a mystery to me. She's a really nice, decent lady. Have you spoken to her yet?"

"Laurie did." Dantzler pointed toward the other mourner sitting alone, this one much younger and prettier. "Who's the good-looking lady?"

"That would be Cheryl Likens. She is Colt's current paralegal, and if the grapevine is accurate, his latest main squeeze. I've never personally dealt with her, but rumor has it she is not a candidate for a Rhodes scholarship. Dumb as a rock. Of course, she would have to be to sleep with Rogers."

"That's what Barbara told Laurie. She said we could rule Cheryl out as the shooter based on sheer stupidity."

"Good old Barbara," Sean said, chuckling. He nudged Dantzler in the ribs. "Come on, Jack, let's get out of here. I can feel the slime growing on my body."

The funeral and the graveside service conducted the next morning also turned out to be a waste of time and effort for Dantzler and the Homicide team. Thirteen people showed up for the funeral, five made the trip to the cemetery. In all, ten of the thirteen were women. Only one attorney had the courage to make an appearance at the gravesite, and according to Sean, the man had been retired for many years. The other two men were photographed and later identified as distant cousins of Rogers.

*****

"Well, that was a chunk of my life I'll never get back," Milt said when the group gathered later that afternoon in the War Room. "Just another reason why I need to sign those papers, turn in my badge, and join Charlie Bolton on his fishing boat."

"You talk about depressing," Eric said, loosening his tie. "To live all those years, work as an attorney, get murdered in a most brutal way, and have virtually no one show up at your funeral service. I don't care how much of a bum the guy was, that's sad."

"You reap what you sow in this life, Eric," Milt said. "That's something I firmly believe."

"So do I. But, still, to have no one grieve for you when you're gone. Man, that's so . . . sad."

Laurie said, "Did you see Barbara Tanner, Eric? That was no act. Those tears were real. She's gonna miss the man."

"Think Cheryl Likens will miss him?" Milt said, grinning.

"Are you kidding? She'll have a new sugar daddy within a week, if she doesn't already have one."

"Maybe you should make a play for her, Milt," Scott said. "Obviously, she prefers older guys, and you certainly fit into that category."

"Scott, I'd go broke buying Viagra trying to keep up with a woman like Cheryl Likens. No, no, Scott. I need a woman, not grief or trouble. She'd be grief *and* trouble."

Dantzler entered the room and the mood suddenly turned somber. He went to the end of the table, pulled back a chair, but didn't sit. Instead, he leaned against the wall, his dark, tired eyes staring into space. After a minute of silence, he pushed away from the wall, sat, and scooted the chair forward.

"Sorry for putting you through an ordeal like this," he said. "I know you all had better ways to spend your time than hanging out at Colt Rogers's funeral service. Sean Montgomery warned me it would be a waste of time. I should've listened to him."

"The next big dinner tab is on you," Milt said. "And the bar bill. Speaking of which, I could certainly use an alcoholic beverage right about now."

"Later," Dantzler said. "What I want from you now are thoughts or ideas about this case. That goes for all of you. Give me anything you've got, no matter how out there you think it might be."

"It's really not very complicated," Laurie said. "If you're convinced the killings in 'eighty-two and these two recent killings were done by the same person, then we just need to dig deeper to find the missing link. If there is one."

"I still say you should pressure Eli for a name," Milt said. "Give him your assurance that if he coughs up the name, we'll protect his family. We'll make sure they are never in harm's way."

"How can I make that assurance, Milt?" Dantzler argued. "I have no clue what we're up against here. For all I know, the killer could be part of Murder Incorporated or the Russian mob. At any rate, you can forget about Eli giving us a name. It's not gonna happen."

"Well, then, our only option is old-fashion hardcore detective work.

Tell us what you want us to do."

"Same plan as before," Dantzler said, standing. "Eric and Scott on the obits, Laurie digging into Devon Fraley's past, you going through Colt Rogers's files. Check with Barbara Tanner. If she's up to it, get her to assist you."

"What about you?" Eric asked.

"Rachel Foster phoned me a few minutes before I came in. She has me set to meet Tommy Whitehouse tomorrow afternoon. He was a hard dude to track down, and given his checkered past, I'm not sure what to expect from him. I doubt he'll give me anything worthwhile, but who knows? Maybe he'll surprise me. Then sometime on Thursday, Milt and I are going to talk with Johnny Richards."

"He wasn't at the funeral today, was he?" Eric said.

Dantzler shook his head. "No. And based on the names listed in the guestbook, he didn't come by the funeral home last night, either."

"Some friend."

"Hell, after what I saw today," Milt said, "I don't think Colt Rogers had any friends."

CHAPTER THIRTY-TWO

Of the three Whitehouse children, the one who most intrigued Dantzler was the one he had yet to meet—Tommy.

There was no mystery why this was so. Tommy Whitehouse's story was a mirror image of Dantzler's uncle Tommy Blake, another charmed golden boy who stumbled somewhere along life's road and became a lost soul.

Tommy Blake had been Dantzler's idol, his hero, his mentor. It was Tommy who taught him how to play tennis and baseball. It was Tommy who instilled in him a love for learning. It was Tommy who helped him become a man. Tommy Blake was one of those charmed individuals who had star quality written all over him. Graceful, strong, quick, fearless, and intelligent, he was seen as a can't-miss Major League shortstop or a Rhodes scholar. All doors were open to him. All he had to do was pick the one he wanted to enter. He chose baseball, signing a contract with the Los Angeles Dodgers on the day he graduated from high school. His impact was immediate, his talent enormous, and within two years he had moved rapidly up the ranks within the Dodgers' organization. Then, while playing for the Triple A club, disaster struck.

A career-ending knee injury and the death of Sarah Dantzler, his beloved sister, with whom he was especially close, slammed those doors shut. After his playing career ended, an addictive personality emerged. Tommy Blake, disillusioned and adrift, traded his dreams of glory for drugs, alcohol, and a series of unsuccessful relationships with women. He was, Dantzler knew, a haunted, tragic figure.

Not unlike Tommy Whitehouse, who, according to Rachel, was so devastated by Eli's situation that he "shut down, checked out, and extinguished the light of brilliance that shone within him." Rachel had used words like lost, haunted, and tragic when describing Tommy. They were the same words Dantzler often used when describing his uncle. Tommy Blake and Tommy Whitehouse were, in Dantzler's mind, two of life's great magnificent maybes, men whose vast potential would never be realized.

Dantzler spent a week trying to connect with Tommy Whitehouse. He phoned numerous times, and stopped by the duplex at least once a day. Tommy never responded to Dantzler's calls, nor did he answer the door when Dantzler went by the place, even though on at least three of those visits, Dantzler was certain Tommy was inside. Only through Rachel's efforts did Tommy reluctantly agree to meet Dantzler.

Pulling up in front of the duplex, Dantzler saw Tommy peering out from a front window. Based on what he had learned from Rachel, Dantzler wasn't sure how much pertinent information he would get from Tommy. But he was sure of one thing. An hour from now, when he walked out of the duplex after meeting Tommy Whitehouse, he would be sad and depressed. Exactly the way he felt every time he walked out of Tommy Blake's apartment.

When Tommy opened the door and stepped onto the small porch, Dantzler felt as if he were looking at the face of his uncle Tommy. The similarities were eerie, almost identical. Dantzler wondered if perhaps they were for all lost souls. The sad eyes ringed by dark circles, eyes that seemed to view everyone and everything with suspicion. The gaunt face and pale skin, the black hair sprinkled with gray, the body thin but still muscular. The aura of lost hope. And yet, Dantzler recognized something in Tommy Whitehouse that he always saw in his uncle—despite the damage inflicted by time and abuse, more than a hint of youthful beauty was still present. The golden boy was lost, but not completely vanished.

Tommy nodded and waved Dantzler in without speaking. He followed Dantzler into the den and sat in a leather chair. Dantzler awkwardly stood in the middle of the room for several moments before finally settling into a wicker chair across from Tommy.

Dantzler could tell Tommy had been drinking. There were no overt signs, no alcohol in sight, no smell, but Dantzler had enough experience dealing with his uncle to know almost instinctively when an alcoholic was covering up his drinking. Tommy Whitehouse had probably begun hitting the bottle early in the day. Or maybe he had been drinking all night. With alcoholics, so good at concealing their symptoms, it was often difficult to know when the first drink of the day was taken. Tommy was not yet drunk, but he was heading in that direction.

Tommy cleared his throat, said, "I remember you from when I was a kid. You were this big tennis hero, the court prince who won all those tournaments. You were one of my idols. You and Johnny Bench."

"Johnny Bench, huh? That's heavy-duty company you're putting me in with. The guy was the best."

"Yes, he was." Tommy dug into his shirt pocket, pulled out a roll of Certs, and popped one into his mouth. "Baseball was my best sport, but I did play a lot of tennis, too. I was pretty good, in fact. Not like you, of course, but, you know, I could hold my own. I have a racket somewhere—Rachel probably has it stored at her farm—that Pancho Gonzalez autographed for me. He was in Cincinnati for a tournament and I got him to sign it. Did you ever meet him?"

"I hit with him once at a juniors tournament in Las Vegas when I was twelve. After I'd won a couple of early matches, I was on one of the practice courts when he showed up. He watched me hit for a few minutes, then asked if I would mind hitting with him. I couldn't believe it. Pancho Gonzalez asking to hit with me. I'm thinking, okay, this has to be a dream. But it wasn't . . . it was real. I hit with him for about an hour. One of the great moments in my life."

"Did you win the tournament?"

"Runner-up. Lost seven-five in the third set. Skinny little left-hander named McEnroe beat me."

"Bummer."

"Did Rachel tell you why I wanted to speak with you?" Dantzler asked.

"Something to do with my father, right?"

"Yes."

"Why?"

"Because I believe he is innocent and I'm trying to uncover the truth."

"Good luck."

"Do you think he's guilty?"

Tommy shrugged. "No, I don't. But a ton of evidence says he is."

"True," Dantzler said, "But after looking into it—"

"Would you excuse me for a second?" Tommy said, standing. "I'm in desperate need of a drink of water."

"Sure. I'm in no hurry."

Tommy was gone less than two minutes before returning to his chair. He popped another Certs into his mouth, leaned back, and hands clasped behind his head. "What were you saying, Detective Dantzler?"

"When did you start drinking again?" Dantzler said.

"What makes you think I'm drinking? Didn't Rachel tell you? I haven't touched a drop in almost six months."

"Cut the denial act, Tommy. You had a drink. I know you did."

"I had water."

"You had booze."

"Okay, so I had a drink. So what? It's not the end of the world. Anyway, I've got it under control now. I know when to stop."

"You're an alcoholic, Tommy. You should never start."

"When did you become my AA counselor?"

"I'm not."

"Then put the brakes on your stop drinking lecture and get back to being a detective. You want to know about Eli, ask about Eli."

"All right. Let's talk about the night of the murders. Where were you when they happened?"

"At home, in my room, watching TV."

"How did you find out about it?"

"When the phone call came, I heard a lot of noise coming from downstairs. I went down to see what was going on. Mom told me something terrible had happened at the barn on Eli's property. She said Eli was on his way to the scene. I didn't find out about the two guys being killed until the next morning. I think Isaac came by the house and told me."

"Did you know either of the two victims?"

"Never met either one."

"Do you think Isaac knew them?"

"You'd have to ask him. But I rather doubt it."

"Why do you say that?"

Tommy laughed. "Because Isaac only associated with the upper crust of society, if you get my drift. Those two guys were a few levels below his standard."

"What's your relationship with Isaac?"

"We have the same DNA."

"You're not close?"

"No, Detective Dantzler, we aren't close."

"Did you know Greg Spurlock or Angie Iler? They were the ones who discovered the bodies."

"No. I didn't know them."

"What was your initial reaction when you heard your father was being charged with the crime?"

"I thought the cops were crazy."

"Why did you think the cops were crazy?"

"There is no way Eli Whitehouse would tie up two total strangers, put a twenty-two caliber pistol to the back of each one's head and systematically blow them away. That's more than preposterous; it's insane. And all that crap about drugs? Eli hated taking any type of medication, including prescription drugs. The notion he was involved in some kind of drug deal gone sour is off-the-charts preposterous. Nothing about that entire scenario added up. Nothing."

"You've obviously given this a lot of thought," Dantzler said. "Give me your version of a scenario that does make sense."

"Someone murdered those two guys and then set my father up to take the fall."

"I agree with you. But that leaves me with two obvious questions. First, who is that someone, and second, why did Eli take the fall without putting up a fight?"

"Hey, I'm just a drunk, remember? You're the cop. You find the answers."

"You knew the combination to the safe, didn't you?"

"Yeah, we all did. So did Abe Basham, Eli's attorney. And there may have been one or two others who knew, but I couldn't swear to that."

"Eli kept the gun in the safe, didn't he?"

"Yes."

"On the night of the murders, Eli swore the gun was in the safe. It wasn't. How do you think it came to be missing?"

"Well, obviously, someone opened the safe and took it."

"Who, other than family members and Abe Basham, could have taken the gun?"

"I don't know."

"Tell me about your relationship with Eli," Dantzler said.

"He was a preacher. I was a cocky, headstrong fifteen-year-old kid. You do the math. We got along, but there were definitely moments when we clashed."

"Sounds normal." Dantzler noticed a lone photograph on the table next to Tommy's chair. "Is that you and Eli?"

Tommy picked up the photo and stared at it for almost a minute. His eyes clouded over with tears. Finally, he placed the photo back on the table.

"Me and the old man," he said. "Back in the day."

"Rachel tells me you've not been to the prison once since Eli was incarcerated. Twenty-nine years without seeing your father. That's a harsh sentence for both of you."

"I don't want to see my father behind prison bars. I'd prefer to remember him like this." Tommy pointed to the photo of him and his father. "And for him to remember me like this. Before the nightmare began."

"You do know he has terminal cancer?"

"Rachel told me."

"I'm sure he would love to see you."

"Then clear up this case before he dies, because that's the only way I'll see him. Free, not in a cold prison cell or a prison hospital."

"Can you think of anyone who would want to do this to Eli?"

"No."

"No enemies you can think of?"

"Eli didn't have enemies, only followers."

"I hate to tell you this, Tommy, but he had at least one enemy. This situation didn't happen in a vacuum. Somebody made it happen."

"Had to be an outsider."

"You mean, not someone in Eli's congregation?"

"No. I mean someone from outside of this area."

"Why would a stranger want to set Eli up?"

"That's the million-dollar question, isn't it?"

"Has anyone you're familiar with died within the past three weeks? Maybe someone Eli knew? A friend of his from the old days, or a former member of his congregation?"

"Why are you asking me a question like that?"

"Because Eli told me the answer to this mystery could be found in the *Herald's* obituary section. We've checked out the backgrounds of everyone who died within the time frame given to us by Eli and we've come up empty."

"To be honest with you, I rarely read the newspaper anymore. Occasionally, I'll look at the Sports Section, but that's about it."

Dantzler thought for a few moments, then said, "The last time I visited Eli, right before I left, he said something strange. He said, 'think of Jesus's empty tomb.' Do you have any idea what he might have meant?"

"I don't know. Could be he was telling you his prison cell—his tomb —will be empty after this nightmare ends."

"You could be right."

"You don't sound convinced," Tommy said.

"I think Eli was trying to direct me down a path leading to the truth. My problem is, I can't seem to find that path."

"My father is innocent, Detective Dantzler. That much you can be sure of."

Dantzler stood, took a card from his coat pocket, and handed it to Tommy. "If you think of anything that might be helpful, call me at either of those numbers. Anytime, day or night."

"I would appreciate it if you didn't tell Rachel about the drinking," Tommy said. "I've disappointed her enough times already."

"She's not concerned about you disappointing her," Dantzler said, stepping outside. "Her only concern is that you keep disappointing yourself."

"Yeah, well, maybe tomorrow will be the day," Tommy said,

lowering his eyes. "The day when an angel of the Lord opens the Seal and all answers are revealed, all tribulations are laid to rest, and all nightmares come to an end."

"That's a nice thought, Tommy. But until the angel shows up, you need to take better care of yourself. Stop drinking and get some help. You're the only one who can end your nightmare."

Those were words Dantzler had said a hundred times to his uncle Tommy. They hadn't worked with him, and they wouldn't work with Tommy Whitehouse. Both men were not only haunted and tragic, they were doomed.

*****

As Dantzler climbed into his Forester, he was unaware of the white Toyota Camry parked on the opposite side of the street a half-block away from Tommy Whitehouse's duplex. Dantzler had no reason to notice the car or the man sitting low behind the steering wheel, his blue eyes partially covered by a black baseball cap. Had Dantzler seen the man, he would not have known him. The two had never met, never been in the presence of each other. In all likelihood, had Dantzler noticed the man, he would have tabbed him as one of the locals who lived in the neighborhood. Most likely a patient father waiting for his wife and kids to join him. He would have been wrong.

The man was a cold-blooded killer.

But Dantzler was not aware of this as he slowly drove away from Tommy's duplex. His thoughts were elsewhere, trapped between the sadness he felt for Tommy Whitehouse and his frustration with Eli's continuing silence. After turning left onto Redding Road, unable to shake his dark mood, he glanced up at his rear-view mirror.

Only one other car in sight.

A white Toyota Camry.

CHAPTER THIRTY-THREE

For more than four hours, from five p.m. until a little past nine, Dantzler read the Bible. New Testament, the four gospels. But unlike his previous reading, when he concentrated solely on the section detailing the women discovering Jesus's empty tomb, this time he did a complete reading of the four books. He did, however, make one slight swerve from standard procedure. Knowing most biblical scholars are in agreement that Mark's account was the first gospel written, he began with that one. Next, he read Matthew and Luke, followed by John's very late gospel, which scholars estimate may have been written more than a half-century after Jesus's death.

Finished, he looked at the yellow legal pad on the table next to the Bible. It was blank, not a single notation. This came as no surprise. He hadn't really expected to learn anything from this most recent reading that he didn't already know, and he hadn't. *Think of Jesus's empty tomb* was as much a mystery to him now as it had been for those frightened women two-thousand years ago.

Nothing he found was going to move Eli's case forward one inch.

Dantzler closed the Bible, went into the kitchen, and mixed a Pernod and orange juice. He took a couple of sips, thought about getting something to eat, maybe ordering Chinese, but decided it was too late for a big meal. Alcohol would have to suffice for now.

When he came back into the den, he was surprised to see Laurie standing by the door, a single key dangling from a silver ring. "You're quieter than a damn cat burglar," he said, sitting at the table.

"Have the guts of a cat burglar, too."

"You keep sneaking in here like this and you'll be dead as a cat burglar."

"Do cat burglars have nine lives?"

"Keep this up and you'll find out."

She walked to the table, picked up his glass, and sniffed. "Yuck, that is disgusting. How can you stand to drink this nasty stuff?"

"How can you not?"

"Easy." Laurie looked at the Bible resting on the table. "What's with the Bible study?"

"I'm thinking of joining the ministry."

"Bad idea."

"Yeah? Why?"

"Doesn't suit you. You were born to put bad guys away, not save bad guys' souls."

"I was born to play tennis."

"And now look at you—a Bible-reading Homicide dick." She sat, dropped the key into her purse, said, "Learn anything new?"

"Nothing that will help me solve Eli's mystery."

"How inconsiderate of Matthew, Mark, Luke, and John to leave the great Jack Dantzler dangling. To make his life more difficult."

"Exactly what I was thinking."

"Well, those guys had their own mystery to solve." Laurie pulled the Bible closer to her and opened it. "Would you read the Bible if you didn't think it might help you solve a case?"

"I never *read* the Bible. I *study* it. More than you might think."

"Do you believe in God?"

"Eli asked me the same question."

"And your response?"

"Said I believe in a Creator. A God beyond the God of the Bible."

"Sounds rather impersonal," Laurie said. "Do you believe God loves us?"

"I don't see much evidence that he does."

"The evidence was nailed to a cross."

"Lots of people agree with you on that."

"You don't?"

Dantzler paused for a moment, and then said, "Look, I don't doubt Jesus was crucified. And maybe Jesus honestly saw himself as the Messiah. I don't know. But what I cannot believe is that God came down to Earth in human form and allowed himself to be murdered. To essentially commit suicide. That's beyond my ability to comprehend. God is God, and if he truly is the Almighty, the died-on-the-cross scenario simply doesn't work for me."

"Jesus or God or . . . whomever—died for our sins," Laurie said.

"That's yet another bone of contention for me."

"What do you mean?"

"The notion that a human being had to suffer and die—be murdered —to atone for the sin of eating an apple. To me, that's a grotesque basis upon which to build a religion."

Laurie shook her head. "I think it's a lot more complex than that. I mean, Jesus died to atone for *all* of our sins. Not just Adam's. Anyway, why are you harping on this? You probably don't even believe the Garden of

Eden story in the first place."

"It's pure fiction. But good fiction—smart, wise, the kind that places a lesson and a moral inside a marvelously told tale."

"And what is that lesson?"

"Bad things can happen when you disobey or defy orders."

"So, Adam and Eve weren't sinners in your judgment, right?"

"They were disobedient children, nothing more."

Laurie laughed. "Am I safe in assuming that Detective Jack Dantzler would not arrest Adam and Eve?"

"What law did they break? None. They ate a damn apple, that's all. Nope. If I arrested anyone, it would be God. For mass murder. You do remember the great flood, don't you? When every man, woman, child, and animal on Earth was killed? Except, of course, for Noah and his gang. I'd love to get God in the interrogation room and query him about that particular act of madness. See what his answer would be."

"Well, while you're drawing up your list of questions and readying the polygraph machine, I'm going to bed." Laurie kissed him on the lips. "You are more than welcome to join me. Just understand that sex will have to suffice. I will offer no answers to the great mysteries haunting you. Not those concerning Eli, not those concerning God. This is my final offer. Take it or leave it."

Dantzler finished his drink and stood. "I'll take it."

"Excellent. Now let's see how much sin we can commit."

CHAPTER THIRTY-FOUR

Ten-forty. The Camry, a rental from Avis, needed to be returned before midnight or else he would be charged for another day. No sense wasting good money when you don't have to. Anyway, nothing was going to happen tonight. He'd known this the instant the good-looking chick showed up an hour or so ago. Her unexpected arrival quashed any plans he had.

The man had come with a single purpose in mind—to kill Jack Dantzler—and that simply couldn't happen now. No way. Taking out a second victim—another *cop* at that—would be doubly difficult to pull off, and it would create a whole new set of problems. He was certain the woman wasn't going anywhere. Around ten-fifteen, Dantzler's house went dark, except for a single light, probably from the bedroom, and that could only mean one thing—she was staying the night. When the light went out a few moments later, the man closed the book on eliminating Dantzler tonight.

He sat low in the front seat, a dark baseball cap pulled down over his eyes, and thought about things. About how the best plans can get screwed up at the last instant. How things rarely go as planned. An hour ago, he was all but certain that killing Dantzler was a done deal. He'd have gladly given any taker twenty-to-one odds it would happen. But things change, alternatives have to be mapped out, contingencies considered. Sometimes you improvise, sometimes you punt. What you never do is make a mistake. Being careful, smart, patient—those were critical elements, and he possessed them in great quantities. He had to have them to do the things he'd done and still be a free man.

Still be alive.

He had turned onto Dantzler's street at dusk, just ahead of a pop-up shower lasting maybe ten minutes, parked two hundred feet past the house, on the opposite side of the street. His plan was to wait until total darkness—a cloudy sky blanketing the moon would add to his cover—then go to Dantzler's house. Dantzler, like any smart cop, would be wary of an unexpected late-night visitor. He'd want to know who the visitor was, and what purpose the visitor had for being there. The man would say he was there with information relating to the Eli Whitehouse case. Upon hearing that, Dantzler wouldn't hesitate to open the door.

The man would step inside, .38 with a silencer in his right hand concealed behind his back, and wait until Dantzler closed the door. When Dantzler turned around, the man would shoot him point blank in the heart. Then, for insurance, he would put a bullet in Dantzler's brain. After that, he would remove two graying hairs from a small plastic bag and put them on Dantzler's body, most likely on his shirt, where the crime scene folks were sure to find them. When they did, and when they ran the hairs for DNA, the name of a loser with a long criminal history would pop up, and he would be arrested for Dantzler's murder.

Killing a cop was always risky business. He'd killed two in his past life, and with each one the heat came fast and hard. You had to be extra careful when rubbing out a man who carried a shield, especially a cop with Dantzler's status and reputation. The boys and girls in blue don't like it when one of their own gets blown away. When it does happen, they are prepared to track a suspect into the gates of hell if that's what it takes to put the bastard away.

Risky, yes, but in this case absolutely necessary. He had to shift the focus away from the Eli Whitehouse case, and taking out Dantzler would make that happen. Hell, the entire Lexington police force, not just the Homicide guys, would stop whatever they were doing and concentrate solely on catching Dantzler's murderer. They'd vacate the police holy of holies—Dunkin' Donuts—to track down a cop killer. Eli Whitehouse, whose case meant nothing to anyone but Dantzler, would get lost in the shuffle, and with Dantzler out of the way, no one would give a damn about Eli or the case.

He'd be home free.

Only two other people knew the whole story, the truth about him and the murders. One was soon to die, and the other was bound to silence, knowing a slip of the tongue would result in catastrophic consequences for a number of innocent people. There was no way that was going to happen.

He started the car and slowly drove down the street, past expensive houses where innocent people lived safe lives, unfamiliar and unconcerned with the kind of evil he could unleash. He smiled, cool and calm, like always. Things didn't work out tonight like he'd planned, but there would be other nights. He would bide his time, wait until the right moment, then strike. And when he did make his move, the outcome would not be in doubt.

Jack Dantzler would be dead.

CHAPTER THIRTY-FIVE

A low pressure front, arriving from the west a little before daybreak, brought a steady rain accompanied by thunder and lightning. The TV weather folks predicted a brief stay for the front, saying it would move through well before noon, followed by bright sunshine. Unfortunately, the front didn't get the memo. Judging by those gray clouds extending from horizon to horizon, the rain was here to stay.

Dantzler lumbered out of bed at seven, careful not to wake Laurie on her day off, showered, dressed, and headed to Coyle's for a light breakfast. As Dantzler was finishing his meal of toast, eggs, bacon and orange juice, Randall Dennis, a long-time friend and frequent tennis foe, came into the restaurant wearing his accustomed frown. Spotting Dantzler, Dennis's frown quickly gave way to a huge grin. After carefully navigating a maze of customers, waitresses and tables, he made it to Dantzler's booth without incident.

"How about we bang the little yellow ball around tonight?" Dennis said, sliding into the booth. "I'm feeling good about my game now. Tonight could be the night I break through . . . take a set from you."

"Randall, you've been 'breaking through' for twenty years. Fact is, you couldn't take a set from me if I played you left-handed. You need to give up that quest and move on to something more attainable, because you are never gonna beat me."

"You cocky so-and-so. I'd sell my soul to Lucifer this very instant if it meant beating your ass."

"Lucifer's evil, but he's not stupid," Dantzler said, standing and patting Dennis on the shoulder. "He's not about to climb aboard your ship."

"It's going to happen, Jack. One of these days I'll surprise you. Just wait and see."

"Keep dreaming, Randall. Keep dreaming."

*****

Before leaving Coyle's, Dantzler phoned Milt at the office and told him to be at the front entrance of the police station in five minutes. When Dantzler pulled up, Milt streaked for the car, using a soggy newspaper as an umbrella. Once in the car, he shook his head like an old dog, splattering water in all directions.

"Damn monsoon," he said, wiping water from his face. "Reminds me of Nam. Over there we got shit like this twenty-four hours a day for three solid months. That was some serious rain."

"Dan said the rainy season was a blessing. Said you did less fighting when the monsoons hit."

"Yeah, that's a fact." Milt rolled up the newspaper and laid it on the backseat floorboard. "Where are we going?"

"To talk with Johnny Richards."

"Oh, yeah, Colt's no-show pal. Almost forgot about him. What's his story, anyway?"

"Don't know, really. That's why we need to talk to him."

"What does he do for a living?"

"He owns a small bar—Johnny's Tavern—in the Meadowthorpe Shopping Center."

"Where, exactly, in Meadowthorpe?"

"I don't know. Somewhere between the restaurant on one end of the strip and the liquor store on the other end. In the middle."

"Huh. You know, me and Dan used to hang out at a dinky little joint in Meadowthorpe. This was back in the late seventies, early eighties. But damn if I remember it as Johnny's Tavern. Back then it went by another name. What the hell was it? Oh, yeah, now I remember. Sneaky Pete's. Little wop named Pete Marconi owned it. Small as a turd, mean as a snake. I suppose that's why me and Dan were so fond of him."

"For cops, you guys did tend to bond with a lot of shady characters."

Milt laughed. "You know, Dan clocked a guy coming out of that liquor store one night. The guy, totally shitfaced, recognized Dan from somewhere. Knew Dan was a cop. Anyway, the stupid hillbilly walks up and gets in Dan's face, cussing, spitting, threatening like crazy. At some point, he made the mistake of pushing Dan. Now, Dan had a six pack of Bud in his right hand at the time, and he wasn't about to drop the beer. Rule number one is, you never drop the alcohol, no matter the circumstances. So Dan came around with a perfect left hook to the poor slob's chin. Bang, down he went, like he'd been shot. Out cold. Dan just looked at me and laughed and said something like, 'wonder what his problem was?' A great moment, one of many we had together."

"You guys were a rowdy pair," Dantzler said. "Rich says it's a miracle you didn't end up dead."

"Ah, shit, Rich doesn't know the half of it. Hell, me and Dan were crazy *and* fearless. That can be a deadly combination." Milt turned serious. "When I think of the stunts we pulled, the dangerous situations we put ourselves in, the women we chased, half of them married, and then I look at a kid like Scott, how young and innocent and conservative he is, I can't decide whether to be proud or ashamed to still be walking upright. I do know we were awfully lucky to come through it all unscathed."

CHAPTER THIRTY-SIX

The Meadowthorpe Center was less than three miles from downtown Lexington, on the right, going out Leestown Road. It consisted of a straight row of small businesses housed in old buildings, none of which exuded a hint of glamour or newness. The lack of modernity and present-day charm didn't seem to be a hindrance to the various businesses or those folks living in the Meadowthorpe neighborhood. The locals kept the businesses alive and thriving.

The restaurant and liquor store served as bookends for the row of businesses. In between were a used book store, an antique shop, ice cream parlor, pool room, real estate office, and a clothing consignment store. Johnny's Tavern was located squarely in the middle.

"Yep, that used to be Sneaky Pete's place," Milt said. "Except for the name change, it looks exactly like it did back when me and Dan frequented the joint."

Joint was an appropriate term for describing Johnny's Tavern. The place was small, consisting of a bar with half-dozen stools, four round tables and three vinyl-covered booths. With no windows and very little, if any, obvious ventilation, the smell of cigarette smoke and body odor clung to the walls and ceiling like an extra coat of paint. An ancient jukebox, wedged between the bar and the first booth, looked as though it probably hadn't worked since Sinatra was wooing the bobby-socks crowd back in the 1940s.

A pair of old geezers sat at one end of the bar, each one nursing a mixed drink. Not yet eleven a.m. and they were already on the road to alcohol oblivion. A lone man sat at the opposite end of the bar, pencil in one hand, punching numbers on a calculator with his other hand, and what appeared to be a ledger book spread out in front of him.

The woman behind the bar had just finished slicing lemons into small pieces and was about to do the same to several limes. She was on the verge of moving from middle-age to senior citizen, with straw colored hair, thin lips, penciled eyebrows, and easily the biggest bosom Dantzler and Milt had ever seen.

"What are you having, gentlemen?" she said, her voice surprisingly warm and friendly.

Dantzler held up his shield. "We would like to speak with Johnny

Richards. Any chance he's here?"

The man at the end of the bar closed his account book and stood up. "I'm Johnny Richards. What can I do for you?"

"I'm Detective Jack Dantzler, this is Detective Milt Brewer. If you have a couple of minutes, we would like to ask you a few questions."

"No problem. I have a small office in the back where we can talk in private, or we can do it out here. Your call."

"Out here will be fine." Dantzler nodded toward the table nearest the front door. "How about the table over there?"

He and Milt sat first, joined moments later by Richards, who remained standing.

"You guys want something to drink?" Richards asked. "Coke, ginger ale, club soda?"

"We're good," Dantzler answered.

"You sure? I'm getting a Coke, and I'll be more than happy to get you something."

Dantzler shook his head, keeping his eyes on Richards, who walked behind the bar, shoveled ice into a glass, and filled it with Coke. He whispered something to the big-bosom bartender, triggering a smile from her, before heading back to the table where Dantzler and Milt were seated.

Richards was, Dantzler guessed, in his mid to late forties, although he might be slightly younger. He looked to be in excellent shape, whatever his age. More wiry than thin, he was one of those lucky guys who could probably eat a ton of food and drink buckets of beer and never gain an ounce. His hair was dark brown, with a scattering of gray around the sides, and his eyes were quick and alert.

Dantzler sized him up as a smart guy who didn't miss much. He also figured him to be a guy who, if backed into a corner, knew how to take care of himself.

"So, Detective," Richards said, addressing Dantzler, "what questions do you have for me?"

Before Dantzler could answer, Milt jumped in.

"How long have you had this place?" he asked, looking around. "I used to come here when it was known as Sneaky Pete's."

"I bought it from Pete in nineteen-eighty. October."

"You sure about that? I was here after 'eighty and it was still Sneaky Pete's."

"Pete wouldn't sell me the place unless I made him two promises. First, he got five percent of the gross straight off the top, and, second, the place retained the Sneaky Pete name until his death. He died in 'eighty-eight.

That's when I changed the name."

"Where are you from?" Dantzler said. "I can tell by your accent you're not from around here."

"Chicago."

"What brought a Windy City boy to Lexington, Kentucky?"

"Opportunity. I was bouncing around, tending bar at several Chicago watering holes, going nowhere fast, when I had a chance to buy this place. I'd saved a little money, not nearly enough to buy a bar, but I had one of those lucky breaks that come along at just the right time. An uncle of mine made some serious money playing the stock market, and he was crazy enough to back my venture. I'd still be in Chicago working God knows where if it weren't for him."

"Thirty years owning a bar—that's a long life in this business," Dantzler said. "You must be doing all right."

"This place is too small for me to ever get rich, but I do okay," Richards said. "We're essentially a neighborhood bar, so we have a solid core of regulars. We treat them right and they keep us going. Works out good for everyone."

"How well did you know Colt Rogers?" Dantzler said.

"Very well. He was a close friend. He's also the reason why I ended up in Lexington."

"If he was such a close friend," Milt interjected, "how come you weren't at his visitation and didn't attend his funeral?"

"I don't much care for funeral homes or funeral services," Richards said. "Too damn depressing. I prefer to remember someone as they were when they were alive and vibrant, not when they look like a wax dummy in a coffin."

Dantzler said, "Was Colt your attorney?"

"Unoffically, I suppose. He wasn't on a retainer, but if I had a legal issue or legal question, he was always available to help."

"You said he was the reason why you ended up here. How did that come about?"

"I met him at the 'seventy-nine Kentucky Derby. I'd come down with my uncle and several of his friends, all of whom were pretty big high rollers. One of those guys was acquainted with Colt. We sat at his table and watched the race. The great Spectacular Bid captured the roses that year. At some point during the day, Colt and I got to talking. It didn't take him long to figure out I was the poor guy at the table. He asked me what I did for a living and what would I like to do. The only thing I knew was bartending, so I told him I'd like to have my own place. About a year later, he called to let me know this place was on the market. I came down, met with Colt, and we got together with Pete. He laid down his terms, which I thought were way beyond my means. However, when I told my uncle about it, he just said, 'okay, kid, if you want it, and if you'll work at it, I'll give you the cash.' I took over in October, nineteen-eighty. Been here ever since."

Richards shifted in his chair and turned back toward the bar. "Hey, Sally, could you bring us a couple of Cokes, please? Thanks."

"How well do you know Eli Whitehouse?" Dantzler asked.

"I don't know him at all, really. Why do you ask about him?"

"Because the warden told us you frequently accompanied Colt Rogers when he visited Eli at the prison."

"The warden has a much different definition of frequently than I do. I only saw Eli Whitehouse maybe five or six times, tops."

Dantzler waited until Sally placed the two Cokes on the table before continuing. "Why were you at the prison in the first place?"

"Colt owns—owned—a cabin on Kentucky Lake. He used to go down there one or two weekends each month, sometimes to fish, but mostly to spend time with whatever floozy he was hanging out with at the time. I don't fish, and I was never unfaithful to my wife, but on a few occasions over the years, he would take me along with him. He'd fish, I would drink Jack Daniels. Anytime he went down there, he always stopped at the prison to meet with Eli Whitehouse. Rather than sit in the car, I would go inside with him."

"What did Colt and Eli usually talk about?"

"Not much, to be honest with you. Truth is, I don't think Eli cared much for Colt. At least that's the impression I got."

"Why do you think Eli disliked Colt?"

"Colt always had a briefcase filled with papers, documents he wanted the old man to sign. And Eli wasn't about to sign anything. Normally, I didn't pay any attention to their conversation, but I do recall one time when Eli yelled at Colt, telling him in no uncertain terms he would never—*never*—sign his name to any piece of paper Colt put in front of him, not even if it came from God himself."

"How did Colt react?"

"Didn't faze him in the least. I'm sure he was certain Eli would eventually wear down and sign the papers. Colt was something of an optimist."

"Where were you when Colt Rogers was murdered?" Dantzler asked.

"Since I don't know precisely what time he was killed, I couldn't put my hand on a Bible and give you a definite location. However, it happened on a Friday night—one of our busiest nights—so I do feel confident in saying I was here in the bar."

"Are you aware of anyone who might have wanted Colt Rogers dead? A pissed-off client, an angry business associate, some thug with a grudge, a jilted ex-lover?"

"I do remember one guy—I don't know if he was a client or not—who came into Colt's office intent on doing some serious harm. He was a big, scary-looking dude, you know, one of those hard-ass types with muscles on top of muscles. He stormed in and pinned Colt against the wall, ranting and blubbering like an insane man, saying if things didn't work out he was going to make Colt pay dearly. Colt was scared shitless, and he had every right to be. I somehow managed to get in between them and talk to the guy. Tried to calm him down, but I didn't do much good. He left, but he was cussing and threatening Colt all the way out of the office."

"Any idea what he meant when he said 'if things didn't work out'?"

"No. I didn't ask and Colt never volunteered the information."

"When did this happen?"

"Oh, not too many years after I got here. I'd say 'eighty-five or 'eighty-six. Sometime around then."

"Do you recall the guy's name?"

"Keith, Kurt . . . something along those lines. Started with a K, I do remember that. Kevin—that's it. The guy's name was Kevin."

"Remember his last name?"

"I'm not sure I ever heard his last name. What I can tell you, though, is Colt worried about the guy for several weeks after the incident. Even started carrying a gun."

Dantzler stood, took a card from his shirt pocket, and handed it to Richards. "If you happen to think of anything else that might be helpful, call me at one of those numbers. And thanks for talking to us. You've given us some interesting information."

"Just catch the scumbag who killed Colt," Richards said. "Colt wasn't a perfect man, and no one knew it better than I did. But he didn't deserve to be gunned down in cold blood."

"No one does," Milt said. He took a five dollar bill from his wallet and laid it on the table. "For the Cokes."

"On the house, Detective," Richards said, sliding the bill toward Milt. "I can handle the cost of two Cokes."

"We always stayed on the up and up with Sneaky Pete," Milt said. "We didn't take freebies from him and we aren't taking them from you."

"As you wish, Detective."

*****

When they were back in the car, Milt said, "What's your take on this Kevin dude who went after Rogers?"

"It's not much, but at least it's something." Dantzler pulled the car out onto Leestown Road and headed toward downtown. "When you were going through Rogers's files, did you run across any clients named Kevin?"

"None that caught my attention."

"You'll need to go through them again. See if you can find this Kevin."

"Drop me off at Colt's office and I'll do it this afternoon."

"That can wait," Dantzler said. "I want to get with Barbara Tanner, see if she remembers the guy. If she does, it'll save us a lot of time."

"Sounds like a solid plan to me."

CHAPTER THIRTY-SEVEN

Even in a pair of cut-off jeans and a ratty University of Kentucky T-shirt, hair pulled back tight in a ponytail, her face streaked with dirt, Barbara Tanner looked much better today than she did the last time Dantzler saw her. Life and hope had returned to her eyes, and judging by the big smile on her face, sorrow and despair had vanished.

She had, Dantzler sensed, weathered the storm surrounding the death of her boss about as well as possible. Good for her.

Barbara invited the two detectives in, asked if they wanted something to drink—they declined—and apologized profusely for the mess in the house and for her sloppy appearance.

"I'm cleaning places that haven't been touched in years," she said. "It's simply dreadful, the dirt and dust and cobwebs I'm finding. I should be horse whipped for neglecting things this long. It's unforgivable."

"You look really good," Dantzler said.

"Oh, I can't begin to tell you how excited I am," Barbara answered, beaming. "When Mr. Rogers died, I was scared to death about being out of work. At my age, in this terrible economy, I thought it would be really difficult finding full-time employment. But you know what? I had three job offers the day after the funeral. All of them with really good, respectable firms. I couldn't believe it."

"That speaks volumes about your reputation within the legal community," Dantzler said. "Have you made a decision yet as to which offer you'll take?"

Barbara nodded, said, "I begin work Monday at Adler, James, and Young. Doing basically what I was doing for Mr. Rogers, but with a bigger paycheck and better benefits. I really lucked out, didn't I?"

Adler, James, and Young—Sean Montgomery's firm. No doubt Sean had a big hand in this deal. "Getting someone with your talent and experience," Dantzler said, "I would say they also lucked out."

"Well, I'm just very thankful. It goes to show good things sometimes come out of bad situations."

"Listen, Barbara, I need to ask you about a guy who may have been one of Colt Rogers's clients. If he was a client, it was probably a long time ago. Twenty, twenty-five years, maybe."

"What's his name?"

"I only have his first name. Kevin."

"Hmm. Let me think. Off the top of my head, I can't remember any clients named Kevin. Do you know what he looked like?"

"Big, strong, heavily muscled. Had a hot temper and wasn't good at controlling it. He came into the office once and directed some serious threats at Colt."

"You know, that does trigger a memory. But the man I'm thinking of, well, Mr. Rogers represented him just prior to when I began working at the firm. I only got in on the tail end of their association, so I really didn't know him. But the man I'm thinking of—his name wasn't Kevin. His last name was Stone, but . . ."

"Ah, shit," Milt yelled, slapping his palm against his forehead. "Kevin Stone—why didn't I think of him? Went by the name Rocky."

"Yes, yes, that's him," Barbara said. "Rocky Stone."

"The name sounds familiar," Dantzler said. "But I can't quite place it."

"He was a local kid, a boxer," Milt said. "Pretty damn good fighter, too. Light heavyweight. I saw him fight once at the Continental Inn, back when they used to hold professional matches there. Knocked his opponent out in the second round. Johnny Richards was dead on when he said Colt Rogers had every right to be afraid. Rocky Stone was one tough gorilla. Crazy, too. He once got into an altercation in the Continental Inn bar and it took five cops to get him under control. They said he was slinging those guys off like they were raindrops."

"What happened to him?" Dantzler asked. "His boxing career, I mean?"

"Hell, who knows? It's no secret boxing is a crummy, dirty racket run by crummy, dirty people. My guess is he got used, abused, and taken advantage of as long as he could make some unscrupulous promoter or trainer a few bucks. Once he was no longer a financial asset, he got pitched out like dirty laundry. Rocky Stone—damn, hadn't thought of him in ages. He had some real potential, could have been a big-time contender under the right circumstances."

"If I'm not mistaken he ended up going to prison," Barbara said.

"He did," Milt said, nodding. "Got pinched for armed robbery up in the Cincinnati area. He and another guy robbed a string of pharmacies, took cash and drugs, maybe shot up one of those places. If I recall correctly, he got hit with a pretty long stint."

"Is he out now?" Dantzler said.

"I don't know, but I've got to believe he is."

"Was Colt Rogers his attorney?" Dantzler asked Barbara.

"I think he was. Yes."

"We need to find out all we can about this guy," Dantzler said. "And if he has been released from prison, we certainly need to speak with him."

"I'll check the records," Milt said, writing in his notepad. "Get all the paperwork, speak with his PO and try to nail down an address."

"Good."

"Do you think he might be the one who killed Mr. Rogers?" Barbara said to Dantzler.

"I don't know. But from what you and Milt have been telling me, and given his past criminal history, he's definitely a person of interest."

"Well, I certainly don't want to wish ill of anyone, but if he is the man who killed Mr. Rogers, I hope he burns in hell forever."

Milt laughed out loud. "Come on, Barbara. Don't hold anything back. Tell us how you really feel about it."

*****

"I've got a good feeling about this," Milt said when they were back in the car. "Rocky Stone is mean enough and crazy enough to be a shooter."

Dantzler was less enthusiastic about the possibility. The lion in his path was the twenty-nine-year gap between the first set of killings and the recent murders. In his mind, he couldn't build a bridge that would connect them. And even if Stone did murder Colt Rogers and Devon Fraley, it didn't lock him in as the shooter of those two kids in Eli's barn. But if he was the shooter, why would Eli keep silent all these years? Why would he spend his life in prison for a thug like Stone? There were too many questions yet to be answered before Dantzler's excitement matched Milt's.

Still, they now had a focus point—Rocky Stone—and that's better than nothing.

Yet—

"I don't know, Milt," Dantzler finally said. "There are a lot of dots that need to be connected. I wish I were as positive as you are."

"You're a negative prick, and always have been. You and Dan were a lot alike that way, damn prophets of doom, the both of you." Milt chuckled softly. "Not at all like me, Mr. Positive."

"Yeah, you're a real sunbeam of joy, Milt."

"Think about it, Ace. This could turn out to be the ray of sunshine we need in order to solve this sucker. Certain elements do fit. Rocky Stone is a convicted felon, he's violent and . . ."

"You're jumping ahead of yourself, aren't you? We don't even know if he's out of jail. For all we know, he could still be locked up. Or if he is out, he could be living a thousand miles from here. Hell, he might even be dead. No, Milt, I'll keep my excitement in check until more facts are known."

"His name fits, too," Milt added, undaunted by Dantzler's skepticism. "Think about it. From what you told us after reading the Bible. You said the name Stone was one we should be looking for. Well, you got it."

"Yeah, that part I like," Dantzler admitted. "But for it to work, if we're going by what Eli told us, then we've somehow got to link Rocky Stone to the obituary page. If we can't do that, then it's just a weird coincidence."

"This is no coincidence."

"Once we do make the connection—if we *can*—then we're still only halfway home. Our next step would be to link Stone to those two kids who were killed in 'eighty-two. Again, if we can't make the connection, this whole thing falls apart faster than a cracked egg."

"Thanks, Ace."

"For what?"

"Taking away all my sunshine."

"Welcome to the dark side, Milt."

*****

Back at the station, Dantzler spent a few minutes briefing Captain Bird on what he learned from talking with Johnny Richards and Barbara Tanner. Bird was skeptical but intrigued. He remembered Rocky Stone as an up-and-coming boxer, but had only a vague recollection of his criminal activities. When told that Stone spent a long stretch in prison for armed robbery, Bird shrugged, went back to filling out forms, and mumbled something about not being surprised that a former pugilist ended up in legal trouble.

After leaving Bird's office, Dantzler joined Milt, Eric, and Scott in the War Room. Milt had already brought the two younger detectives up to speed before Dantzler walked in. Scott was excited about the news, Eric wasn't.

"We're heading up a blind alley on this one," Eric said. He was standing by the coffee pot, holding an empty cup. "I've been through those obituary notices five times and there is no one named Stone anywhere to be found. If this Stone guy killed Rogers and Fraley, then we're looking for two shooters, not one."

"There is only a single shooter," Dantzler said. "I don't like Stone as a candidate for the two most recent murders or the first two."

Milt said, "Stone kills those young kids for who knows what reason. Maybe it was a drug thing, maybe it was something else, maybe they just pissed him off. But he kills them and gets away with it. Fast forward a few years and he gets pinched for the armed robbery thing, goes away for almost twenty years. That's plenty of time to build up a lot of hatred and resentment toward the attorney who couldn't save your ass. He gets out, thinks about it a little bit, maybe adds a little booze to boost his hate level, decides it's time to settle old accounts. He kills Rogers. Fraley, the poor temp, overhears his name, or maybe she knew he was coming in, so Stone has to take care of her too. What's so difficult to believe about that?"

"Milt, if I had ten dollars for every maybe in that speech, I'd buy myself a steak dinner tonight at Malone's," Eric said. "It will take some serious evidence before I'm convinced Stone killed those two guys twenty-nine years ago. And I doubt we'll find it."

"Know what's missing from your scenario, Milt?" Dantzler said. "Eli Whitehouse. How does Rocky Stone fit in with Eli? Why would Eli go to prison for a nobody like Stone? Give up his freedom, his family, his congregation? It makes no sense."

"Like you said from the start, Eli did it because he's afraid. Not for himself, but for his family. Rocky Stone is, as we all know, a scary dude."

"But why did Stone kill those two kids?"

"Hell, Jack, I don't know. That's what we've got to find out. We need to make the connection."

"There is no connection, Milt," Eric said.

Milt ripped a piece of paper from a legal pad and stood. "Let me call Stone's parole officer, see if I can come up with an address. That will at least answer the question regarding his whereabouts."

"Why didn't the guy use his cell phone?" Scott asked, after Milt left the room.

"A dinosaur like Milt never thinks cell phone first," Eric said.

"Can't imagine thinking otherwise," Scott said, shaking his head.

Ten minutes later, Milt came back into the room, waving the paper like a flag. "Stone lives on Alexandria. Let's go pay him a visit, Ace."

"We're *all* going," Dantzler said. "Everybody wears a vest. Stone is obviously a force to be reckoned with, so we're taking no chances."

"I've never worn a vest," Scott said.

"Get used to it, Rookie," Milt said. "You're not writing parking tickets anymore."

CHAPTER THIRTY-EIGHT

"What else did Stone's PO tell you?" Dantzler said to Milt as they turned onto Alexandria Drive. They were in Dantzler's Forester, followed by Eric and Scott in an unmarked police cruiser. "Anything I need to know before we talk to him?"

"Stone is unemployed—surprise, surprise—drives a red Ford pick-up, has three ex-wives, a couple of grown kids he never sees, and has been good about meeting with his parole officer. He belongs to a once-a-week prison support group but rarely attends. He's come up clean on all his drug and alcohol tests. According to the PO, Stone has been minding his manners and staying out of trouble."

"Sounds like a real prince," Dantzler said, adding, "how does he get by financially? He has to have income from somewhere."

"He lives with a woman named Consuela Lopez. She has her own business—cleans houses, office buildings, condos . . . that sort of thing. Has three full-time employees and a legion of part-timers. Her financial records indicate she makes pretty good money, more than two-hundred K per year, which is sufficient enough to support Stone and her two kids. Stone may be an ex-con and a brain-dead former boxer, but he's no dummy. He was smart enough to reel in a fish with money."

"Nice setup. Wouldn't mind landing a deal like that myself."

"Bring it up with Dunn," Milt said. "She'll support you."

"Right. And I'll win Wimbledon this year."

"How's that working out for you guys, anyway? Everything cool?"

"Jury's still out."

"Is Rich the problem?"

"One of them."

"Tell you what, Ace. I wouldn't worry too much about what Rich thinks. If things do work out between you and Dunn, Rich will have to accept it and deal with it. In the final analysis, it's really none of his business."

"I doubt he would agree with you."

"What's he going to do? He's not going to fire you, the best homicide investigator the department has ever had. And Dunn's a rising star. He's doesn't want to lose her. I say go for it and let the chips fall where they may."

Dantzler was in no mood to discuss his private life. "Let's worry about Stone today. Okay? We need to stay focused on him, not on my relationship with Laurie. That can wait."

"How do you want to handle it?" Milt asked.

"Straightforward. We'll go up on the porch, announce our presence, and tell Stone we only want to talk. Eric and Scott will cover the back, in case he decides to rabbit. Did his PO say whether or not Stone has any weapons?"

"He didn't say, but, hell, he wouldn't know if Stone is armed or not. Stone's an ex-con, he's not supposed to own weapons, but . . . we all know about ninety-nine percent probably do. If he has one gun or ten he's not about to tell his parole officer. We definitely need to be cautious."

*****

"Which house is it?" Dantzler said, slowing the car to a crawl.

"That one," Milt said, pointing to his left.

The red brick house, which sat on the corner of Alexandria and Palms Drive, was virtually identical to other houses along the street. It was small and neat, probably three bedrooms and two baths, with a two-car garage and a perfectly manicured front lawn. A flowerbed consisting of a rose bush and azaleas surrounded by Creeping phlox ran parallel beneath a front window. Two wicker chairs and a swing sat idly on the concrete porch, adding to the cozy quotient.

Dantzler studied the house while waiting for Eric and Scott to join them. Although the layout seemed simple enough, one aspect troubled him—a five-foot high wooden fence that enclosed the back yard. Not being able to see what might be happening behind the house was cause for concern. If the fence was locked from the inside it could spell trouble. His plan was to have Eric and Scott cover the back, and if Stone did decide to bolt, and if he did come out firing a weapon, the two detectives might not know what was happening until it was too late. They would definitely need to be alert.

"That damn fence could pose a problem," Milt pointed out.

"Precisely what I was thinking," Dantzler said. He turned to Eric. "Eric, you and Scott circle around to the back of the house. Check out the fence, see if it has a door or gate. Make sure you know if it's locked, or if it opens from the inside or outside. Either way, stay on your toes. Don't get caught by surprise."

While Eric and Scott were making their way around back, Dantzler and Milt walked up the sidewalk toward the house. Halfway there, they noticed a man peeking out from behind a curtain. He watched the detectives for several seconds, let the curtain drop, and disappeared.

"Was that Stone?" Dantzler asked.

"Couldn't tell."

As they stepped onto the porch, the front door opened just enough for them to see the side of a man's beefy face. He had a patchy beard, a deep scar above his upper lip, and dark blue eyes.

"I know you guys are cops," the man said, his voice gruff and scratchy. "I've been told you were coming, and I ain't got nothin' to say to you."

"Are you Kevin Stone?" Dantzler said.

"*Rocky* Stone."

"Rocky, I'm Detective Jack Dantzler and this is Detective Milt Brewer. We're with Homicide. We would like to ask you a few questions, if you don't mind."

"You can't come charging in here like this," Stone said, angrily. "This ain't Russia."

"We're not charging in, Rocky. We only want to talk, that's all."

"I don't have anything to talk about, 'cause I ain't done nothin' wrong. I've been clean ever since I left the joint. Ask my parole officer."

"We did, and he had positive things to say about you. But, still, we need to ask you a few questions."

"Questions about what?"

"It would be a lot better if we could talk inside. Why—"

"I'm not talking to you, I don't have to talk to you, and that's that. So, *amscra*."

"Come on, Rocky. Don't make this difficult. Sooner or later you're gonna have to talk to us. Let's do it now and get things cleared up. Then we'll be out of here."

"What do you want to talk about?"

"Colt Rogers, for starters."

"Colt Rogers? That sniveling weasel? I ain't got nothin' to say about him, except that I'm glad he's dead."

"We need to talk about that, Rocky."

"Wait a minute. Homicide? You're tryin' to pin his murder on me, aren't you? No way. I'm happy he's dead, but I didn't kill him."

"Then here's your chance to clear it up, once and for all."

"Yeah, right, like you guys are gonna believe me."

"You tell the truth, we'll believe you."

"That's bullshit and we both know it."

"It's not bullshit, Rocky. We'll listen to what you have to say."

"You bastards ain't nothin' but bullshit artists."

"Tell you what, Rocky. You let us in and agree to talk, here's what I'll do. I'll call ahead and line up an attorney to sit in with us. You won't even have to ask for legal representation. That's a deal I've never made before. What do you say?"

"Same thing I said before . . . you're a bullshit artist."

"No, I'm not. You don't have to say a thing until the attorney gets here. You have my word on it."

"Yeah, well, how much do you think your word means to me? Less than nothing, that's how much. And if I did believe you, what kind of lawyer would you call? Another money-grubbin' loser like Colt Rogers? No, thanks."

"Open up, Rocky," Dantzler said, forcefully.

"Go away. I ain't sayin' nothin'."

"We're not leaving, Rocky, so you might as well let us in."

"Go to hell."

"Open the door, Rocky."

"Sure. Let me unhook this chain."

Seconds after Stone closed the door, Dantzler and Milt heard two familiar sounds—the dead bolt closing and a bullet being jacked into the chamber of a weapon.

"Gun," Milt said, ducking to the side of the door. "The dumb bastard's gonna make this difficult."

Dantzler, Glock in his right hand, leaned across and banged on the door with his left fist. "Don't be crazy, Rocky. Nobody is accusing you of anything. All we want to do is get some facts straight."

Silence.

"Rocky, open up," Dantzler yelled. "Let's talk."

Dantzler pressed an ear against the door, listened, and heard the sounds of movement coming from inside the house. A chair scraping the wooden floor, Stone laughing out loud, footsteps, a door slamming shut.

"He's bolting," Dantzler said, turning the doorknob. "Godammit, he's jammed the door shut."

"This is gonna get ugly," Milt said. "Knew I should've put in those damn retirement papers."

From behind the house a sudden burst of gunfire shattered the quiet. After a few moments of silence, more gunfire erupted, another staccato burst, followed by silence. Dantzler could tell from the sounds that Stone was exchanging fire with Eric and Scott. He also knew Stone had far more firepower than the two detectives.

"That's an automatic," Milt said, reading Dantzler's mind. "I guess that answers our question about whether or not he's armed."

Staying in a crouch, Dantzler and Milt moved quickly toward the back, hugging the fence like a pair of rats. Ten feet from the end, they saw Stone send a hail of bullets toward Eric and Scott. Stone turned and ran past a big oak tree, pausing long enough to insert a new clip into his rifle, then headed for the street, stopping every few yards to spray more bullets at the detectives.

Dantzler reached the end of the fence and immediately looked to his left. Eric, partially hidden behind a girl's bicycle, was on one knee, gun in his right hand firing at Stone while keeping his left hand pressed against Scott's chest.

"Oh, shit, Scott's been hit," Dantzler yelled to Milt. "Call for backup and go help Eric. Keep that damn kid alive, Milt. I'm going after Stone."

Milt went left toward Eric and Scott, cell phone at his ear, screaming orders for backup and an ambulance. Cramming the phone into his pocket, he knelt next to Eric, who now had both hands on Scott's wound. Scott was alive—barely. His eyes were open, he was white as a snowman, but he was breathing.

"You hang in there, Rookie," Milt said, putting his hands over the wound. "Medics will be here in seconds. Keep those eyes open, hear me? That's an order."

Scott smiled and winked and passed out.

CHAPTER THIRTY-NINE

Dantzler was about to cross Palms Drive when he saw Stone dart between two houses, veer to his right, and disappear behind a large storage shed. Dantzler crossed the street, took cover behind a black Honda Accord, and checked the clip in his Glock. As sirens wailed in the distance, Dantzler duckwalked past the Honda, using a row of cars for cover, until he was even with the opening Stone had taken. He raised his head in an effort to see Stone, but had to duck down quickly when a new burst of gunfire shattered the car's front windshield and blew out the right front tire.

Dantzler returned fire, waited for a second assault from Stone, and was surprised when nothing happened. Briefly, he entertained the thought that one of his bullets had wounded or killed Stone. But that was, he knew, only wishful thinking. Stone was too well protected by the shed to have been hit. Seconds later, Stone made it official that he was alive and well by rattling off another dozen shots, all of which did further damage to the car protecting Dantzler.

When the shooting stopped, Dantzler peered over the car's hood and saw Stone running hard between the houses. Dantzler gulped in fresh air to refill his burning lungs, stood up, and began to give chase. As he reached the opening between houses, he heard noise coming from behind. Turning, he saw Eric moving at blinding speed, gun in his bloody right hand, a hard look of hate on his face. Before Dantzler could say a word, Eric raced past, quickly closing in on Stone, who had made the crucial mistake of running into an alley with no exit.

Realizing he was trapped, Stone, now desperate and panicked, swung around, steadied himself, and prepared for what he had to know would be his last stand. Screaming like a mortally wounded animal, Stone lifted his rifle and took dead aim at Eric.

Then in a flash Stone's head came apart. Blood, bone, and brain matter painted a grotesque mural on the side of the house Stone was standing in front of. The rifle fired skyward as it flew from his hands. Stone tumbled to the ground, right leg twitching for several seconds, his shattered head at the center of an expanding pool of blood. After several more seconds, the twitching stopped and his breathing ceased.

Eric had ended the rampage with a single shot.

Dantzler got to Stone's body first. Out of habit, he kicked the weapon, a .223 assault rifle, away from Stone's right hand. He thought about checking for a pulse, but knew it wasn't necessary. Kevin "Rocky" Stone was a goner.

"You okay?" Dantzler said to Eric.

"Never felt better."

"That was some serious cowboy shit you pulled, Eric. You should be thankful you aren't the one lying on the ground."

"He shot my partner. I had to go after him."

"Is Scott still alive?"

"Yeah. But he's hurt bad."

"You know, Eric, if I wasn't so damn relieved, I'd be pretty pissed at you."

Eric nodded, started to say something, but didn't.

Dantzler put an arm on Eric's shoulder and said, "But eventually I would get over it."

*****

The man watched with delight as the deadly scene unfolded in front of him like a wild big screen cops-and-robbers shootout. And damn it had all happened so fast, like a lightning bolt from the sky. First nothing, now this. Amazing. Less than twenty minutes ago, this had been a quiet, peaceful suburban neighborhood; now it was a war zone. He had anticipated drama, even as he followed Dantzler to Stone's house, but he had never expected action of this magnitude. This far exceeded his wildest expectations.

Keeping his head low, baseball cap shadowing his blue eyes, he watched as two police cruisers and an ambulance zoomed down Alexandria and turned onto Palms Drive. Sirens wailed, detectives and uniformed cops arrived like storm troopers, intent on getting in on the action. Medics showed up, hoping to save the wounded. All part of a scene that had dissolved into chaos and bedlam and pandemonium, fueled by the combined energies of death and madness and fear. Curious neighbors stepped out of their houses, all eagle eyes, desperate to get a closer look at what had just happened. Frightened mothers ran screaming and crying, grabbing up young children and herding them to safety. Above, a helicopter from one of the TV stations hovered like a mechanical raven waiting to swoop down and photograph the chaos. A live, real-time video game for the viewing audience. Tonight's ratings would be sky high.

Beautiful, the man said to himself, just peachy. He smiled and shook his head. Leave it to a worthless nobody like Rocky Stone to cause this kind of madness. Like the TV ad says, shit like this is priceless.

What the man didn't know, and wouldn't be able to find out until later, was the outcome of all the gunfire. Somebody had been killed, that much was a given. He'd been in similar situations, where bullets were flying in all directions, and it was rare when there wasn't at least one casualty. But who? Was Rocky dead? Dantzler? One of the other detectives? Maybe, he thought, they were all dead. Now, that would be peachy.

Regardless of the outcome, whether Dantzler was alive or dead, the man realized his course of action had been altered. Thanks to today's events, a heavy and dangerous burden had been lifted. After today, there was no longer a pressing need to eliminate Dantzler, even if the famous detective had been lucky enough to survive the gun battle. Given what happened today, and given the facts that would be uncovered in the next few days, Dantzler would have no choice but to close the file on Rocky Stone.

And Eli Whitehouse.

The man's smile widened.

He was now free and clear.

CHAPTER FORTY

Dantzler remained at the scene until well after dark, overseeing the removal of Stone's body, the collection of evidence—early estimates had it at more than a hundred rounds fired during the skirmish—and rehashing the series of events for Don Andrews, the new guy in IAB. He also made a point to be on hand when Eric had his initial debriefing with Andrews. Dantzler wanted to make certain Andrews understood it was a good shoot. After hearing the evidence and walking through the crime scene with Dantzler and Eric, Andrews's preliminary assessment was that Eric had acted within the proper guidelines.

At nine-fifteen, with little left to do except stand around and watch the capable crime scene techs do their thing, Dantzler hopped in his car and headed for the hospital. Turning onto Alexandria, he saw Eric standing on the sidewalk in front of the Lopez house, talking with three uniformed officers. Some of Scott's old buddies, no doubt bent on hearing all the gory details of the bloody gunfight, each one expressing disappointment at having not been involved while secretly thankful they weren't.

Dantzler pulled up next to the sidewalk and motioned for Eric. "Go home, Eric. Get some rest. Tomorrow will be a long day. You'll need to be sharp."

"I will," Eric said. "But first I need to check on Scott."

"No, you need to go home. That's an order."

"But . . . he's my partner."

"Go home."

"Shit," Eric said, walking away.

Arriving at the hospital, Dantzler couldn't find an empty space so he reluctantly parked in a handicapped spot. Hurrying from his vehicle, he entered the hospital through the emergency room, badge out, fully prepared to bulldoze any media person foolish enough to stick a microphone or camera in his face. It had already been a long, strenuous day, and it was still a long way from over. He wasn't about to rest until he knew Scott's status. Given the seriousness of Scott's wound, it could be hours before anyone knew anything for certain.

In the emergency room, Dantzler spied Kathy Ramsey, a nurse he recognized from the Tennis Center. Pulling her aside, he asked where Scott would have been taken. Kathy said Scott was in surgery on the second floor. Dantzler didn't ask for further details, and she volunteered no additional information. He thanked her and headed for the elevator.

Predictably, the waiting area was standing room only, the visitors evenly divided among family, friends, and police personnel. Dantzler eased to the right, where Laurie was talking to Richard Bird and Bruce Rawlinson. She waved and forced a smile when she saw Dantzler coming her way. Dantzler nodded, and then turned his attention to Scott's family.

Scott's father was leaning against a wall, head down, eyes directed straight at the floor. Judging by his attire—slacks, polo shirt, loafers—he had probably been on the golf course when word came that his only son had been seriously wounded in a shootout. He was a big man, much like Scott, and it was easy to see a strong resemblance between father and son. It was also impossible to miss the concern written on his face.

Mrs. Crofton, hands clasped together, prayer beads wrapped around her fingers, sat between her two daughters and a priest. None of them spoke, and they all had that dazed, faraway look so often seen in hospital waiting areas or hospital chapels, those solemn places where hope and despair and fear and uncertainty swirl around inside a person like an EF5 tornado.

Waiting for a life-or-death medical report on a loved one was, Dantzler knew, nothing less than hell on earth. And when it was the parent waiting for news concerning the fate of a child, the worry and anxiety and panic factors multiplied ten-fold. Losing a child was every parent's worst fear.

All heads turned when the automatic door opened and one of the surgeons came into the waiting area. He immediately located the Croftons and went directly to them. As the doctor huddled with Scott's family, Bird and Dantzler moved closer to the group, stopping just outside the circle but close enough to hear the news.

Good news.

The surgery went well, the doctor said, and Scott's life was no longer in danger. There had been significant blood loss, Scott's collarbone had been shattered by the bullet, and there was the remote possibility of permanent nerve damage in the shoulder or arm. That wouldn't be determined until later. But if there was no infection or unforeseen complications, Scott stood an excellent chance of making a complete recovery. All things considered, the doctor concluded, Scott Crofton was one very lucky young man.

"Thank God for small miracles," Bird said as Scott's parents and sisters hugged each other. "No, let me amend that. Thank God for big miracles. I certainly wasn't counting on news this positive."

"Based on how he looked at the scene, neither was I." Dantzler motioned for Laurie. "Get Eric on the phone and give him the news. I'm sure he's dying to know what's going on."

Laurie stepped away from the crowd, opened her cell phone, and began punching in numbers.

"Where is Eric?" Bird asked.

"I sent him home," Dantzler said. "Actually, I had to order him to go home. Made Milt follow to make sure he went to his house rather than come here."

"Tell you something, Jack. If I'd been in Eric's shoes, just witnessed my partner being gunned down, I would've told you to go straight to hell. Then I would've come straight to the hospital."

"That's pretty much what Eric said. But I felt he'd been through enough today. He's going to have a helluva day tomorrow, so I thought it best for him to get some rest." Dantzler watched Laurie snap her cell phone shut. "You give him the news?"

"Yeah, him and Milt," Laurie said. "Eric kinda sounded like he was fighting back tears. I got the feeling he didn't think Scott had much of a chance."

"That makes two of us," Dantzler said. "We can thank Eric and Milt for saving Scott's life. They kept him from bleeding out."

Dantzler checked his watch. It was just shy of ten-thirty. Taking out his cell phone, he punched in some numbers. After three rings, Charlie Bolton answered.

"You still have any Anchor Steam in the fridge?" Dantzler said.

"Always."

"You smell like dead fish?"

"Not that I'm aware of."

"I'm on my way."

CHAPTER FORTY-ONE

"Heard the Crofton kid was hit pretty bad," Charlie said after he and Dantzler were seated at the kitchen table. "How's he doing?"

"He lost a lot of blood, and there could be some nerve damage to his left arm, but the doctors are optimistic he can make a full recovery. Infections and blood clots are the big concerns at this stage."

"Sounds encouraging. I'd heard he was hanging on by a thread and would be lucky to pull through."

"It was dicey until they got him stabilized."

"How is Eric handling it?"

"He's fine."

"You need to keep an eye on him for the next few days, make sure he's okay. Taking a human life, even a scumbag's, is something that can eat at a person's insides, make 'em go a little screwy. I've known cops who thought they were handling it okay, then at some point the realization of what they had done hits them like a runaway locomotive and they fall apart. It can slip up on a person, kick 'em into crazyville."

"Trust me. Eric won't fall apart."

"Word is he was pretty heroic during your little firefight."

"He was also very lucky."

"Luck ain't a bad thing to have on your side, especially in a situation like the one you guys were in."

"You should have seen him, Charlie, when he was charging at Stone. He had this look on his face that . . . that was pure hatred."

"A little hate mixed in with luck—nothing wrong with that. Hell, if my partner had just been shot, I'd have a good deal of hate inside me. It's only natural."

"Yeah, maybe you're right. But you don't charge straight at a guy who's aiming an assault rifle at you. That's nuts."

"I say give Eric a medal. He lowered the number of scumbags in the world by one." Charlie drained his beer and set the bottle on the counter. "He also closed the Eli Whitehouse case for all of us."

"I'm not so certain of that."

"Why am I not surprised that you disagree with me?"

Dantzler shook his head. "It simply doesn't play out for me that

Stone is the shooter. Not those killings in 'eighty-two, not the recent ones. It simply won't compute for me."

Charlie said, "He kills those two boys in Eli's barn, goes away to prison, the trail goes cold, he gets out of the joint, kills Rogers for who knows what reason, then has to take out the temp lady as insurance. That computes for me."

"Come on, Charlie. There's no way you buy that theory. Stone had the IQ of a frog. You want me to believe he could kill four people, manufacture and plant evidence, and get away with it?"

"He didn't get away with it, Jack. He's lying dead on a slab in the morgue."

"But we didn't catch him, Charlie. He bolted, got himself killed. We had nothing on him, nothing at all. If he had come in quietly with us, allowed us to interrogate and investigate, I would bet my pension we wouldn't have found a scintilla of evidence connecting him to the killings in 'eighty-two or the most recent killings. We would have had nothing to hold him on. A first-year law student would have had him back on the street before you could say Perry Mason."

"Need a replacement for that dead soldier?" Charlie said, standing. "I'm having another one."

"Sounds good." Dantzler finished his beer and dropped the empty bottle into the wastebasket. "Tell me, Charlie, do you really believe a blockhead like Rocky Stone would be capable of committing a double murder and then have the smarts to keep it quiet for twenty-nine years? I sure don't believe it."

"You're assuming he did keep it quiet and didn't spill his guts to someone along the way. Sure, he yapped about it. I'll grant you that much. Probably bragged to a dozen guys over the years. Bums like him see crime as a badge of honor, so they brag about it. But those he confided in either didn't give a shit, or they weren't impressed, or they were too afraid of him to squeal. His secret stayed buried."

"Charlie, if I thought for a second you believed a word of that, I would slap you upside the head. Try to knock some sense into you. Your theory has more holes in it than two dozen golf courses."

"What holes bother you the most?"

"For starters, there's no connection between Stone and those two boys killed in the barn. And there is no connection between Stone and Eli Whitehouse. Even if I conceded that Stone killed Colt Rogers and Devon Fraley, and I don't concede it, there is nothing to link him to those first two murders. And that doesn't even begin to touch the major hole in your theory

—those fingerprints on Eli's gun. How could an idiot like Stone get the gun out of the safe in the first place? And do you want me to believe he was intelligent enough to use the gun, somehow manage to get Eli's prints on it, and leave it at the crime scene? You don't buy that and neither do I."

"You know what you've done, don't you, Jack? You just validated the jury's verdict. Based on what you laid out for me, Eli is guilty as sin. He's the only one who could have killed those two kids in 'eighty-two. But you don't buy it and neither do I."

"No, I don't."

"And we both know he didn't kill Rogers or the Fraley woman. So, it can only mean we are looking at two shooters."

"No, there's only a single shooter, Charlie. A pro, a hit man. I'm sure of it. There's a connection that ties these four killings together, a link, and I can't find it. But it's out there, waiting to be uncovered."

"Go talk to Eli again."

"He won't tell me. He's afraid to."

"Jack, this may turn out to be one of those times when you are going to have to do the one thing all detectives detest—walk away without finding the answer. I know that's like telling you to cut off an arm, but sometimes the good guys don't win. It's a simple and painful fact of life. If Eli won't help, you have no choice but to close the book on this one. Otherwise, it's going to eat you up inside."

"What . . . and lay all this on Rocky Stone?"

Charlie shrugged.

"I'm not walking away, Charlie. Someone out there has murdered four people and is still walking around free. I won't rest until I bring him in."

"Then you might not get much rest."

CHAPTER FORTY-TWO

Charlie was right.

Dantzler didn't get much sleep during the night, and what he did get was far from restful. Mostly, there were brief periods of dozing interspersed between longer periods of wakefulness. There were other moments when he wasn't certain whether he was asleep or awake. Either way, the previous day's events ran through his mind like a TV news loop that keeps repeating itself over and over. He tried to shut it down but despite his best efforts he couldn't. It played on and on, a newsreel filmed in hell.

Clear, vivid, dream-like images: Stone emerging from behind the fence, firing his weapon in all directions . . . Scott lying wounded and bleeding on the ground . . . chasing Stone across the street . . . seeing Eric flying past, hate etched on his face . . . Stone's head exploding.

By five-fifteen, with hope for meaningful sleep now out of the question, Dantzler dragged himself out of bed and into the shower. The hot water felt like sharp needles being driven into his body, but the shower, more necessary than refreshing, served a dual purpose—it woke him up, and it melted away the previous night's dreamy images. After dressing, he downed a bialy and a glass of orange juice, jumped in his car, and went to the office.

Bleary-eyed but wired, Dantzler was his desk by six-thirty, sitting alone, methodically working his way through a stack of long-neglected messages. The Homicide section was quiet, exactly how he wanted it. He felt miserable, as though he was in the midst of a supernova hangover. His head screamed, his eyes burned, and neither showed signs of letting up anytime soon. Worse still, his stomach felt like Mount Vesuvius, ready to erupt at any moment. Clearly, his medicinal holy trinity of Tylenol, Visine, and Pepto-Bismol were not worthy opponents against what ailed him this morning.

His first order of business was to call the hospital and check on Scott's condition. The ICU charge nurse informed him that Scott was still heavily sedated, but his vital signs were good, he had no fever, and he seemed to be resting comfortably. Barring unforeseen complications, she concluded, Scott would likely be moved out of ICU within the next twelve hours. Dantzler thanked her and hung up.

From nine to eleven, Dantzler and Eric met with Don Andrews of IAB, Jeff Rosen, the chief of police, and Captain Bird, carefully reviewing the previous day's events, getting it all on the official record in case questions arose. There shouldn't be any questions, but . . . a black man had shot and killed a white man, and regardless of the circumstances or the victim's shady background, anytime race is a factor, the potential for trouble hovered like some unforeseen powder keg set to explode at a moment's notice.

Because of the potential for trouble, the narrative had to be nailed down, it had to be accurate, and it had to be above board in every way. To ensure that it was, the interview was recorded on video. By capturing it on tape, along with the date and time, no one could be accused of doctoring or altering the testimony.

By a stroke of pure luck, the testimony given by Dantzler and Eric—and later by Milt—had eyewitness corroboration. Neighbors Manny Sanchez and Byron Stoddard happened to be standing on Stoddard's back porch when Stone began firing at Eric and Scott. They saw it all unfold, Scott going down after being hit, Stone racing across the street like a wild madman, Dantzler giving chase, Eric ending it all with a single shot to Stone's head.

The Sanchez/Stoddard testimony wasn't necessary, but it certainly couldn't hurt. In today's world, where race always seems to work its way into every equation, anything that could blunt potential trouble between blacks and whites was more than welcomed.

By noon, Dantzler was starving. He collared Eric and offered to buy his lunch. Eric quickly agreed. Until Eric was officially cleared by IAB, he was saddled with desk duty, which translated into answering phone calls, taking and delivering messages, and generally catching a lot of grief from his fellow detectives, who quickly christened him "Mr. Secretary." The good-natured ribbing did little to placate Eric's grumpiness. Like Dantzler, Eric was a man of action, greatly preferring leg work—real detective challenges—to sitting behind a desk shuffling papers. He would remain grumpy until he was allowed to get back in the field.

When they returned to the office, Dantzler went by his desk, grabbed a handful of folders, and went into the War Room. He hadn't been in there more than ten minutes when Milt burst through the door holding a single file over his head and smiling like a young kid who had just been told he could have the biggest ice cream cone.

"Jack, you aren't gonna believe what I'm about to lay on you," Milt said, beaming. "First, though, you need to sit down. If you're standing when you hear what I've got to say, you'll fall down and bust your keester."

"Okay, Milt," Dantzler said, pulling back a chair and sitting. "What do you have that's so earthshaking?"

"You won't believe this, Jack."

"Spill it, Milt, before I choke it out of you."

"The late, departed Kevin Stone, a.k.a. Rocky, was Eli Whitehouse's nephew." Milt tossed the file onto the table. "His mother, Grace, was Eli's older sister. She died of a massive stroke when Rocky was seven. Rocky was raised by his father, Vince. He was a plumber, owned his own business. No paper on him whatsoever. Unlike his wayward son, Vince was a law-abiding citizen. Paid his taxes, went to church, kept his nose clean. He died of a heart attack in 'ninety-four."

This was big news, and Dantzler remained silent as he let it sink in. But big news didn't necessarily translate into important news. It might mean an end to the case, or it might mean nothing at all. He let it roll around in his head for several minutes, hoping a clear meaning might emerge. It didn't. Instead, he was bombarded with more questions.

"Well, what do think, Ace?" Milt finally asked.

"Interesting."

"Interesting? That's the best you can come up with?" Milt picked up the folder and pointed to it. "This is way more than interesting. This settles it, Jack. Rocky Stone killed those two kids in 'eighty-two, he killed Colt Rogers, and he killed Devon Fraley. Case closed."

Dantzler remained silent.

Milt continued, "Rocky not only knew Eli, he was related to him, which means he had access to Eli's house, to the safe, the gun. He—"

"You don't know if he ever set foot in Eli's house."

"He was family, Jack. Eli's nephew. I think we can safely assume he visited the Whitehouse residence."

"I prefer facts to assumptions."

"It plays, Jack. Rocky kills those two kids, leaves the gun at the scene, knowing Eli will take the fall, which is exactly what happened. Flash forward to a couple of weeks ago. Rocky gets pissed at Rogers, takes him out. Devon Fraley must have known or heard something, knew Rocky was coming to see Rogers, so she had to be silenced as well. It all falls into place. He's the thread running through this entire scenario, from then to now."

"Sorry, Milt, but I'm not buying any of it."

"Why not?"

"To begin with, you're crediting Rocky Stone with a lot more IQ points than I'm willing to give him. I don't think he possessed the gray matter necessary to do all the things you say he did."

"You don't have to be smart to pull a trigger."

"True. But it does require a certain level of intelligence to do the other things you say Rocky did. Get into the safe, secure the gun, make sure Eli's prints were on it, find the two victims, lure them to the barn, tie them up, kill them, set the barn on fire, and get away without being seen. Then he has to do something equally challenging. He has to keep it quiet for twenty-nine years. And what about the thirteen hundred dollars Greg Spurlock took off the two bodies? Can you see Rocky Stone, a washed-out pug and ex-con, leaving a wad of cash lying around? I can't. Why would he set up Eli, a relative? And can you see Eli spending three decades years behind bars for a loser like Rocky Stone? No way. Not even if Stone was kin."

Dantzler shook his head. "And that's only for openers, Milt. I can point out another dozen reasons why I'll never be convinced Rocky Stone killed those four people."

"If Stone was innocent, why did he run?" Milt said. "Why did he open fire?"

"Because he was stupid."

"Well, duh."

"He hated cops, saw us as a threat to his freedom, and wasn't about to let us put him behind bars again. He would rather go toe to toe with us than go back to prison." Dantzler was quiet for several seconds, then said, "Don't you find it interesting that Stone had the rifle and ammo right there in the living room?"

"No, not really."

"Well, I do."

"What are you saying, Jack?"

"Something Rocky said when we first got there has stayed with me. He said, 'I've been told you were coming, and I ain't got nothing to say to you.' How did he know we were coming?"

"He saw us out on the street in front of his house. The four of us, huddled together, talking. He's an ex-con—he could spot a cop a mile away. Hell, he could smell a cop a mile away."

"That's possible."

"But you don't sound like you believe it."

"I don't. I think he meant exactly what he said—he knew we were coming to see him."

"Other than the four of us, who knew we were going to see Rocky?"

"Rich knew. Laurie. Bruce Rawlinson. I told Charlie Bolton. And I'm sure others knew as well. It wasn't like some big secret."

"You're inferring there is a leak in the department."

"Stone knew we were on the way. So, yeah, there's a leak somewhere."

"Jesus, now we're not only fighting the bad guys on the outside, we're fighting the enemy within. That pretty much sucks." Milt scratched his head and grimaced. "You have a candidate for who the snitch might be?"

"No. But I'll wager you this," Dantzler said. "The snitch, whoever he turns out to be, is the person who killed those four people."

CHAPTER FORTY-THREE

There were times when Dantzler cursed his own stubbornness. This was one of those times.

His stubbornness placed him squarely at odds against his colleagues, all of whom were willing to convict Stone for the Colt Rogers and Devon Fraley slayings. They also believed that given his kinship to Eli, and his access to the murder weapon, Stone was a likely suspect for the murder of those two boys in 1982. Although none of them believed deep in their heart of hearts that Stone was the lone killer, they were willing to cast aside their true feelings and grant him that distinction.

Sympathy had replaced evidence.

All Dantzler had to do was sign off on it and both cases would be closed. Like that, simple as snapping his fingers. Sealed, air tight, official. With Dantzler's blessing, the late Kevin "Rocky" Stone would forever be remembered as a four-time murderer.

But marching in lock-step with the crowd wasn't part of Dantzler's nature. It never had been, and he wasn't about to change now. This was especially true when he was certain the crowd was marching in the wrong direction and to the beat of a misguided tune. If he was deemed an outsider, a lone wolf, so be it. He would always stand his ground against an erroneous consensus.

If Dantzler gave the green light, and if Jeff Rosen agreed—which he would—then Kirk Foster could go to his boss, the governor, and have him sign the required documents necessary to free Eli. Within a matter of hours, John Elijah Whitehouse, the Reverend, would be released from prison and allowed to return home, to be reunited with his family, to live out his final days being cared for by his loved ones.

But as much as he wanted to, Dantzler wasn't about to sign off on it. He couldn't agree with the prevailing sentiment. There were, he argued, too many stumbling blocks standing in his path. For starters, he couldn't convince himself that the easy way was the correct way. In his experience, it was usually the exact opposite. The hard way typically turned out to be the correct way. Also, nothing had changed evidence-wise, a fact his colleagues seemed willing to overlook or dismiss. Dantzler wasn't prepared to take that leap, regardless of any sympathy or empathy for Eli.

Empathy is never enough to overturn a jury verdict.

No, Eli didn't kill Rogers and Fraley, and Dantzler remained convinced the old man didn't kill those two young boys, either. But the mountain of evidence said otherwise, that Eli did in fact kill Osteen and Fowler. Until or unless Dantzler could bring down that mountain, Eli had to remain in jail. As a detective, he was bound to the evidence, not to the tug of his heart.

Dantzler was now the lone voice arguing against laying the four murders on Kevin Stone. That made his the lone voice keeping an innocent man behind bars.

He felt like a traitor to his own cause.

*****

Dantzler pulled up next to the Church of the Holy Father, got out of his car, and walked around to the front door. Standing outside, he could hear a voice coming from inside the church. He opened the door slightly and peered inside, fearing he had arrived in the middle of an evening service, or possibly a funeral. But he hadn't. The church was empty, save for Isaac Whitehouse, who was standing alone in the pulpit, reciting a passage from Paul's letter to Galatians in a deep, melodious voice.

Isaac stopped speaking the moment he saw Dantzler open the door and step inside the church. Closing his Bible and notebook, he waved Dantzler forward. Stepping down off the stage, Isaac stopped at the second row of seats, leaned over, and picked up a small tape recorder. After turning off the recording device, he extended his hand to Dantzler.

"It's an old habit of mine to record my sermons in advance," Isaac said. "I'll listen to it several times between now and Sunday, make a few notes, pick out the obvious flaws. This way, I have the opportunity to critique it, to see if I'm being redundant, of if I am using certain phrases too often, or being plain old boring. There's nothing worse than a dull sermon. This gives me some idea of the strengths and weaknesses before the curtain goes up on Sunday."

"Sorry if I interrupted," Dantzler said.

"Don't apologize. I was almost finished. And to be honest with you, it wasn't going particularly well. I'll record it again later this evening, after I do a major overhaul." Isaac pointed to one of the pews. "Have a seat, Detective. Or if you prefer, we can go to my office."

"This will be fine," Dantzler said, sitting. "Did you hear about your cousin, Kevin Stone?"

Isaac nodded. “Rachel told me. A real tragedy, Detective Dantzler. A sad end to a sad life.”

“Will you preach at the funeral?”

“There won’t be a funeral per se, only a brief graveside service. But, yes, I will say a few words for Kevin. He was, after all, family. I feel it’s my responsibility to help lay him to rest.”

“I’m sorry for your loss.”

“Thank you.”

“Where will he be buried?”

“He won’t be. Believe it or not, Kevin had a will. He wanted to be cremated and have his ashes scattered over his mother’s grave.”

“Mind my asking who is paying for the cremation?”

“Rachel and Kirk.”

“When was the last time you saw Kevin?” Dantzler asked.

“Let me think about that. Oh, five years ago, maybe. I only saw him once or twice after his release from prison.” Isaac looked away. “I know you’ll find this hard to believe, Detective Dantzler, but Kevin was one of the nicest, sweetest young kids you could ever hope to meet. He was two years older than me, and when I was young—I’m talking really young—Kevin was my big hero. He was only six or seven, but I thought he was just so cool. And he always treated me like a kid brother, his best pal. Then Aunt Grace died and everything changed. His father, Vince, was a great guy, but he was simply too busy to keep a close watch on Kevin. Vince was a plumber and an electrician. He worked all the time. *All* the time. And to be perfectly frank, Vince lacked good parenting skills. He was a good guy, a mediocre father.

“About a year or so after Grace died, this would be when Kevin was eight or nine, he began hanging around with the wrong crowd,” Isaac continued. “That’s when he drifted away from us. Sadly, it meant drifting away from the very people who could have helped him through what had to be a difficult time.

“Was Kevin close to his mother?”

“Yes, very close. And she had terrific parenting skills. Once she was gone, Kevin had no one who could help him channel his anger and frustration.”

“My father was killed when I was six, my mother when I was fourteen. I know something about anger and frustration.”

“I didn’t know. It must have been horrible for you.”

“Did Eli try to help?” Dantzler said.

“Eli and my mother both tried. They even asked Kevin to move in with us full-time, said it would be the best thing for him. Vince agreed. But

Kevin didn't want to, and I suppose none of the adults felt like pushing the issue. In retrospect, it was a mistake letting him have his way. Left alone, Kevin became a street kid, hanging out with and influenced by the wrong people. He also became mean, bitter, and exceptionally hot-headed. It didn't take much for him to explode."

"Yeah, I know."

"Are you the one who shot Kevin?"

"No. But only because someone else shot him first."

"Rachel said a detective was wounded. How is he doing?"

"Barring complications he should be okay. He was very lucky."

"I'll say a prayer for him."

Dantzler said, "Back in 'eighty-two, did Kevin spend much time at your house?"

"By then, he had become a professional boxer and was doing quite a bit of traveling. He was hardly ever in our house. Why do you ask?"

"I'm looking at him as the possible shooter of those two kids in Eli's barn."

"You're putting me on, right?"

"It's not possible?"

"Kevin may have killed them with his fists, but not with a gun. And certainly not with Eli's twenty-two. That simply could not have happened."

"Why not?"

"Kevin didn't have access to Eli's safe. He didn't have a clue where the safe was located. Only a handful of people did." Isaac let out a deep sigh. "Are you convinced Eli is innocent?"

"Yes."

"Eli is fortunate to have you in his corner. You and Rachel."

"What about you? Aren't you in his corner?"

"I've seen the evidence against Eli, Detective Dantzler, and it is overwhelming. I can only believe what I see."

"You believe in God, but you can't see him." Dantzler stood. "We believe what we want to believe, Brother Isaac. For whatever reason, you don't want to believe Eli is innocent."

Isaac remained silent as Dantzler left the church.

CHAPTER FORTY-FOUR

Working a closed case was like performing open-heart surgery on a corpse: no matter how many faulty arteries you replaced, the patient didn't get any better.

Right now, Dantzler's patient, the Eli Whitehouse case, was barely on life support.

In a career that spanned more than twenty years, he had never worked a case this frustrating or this perplexing. Most cases had doors he could open, paths he could follow, evidence he could pursue. Not this one. This case offered nothing. There was nowhere to go, no new direction to turn, no fresh ideas. Dantzler felt like a painter who was staring at a blank canvas without a single brush to work with.

"That's some look you have on your face, Jack," Laurie said, stepping into the War Room. "You look like a man pondering the mystery of the universe."

"That might be an easier mystery to solve than this one," Dantzler said. He was sitting at the table drinking a Diet Pepsi. "Remind me again why I was dumb enough to take on a closed case."

"Because you are convinced an innocent man is behind bars for a crime he didn't commit, and that's a situation you cannot tolerate. A very noble undertaking on your part, regardless of how this case turns out."

"Oh, yeah? Well, let me clue you in on something. For all my efforts, all of *our* efforts, we haven't changed a damn thing. The evidence as it now stands points directly at Eli Whitehouse as the shooter of those two kids in 'eighty-two. And we aren't even close to catching the person who killed Rogers and Fraley. All this work and we've accomplished nothing. We're still standing on square one, stuck in neutral."

"I know."

"And what makes it especially frustrating is Eli could end it all by simply giving us a name. Two words from him and we have the shooter of four people. Three cases solved. And Eli could walk out of prison a free man. But he won't. The one person we're all trying to help refuses to help himself. Thinking about it makes me want to walk away."

"It'll never happen."

Dantzler shook his head. "No, I can't walk away, not as long as I remain convinced Eli's case is connected to the Rogers and Fraley murders. Four people are dead—their families deserve answers."

"Tell me, Jack. Have you seriously considered the possibility Eli did kill those two boys in 'eighty-two? That he is guilty? You've even admitted that nothing about the evidence has changed or been disproved. Maybe there is no new evidence. Maybe the verdict was the correct one." Laurie sat across from Dantzler. "That would, of course, mean there are two shooters. It would also mean that by focusing all our attention on Eli's case, we've placed too much emphasis and aimed too many resources in the wrong direction. By doing so, we've given the Rogers/Fraley killer a big advantage."

"There is only one shooter."

"Okay, so who are the suspects?" Laurie asked. "If you've ruled out Kevin Stone, who's next on your list?"

"I have no answer," Dantzler admitted. "And at this point, I have nowhere to turn."

"Eli is your salvation."

"I thought I was supposed to be his."

"Why not approach him one more time? See what he'll do?"

"Won't work."

"Can't hurt to give it one more shot. Who knows? He might have a change of heart."

"Waste of time. Eli is not giving us the name."

"So . . . what will you do?"

"What I've always done." Dantzler stood and picked up the stack of files from the table. "Go back over the case—all three cases—and study them again from top to bottom. Keep my fingers crossed that something new or enlightening jumps out. At this stage of the game, it's the only thing I can do. The only thing I know how to do."

*****

Dantzler went home, arriving seconds ahead of a soft, gentle spring shower as pleasant as it was unexpected. An hour later, the rain had passed, the night air was warm and sticky, and he was standing on his deck, drink in hand, looking out at the lake, feeling one of those funky moods beginning to sneak up on him like an invisible assassin closing in from behind.

He sipped his Pernod and thought about the case. More specifically, he thought about Isaac Whitehouse, the one name that kept popping up on his detective's radar. Of all the players in this drama, Eli's eldest child was the most mysterious and the most bewildering. His actions, his beliefs, seemed so unnatural, so unlike those of a normal child. So unlike those of his siblings.

Rachel was convinced of Eli's innocence, and Tommy, despite his personal problems, indicated he also felt Eli had been wrongly convicted. Not so with Isaac, who, during his two meetings with Dantzler, showed not an inkling of love or affection for Eli, only a grudging respect for the old man's preaching ability. He refused to believe Eli might be innocent, and even more troubling, he displayed an almost total indifference to the possibility his father could leave the prison and die a free man.

It was almost as if Isaac wanted his father to remain locked behind those steel prison bars until his last dying breath.

Not even the biblical Isaac held such a harsh opinion of his father Abraham.

Dantzler tried to dismiss Isaac Whitehouse as a suspect in the murder of those two boys in 1982, but he couldn't. His instincts wouldn't allow it. Did he see Isaac as the shooter? No. Dantzler quickly ruled out that possibility. But ruling Isaac out as somehow being involved in the crime wasn't so easy to do. As Dantzler saw it, there were several critical factors preventing a quick dismissal of Isaac as a suspect.

To begin with, Isaac knew the combination to the safe, which gave him access to the .22. He could easily have gotten the gun and given it to the shooter, having made sure Eli's prints were on it. Given Isaac's apparent apathy toward his father, such action, although unlikely, was not beyond the realm of possibility.

Also, Isaac was only a couple years younger than the two victims, and although he denied knowing them, it didn't mean he was telling the truth. They may have been friends, or at the very least, acquaintances. If so, and if a link could be established, it enhanced the likelihood that Isaac was somehow involved. If nothing else, it would prove him to be a liar.

And having been involved in the crime, Isaac could be counted on to remain silent all these years.

But why would Isaac help perpetrate such a crime? Did he really hate Eli enough to watch him sent to prison for a crime he didn't commit? Was Isaac that bitter, that cruel and uncaring? And if Isaac was involved, who was he covering for? Who was he protecting? Who was the shooter?

So many unanswered questions, so many dots yet to be connected.

Dantzler went into the kitchen and made another drink. Sitting at the table, his thoughts kept coming back to the two meetings with Isaac. During those talks, Isaac demonstrated no love for his father, but neither had he displayed any outward or overt signs of hate. Or at least, none Dantzler could detect. More than anything, Isaac seemed indifferent, almost strangely removed from his father's plight. It was as though he simply didn't care what happened.

But was Isaac Whitehouse an accessory to a double murder? Was he so hate-filled, so heartless, that he was willing to ruin his own father's life? Could any son feel so much animosity toward his father?

Dantzler cringed at the thought. Hating a parent was unnatural, and harboring enough hatred to help send a parent to prison was even more unnatural. But . . . if twenty-five years as a detective had taught him anything, it was this: human behavior is the ultimate mystery.

CHAPTER FORTY-FIVE

At a little past eleven p.m., a second thunderstorm, this one accompanied by heavy winds, drove Dantzler off the deck and into the house. Once inside, he mixed another drink, settled into the recliner in the den, and began surfing the tube for something worthwhile to watch. His first stop was The Charlie Rose Show, the most intelligent and enlightening of the interview programs, and one that rarely failed him. However, that wasn't the case on this night. Tonight, Charlie was talking to the director and two actors from a new movie based on a graphics novel. Dantzler had no interested in that. Things didn't improve with a switch to usually reliable CNN, or to any of the other cable networks, where, for the most part, there was a lot of screaming and finger pointing between liberals and conservatives, Democrats and Republicans.

So much for intellectual and civil debate.

In the end, Turner Classic Movies came to the rescue, as it often did at this late hour. After giving the remote a solid workout, Dantzler landed on *White Heat*, the classic black and white gangster flick starring the great Jimmy Cagney as Cody Jarrett, the psychopathic criminal with the mother fixation who yells "made it, Ma—top of the world!" just seconds before he's blown to smithereens in spectacular cinematic fashion. It was one of Dantzler's all-time favorite movies, and certainly his favorite Cagney performance.

Dantzler was enough of a movie buff to know every serious actor from Brando on down idolized Cagney. The legendary director Stanley Kubrick rated Cagney as one of the five greatest movie actors of all-time, and with good reason. Cagney never let you down. Energy and truth were at the heart of Cagney's acting. No matter the situation, or how lame the dialogue, he was always believable. For Dantzler, ten minutes of the marvelous Cagney was preferable to the endless, numbing hours of barking, biting, and screaming constantly found on the major cable networks. It wasn't even a close contest.

After Cagney went up in flames, Dantzler turned off the TV and relocated to the kitchen. For the next half-hour he waded through a stack of unopened and long-neglected mail, separating the important (bills, bank statement) he had to address from the unimportant (credit card offers, various coupons, the Watchtower), which accounted for the ninety-five percent he could deep-six without bothering to open.

With the mail taken care of, Dantzler thought about finding another movie to watch. But the chances of running across a worthy follow-up to Cagney were slim to none. Instead, he decided to take another look at the obituary information Eric had gathered. It was tedious grunt work, and his previous studies had yielded nothing helpful, but he felt compelled to pore over the information one more time. Or ten more times, if necessary. After all, according to Eli, this stack of clippings was where the answer to the mystery could be found.

All Dantzler had to do was find it.

Two hours later, having gone through every obit notice in the three folders, he was still batting a solid zero. There was simply nothing linking anyone mentioned in any of the obits to the Eli Whitehouse case. If, indeed, Eli's secret was hidden within these pages, it was beyond Dantzler's grasp.

When Dantzler set the three folders aside, he noticed a fourth folder, one not nearly as thick as the others, lying on the table. At first he was puzzled; the folder seemed to appear almost out of nowhere. Then it dawned on him what he was looking at. The folder with the female obituaries he had asked Eric to check out. Staring at it, he realized he had never studied its contents.

Could it possibly be?

Dantzler opened the folder and took out the stack of newspaper clippings, photographs, and notes Eric had written. Slowly and methodically he began reading the obits, which had been arranged alphabetically by Eric, beginning with Adcock, Shirley.

More than halfway through the stack, having uncovered nothing of interest, Dantzler turned the page and picked up the next obit notice.

And there it was, plain as day, exactly like Eli said.

Holy shit, Dantzler muttered out loud, his heart pounding like a timpani drum. *Holy shit*, he repeated.

He looked away, then back down at the newspaper clipping, blinking several times to make sure that what he was looking at was no sleep-deprived vision. It wasn't; this was the real thing. Hands trembling, suddenly wide awake, adrenaline pumping, he picked up the single piece of paper.

And began reading.

RICHARDS

Mary Magdalene Richards, 54, loving wife of Johnny Richards, departed this life on April 7, 2010, after a brief illness. Known to everyone as Maggie, she had a strong devotion to family, a great appreciation of the arts and a love of Nature's beauty. Maggie was born on June 18, 1955, in New York City, where she met and fell in love with her husband, whom she married in 1976. She worked in the HR Department at the VA Hospital for many years, eventually retiring in 2005. Maggie is survived by her husband; two sisters, Annabella Donetti of New York City and Gabriella Terranova of Atlantic City, N.J.; six nieces and three nephews. Funeral services will be held at Kerr Brothers Funeral Home in Lexington on April 9 beginning at 10 a.m. Burial will be in the Lexington Cemetery. Donations on behalf of Maggie Richards may be made to the Markey Cancer Center.

Dantzler had been right. Eli's whispered dictate held the key that unlocked the mystery.

Think of Jesus's empty tomb.

Mary Magdalene.

The only woman mentioned in all four Gospel accounts of the women discovering the empty tomb, and the first woman to see the resurrected Jesus.

Eli had given the perfect clue. *Mary Magdalene.* And now, Dantzler had finally uncovered it.

The pieces fell into place, the jigsaw puzzle solved.

Mary Magdalene Richards.

Johnny Richards.

The shooter.

*****

Three-thirty in the morning and too wired to sleep.

Dantzler paced, plotting strategy, putting together his next move, mentally constructing his plan of attack. He was buzzed, alive with excitement, anxious for daylight to break. Anxious to go for the jugular.

To put away a four-time killer.

To free Eli Whitehouse.

During crucial times like this, Dantzler often approached matters from a tennis player's perspective rather than from a detective's point of view. He saw the case through a tennis player's mental lens. In so doing, his understanding of what it took to win was elevated to the highest level, just as it was when he squared off against a talented foe. *Crunch time is my time*. That had always been his mantra. When the match was on the line and the outcome still in doubt was when he played his finest tennis. It all came down to will; the player with the strongest will usually emerged victorious. And Dantzler always felt his will was stronger than that of any opponent. The instinct for dominating a foe was as much a part of him as the blood flowing through his veins.

He detested losing. It wasn't an option.

As with countless tennis matches throughout his life, he now faced one of those pivotal moments where the outcome would likely be decided by how he played his next shot. Everything was riding on his next move, his next piece of strategy. He hadn't arrived at match point—he hadn't come that far just yet—but his next barrage of shots, if executed perfectly, could decide the outcome in his favor.

The trick now was to make no mistakes. Every shot, every move, had to be executed to perfection.

This wasn't pop-the-cork-and-spray-the-champagne-time, but it was close. While there was still much to be accomplished before the flag of victory could be flown, he now held the upper hand. This much he was certain of: he had the slight edge necessary for putting away a worthy opponent. For the first time, he felt in control of the match.

Dantzler smiled.

Victory was now within his reach.

*****

By six-fifteen Dantzler had showered, dressed, downed a bowl of cereal, and made phone calls to Laurie, Milt, and Eric, ordering them to be in the War Room no later than seven-thirty. He offered no specifics other than to let them know there had been a major break in the Eli Whitehouse case. This bit of news was tantalizing enough to rouse the sleepy detectives to life.

Dantzler stood on his deck and watched the sun begin its upward ascent, a bright orange globe carrying with it the promise of a glorious day. A mist hovered over the lake like an ethereal guardian angel. Crickets and loons and frogs sang in unison. The air was still and cool.

For any Homicide detective, answers are always accompanied by questions. In some ways, finding the answer only serves to heighten the riddle. Dantzler now had his answer—Johnny Richards. But exactly *who* was Johnny Richards? Why did he kill those two boys in 1982? What was his connection to Eli Whitehouse? How did he get the murder weapon out of Eli's safe? What was the leverage he wielded that was powerful enough to convince Eli to willingly accept a lifetime prison sentence?

Those questions came at Dantzler faster than a blistering 130-mile-an-hour serve. The answers, he knew, wouldn't come so fast. They seldom did. But it didn't matter to him now. Eventually the answers would be known by him, by Eli, by everyone.

The light of truth always prevails.

CHAPTER FORTY-SIX

"Man, I can't believe I missed something so important," Eric said, shaking his head. "It was right in front of me the entire time and I blew it."

"Don't be so hard on yourself, Eric," Dantzler answered. "Remember, I'm the one who said we should concentrate solely on males. Also, the file was on my desk for a full week before I decided to take a look. If anyone is at fault, it's me."

Dantzler and Eric were sitting across from each other at the War Room table. Milt was at the head of the table, and Captain Bird was standing by the coffee pot. Still a few minutes before nine, yet all four had been at the office for almost two hours. The energy in the room was electric.

"I gotta tell you, Ace," Milt said, pointing at his copy of the obit notice. "I never detected anything hinky or suspicious about Richards when we met with him. From where I was sitting, he came across as sincere and genuine. If he is our guy, he's one cool and confident dude."

"He's a pro, Milt," Dantzler said. "Guys like him don't rattle. He knew exactly how to play us, and he did it with the ease of a smooth, polished actor. I doubt Sean Penn or Russell Crowe could have been more convincing."

"And you're sure he's our guy?" Milt said.

"One-hundred percent."

Bird stepped forward and moved to the table. "Look, Jack, I'm not arguing with you on this, but let me play devil's advocate for a few seconds." He turned a chair around and sat, locking his arms around the back. "There are a lot of questions to be answered before you can nail Richards. First among them—how did he manage to get Eli's pistol out of the safe? If you can't answer that one, your entire case against Richards turns to shit."

"I don't know how he did it, Rich; I only know he did. Just like I don't know why he killed those two kids in 'eighty-two, but he did. I also don't know what he has on Eli that would persuade the old man to spend his life in prison, but he has something. You don't have to play devil's advocate, Rich. I know there are plenty of unanswered questions. It's up to us to answer them.

"But it's all there," Dantzler continued. "Richards was living in Lexington at the time of the first killings. The Colt Rogers connection. The wife named Mary Magdalene. Everything fits."

"It's not *all* there, Jack," Bird countered. "To get the gun, Richards had to know the combination to the safe. If he didn't have the combination, it means someone from inside the Whitehouse family was helping him. That opens a whole new can of worms. And the fingerprints—you seem to be overlooking the fact they were Eli's. If Richards was the shooter, why were Eli's prints get on the gun? What about Devon Fraley? How does she fit into all this? Why would Richards kill her? It's one thing for you to keep saying you *know* these things, Jack, but you're a long way from proving any of it."

"Damn, Rich, you've become more cynical than Milt?"

"Hey, leave me out of this," Milt said, laughing.

"I'm not cynical, Jack," Bird said, walking to the door. "I'm just not as quick to hop on board as you seem to be."

After Bird left the War Room, Eric stood, and said, "He's right, you know. We have a boat load of questions we have to find answers for before we can go after Richards. And right now, we have next to nothing. Let's hope Laurie's research comes up with some interesting finds. If she doesn't, we're screwed."

"What data bases is she checking?" Milt asked.

"All of them," Dantzler said. "She told me she should be done by noon. Let's meet here again at one-thirty."

"See you then," Eric and Milt said in unison.

*****

Back at his desk, Dantzler phoned the state capital in Frankfort, identified himself to the operator, and asked to speak with Kirk Foster. He was immediately put through to Kirk's office.

"If you are calling to set up another tennis match you're wasting your time," Kirk said, laughing. "I learned my lesson the first time around. I'm no glutton for punishment."

"Relax," Dantzler said. "I'm not looking for a rematch."

"Then what can I do for you, Detective Dantzler?" Kirk asked.

"I need to ask a few questions regarding Eli's finances."

"What makes you think I know about Eli's finances?"

"When I met with Eli, he told me you are in charge of his business affairs."

Kirk was silent.

"Eli also made it clear that none of his children are aware of this," Dantzler continued. "That doesn't have to change. There is no reason for them to know we talked."

"What is it you want to know, exactly?"

"How will Eli's estate be divided after he's gone?"

"Evenly. Each sibling gets one-third of everything. Straight down the line."

"What do you estimate his net worth to be?"

"Including everything—land, physical properties, stocks—it's close to ten million."

"I assume you are executor of the estate."

"Yes, I am." Kirk said. "But all decisions regarding the sale of land and/or properties, or the disbursement of money, will be made by the three children. It is Eli's wish, and this is clearly stated in his will, that all decisions are to be based on a majority rules basis. In the unlikely event a clear decision cannot be reached, I have the authority to cast the deciding vote."

"How big a stock portfolio are we talking about?"

"Not big at all. But extremely successful, despite taking some severe hits and suffering substantial setbacks during the past couple of years."

"How does a man behind bars for twenty-nine years invest in the stock market?"

"He doesn't—his son-in-law does. But always with Eli's blessings."

"At any time has Eli directed you to give money to any of his children?"

"Never. He couldn't do that and keep them in the dark about me being executor of his estate."

"Did he ever direct you to give money to Colt Rogers?"

Kirk snorted. "Are you kidding? Eli detested Rogers. Thought he was a low-life criminal. He would never have given Colt Rogers a penny."

"What about Johnny Richards?"

"What about him?"

"Did Eli give him money?"

"Eli gave no money to anyone, Detective Dantzler. That won't happen until after his death. Why are you inquiring about Eli's finances?"

"Some new developments have come to light and I'm trying to get a handle on them."

"In the world of politics, that's known as a non-response response."

"Unfortunately, at the present time, it's the only response I can give. But I can tell you a serious suspect has emerged, one we are very interested in. For obvious reasons, I can't give you a name. The investigation is in the early stages, and it could easily blow up in our faces, so I would also ask you to keep this information to yourself."

"You have my word," Kirk said. "And I appreciate the work you've done on this case, Detective. Nothing would make Rachel happier than seeing her father walk out of prison a free man. An innocent man."

"Nothing would make me happier than putting away a four-time murderer," Dantzler answered.

*****

All eyes were on Laurie when she came into the War Room. Dressed in a black slacks, white blouse, black blazer, and black shoes, her hair flowing down to her shoulders, she looked more like a movie star entering an A-list party than a Homicide detective coming into a drab squad room. A wry smile played on her lips.

"I have good news and bad news," she announced. "The good news is, Macy's is having a forty-percent off sale on shoes beginning tomorrow morning. I plan on being first in line. The bad news is, Johnny Richards didn't exist prior to nineteen-eighty."

"Come again?" Milt said.

"I have checked every possible data base—federal, state, local, military, Interpol—and our Johnny Richards was not on anyone's radar until he arrived in Lexington in October, nineteen-eighty. Prior to that, he's a phantom. Trust me, gentlemen, I have waded through each and every data base in meticulous fashion, and he does not show up on any of them."

"Are you sure?" Eric said. "There must be a million guys named Johnny Richards. Maybe you overlooked something."

Laurie shook her head. "I checked and double-checked and checked again, and I came up empty. Our Johnny Richards ain't who he says he is."

"Well, who the hell is he, then?" Eric said, leaning back in his chair.

"What did you find out about Johnny Richards, post nineteen-eighty?" Dantzler asked.

"Nothing illegal or interesting. He bought the tavern in 'eighty and has operated it successfully ever since. There is a small apartment above the bar, which is also his. The tavern brings in about two-hundred grand a year. Richards also owns a house on Summershade, and a Lexus. His wife, Maggie, died recently, as we all know. They had no children. Maggie worked at the VA Hospital until she retired. She also did some fill-in work for Colt Rogers. Other than that, there really isn't anything worth noting. The man is clean. Not even a speeding ticket."

"No one who changes his identity is clean," Milt said. "You only do it because you're dirty."

Dantzler said, "There are two primary reasons why a man changes his identity. Either he's running away from something he's done, or he's hiding from someone. Johnny Richards, or whoever he is, didn't strike me as a man who would run away from anything. If I'm right, it means he is hiding from someone."

"Hiding?" Eric asked. "From who?"

"Don't know," Dantzler answered. "But all the checkmarks are there . . . new identity, new location, no background data, no past history. And that's not all. I'll make you a wager Richards has undergone just enough plastic surgery to change the way he looked prior to nineteen-eighty."

"Come to think of it, he did have the look of a guy who might've had some work done," Milt said. "Particularly around the eyes."

"All these changes lead me in one direction."

"You're thinking Witness Protection, aren't you?" Milt said.

Dantzler nodded. "That's exactly what I'm thinking."

"Goddammit, that means dealing with the Feds," Milt offered. "That's never any fun."

"The Witness Protection Program comes under the Justice Department banner, with the U.S. Marshals Service doing the actual legwork. It's the Marshals who move the individual around, secure proper documentation, find living quarters . . . that sort of thing. But I'll start at the top, contact someone inside Justice, and see what I can find out."

"Shouldn't we put surveillance on Richards?" Eric said.

Dantzler thought about this for a moment before answering. "Let's hold off on surveillance until we find out more about the guy. If he is in the Program, it could make things a lot more complicated. I want to make sure we know what we're doing and who we're dealing with before we make any moves."

"Damn," Milt said, shaking his head. "I was hoping this would be easy."

"It's only a bump in the road, Milt," Dantzler said. "If Richards is the shooter, and I'm dead certain he is, we'll bring him in. But I have a feeling we can toss easy out the window."

CHAPTER FORTY-SEVEN

Seeking outside assistance on a case was almost always a last-ditch option for Dantzler. Given his druthers, he would never seek help from the Feds. It was his firm belief that he and his fellow Homicide detectives were superior in every way to the so-called "experts," although he did acknowledge that the federal agencies, with their generous budgets and multitude of gadgets, were technologically superior. While some viewed Dantzler's disdain for seeking outside help as arrogance, he countered the accusation with the argument that more hands only make a bigger mess.

But above all else, Dantzler was a pragmatist. In the end, all good cops are. You do what it takes to put the bad guys away, and if it means bending a few rules along the way, or seeking help from outside sources, you do it, regardless of the dent inflicted upon your pride, or the bitter taste such a move might leave in your mouth.

Justice must always outweigh ego.

Dantzler was sitting as his desk when the phone rang. He put down the file he was reading and picked up the receiver. He knew who the caller was—Lisa Kennedy. Earlier that afternoon, he placed a call to her at the Justice Department and was informed she was on assignment in Denver. He left his name and number, and asked that Lisa contact him as soon as possible.

"What a pleasant surprise," Lisa said. "I didn't expect to hear from the guy who saved my ass. How long has it been now? Two years?"

"Almost three," Dantzler said, referring to the Victor Sammael case they worked together. "How are things in your part of the world? I would imagine you've been staying busy."

"Extremely. There simply aren't enough hours in the day. I feel like I'm chasing after something I can never catch."

"You are," Dantzler said, laughing. "The illusion we can make a difference that truly makes a difference."

"Don't tell me that," Lisa said. "If I thought we weren't making a real difference, I would be out the door faster than you can say goodbye yellow brick road. I'd go live on a beach and drink rum all day."

"Now, there's a plan I could fall in love with."

"You may fool some people with such talk, Detective Dantzler, but not me. I've seen you in action, remember? I know how much you care about little things like protecting the innocent and putting bad guys away. And I also know—we both know—that what we do does make a difference. There is nothing illusory about it."

Dantzler laughed, said, "Spoken with the passion of a true believer. J. Edgar Hoover would hold you in the highest esteem."

"Yes. But would he let me borrow one of his dresses? That's the real question." Lisa snickered. "I shouldn't make such crass comments on the phone. You never know who might be tuned in."

"Listen, Lisa, the reason I called is to ask for a favor."

"You name it, you got it. I never say no to anyone who saved my life. What do you need?"

"Your help in identifying a possible four-time murderer."

"Sounds intriguing. But why me? Why not the FBI? That's the kind of thing they excel at."

Anticipating Lisa's response, Dantzler was ready with his answer. For the next fifteen minutes, he gave Lisa a detailed rundown of the Eli Whitehouse case, omitting nothing, unraveling his tale from its opening act, his first meeting with Eli in the prison, through to the death of Rocky Stone. He gave her background information on the murders in 1982, and the more recent murders of Colt Rogers and Devon Fraley. He told her about the Whitehouse children, and how Eli's finances would be divided upon his death. He told her about the obits, the "think of Jesus's empty tomb" clue provided by Eli. Dantzler concluded his briefing by stating his reasons why he was now certain Eli was innocent despite evidence indicating otherwise, and why he was convinced a single shooter was responsible for all four deaths.

With one exception, asking Dantzler to repeat a name, Lisa remained silent throughout. She had been taking notes, waiting until Dantzler finished before asking questions. Only after he was silent for several seconds did she did finally speak.

"Okay, call me a dummy, but I don't see where you need my help. Am I missing something, or is there more to the story?"

"The single shooter—he's who I need you to help me nail down."

"All right. Do you have a name for me to work with?"

"I have an alias—Johnny Richards. I need you to tell me who he really is."

"Why are you so certain Johnny Richards is an alias?" Lisa asked.

"Because prior to nineteen-eighty, when he showed up in Lexington, the man didn't exist. There is absolutely no trace of him in any data base, no paper trail whatsoever. Prior to his arrival here, the man was a ghost."

"Not good," Lisa said, adding, "people don't simply change their identity and 'show up' out of nowhere. When they do, it's usually the result of nefarious circumstances."

"Exactly."

"And you are thinking he is in the Witness Protection Program, right?"

"Has to be. And that's where I need your help."

Lisa thought for a few moments. "I'll look into it from my end and see what I can come up with. Also, I have a good buddy in the U.S. Marshal's Service who owes me about a dozen favors. I'll contact him and pick his brain. In all likelihood, he can find out more than I can anyway."

"Thanks. I really appreciate it."

"What else can you tell me about Johnny Richards?" Lisa said.

"Not much, to be honest with you. He moved to Lexington in nineteen-eighty, bought a bar, which he still owns and operates, and was married to Mary Magdalene Richards. She went by Maggie. Her maiden name was Costello. Says he's from Chicago, but judging by his accent, I'd say New York or New Jersey. About six-foot-one, one seventy-five, brown hair, probably in his fifties. Looks younger, though, and my hunch is facial surgery. Beyond that, it's all a blank. You can see why I need your help filling in those blanks."

"I have a few tasks I still need to clear here in Denver," Lisa said. "Shouldn't take more than another day. I'll get to work on it when I'm done. Meantime, I'll go ahead and call Jeff Walker—he's my contact in the Marshal's Service—and see if he can help us. Or at the very least, put us in touch with someone who can."

"Sounds good. And, Lisa, if it's at all possible, I'd like to work fast on this one."

"I understand. You want to put away another bad guy."

"Yeah. But I would also like to see Eli Whitehouse die a free man."

CHAPTER FORTY-EIGHT

Heavy storm clouds floated above the night sky like giant black zeppelins, hovered briefly before moving on, only to be replaced by bigger, darker zeppelins. Off to the east, sporadic flashes of lightning bumped up against the darkness, pushed it aside for an instant, then vanished, leaving the night even darker than before. Thunder rumbled deep and low—Eli's Yahweh must be suffering from a bellyache, Dantzler thought—and the first drops of rain began to tickle the lake behind the house.

Standing on his deck, glass of Pernod in hand, Dantzler felt like a man who had fallen into a pit of quicksand. He wanted to move—needed to move—but forces beyond his control had him at a standstill. Frustrated and trapped, once again at the mercy of others, and there was nothing he could do about it. Just wait, while watching the minutes and hours tick away.

Two days and he had heard nothing from Lisa Kennedy or Jeff Walker. Not a word, not a peep. Only silence. He was disappointed, but more than that, he was surprised. He knew Lisa, knew she was a pro, true to her word. If she gave her promise, it was good as gold. But Lisa had her own job to do and it had to take priority over helping him. He understood that. He also figured if Lisa had spoken with Jeff Walker, she probably didn't impart the same sense of urgency to him that Dantzler had stressed when talking with her. There was also a good chance Walker handed the case off to yet another agent who might make it a high priority, or just as likely, stick it at the bottom of his to-do list.

The Feds tended to move at their own speed, which invariably meant moving at a slower pace than Dantzler cared for. Usually, it was a crawl rather than a slow pace. Of course, if the situation were reversed, if the Feds needed or requested his assistance, they expected to receive it pronto. Urgency was important if they were the ones seeking answers.

Dantzler flopped down into a chair, sipped at the Pernod, closed his eyes, and listened as the rain began to come down harder. The rain, he knew, was here to stay, and would likely last the night. This was fine with him—he loved the rain and had since he was a small boy. Few sounds were more soothing than rain hitting on the roof. A gentle summer breeze suddenly kicked in, bending the grass, jostling the trees, their branches waving like shadowy arms in the darkness.

Nice, he thought. Peaceful. A rare moment of inner quiet, when the detective voices in his head were silent and his thoughts drifted in other directions. There had not been many moments like this lately, not since he . . . Then quick as the next lightning flash, those detective voices smashed through the barrier, shattering the inner quiet, directing his thoughts back to the Eli Whitehouse case. Back to Johnny Richards.

Back to what was proving to be an impossible, frustrating challenge.

Dantzler had spent much of the past two days poring over the female obituaries. He was all but certain Johnny Richards was the shooter, but he had to make sure. He had to be absolutely convinced he had not leapt at the first clue without giving the full weight of his attention to other possibilities. He wanted to be one-thousand percent positive he was going in the right direction. In his line of work, where a person's fate was at stake, there could be no screw-ups. Ever.

You can't blunder on match point.

His research into the female obituaries uncovered three names he deemed possibilities—two Marys and, incredibly, one Salome. As expected, they turned out to be dead ends. Both Marys were long-time widows, in their eighties, neither of whom had so much as a speeding ticket on their record. They were law-abiding, upstanding citizens in every regard.

So was Salome Renee Garrett, who, according to her obit notice, owned and operated a successful florist business, had never been married, and was survived by her life partner, Becky Allen. Like the two Marys, Salome's record was spotless.

His researched had only confirmed what he suspected all along—Mary Magdalene Richards was the clue Eli hinted at.

And Johnny Richards was a four-time murderer.

*****

Initially, Dantzler had been disinclined to keep watch on Richards. He thought it best to wait until he heard back from Lisa Kennedy, or whomever she handed the case off to. See what they could come up with, which might turn out to be something big or nothing worthwhile or helpful at all.

Despite his conviction that Richards was the shooter, at this stage of the game, barring more pertinent information, round-the-clock surveillance was not in the cards. Captain Bird vetoed the plan in no uncertain terms. Bird argued, and rightfully so, there wasn't enough evidence against Richards to justify a full-court press surveillance-wise, which would involve too much manpower and too much expense, neither of which could be spared unless more relevant information came to light.

Still, Dantzler wasn't about to hang around and do nothing, no matter what Captain Bird said. It was bad enough having to wait for the Feds to get him information regarding Richards; that particular stumbling block was beyond his control. But it didn't mean he had to sit idly by while Richards fled the city, or possibly the country. Doing nothing was not an option at this stage of the game.

Dantzler's plan was simple, cheap, and if not completely satisfying, it would at least keep Richards within his sights. He would have someone drop by the tavern and spend a couple of hours inside, to see if Richards was there, to monitor his movements, and to observe the men and women he interacted with. No tape recorder, no camera . . . just old-fashion cop observation. Eyes on the prize.

Two nights ago, Bruce Rawlinson was the observer, arriving at a little past eight and staying until eleven. He reported back that Richards remained seated on a stool at the end of the bar for much of the night, drinking very little, and only rarely interacting with the clientele. On a couple of occasions, he worked the bar while the bartender took a bathroom break. At nine-thirty, he left the bar, went upstairs, and was gone for approximately twenty minutes before returning to his stool.

According to Rawlinson, Richards "acted normal, just like you might expect a tavern owner to act."

Last night, Dantzler dispatched Laurie to the tavern, telling her to stay as long as she felt comfortable. He also recommended she not go alone. A woman as beautiful as Laurie would need help fending off the many drink offers and Big Bubba advances he knew would come her way. For women frequenting a dive like Johnny's Tavern, there was always strength in numbers. Laurie agreed, taking Annie Westrom, her old colleague in the Missing and Exploited Children's Unit, with her. They stayed for almost two hours, each one nursing a beer, while politely declining the dozen or so sent to their booth by hopeful suitors.

Laurie's report differed little from Rawlinson's. Richards spent the entire two hours perched on a stool at the end of the bar, reading a magazine or newspaper. He had one drink—Jim Beam, straight—briefly spoke to a couple of men, nodded at several women, and helped out once when the bartender took a break. All perfectly normal actions for a bar owner, Laurie concluded.

Although nothing noteworthy had been gleaned from the visits, Dantzler was satisfied he had made the correct decision sending his undercover snoops into the bar. Based on their reporting, he was now sure of two things—Johnny Richards was still in town, and he had no inkling that he was on their radar.

CHAPTER FORTY-NINE

Johnny Richards closed *The Daily Racing Form* and ordered another Jim Beam, this one mixed with Diet Coke. It was almost eleven and the bar was packed, mostly with regulars, the same faces he saw virtually every night of the week. One of the regulars, Patty Morris, a twice-divorced mother of three with a strong yin for vodka, walked past on her way to the restroom, pausing long enough to offer condolences for the recent death of his wife. He thanked her with a nod, saying nothing, because there really wasn't anything to say.

Besides, he had more important things to do than engage in conversation with a vodka-soaked floozy like Patty Morris. Far more important things. Like deciding what course of action to take next.

He had spent the past hour alternating his attention between studying the fillies running at Churchill Downs tomorrow and the two fillies seated in the middle booth next to the wall. He circled his picks on tomorrow's card, noting his wager amount next to each one. But as much as he loved handicapping the ponies, the two-legged fillies dominated his thoughts.

The one seated in profile, the one with short blonde hair and cute turned-up nose, he had never seen before. He had a gift for remembering faces, and hers wasn't one he had run across. She was completely unfamiliar to him. Not so with the other filly, the one he could see dead on, the beauty with the long brown hair and classic movie star beauty. Her, he was familiar with. Her, he had seen before. Twice, in fact.

The first time was the night he sat parked on the street across from Dantzler's house. He had gotten a good look at her face when she stepped onto the well-lighted porch. Her unexpected arrival had forced him to alter his plan to kill the detective. She had no way of knowing it, but she had saved her lover's life. A lucky break for Dantzler. He wondered how she would feel about it if she knew.

The second time he saw her was immediately following the gunfight between Rocky Stone and the detectives. She arrived shortly after the shooting stopped, flashed her shield, spoke briefly with Dantzler, then began interviewing witnesses. Very thorough, very professional, very cop-like.

And now here she was, this detective, this beautiful filly, sitting in his bar, acting all cool and remote and nonchalant and superior. Hanging with her gal-pal, two fun-loving chicks out for a few drinks, having a nice, innocent time in the bar.

His bar.

Tonight.

Coincidence? He didn't think so.

They were here for a reason, and he knew what the reason was—to keep an eye on him. They had been sent by Dantzler to monitor his comings and goings. To keep him within grabbing distance.

Okay, he thought, so now we all know the score. You have me in your sights. No big deal . . . I've been there before.

He grinned.

Let the games begin.

*****

An hour after the two lady cops departed, Richards climbed the stairs to the small apartment above the bar, opened the safe, and began filling a duffel bag with stacks of cash. Close to a million dollars, all in hundred dollar bills. Emergency funds he had accumulated over the years. Get away money.

After the bag was filled and zipped shut, he sat at the wooden table and assessed his situation. He did this without any sense of panic or fear. Those two emotions simply did not exist within him, and never had. From the very start of his career as a killer, when he was still a teen, he had earned a reputation for being cool, calm, and totally in control of his emotions. Sam Giancana once famously called him "the original Ice Man."

If the men he had worked for and against in those bloody days hadn't scared him, a cop like Jack Dantzler sure wasn't about to.

But Dantzler was, he knew, a damn good cop. One of those bulldog types who doesn't know the meaning of the word quit. Who keeps digging until he gets what he wants. No, he thought, Dantzler might not be a man to fear, but he was a man to be respected.

Giving this much thought to a cop, even one with Dantzler's skills and reputation, was out of character for him. He was not a man given to introspection or reflection or self-recrimination. He didn't second-guess himself, either for actions taken or not taken. Beating yourself up served no useful purpose; it only made you weak. And being weak made you vulnerable. Being vulnerable got you killed.

He had never been weak, nor was he a whiner. Whatever happens, happens. He had always understood and accepted this. And regardless of the outcome, you deal with it like a man. Like a *mensch*, the great Meyer Lansky used to say. Lansky also said life comes at you like a Major League fastball. Sometimes you make good contact and bang out a hit. Other times it sails past and you strikeout. You don't gloat when you succeed, you don't cry when you fail. With either outcome you move on.

Richards saw himself as a man with a violent past and a man with no past. Such a dichotomy made him prey on two fronts—those who knew and those, like Dantzler, who sought to know. Falling victim to one meant death, the other meant prison. Neither option was acceptable.

Fully aware that the day might arrive when he would find himself in someone's cross hairs, he had long ago mapped out an escape plan. First, he had to put together a large amount of cash; any escape plan required sufficient funds. He had the money, more than enough, in fact, to get safely out of the country. To elude the predators who aimed to bring him down. With this much cash, he had plenty of options to choose from. Perhaps he would go to Costa Rica or Mexico and buy a small house or villa. Some place warm, close to the ocean.

Second, he would have to destroy the bar, a most regrettable but necessary requirement. He couldn't risk leaving anything behind, not a single note, not an inventory entry, not a trace or shred of anything the authorities could use as evidence against him. Or as a method of locating him. Everything had to vanish completely.

So, in 1986, he paid an old acquaintance, a legendary New Jersey arsonist, to hotwire the entire building. All Richards had to do was flip a single switch, leave the premises, and fifteen minutes later the bar would be swallowed up in flames. Within a matter of minutes, seconds really, the structure—and in all probability much of Meadowthorpe Shopping Center—would be reduced to a pile of ashes.

Third, he had purchased a stolen VW Jetta he kept parked in a small garage behind the bar. If the occasion arose when he needed to make a quick departure, the Jetta would be his getaway vehicle. No one knew the car was in the garage, which he always kept locked. And if the cops did discover the car at some later point, they would have no way of knowing it belonged to him.

If Dantzler had ordered round-the-clock surveillance on him, the cops would be focused on the Black Lexus parked out front. As long as the car was there, the cops would assume he was spending the night in the upstairs apartment. Meanwhile, he would wait a couple of hours, giving the cops enough time to become tired, sleepy, and less alert, and then he would slip out through the back entrance, get into the Jetta, and quietly drive away.

His destination would be Mason-Headley Road on the other side of town. There, buried beneath overhanging trees and concealed behind high rows of bushes, virtually hidden from view, sat a small white cottage. The structure, less than a thousand square feet total, consisted of one bedroom, kitchen, bathroom, and den. It was as unassuming as a house could be. But its location, invisibility, and isolation more than made up for its lack of size and space. A person could drive down Mason-Headley a hundred times and never notice the cottage was there. To see the cottage, the driver had to practically be looking for it.

Isolation was the key; that was the primary reason Richards purchased the cottage in the first place. Being the last house in a long stretch of houses was another selling point. To the left of the cottage was a narrow country road leading to God knows where. To the right, almost three-hundred yards away, sat a much larger house, blocked from view by a wall of oak trees. The distance and trees provided a barrier between him and overly friendly neighbors who might feel compelled to act neighborly. This wasn't likely to happen. Only on rare occasions did those neighbors—or anyone for that matter—ever see him at the cottage.

No living human being was aware that Johnny Richards owned this cottage. Even his beloved wife Maggie hadn't known. It was the one secret he kept from her, the one thing about him she didn't know. The late Colt Rogers was the sole person possessing this knowledge, and that was only because he helped facilitate the deal. Nothing connected Richards to the cottage. The paperwork, the tax records, the deed, all listed the owner as Saul Bergman, a forty-three-year-old independent jewelry dealer from Brooklyn. However, those records failed to show one crucial fact: Bergman was no longer around to fence his stolen gems, having been killed by Richards in the early '70s.

Bergman, a degenerate gambler, owed a huge sum of money to a certain powerful individual, a man disinclined to tolerate an unlucky bum who couldn't pay his debt. When sternly reminded of his obligation, Bergman made the mistake of saying if anyone harmed him or threatened to harm him in any manner, he would go straight to the authorities. He boasted that he had his share of friends in high places, and that he wouldn't hesitate to contact them if necessary. Fatal mistake on Saul's part.

One day later, Richards put a bullet in Bergman's head. He then took the body to a construction site, where Bergman was laid to rest beneath two tons of freshly poured cement. Before dumping the body into the pit, Richards took Bergman's driver's license and Social Security card on the off-chance that at some later time they might come in handy. And they had.

Here, in Lexington, when it came time to buy the cottage. With Colt Rogers shepherding the paperwork, Richards was able to purchase the cottage without anyone knowing he was the true owner. From all perspectives, legal or otherwise, the property belonged to Saul Bergman. And so long as Richards paid the taxes, no one would be the wiser.

Richards grabbed the duffel bag, turned off all lights, and went down into the bar. He walked to the front door and looked out at the parking lot. Empty, except for his Lexus. That didn't mean the cops weren't watching; they could be anywhere. But he doubted they were. At this point, it was his belief that the cops saw him as *a* suspect, not *the* suspect. He was all but certain Eli hadn't given him up; nor did he believe Dantzler had uncovered enough solid evidence to make him the primary target of the investigation. Still, he wasn't about to take unnecessary chances.

He wouldn't torch the bar—not tonight, anyway—but he would drive the Jetta to his place off Mason-Headley. There, he would make a phone call to an old friend in Las Vegas and schedule a time for him to send his private plane to Lexington. Any phone call was, he knew, extremely dangerous, regardless of how much he trusted the person receiving the call. Friends don't always remain friends. But he had no choice. It was his only safe way out.

Once those details were worked out, he would return to running the bar as usual. He would offer no hint that he was aware of being in Dantzler's crosshairs, or that he was, in fact, one step ahead of the detective. When the arrival time for the plane was set, when he was assured of safe passage, he would flip the switch, thus reducing the bar and the shopping center to a pile of ashes in a matter of seconds.

And then he would vanish forever.

CHAPTER FIFTY

By mid-morning the rain was a distant, soggy memory. The sun was steadily climbing in the heavens, its rays pouring down like heated honey. By the middle of the afternoon, the temperature would be in the 90s. A scorcher by any standards.

Dantzler still hadn't heard from Lisa Kennedy or anyone else at the Justice Department, so he decided to swing by the hospital and see how Scott was doing. Having not visited Scott for three days, he felt guilty for being negligent. There had been daily updates from Milt and Captain Bird, but getting second-hand reports didn't absolve him of his neglect. As Scott's immediate superior, Dantzler should have checked in at least once a day.

Dantzler knocked on the door, opened it, and peeked in. Scott was sitting up in the bed, talking to two young women. The room looked like it had been decorated for a kid's birthday party. Balloons hugged the ceiling like a multi-colored rainbow, heart-shaped balloons with "Get Well Soon" written on them were tied to both ends of the bed, and a giant teddy bear rested comfortably in a chair beneath the window. What must have been seventy five cards of all shapes, sizes, and colors stood like a legion of onlookers strategically placed around the room.

Seeing Dantzler, Scott's face broke into a huge grin. "Hey, Detective Dantzler, how's it going?" Scott said, waving his boss in.

"Everything is cool. The better question is, how are you doing, Scott?"

"Being released tomorrow. So I'm feeling good."

"That's terrific news."

"Finally get some good food. Can't wait for Mom's cooking."

"Tired of Jell-O, right?"

"Right."

The woman closest to Scott punched him on his good shoulder. "What are we? Invisible?"

"Oh, yeah, sorry," Scott said. "Detective Dantzler, this is my sister, Amy. And my girlfriend, Molly."

"Pleased to meet you," Dantzler said, nodding at the two women. He looked at Molly, then at Scott. "Didn't know you had a girlfriend, Scott. Good for you. But I have to tell you, she's way out of your league."

"Don't I know it," Scott said, taking Molly's hand. "I'm gonna try to hang onto her, even if she is too good for me."

"You'd better keep her, loser brother," Amy said, adding, "because you'll never find another one like her."

Following Amy's pronouncement, no one seemed to know what to say next. Molly blushed, Amy appeared to be either annoyed or amused—Dantzler couldn't decide—and Scott had the look of a man who had uttered something he now wished he'd kept to himself. Dantzler wanted to laugh but found the strength to restrain himself. He didn't want to embarrass Scott or the women, nor did he want to exacerbate what had obviously become an awkward moment.

Finally, Scott broke the silence, saying, "What about Eric? How is he holding up?"

"Eric's good," Dantzler answered. "You needn't worry about him."

"He saved my life, didn't he?"

"Eric and Milt get the credit. They're your guardian angels."

Scott worked his right hand beneath the cast on his left shoulder and began digging at an itch, grimacing slightly as he did. "Will I still have my job when I get healthy?"

"You mean, will you still be on the force?"

"No. Will I remain on the Homicide unit?"

"Is that what you want?"

"More than anything. It's all I've ever wanted."

"Then, sure, you stay with us. But that's not something you need to worry about right now. You need to concentrate on getting well."

"I was just thinking, getting shot, well, you know . . . it might mark me as a loser, a failure."

"You were wounded in the line of duty, Scott. You were doing your job. People in our business get shot sometimes. Unfortunately, that possibility goes with the territory. Thank God, you survived. You came through it okay. When you get healthy enough to come back, you'll work the desk until the doctors clear you for field duty. Once they do, you'll be back out with us, trying to put the bad guys away."

Scott nodded but didn't say anything.

"Just be forewarned, Scott," Dantzler said, moving toward the door. "Having been wounded is not going to shield you against the slings and arrows Milt will toss your way. Knowing him, he'll probably ride you even harder."

"Wouldn't have it any other way," Scott said, grinning.

*****

Dantzler went from the hospital to the Tennis Center, spending an hour working out on the treadmill, and another hour helping Alice Crawford perfect her serve. It was, he knew, a hopeless cause. But Alice had convinced herself that at age forty-one, with Dantzler's help, she could be the next Martina Navratilova. He didn't have the heart to tell her tennis really wasn't her game.

After concluding his futile efforts with Alice, he showered, dressed, and went to Rafferty's, where he had soup and a salad. Then he headed straight to the office for a one o'clock meeting with Captain Bird. Dantzler had requested the meeting for the purpose of bringing Bird up to date on the case, what he wanted to do, and how best to go about doing it. However, when Dantzler arrived at the office, he was informed that Captain Bird had been summoned to a meeting with Mayor Elizabeth Anderson. Dantzler was only too happy to have escaped an invitation to that little *tete a tete*. The mayor was one tough, no-nonsense go-getter. A pit bull in a skirt was the closest analogy Dantzler could come up with. Having a sit-down with her, especially one she requested, was rarely a pleasant experience.

At three-thirty, Dantzler was alone in the office when his cell phone buzzed. He flipped it open, said, "Detective Dantzler."

"Detective, this is Jeff Walker. I'm with the Department of Justice."

"Lisa told me you might be getting in touch with me. I appreciate the call."

"Sorry it took so long, but . . . it's kinda busy around here these days."

"No problem. Like I said, I appreciate you taking the time to talk to me."

"So . . . you want to know about Johnny Richards, right?"

"Yeah."

"Better get a pen and some paper, Detective. This could take a while."

CHAPTER FIFTY-ONE

Dantzler sat at the head of the table in the War Room, a half-dozen crumpled yellow pages torn from a legal pad spread out in front of him. Laurie and Eric sat to his left, Milt to his right. Captain Bird leaned against the wall at the far end of the room.

They all waited patiently as Dantzler searched through the pages, which he had numbered, getting them in order. Satisfied with his arrangement, he looked around the room, took a deep breath, and began reading.

"Johnny Richards was born Gianni Rinetti in Palermo, Sicily, in nineteen fifty-eight, the son of Enzio and Gabriella Rinetti. Enzio, a physician, died of a heart attack at age thirty-five, leaving twenty-year-old Gaby to take care of their infant son. Beautiful and highly ambitious, Gaby longed to leave Italy and move to Brooklyn, where many of her family members were living. She wanted the good life for her and her son. Gaby's desire was for him to have the same opportunities her relatives had. To experience the most appealing of all enticements—the Great American Dream.

"Obviously, she needed money in order to cross the big pond," he continued. "To achieve her goal meant reaching out to one of her relatives in America, which she did. An uncle."

Dantzler paused, then said, "Carlo Gambino."

"Holy shit," Milt said. "*The* Carlo Gambino? Head of the Gambino Crime Family?"

"He was more than simply head of the family, Milt," Dantzler pointed out. "He was *Capo Di Tutti Capi*, boss of all bosses. Head of The Commission. Which, as everyone knows, is made up of the heads of New York's five crime families."

"Lucky Luciano was the genius who created The Commission back in the thirties," Milt pointed out. "He's the guy who put the 'organized' in organized crime."

"Man, this is straight out of *The Godfather*," Eric noted. "The only thing missing is the damn theme music. So . . . how does Johnny Richards, or Gianni whatever, fit into this?"

"Don Carlo loved Gianni like one of his own children," Dantzler read from his notes. "He doted on the boy, lavished him with expensive gifts, clothes, and toys. Nothing was too good or too costly for little Gianni. Not surprisingly, Gianni, as he grew older, was fiercely loyal to the old man. And as we all know, in Mafia-land, loyalty and respect mean more than anything.

"At some point, Carlo, recognizing Gianni possessed exceptional skills and intelligence, began to view the kid as a potential successor. He undertook the process of grooming the boy for the top spot, introducing him to the heads of other families, letting him sit in on meetings, pointing out potential rivals or threats, giving him Cosa Nostra history lessons . . . that sort of stuff."

Dantzler opened a bottle of water and took a long drink before continuing. "No one knows for sure when or under what circumstances Rinetti made his first hit, but the guess is he was around fourteen or fifteen. What is known for sure is that within the next three or four years he became Gambino's top trigger man. If the old man needed a rival eliminated, the job was given to Gianni. Also, Gambino began to loan Gianni out to other families—for a hefty fee, of course."

"Paid assassin," Laurie said. "What a nice way to spend your teenage years."

"Ah, come on, Laurie," Milt said, chuckling. "We want our young people to show initiative, to earn a few bucks along the way. So he murdered people rather than cut grass or deliver newspapers. That doesn't make him a bad person."

"Shut up, Milt," Laurie snapped. She looked at Dantzler. "Continue, please."

"One of Gianni's most celebrated hits occurred in nineteen seventy-four," Dantzler said. "The victim was Carmine 'Mimi' Scalino, a feared and respected soldier in the Colombo Family. Scalino was notorious for being loud, arrogant, and obnoxious when he got drunk, which he was when he spotted Gambino at a popular Italian restaurant. Scalino approached Gambino and began to insult him in front of others. Gianni made a move to retaliate, but Gambino, calm and dignified as always, stopped him, never uttering that first word. Despite being embarrassed and disrespected in public, Gambino quietly walked out of the restaurant. I'm sure you can guess where this tale is headed. Not long after the incident, Scalino's bullet-riddled body was found at Otto's Social Club in Brooklyn encased in the cement floor. It was common knowledge that Gianni made Scalino pay for disrespecting Gambino.

"In June, nineteen seventy-six, Gianni married Maggie Costello," Dantzler said. "She was a cousin to Frank Costello, another Luciano protégé, and one of Gambino's oldest pals. But according to Jeff Walker, my Justice Department source, Maggie was absolutely clean, wanting nothing whatsoever to do with Mob life. To her, there was nothing glamorous or exciting about it, regardless of how the movies and novels portrayed it. She had seen too many friends and family members either sent to prison or die an early, violent death, neither of which was an outcome she wanted for her husband. She pleaded with Gianni to walk away from the business, and although he was deeply in love with her, he wasn't about to abandon Don Carlo.

"Circumstances changed when Gambino died in October, nineteen seventy-six. All of a sudden, stability was gone, replaced by jealousy and in-fighting. Before his death, Gambino chose his cousin, Paul 'Big Paulie' Castellano, as his successor, a decision that didn't sit well with the family's other underboss, Neil Dellacroce. The Dellacroce followers included familiar names like John Gotti and Salvatore 'Sammy the Bull' Gravano, tough street-wise thugs who viewed Castellano as soft and prissy. They didn't think 'Big Paulie' had earned the right to be Boss of Bosses. He had neither their support nor their respect. As a result, his days were numbered almost from the beginning of his reign as Don. A few years later, after Dellacroce had died, Castellano was gunned down in front of a New York steak house."

"Yeah, I remember that," Milt said. "Sparks Steak House, if I recall correctly. Gotti gave the order, then he and Sammy 'the Bull' sat in a car a block or so away and watched it happen."

Dantzler continued, "With his benefactor dead, and knowing too many power-hungry rivals stood between him and the top spot, Gianni heeded his wife's pleas and left the Gambino family. What he didn't do, though, was stop killing. For the next three years, he was essentially a gun for hire. He is thought to have done wet work for crime families in Las Vegas, Philadelphia, Los Angeles, and New Orleans. And that's a conservative guess. In truth, there were likely many others the Justice Department can't confirm."

"Okay, okay, Jack, enough with Richards's past history," Bird said, still leaning against the wall. "We all know the guy was a Mob hit man. Fast forward to how he got to Lexington."

Dantzler nodded, said, "Sometime late in nineteen seventy-eight an Organized Crime Unit brought Gianni in for the purpose of letting him hear a taped conversation between two West Coast crime bosses. On the tape, one of the bosses commented that a half-million dollar hit had been put out on Gianni and his wife. The reason for the hit is unclear, but Walker suspects it was because Gianni whacked a target the bosses hadn't singled out for elimination. Now, in the world of organized crime, wives and family members are considered off-limits. That's a crucial part of the code. Appalled by this serious breach of ethics, Gianni quickly agreed to testify against both bosses in exchange for being placed in the Witness Protection Program. The Feds, naturally, were only too happy to make the deal. However, when they began to push Gianni for information relating to the Gambino Crime Family, he balked. He had only marginal respect for Castellano, and no respect at all for Gotti, who Gianni knew would eventually muscle his way to the top spot. But there was no way in hell he was ever going to rat against his old family, no matter how much the Feds upped the ante. So, after giving information against the two West Coast bosses, he told the Feds to shove the Witness Protection Program up their ass, moved to Lexington with his beloved Maggie, changed his name and facial looks, bought the tavern, and lived happily ever after."

"That's a pretty ballsy thing to do," Milt said. "To just walk away from federal protection and practically live out in the open. He had to know something the Feds didn't know. He had to have protection from somewhere."

Dantzler stood and stretched his legs. After taking another sip of water, he returned to his seat and said, "Jeff Walker said the same thing. He suspects the hit on Richards was likely taken off because his wife had been included in the original deal. All bosses saw that as a cardinal sin."

"Still, though, a guy like Richards, a modern-day John Wesley Hardin, had to keep looking over his shoulder," Milt said. "I don't care how much he changed his looks. Guy with a reputation like his, there is always some young punk looking to make a name for himself. I can't imagine Richards living a peaceful life."

"Peaceful or not, he's still alive," Dantzler said. "And he's guilty of these four murders. That's the only thing that matters to us."

"Okay, Jack," Bird said, pushing away from the wall. "Where do we go from here?"

"We take all this to a judge and get search warrants for Richards's house, the tavern, and his vehicle. Shouldn't be difficult getting a warrant, given what we know about him. Then we bring him in for questioning. We gather evidence and start building a case against him."

"Does he have *any* protection from the Feds?" Eric asked.

"No," Dantzler answered." And even if he did, the protection doesn't cover crimes he committed here."

"Get those notes typed in readable form and bring them to me," Bird ordered. "I'll take them to Judge Tucker. She'll sign anything I put in front of her."

"Shouldn't we go grab Richards now?" Eric said.

Dantzler shook his head, said, "No. Let's wait for the search warrants. I want to do everything by the book. We cannot screw this up."

"And keep in mind who we're dealing with," Bird added. "This ain't Rocky Stone. This is a cold-blooded assassin who knows every trick in the book. He will put you down without blinking an eye."

CHAPTER FIFTY-TWO

At a little past noon, search warrants in hand, Dantzler gathered his troops in the War Room. He hadn't eaten since yesterday, and dark circles ringed his eyes, but he was wired to the max. Anticipation and excitement pulsed through his body like electric currents, elevating his energy to off-the-chart levels. He always felt charged when a mystery was about to be solved, but rarely had he experienced this kind of excitement. This was something different.

Not wanting to sound supersonic, he took a slow, deep breath, and said, "Milt and Eric will go to Richards's house. If—"

"Take as much back-up as you need," Captain Bird interrupted. "SWAT is on alert, if you want to use them. That's your call, Milt. But make no mistake about it—all of you. I do not want another one of my detectives getting shot. That's an order."

Dantzler waited until he was certain Bird had finished before continuing. "Laurie and I will go to the tavern. This time of day, that's most likely where Richards will be. We'll have back-up, but I want them out of sight. Laurie and I will go in alone. I don't want to spook Richards. We'll tell him—"

"Hell, Jack, you're gonna serve the guy with a search warrant," Eric noted. "You don't think that'll spook him?"

"If it does, it does," Dantzler conceded. "How he chooses to play it is up to him. If he cooperates, great. If not, we don't play nice."

"You're nuts if you think he's gonna cooperate," Milt said. "A guy as wary as Richards will go on the offensive in about two seconds. You need to go in barking, not asking."

"Jack, I have to agree with Milt on this," Bird said. "I think the smart play is to go in with back-up. A show of force is not necessarily a bad thing."

"We're not there to arrest the guy, Rich," Dantzler argued. "At this stage, we don't have enough hard evidence to arrest him. We're only there to talk to him and to search the premises. Unless he fails to cooperate, I see no need to go all Atilla the Hun on him."

"Play it the way you feel most comfortable," Bird said. "Just don't take any unnecessary chances. That's all I'm saying. And keep in mind who we're dealing with. The guy was Carlo Gambino's right-hand man. He's bound to have a few deadly tricks up his sleeve."

*****

Dantzler and Laurie drove away from downtown, in the direction of Meadowthorpe Shopping Center, with three police cruisers tailing close behind. Turning right off Leestown Road, Dantzler led the procession to a service station, parked, got out of the car, and met with the six uniformed officers. He ordered two officers to position themselves at each end of the shopping center, two stationed in the front parking lot, and two in the alley behind the tavern. After giving the six men a detailed description of Johnny Richards, he and Laurie got back in the Forester and drove to the tavern.

"That's Richards's Lexus," Laurie said, pointing. "Means he's here."

"Stay alert," Dantzler warned, although he knew the warning was not necessary. "And never take your eyes off Richards. If anything looks even the least bit hinky, do what you have to do. Don't let him shoot first. He won't miss."

*****

Inside the tavern, Sally, the big-bosom bartender, was conversing with two male customers standing at the end of the bar where Richards normally sat. Judging by the intense look on her face, and the interest shown by the two men, the tone of the conversation was serious. As Dantzler moved closer to the trio, he thought he detected tears in Sally's eyes.

When Sally looked up and saw Dantzler, she immediately came out from behind the bar, threw up her hands, and began to weep openly. "I don't know where Johnny is. He's not here, and he's not at his house. Something bad must have happened to him."

Dantzler gently took her by the arm and led her to a chair. He sat across from her, while Laurie remained standing behind him.

"Isn't that Richards's Lexus in the parking lot?" Dantzler asked.

"It is," Sally said, sobbing.

"Does Richards have a second vehicle?"

"Not anymore. He had a Mazda, but he sold it when Maggie died."

"You're positive he sold it?"

Sally nodded. "Yes. To my nephew Eddie. Eddie Clayton."

Dantzler said, "When was the last time you saw Richards?"

"Two nights ago." Sally pointed at Laurie. "The night she was in here."

"Do you have a key to the upstairs apartment?"

"Yes. But he's not up there. I've checked." She wiped her eyes with the front of her apron. "I'm not related to Johnny, but am I allowed to file a missing persons report? If so, you can get a real search underway."

Dantzler looked up at Laurie. "Call the officers and have them meet in the parking lot. Tell them to go ahead and search the vehicle. Then phone Milt and let him know what Sally has told us. Have him make sure Richards is not in the house. Tell him—"

"He's not at his house," Sally insisted. "I know, because I went by there last night and again this morning."

"The house on Summershade?"

"Yes."

"Do you have a key to the house?" Dantzler said.

"No. But I knocked until my knuckles bled. And I looked in all the windows. He's not there."

Dantzler dug into his coat pocket and pulled out two envelopes. "These are search warrants. One for the bar and upstairs apartment, one for the Lexus. Given the circumstances and the fact you've asked us to file a missing persons report, I don't need these warrants to search the premises. However, for the sake of protocol, I'm giving them to you anyway."

"Search warrants?" Sally said, taking the two envelopes from Dantzler. "Why on earth do you need search warrants? Johnny's not here. I already told you he's missing."

"I can't discuss the details, Sally," Dantzler said. "What I can share with you is that we're in the middle of an investigation involving Johnny Richards. That's why we need to search the bar, apartment, and car."

Sally's confusion was quickly replaced by anger. Her face reddened and her eyes welled with a new wave of tears. Kicking the stool, she stood and aimed a finger at Dantzler.

"You have no cause to harass Johnny," she screamed. "He has done nothing wrong. Johnny Richards is the nicest, kindest gentleman I have ever known."

"Then he has nothing to worry about," Dantzler said, not wanting to extend the argument. "Let us do our thing and we'll be out of here."

"Will you at least put out a missing persons report?" Sally said, bottom lip trembling. "Can you do that for me?"

"Yes."

Dantzler was about to say something to Laurie when Craig McKinley, one of the uniformed officers, came into the bar.

"We found something of interest in the vehicle, sir," McKinley said.

"In the trunk, wrapped in a plastic bag. A forty-four."

"Same caliber the killer used to take out Colt Rogers," Laurie said.

"Bingo." Dantzler said. Then to McKinley, "Log the weapon and take it to ballistics. Tell them to match it against the bullet that killed Colt Rogers. And tell them I want the results yesterday."

"You got it," McKinley said, turning and heading for the door.

Dantzler's cell phone chirped. The caller was Captain Bird. "Yeah, Rich, what's up?"

"You and Laurie need to get to TAC Air ASAP," Bird said. "There's something here you need to see."

"Can't it wait, Rich? We're about ready to begin searching the bar and apartment."

"Forget that for the time being. What I have to show you is far more interesting."

CHAPTER FIFTY-THREE

Johnny Richards's body lay on its side in the Jetta trunk. His hands were tied behind him, his legs bound at the ankle. There was a single bullet entry to the back of his head.

Just like those two kids in the barn, Dantzler thought to himself. *What goes around, comes around. Maybe there was justice after all.*

"What did Joe Louis say?" Bird said. "You can run but you can't hide. Looks like the Brown Bomber was right."

"Who found the body?" Dantzler asked.

"Couple of executive types arrived back from a business meeting in Houston," Bird answered. "Their car was parked next to this piece of shit Jetta. One of the guys noticed blood pooled beneath the trunk. He reported it to the lady at the front desk. She phoned us. Officers Bradley and Cline were first on the scene. They popped the trunk, found Johnny-boy."

"Who do you think did this?" Laurie said.

"Believe me, we'll never know the answer to that one," Bird answered. "And you know what? I don't give a shit. This murder has been on hold for more than thirty years. It was destined to happen sooner or later. Somebody got even, that's all I can tell you. Old debts were collected. And with the enemies Richards made over the years, the crowd he ran with, there's no way we'll ever know who pulled the trigger."

"But Richards was a pro," Laurie reminded. "He was clever enough to stay alive all these years despite having a target pinned on him. I can't help but wonder how he ended up like this. I mean, who could have outsmarted him?"

"Someone he trusted," Dantzler said. "Someone with a private plane. Richards contacted the person, asked him to fly in and pick him up. Once the plane showed up, Richards would have instructed the man to fly him wherever he felt safe enough to live. But . . . he got a bullet rather than a boarding pass."

"How did the shooter get Richards into the car?" Laurie asked.

"Easy," Dantzler replied. "He tells Richards the plane needs to be refueled, or he needs to grab a bite to eat. Something believable. Richards agrees. Remember, he trusts this person. At some point, the guy pulls a gun on Richards, orders him to drive to some deserted place, ties him up, puts him in the trunk, and shoots him. He drives back here, parks, gets in his plane, and flies home. Execution accomplished."

"The moral of this lesson is be careful who you trust," Bird said, adding, "but whoever the shooter was, he has my sincerest thanks."

Laurie said, "If ballistics can match the forty-four we found in Richards's Lexus with the slug that killed Colt Rogers, then that should bring down the curtain on at least one of these last two murders."

"You found a forty-four?" Bird said. "It'll match. You can take that to the bank."

Dantzler stepped away from Laurie and Bird, took out his cell phone, and punched in Kirk Foster's number. Kirk answered immediately.

"Call your boss and have him signed the proper papers," Dantzler said. "It's time to bring Eli home."

After Dantzler put his phone away, Bird approached him, a stern look on his face. "You're jumping ahead of yourself, aren't you, Jack? Way I see it we only solved the Rogers murder. That's it. We can't be certain Richards killed Devon Fraley, although there is a high probability he did. But nothing has changed regarding Eli. His prints are still on the gun used to commit those murders in 'eighty-two. The bottom line is, we don't have the answers to who killed those two kids in the barn, answers we need in order to prove Eli's innocence."

"No. But I know where those answers are."

CHAPTER FIFTY-FOUR

Dusk. To the west, the sun dipped deeper into the horizon. In a matter of minutes, it would disappear completely. The evening sky hung low over the city like a protective blanket. The air was still, as though the Earth and everything on it had ceased to breathe. The only sound came from a regal robin proudly perched on an overhead wire.

Dantzler cut the engine and climbed out of his car. The adrenaline rush that fueled his energy had long since passed, leaving him weary to the bone, hungry, and badly in need of sleep. But none of this mattered now. This was, he knew, the final step on a journey that began when a dying man proclaimed his innocence in a prison gymnasium.

Slowly, he pushed away from the car and walked toward the duplex.

Up those steps, behind the door, was where he would uncover the truth. In there, the secrets would be revealed. Here, at last, he would find answers that had eluded him. Who killed those two kids in 1982, why they were killed, how the killer managed to get Eli's gun, and why an innocent man would quietly agree to spend his life in prison.

Those answers would come from the lonely, tortured soul who for three decades had lived in his own private hell.

Tommy Whitehouse.

Tommy opened the door before Dantzler stepped onto the porch. He was dressed in cut-off jeans, tank top, and white sneakers. He held a plastic cup in his left hand. After motioning Dantzler into the house, Tommy closed the door, moved in front of Dantzler, and held up the cup.

"Dr. Pepper," he said, sitting. "Straight. You can check it if you like."

Dantzler sat in the chair across from Tommy. "Your father is being released from prison, Tommy. He should be home sometime tomorrow."

"Rachel called thirty minutes ago. She and Kirk are already on their way to the prison. They're flying down in a private jet. She hopes to have Eli home by midnight." He swallowed hard and looked away. "She asked me to go with them, but . . ."

"I'm sure your father will be thrilled to see you," Dantzler said.

"I don't know about that."

Dantzler leaned forward. "I need the truth, Tommy. All of it."

"Truth? About what?"

"About what happened in nineteen eighty-two."

"What makes you think I know anything about what happened?"

"Come on, Tommy. You've had to keep dark secrets bottled up inside you for too long now. It's time to let go of those secrets and come clean about what happened. About everything."

"I don't know what you're insinuating, Detective Dantzler. Or why you think I have the answers."

"Because of the way you changed, the drinking, your self-imposed estrangement from your father. None of it happened by accident or without a good reason. Something catastrophic triggered it. Also, when we first met, you said something very interesting. You said, 'my father is innocent, Detective Dantzler. That much you can be sure of.' Now—"

"I'm sure Rachel said the same thing,"

"Yes, she did. But for her, it was more hope than anything. Not with you. When you said those words to me, you were stating a hard, cold fact."

Tommy set his cup down, leaned back, and washed his face with his hands. After almost a minute of silence, he finally said, "I can't tell you what I know. And I wish you would go away and leave me and my family alone. If you persist in this quest, people are going to get hurt."

"Johnny Richards is dead," Dantzler said. "His body was found in the trunk of his car about an hour ago. He's no longer a threat to you or your family."

Tommy nodded but remained silent.

"I suspect Richards killed those two kids in 'eighty-two," Dantzler continued. "But I can't know for sure unless you tell me what happened. You have to fill in the missing pieces."

"If I do, if I tell you everything, no one in my family will ever speak to me again." Tears dripped from Tommy's eyes. "And they would have every right to hate me. For the pain and suffering I caused them."

"I don't think so. In fact, I'd say you've got it all wrong."

"How could they forgive me when I can't forgive myself?"

"The truth, Tommy. How was Richards able to orchestrate all of this?"

Tommy took a drink from the cup and put it down. "I had been shooting some hoops at the YMCA gym. I was in the locker room getting dressed when I heard these two guys talking. We were the only three people in there at the time. I could see them in a mirror, but they couldn't see me. Anyway, one of the men, not Richards, started telling Richards that if he didn't cooperate and testify, he could get into a lot of trouble. The man said to Richards, 'How many men have you killed? Thirty? Forty? Well, we're willing to look the other way if you'll testify against the Gambino family. This offer comes from high up.' Richards laughed and said something like, 'You can take your offer back to where it came from and tell your boss I said no deal. Never.' It was obvious Richards wasn't at all afraid of the other man."

"Did you by any chance get the second man's name?"

"No."

"Ever see him again?"

"No."

"Okay, what happened next?"

"The other man takes off, leaving only me and Richards in the locker room. I'm more than a little nervous after hearing all the stuff about him killing forty people, so I want to get out of there pronto. But as I started for the door, I accidently dropped my basketball. I grabbed the ball and made a beeline for the door when I hear Richards saying, 'Come here, kid. Now!' I froze like a statue. I wanted to run but couldn't move at all. It's pretty scary seeing a man who has killed forty people coming toward you."

"What did Richards do?"

"Nothing. He asked me what I heard. Naturally, I told him I didn't hear anything. Then he asked me what my name was and where I lived. I told him. After I gave him the information, he patted me on the shoulder and told me to get lost."

"Do you think he believed you when you told him you didn't hear anything?" Dantzler asked.

"At the time I wasn't sure. Nor did I care. I only wanted out of the locker room. But given what subsequently happened, he obviously didn't believe me. Or maybe he simply wasn't willing to take a chance either way."

"What did happen next?"

"A couple of days later, I'm walking home after baseball practice and this car pulls up next to me. It's Richards. He orders me into the car, says we need to talk about a few things. I get in, thinking we'll talk right there in front of the baseball field, where I felt fairly safe. But he takes off. Now I'm scared shitless, thinking maybe I'm gonna be victim forty-one. We drive down to the University of Kentucky campus, to the football stadium, where he parks in a vacant lot. Then he tells me he's been doing a lot of research, and that he knows everything about me and my family. I listen, don't say a word, still unsure if I'm going to live or die. Next, he wanted to know if my father owned any weapons. I told him Eli had a Winchester rifle and a twenty-two pistol. He asked if Eli had used the twenty-two recently. I told him I thought he had. He then told me to get the twenty-two, and to make sure to not touch the handle when I picked it up. He said I had until the next day to get the gun and give it to him. He also said if I didn't get the gun, or if I told anyone about this meeting, bodies would fall. After that, he took me back to the practice field."

"So you got the gun out of the safe," Dantzler said. "Did you meet Richards the next day?"

"Yes. Behind Turfland Mall."

"What did Richards tell you?"

"He told me that no matter what happened in the next few days I had better keep my mouth shut. He said only two people in the world know about any of this, and if I uttered a single word implicating him he would methodically murder every member of my family, beginning with little Rachel. He added that they would suffer in such a horrible way that they would plead with him to finish them off. I had no choice but to believe him and to do what he said."

Tommy's eyes glazed over with tears. He hung his head, saying nothing for more than a minute. When he finally lifted his head tears streamed down his cheeks.

"Three days later, two boys were dead and my father had been arrested for murder. And I could only watch, couldn't speak up, even though I knew the truth. I was afraid, a coward. All these years . . . how could my family not hate me for what I allowed to happen?"

"You were a terrified kid trapped in an impossible situation." Dantzler said, putting a hand on Tommy's shoulder. "And believe me, Tommy. Johnny Richards would have done exactly what he said he would do had you pointed a finger at him. He was a ruthless killer."

"Still . . . I should've handled it differently."

"I don't know what more you could have done."

"Something . . . anything."

"Do you think Eli knew it was you who took the pistol?"

"No."

"Well, he had to know something," Dantzler said. "There had to be a reason why he took the fall for a crime he didn't commit."

"Colt Rogers met with my father the day after he was arrested. He's the one who passed along the threats Richards made against my family. Eli had to silently swallow the medicine or risk the chance everyone in his family would suffer and die."

Dantzler stood. "Thank you for telling me this, Tommy. I know it was painful, and I know this situation has caused you more agony than I can imagine, but you've helped me solve the puzzle."

"Am I in any kind of trouble?"

"Why would you be in trouble? You didn't break any laws. The way I see it, you're the hero in all this."

"Heroes aren't cowards."

"You're no coward, Tommy," Dantzler said, opening the door. "You had a decision to make and you chose the only path you could. And it was the right path."

"I hope God's judgment is as generous as yours."

"You need to see Eli. He misses you more than anyone. The two of you have a lot of ground to make up and not much time to do it. Make the move. Go see him."

"I don't know. I'm not sure I can ever look him in the eye again.

CHAPTER FIFTY-FIVE

Dantzler arrived home at nine-fifteen, quickly undressed, and fell down on the bed. He was out as soon as his head hit the pillow. He awoke at eight-thirty the next morning. Almost twelve hours of uninterrupted sleep. Unheard of for him.

Nothing revives a worn-down body faster than a good night's sleep and a full breakfast. Following a lengthy shower, he dressed, grabbed the newspaper, and headed downtown to Coyle's Restaurant for a late breakfast. After making a couple of phone calls, he checked the time—eleven forty-five —and left the restaurant. He had one stop to make before his one o-clock meeting with the Whitehouse clan at Rachel's farm.

The family had questions, and it would be up to him to provide the answers. After all, he was the only one who knew all the details.

Ninety minutes later, opening the door to Rachel's house, Dantzler was met by a host of people, many of whom he had never seen before. Eli sat in a huge leather chair, looking every bit like an ancient prophet being attended to by his many followers. He also looked much healthier than he did during his previous meetings with Dantzler. His hair and beard had been trimmed, his skin had some real color to it, and his eyes sparkled. To his left, a nurse inspected tubes and various other connections, making sure he was getting his medication. On the opposite side, Rachel adjusted a pillow behind his head. Kirk stood next to her, holding a small plate that contained what remained of a piece of chocolate cake. Also in the room were six younger people—three boys, three girls—ranging in age from mid-teens to mid-twenties. Dantzler didn't recognize any of them. Eli's grandkids, he presumed.

Isaac sat on a couch ten feet away from Eli, staring straight ahead, his face showing no emotion. Dantzler could only wonder what thoughts were going through Isaac's head at this moment. Was Isaac happy, sad, jealous, envious—Dantzler couldn't begin to know. Probably all of that and more.

When Dantzler pushed the door open wider and Tommy Whitehouse stepped into the room, everything came to a halt. No movement, no talking, just a roomful of stunned people standing like statues. Dantzler wasn't sure if anyone in the room was even breathing. It was, he felt, like a movie freeze-frame moment. Amid the silence, all eyes went from Tommy to Eli. Back and forth they went, from son to father, no one quite certain what to say or do. No one sure what would happen next.

Then Eli spread his arms like some majestic prehistoric bird, and in a voice clear and strong, he shattered the silence with a single word:

"Thomas."

Hearing his name, Tommy ran to his father, knelt in front of him, wrapped his arms around his father's emaciated body, and buried his head into the old man's chest. Eli folded his arms around the son he had not seen in twenty-nine years, leaned forward, and kissed Tommy on the cheek.

Tommy, weeping uncontrollably, kept repeating, "I'm sorry, I'm sorry, I'm so, so sorry for what I've done. Can you ever forgive me?"

Eli lifted his son's head, looked him in the eye, and said, "You have no reason to ask for forgiveness. You did nothing wrong, nothing that requires forgiveness, from me or anyone else."

"I'm so sorry," Tommy said. "I'm sorry for failing you. It was me . . . I took the gun from the safe."

"I know," Eli said. "But you only did it because you had no other choice. It was the same with me. I had to stay silent, remain in prison, because the alternative meant death to our loved ones. Neither of us could allow such a terrible thing to happen."

Rachel, confused by what she was hearing, knelt next to Tommy, putting her arm on his shoulder. Kirk moved next to Rachel and held her hand. Isaac, his facial expression unchanged, remained seated on the couch.

"Hold you head high, Thomas," Eli ordered. "You are my son, in whom I am well pleased."

*****

A few minutes later, the nurse ordered Eli to get some rest. He agreed, telling his children he was tired and needed to lie down for a while. The nurse, with Rachel's help, lifted Eli into his wheelchair. After another check on the tubes and connections, with the nurse following close on their heels, Tommy rolled his father into a side bedroom.

While Tommy remained at his father's side, Dantzler, Rachel, Kirk, and Isaac sat at a long oak table in the dining room. Judging by the food remaining on the table, this was where the homecoming celebration had been held. There were finger sandwiches, a vegetable tray, several different kinds of fruit, and the remains of a cake with "Welcome Home, Eli" on it.

Rachel requested the sit-down, saying she wanted to know exactly what had happened twenty-nine years ago. "Did Tommy really take the gun from the safe?" she asked Dantzler.

"Yes."

"But . . . why?"

Dantzler paused for a few seconds, assessing how he should lay out the full story to the Whitehouse family. The best way, the only way, was to start from the beginning and give the details in narrative form. Otherwise, he would be bombarded with a multitude of questions. That would only serve to bounce the story from place to place, making it all the more confusing.

"Let me go back to the beginning and take you through the entire story," he said.

And that's what he did, starting with a detailed biographical sketch of Johnny Richards. Who he was and how he made his living as a Mob hit man. He told them how it all began when Tommy inadvertently overheard the conversation between Johnny Richards and the other man in the YMCA locker room. How Richards then confronted Tommy, ordering him to get the gun out of the safe. How Richards promised Tommy that if he talked, everyone in the family would be tortured and killed. How Richards sent Colt Rogers to Eli with the same promise of death if Eli fought the charges. How Richards killed Rogers and Devon Fraley, and attempted to set up Rocky Stone as the murderer. How Eli's clues, difficult as they were to figure out, eventually led the authorities to Richards.

Dantzler ended his tale by informing them that Richards was dead.

"So, Eli was right," Rachel pointed out. "Tommy had no other choice."

"If Tommy or Eli had spoken up, none of you would be sitting at this table right now," Dantzler said. "You would all be dead. Johnny Richards would have done exactly what he said he would do."

"And the two kids Richards killed in the barn? How did they fit in to all of this?" Kirk asked.

"They were unlucky victims," Dantzler answered. "Richards needed to ensure Tommy's silence. He did so by killing those two boys and then framing Eli for the murders. Where Richards found the two kids is anyone's guess. All we know is he did find them. He lured them into his car—maybe with the promise of drugs—drove them to the barn, tied them up, and executed them. Then he left the gun at the scene. And, of course, the gun had Eli's fingerprints on it. Those prints, along with Eli's refusal to defend himself at his trial, led to the inevitable guilty verdict."

"Diabolical," Rachel said, more to herself than to the others. "And to think what all this did to poor Tommy."

*****

Later, the nurse and Tommy came out of Eli's bedroom. Tommy walked into the dining room and told Dantzler that Eli would like to speak with him. Dantzler excused himself and went in to see the old man.

"Thomas will be all right now, won't he, Detective?" Eli said, his voice still strong and clear.

"I don't know, Eli. He has a serious alcohol problem. That's not easy to overcome. His road to recovery, provided it's what he truly wants, will be difficult and painful. But . . . after seeing you again, after unloading such a heavy burden, maybe the road will be a little easier."

"The suffering that child experienced all these years," Eli said, shaking his head. "Only Job suffered more."

"Were you aware that Tommy took the gun from the safe?"

"Not at first. But it didn't take a genius to figure it out. Not after Tommy fell like beautiful Lucifer from heaven. It could only have been Tommy."

"What did Colt Rogers say when he came to visit you the first time?"

"He said if I chose to fight the charges against me every member of my family would be murdered. So you see, Detective. Like Tommy, I had no choice but to remain silent and endure as best I could."

"Why did you wait all these years before revealing the truth? You could have done it ten, twenty years ago. Why didn't you?"

"I was a coward. And I feared for my family."

"That's a terrible punishment you put on yourself. On your family. Was it worth the price you paid?"

Eli shrugged.

"Why now, Eli?" Dantzler asked. "You could have let this thing play out and no one would be the wiser."

"I figured I would be dead by the time you uncovered the truth. Coward or not, I wasn't about to go to my grave without freeing Thomas from the terrible hell he was living in. He had suffered enough for the sins of others."

"Johnny Richards is dead."

"Forgive me if I refrain from saying a prayer on his behalf."

"Jesus's empty tomb, Mary Magdalene—excellent clues," Dantzler said. "But why so cryptic? So evasive? You could have made it a lot easier by simply giving me a name."

"I had faith you would figure it out."

"Why were you so certain I would take the case?"

"Because you're a Gnostic."

"What does being a Gnostic have to do with anything?"

"Gnosis, as we both know, means knowledge. And knowledge leads to the truth."

"I still don't follow."

"What was your answer when I asked if you possess gnosis?"

"I chase it but I don't always catch up to it."

"You're a seeker, Detective Dantzler. You seek knowledge, truth . . . God. I knew the truth—that I was innocent—and I had confidence you would uncover it."

"Your faith is admirable, Eli. Misplaced, perhaps, but admirable."

"Is my faith in Tommy's recovery misplaced?"

"Only time will tell. But I'll keep my fingers crossed that your faith will be rewarded."

"Are you familiar with the concept of *tikkun*?"

Dantzler was startled by the old man's question. "I'm surprised you know Kabbalah."

"Many paths lead to God, Detective. I try to travel as many as I can."

"During the process of Creation, the vessels containing the strict light of God's judgment were not able to contain the light. Therefore, the vessels broke, shattered. *Tikkun* means restoration or redemption. The mending of those shattered vessels."

"Very good, Detective Dantzler. My son, Thomas, is broken and shattered, but he will be restored. My faith in that is absolute."

"Like I said, Eli. I hope you are right."

"You're a good man, Detective," Eli said. "And not nearly so far removed from the Almighty as you would like us to believe. I suspect you'll keep running away from God until you eventually bump into him."

*****

As Dantzler was preparing to leave the house, Rachel met him at the door. She leaned up and kissed him on the cheek.

"Thank you, Detective Dantzler," she said. "Thank you for proving my father's innocence, and for freeing Tommy from his terrible burden. Thank you for giving my family back to me."

Dantzler stepped outside, opened his cell phone, and called Laurie. He told her to meet him at Malone's Steak House in an hour. Then he closed the phone, put it in his coat pocket, and walked toward his car. A huge smile crossed his face.

Never had he been happier than he was at this moment.

Acknowledgment

Much of the inspiration for certain aspects of this story came from Harold Bloom's great book, *Jesus and Yahweh: The Names Divine*. I highly recommend Professor Bloom's book to anyone willing to be enlightened and challenged. It is terrific. Thanks to Clay Stafford and Beth Terrell at the Killer Nashville Writers Conference. It was there that *Gnosis* was given its first breath of life. And as always, I want to thank my small band of family and friends who have always believed in me, and have been loyal from the beginning: Julie Watson, Sarah Small, Ed Watson, Wanda Underwood, Christina Young, Suzanne Slinker, Denny Slinker, Jimmie Nell Jenkins, Grant Sparks and, most especially, my aunt Bobbie Watkins. Lastly, I want to thank my good friend Theresa Little for helping me out with the landscaping, and with a thousand other things. Theresa was beyond wonderful, and she was taken from us far too soon.

Author's Bio

Tom Wallace is the author of two previous mysteries featuring Detective Jack Dantzler—*What Matters Blood* (2004) and *The Devil's Racket* (2007), both set in Lexington, Kentucky, where Tom lives. He also wrote the thriller, *Heirs of Cain* (2010).

Tom spent many years as a successful, award-winning sportswriter in his native Kentucky. He authored five sports-related books, including the highly popular *Kentucky Basketball Encyclopedia,* an in-depth history of the University of Kentucky's legendary hoops program.

Tom, a Vietnam vet, is an active member of Mystery Writers of America and the Author's Guild. His Web site is http://www.tomwallacenovels.com.

ANON
A NOVEL OF CORPORATE TERROR
BY PETER GIGLIO

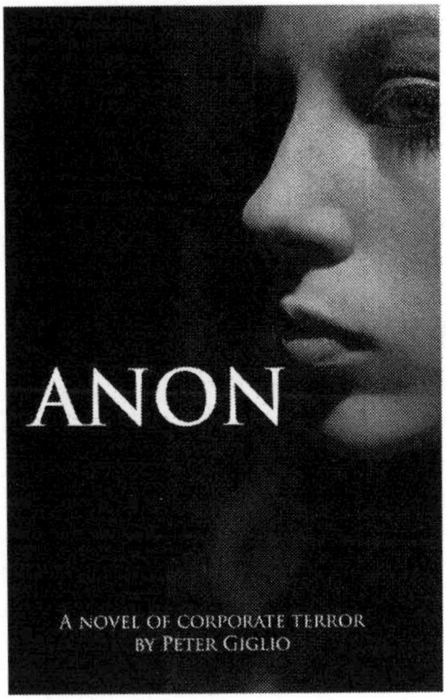

"An invigorating new hand with the poise, polish, and precision of an established old hand, Peter Giglio arrives on the genre fiction scene with force and vitality. He's a natural, a keeper, and a clean shot of oxygen."
—Eric Shapiro, author of Stories for the End of the World and director of Rule of Three

ISBN# 978-0615498201
$14.99
Trade Paperback
Horror

Rory Ellison, victim of his own misdeeds, wallows in misery. Then a door opens. Now he's got a new job, a dream assignment to rewrite the darkest mistake of his past, and a strange new companion in his head. Wielding powers beyond his comprehension and control, Rory returns to …

… Faith. She possesses the perfect husband, kids, and home. But when Rory falls back into her world, old wounds open wide, shattering her ideal life.

At the center of the mayhem stands Anon, a seemingly benevolent organization with a sinister past of its own. "Helping you realize your dreams sooner," the company promises. But what do they stand to gain? How far will they go to get what they want? And if they make dreams a reality, what about nightmares?

Only Michelle, a young girl with a strange gift, can defeat the evil threatening her family. But she must face fear, work with the ghosts of her enemy's past, navigate a maze of terror, and make the tough choice to grow up too soon in a world filled with evil and indifference.

Hold on tight! Anon—a tale of corporate and familial terror—is unlike anything you've ever read.

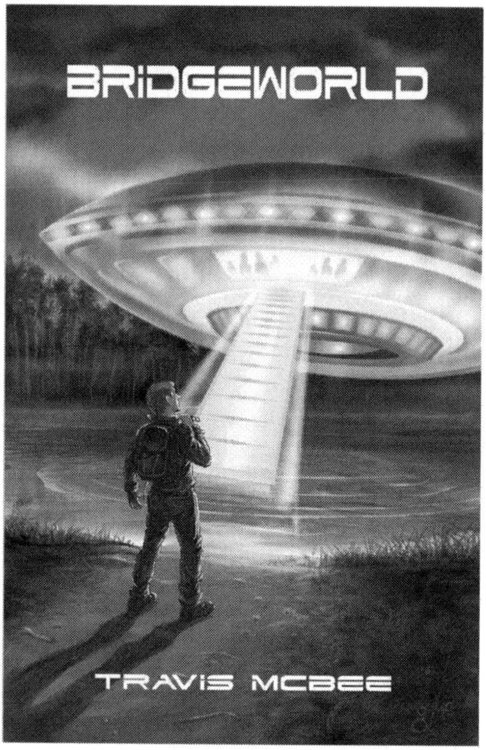

BRIDGEWORLD
BY
TRAVIS MCBEE

ISBN 978-0615504452 Young Adult
$14.99

William Haynes was the type of guy that everyone either wanted, or wanted to be. He was an honor roll student and captain of his middle school football team. He was dating the most popular girl in the school and had dozens of friends. Yes, life was perfect for Will…that is until a strange man shows up and forces his parents to reveal a secret they have kept hidden since he was born. He is told that he has been given a scholarship to a prestigious private school that his parents attended, a private school that happens to be in space. Will must choose between a life many would die for and a life none could imagine. A life where he is no longer perfect, where he must make new friends, and where he must survive a school rivalry like no other.

Secret by Morinda Montgomery

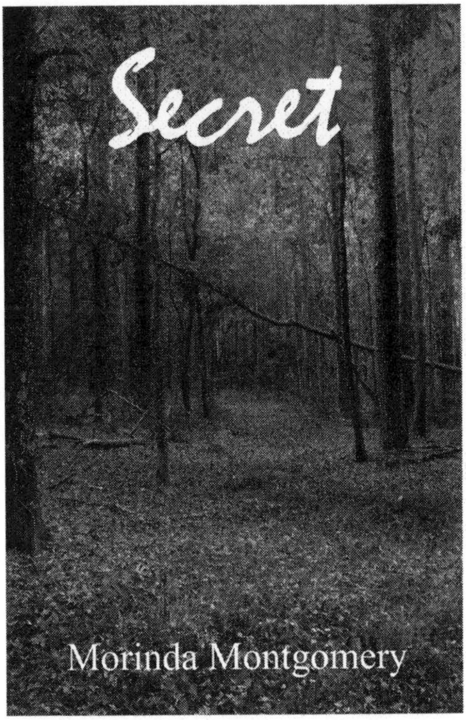

ISBN: 978-0615499505

Paranormal Romance

$14.99

What do you get when you arrange a marriage between fire and ice?

Morgan's world is turned upside down when she is forced into an engagement to Brian DeMacleo. Brian is an infuriating, overbearing, conceited, arrogant bastard who does nothing but treat her like a child. Not only does Brian have to deal with his...condition... but now he has to deal with the lovely Morgan. Or rather, the not so lovely as personality goes. The woman does nothing but argue and try to irritate him.

Steam, and lots of it.

At least they can find some common ground in that neither of them wish to get married. They will get out of the marriage no matter what it takes. But can they keep their secrets as the moons cycle continues?

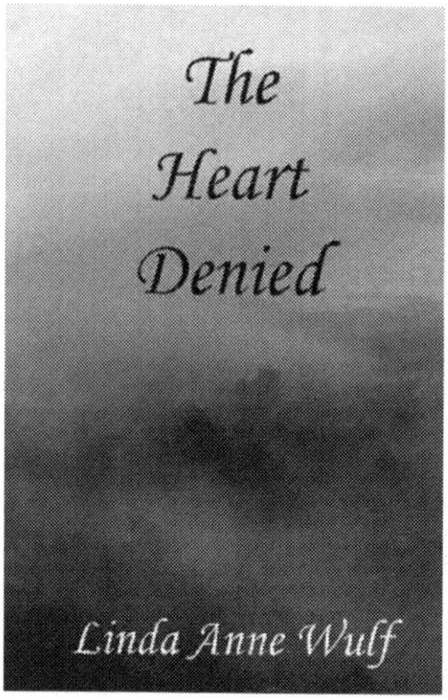

The Heart Denied by Linda Anne Wulf

ISBN 978-0615432427
Trade Paperback
$14.99
Historical Fiction

In 1728, THORNE NEVILLE leaves Oxford University and one devastated courtesan to take his deceased father's title, occupation, estate and advice--that being to marry the Viscount Radleigh's convent-schooled daughter, and thus spare himself the potential heartache of a love match. Having watched his father grieve away eighteen years for his dead mother, Thorne grimly understood that advice--though he doubts it will matter. His own heart was buried years ago, along with his childhood love. But Thorne is about to learn that fate doesn't bow to plans, and that denying his heart will cost not only him, but others as well. The lesson involves four strong-willed women:

KATY, the spirited courtesan who loves him and plots to conceive his child;

GWYNNETH, the rebellious wife whose preference for convent vows over marriage vows makes Thorne's domestic life hell;

CAROLINE, the sultry socialite who not only schemes with Thorne's half-brother to ruin him, but tries to seduce Thorne while pretending to be Gwynneth's dearest friend;

ELAINE, the chambermaid who must at all costs keep Thorne from guessing her true identity.

As Thorne's carefully constructed world disintegrates in a succession of murder, rape, suicide and betrayal, he must begin the painful recovery of his heart, in order to rediscover the woman who has held it for so long.

Andraste

by

Marisa

Mills

ISBN: 978-0615493787
Young Adult

Available in
Print and Ebook!!

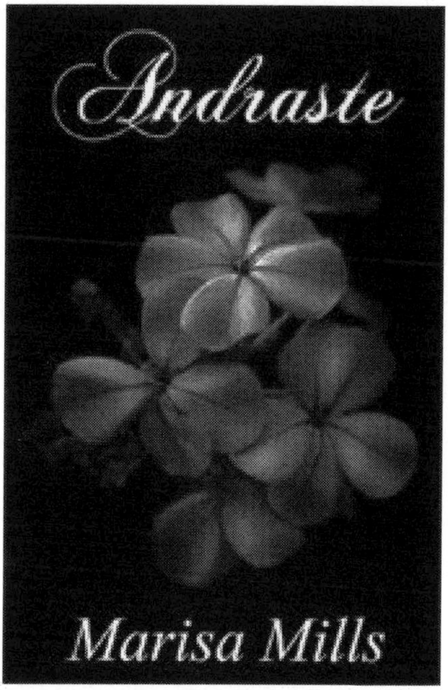

All is not as it appears

Andraste, the daughter of an elfin prince and fairy queen is Fate's Beloved, blessed with an incredible prophecy naming her as the one who can vanquish the Abatu Empire. She has spent her life preparing for the day when she would leave her homeland and fulfill her destiny. That day has come, but there are a few things Andraste doesn't know. Her prophecy is a carefully-constructed lie, and beneath the beauty and civilization of her mother's fairy country, there lie ancient prejudices and secrets. Traitors live within the castle walls, but Andraste can't help but wonder who's worse: the vampire empress conquering the world, or the deceitful fairies she's fighting to save.

12228308R00147

Made in the USA
Lexington, KY
30 November 2011